SPURN ME

IMMORTAL VICES & VIRTUES: SHADOW SHIFTER BONDS

BOOK FOUR

AMANDA PILLAR

Spurn Me

Amanda Pillar

Edited by: Theresa Schultz

Proofread by: Rachel Theus Cass

Discreet Edition Cover Art by Manuela

Regular Edition Cover Art by Urban Rex Designs

Paperback ISBN: 978-0-6487935-3-3

Hardback ISBN: 978-0-6487935-4-0

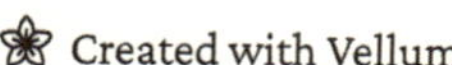

To my imagination, without which, this book would not exist.
May it continue to be unpredictable and slightly terrifying.

“The boundaries which divide Life from Death are at best shadowy and vague. Who shall say where the one ends, and where the other begins?”
— Edgar Allan Poe

INTRODUCTION FROM KIERAN ASPEN

CO-RULER OF THE HOUSE OF DEATH AND DIAMOND

Most people like to start a story at the beginning.

I am not most people.

Sure, I could tell you about the portals and how they connect to Earth. Or about the Houses and how the world works. But you can just read the next chapter for that crap. Or better yet, go read Season One of this series. (Yeah, yeah, I'm breaking the fourth wall and all that. Just go with it.)

I am not here to give you a boring history lesson.

No, that's for Oberon, who is more annoying than jock rash.

This story begins with *me*.

It's my origin story, if you will.

Which is a pretty fucked-up tale, truth be told. And a bit heavy for the start of a book, but them's the breaks, kids. So, I'll give you the *Cliff's Notes* version:

You see, my mother was one of the rare humans left on Earth. She found her mate, who was the brother of King Elias, ruler of the House of Blood and Beryl. Mommy dearest agreed to become a vampire so she could spend eternity with her mate. Halfway through the transformation, my sperm donor, a necrophiliac-loving death fae, found her. He then kidnapped her, impregnated her, and kept her on the edge of transformation for nine months.

All for the sake of "science."

I don't know about you, but the science I learned about had less to do with fucking corpses and more to do with playing with baking soda and vinegar. Or studying electrons and $E=mc^2$. Yeah, I liked physics more than I did chemistry.

Anyway.

I was the result of the illegal and immoral "experiment."

Mom escaped with me, back to her mate. Who was as joyful as you can imagine having his mate returned to him...but the baby she brought home...well, that didn't go down as well. But that's a whole different story.

Many years later, after I'd already started working for my step-uncle, Elias, as an "information specialist" (AKA torturer), my sperm donor kidnapped and tortured me. Because that's what you do with your half-vampire, half-death fae progeny. Apparently.

I may have held the teeniest, *tiniest* grudge.

Suffice to say, the bastard is deader than dead. Like, no chance of resurrection, even for the most powerful necromancer or death fae out there. I even did the worst of the worst and cremated him (which is stupid, because I'd have thought a slow and painful death would be much worse than cremation). I then pulverized his bones, before sinking all that ash and dust over the Mariana Trench.

And that, I thought, was that.

The end.

I had successfully destroyed him *and* his bloodline (except for, well, me).

But that's where I was wrong.

You see, I didn't know he had a mate.

And that his mate survived his death.

GLOSSARY

The Houses

House of Air and Amythest
House of Blood and Beryl
House of Death and Diamond
House of Earth and Emerald
House of Fire and Fluorite
House of Gold and Garnet
House of Sea and Serpentine
House of Spirit and Sapphire
House of Destiny and Dragomir

No Man's Land

No Man's Circus – Portland, Oregon
The Crossroads – St Louis, Missouri

The Portals

Himalaya Portal – Opens to a world of Gods
Sahara Desert Portal, Africa – Opens to the Witch World, the Old Country
Portland Portal, Oregon – Opens to the Shifter World, Arcadia

Amazon Portal, South America – Opens the Angels/Demons World, Celestia/Soleil
Near Fiji Portal, Pacific Ocean – Opens a world of Merpeople
Giant's Causeway Portal, Ireland – Opens to the Fae World, Avalon
Melbourne Portal, Australia – Opens to a Shapeshifter World, Vuulectus
The Crossroads Portal, Missouri – Opens to Tartarus

Portal
No Man's Land
Fire & Flourite
Air & Amethyst
Spirit & Sapphire
Sea & Serpentine
Death & Diamond
Blood and Beryl
Gold & Garnet
Earth & Emerald

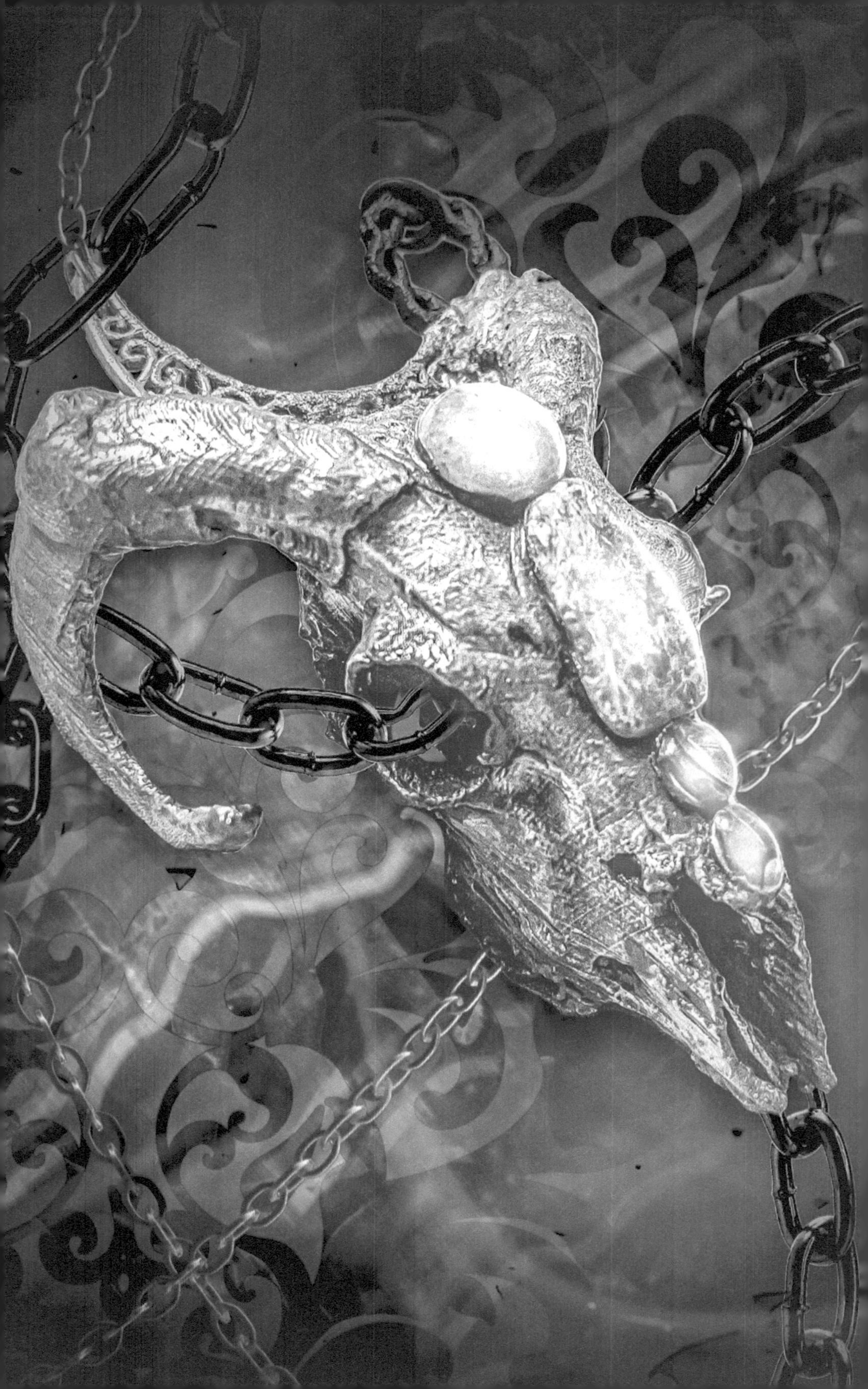

CHAPTER 1
OBERON

AVALON, OVER FIVE THOUSAND YEARS AGO...

Oberon Ó Duibh's life was damned near perfect. Standing on a marble dais above the most powerful fae in the world, he watched as fear flickered across their faces.

The platform beneath his feet held swirling veins of gold and silver, its surface embedded with precious gems, each stone picked to represent the colors of the three royal fae bloodlines: black, green, and white. A cavernous hall stretched out before him, the high ceiling held aloft by soaring columns of cloud-white marble.

The hall boasted a large assembly of fae, split down the middle by a long, embroidered purple carpet, which led from the enormous double doors to the steps of the dais. It was where the new High King and High Queen would walk once their coronation was complete. It was also where they would greet their subjects, and where the Lower Court kings and queens would swear their fealty to their new rulers.

Malice, awe, and envy were almost scents in the air as the coveted High King's crown was held above Oberon's head by a chanting official dressed in the yellow of a High Court noble. Oberon could feel the weight of the audience's stares, from the fierce gazes of the fire fae to the icy glares of the death dealers. Gowns and skin tones varied from purple to black, white, pink, green, red, and even gray—although some of the fae didn't even *have* skin. And there were crowns aplenty in sight.

But all Oberon could think about was how he'd seemingly gotten everything he'd ever wanted, and more. He'd taken on the world and won. He'd not only acquired the throne, but also a mate and power.

So. Much. Power.

His entire life had been about this moment, about becoming High King of Avalon. But even he could have never imagined it happening like this. With the world at his feet, and a worthy mate by his side.

A series of sharp stings bit into his head when the base of the strangely feather-light crown settled on his white hair, as if a dozen previously hidden spikes had burst forth to drill into his skull. He smiled as pain seared through his veins, welcoming the agony, as it symbolized the start of his trial by magic—the last and only step before he became High King.

Oberon's heartbeat turned sluggish while the crown's magic—or poison—began to work its dark enchantment. The oxygen in his lungs vanished, the metal on his head heating to near-intolerable temperatures, the bitter stench of burnt hair thickly coating the air. Light was stripped from his field of vision and the surrounding soundscape dimmed to nothing. He was vulnerable now, more vulnerable than he'd been in his entire life, aside from as a mere babe.

Without thinking, he drew on the magic from the world beneath his feet, forcing air to surround him, replacing the vacuum in his lungs and the one cocooning his body. Sound rushed in, pleasant after only the pounding of the blood in his veins. The low chanting of the officials on the dais was offset by the quiet, pained gasps of his mate. His stomach clenched at the evidence of her distress, but he gritted his teeth against the urge to help. This was a test he could not assist her with. She either passed or she died.

Fight, Titian. Beat the crown, he urged her silently, even though telepathy was not an ability he possessed.

The metal crown grew white-hot during his moment of distraction, and as the stench of keratin intensified, he refocused. Reaching out beyond Avalon's atmosphere, he harnessed power from the frozen depths of space to cool the near-molten crown and the heat in his veins. He may not have needed to draw from space itself, but he chose to demonstrate his true power and skill in this magical test. All fae were children of the stars, but only Celestials could wield the power of space itself. Finally, he wove light into existence, borrowing the power from the binary stars in Avalon's solar system, Grian and Suil. His vision returned to normal, and he blinked past the sudden brightness.

The crown had tested him, verifying he was a Celestial, the rarest kind of fae—and the *only* type of fae allowed to rule as High King or High Queen.

He turned his head to look at his mate, his Titian. Her body was eerily still, although her exceptional beauty had not dimmed, despite her skin's pallor. He was awestruck anew by her, suddenly able to understand why she had inspired artists to compose poetry about the slender line of her neck, sonnets to the shape of her lips. But only he knew how they tasted, how they felt under the skin of his fingers.

All her other lovers were dead.

Most killed by her own hand, some by his.

His Titian was nothing, if not vicious.

Her sea green eyes remained unfocused as she battled magically with the crown, her chest barely rising with each breath, the silver and white of her dress engulfing her delicate frame. The metal of the silvery crown glowed white-hot against her golden-blonde hair, the rare gemstones set within luminescing in bright, random colors. It made the crown's small, intricate details difficult to discern—the stylized crescent moons, stars, and planets awash in the glow.

The officials continued chanting as the seconds turned into minutes. Delicate beads of sweat formed on Titian's forehead as she continued to battle for her right to wear the High Queen's crown. The only constraint to a Celestial's power was the fae's own ability to wield magic, and what Titian lacked in raw magical ability, she made up for in intelligence.

You can do it, he thought, willing her to victory.

The crowd of fae below began to grow restless as the minutes continued to tick by. Their whispers died when he turned to them, sweeping his dark gaze over the throng.

They think she is going to fail.

No.

Titian was a Celestial.

She could do this.

Five more minutes dragged by.

He stepped toward her, ignoring the warning glares of the surrounding officials. They continued to chant, although they watched him like kelpies did hapless strangers. But he didn't need to move any closer. He reached deep inside himself, within his mind and heart, seeking where he felt the mate bond. There it was, glimmering and strong. It looked like a mixture of gold and silver, white and black, to his inner eye. The colors of their magic, and their bloodlines.

Carefully, he pushed some of his power through the bond, trying to channel it to her. He wasn't sure if it would work, but he couldn't stand by and watch her fail. He didn't want to be High King without her by his side.

My, how you've changed, he thought to himself, as he pushed magic toward her. Until three years ago, his greatest desire had been to become High King, with Titian Geal and every other member of her family dead at his feet. Even better, he'd dreamed that the Ó hUainín family lay lifeless next to them.

For over five thousand years, the three royal bloodlines had been at war, vying for the throne. Nowadays, the battle was more clandestine; assassins in the dark and poisons after dinner versus all-out battle. But it was a war, nevertheless. The Ó Duibh, the Geals, and the Ó hUainín had been grappling for power ever since they realized the key to producing Celestials lay in their blood.

Until Oberon's and Titian's births, there hadn't been a new Celestial in close to three hundred years. They'd been raised to hate each other with a fierce passion. But they hadn't met face-to-face until the day he'd been sent to kill Titian in her sleep.

The mate bond had kicked in the minute he'd laid eyes on her. He would have died for her in that moment.

It had taken time, but she'd come to accept him and their bond. Love him, even.

The unnatural pallor of her skin began to change, responding to the power he'd fed her. The sweat droplets on her forehead vanished, and the taut lines of her body softened.

A bare five minutes later, Titian's eyes opened, victory and pride shining forth as she stared out toward the sea of fae beneath the dais. He stepped closer to her, ignoring the glares of the officials. Picking up her delicate hand, he raised it to his lips, pressing a soft kiss to her knuckles, before he turned her palm over and pressed a hotter, wetter kiss to her inner wrist.

"We did it," he murmured, awestruck by the triumph shining from her sea green gaze.

"Yes, we did." She gave him a small, enigmatic smile, one that made his cock stand to attention. Thankfully, his ceremonial robes hid the physical response.

As one, they turned toward the crowd below, staring down at the leaders of the fae, the kings and queens of the Lower Courts, and the rulers of the Wild Fae. Titian's fingers entwined with his own, and warmth trickled through his formerly frozen heart.

The official who had placed the crown on Oberon's head stepped forward. The male fae was dressed in yards of rare spider silk, his dark green hair gleaming in the light. He clapped his hands three times, the sound stark and loud in the now-silent hall.

Then the fae bowed low, his body almost bent in half. When he stood, his voice rang over the crowd. "All hail Their Majesties, Oberon Ó Duibh and Titian Geal, the High King and High Queen of Avalon, granted by right of the Celestial Crown, Sovereigns of the Abyss, Rulers of Elysium, and Protectors of the Lower Courts and Wild Fae."

It was done.

He'd prevailed.

He'd won everything.

CHAPTER 2
OBERON

Oberon entered Titian's bed chamber and came to a stop before her large four-poster bed. Made from ivory collected from a long-dead sea monster, the bed had room enough for six. But it would only ever host him and his mate.

His bed was made from the darkest of ebonies, carved to resemble a nightmare come to life. He preferred her chamber; decorated in whites and silvers, with soft pastel accents, it spoke of warmth, of *her*. His quarters spoke of death and gloom, something which probably would have appealed to him prior to being mated.

Between them, they had agreed that Titian's chambers would be theirs, since the High King and Queen did not share a room. In fact, the staff had been aghast when he requested a new suite be prepared for the two of them. Titian had suggested that they keep separate quarters for now, that they play the long game: grant the staff and nobles the illusion that they had some power, some control over the royal couple, when in fact, they would bend to *their* wishes.

He loved her cunning, how she thought ahead.

Titian walked toward him from her bathing chamber, her long hair cascading around her sleekly muscled body in waves of golden silk. She was dressed in a simple white silk slip, the thin straps over her shoulders barely able to hold up the material. His gaze lingered on her breasts, her hard nipples, before sweeping over her hips and down her long, long legs.

How he wanted her.

Titian came to a stop before him, running a hand down the front of his chest. He hadn't completely changed out of his outfit from earlier. He still wore the crown—it hadn't let him remove it—fancy black silk pants and shirt, but he had discarded the embroidered ceremonial tunic. However, he'd kept his favorite iron blade in the sheath at his hip. He never went anywhere without it. Even though he could form a star-blade from nothing more than air, he liked the feel of the heavy metal in his palm. It centered him, and it reminded him of how fragile life was.

He'd spent too long expecting a knife in his back to relax his guard now, even with the mate who he would trust with his heart, his life.

Titian's voice was a low purr as she undid the buttons of his shirt. "Your Majesty." Her sweeping palm stopped over his heart. Her hand formed a claw and her sharp fingernails dug into his flesh, slicing through the fabric of his shirt. He inhaled at the sting and the scent of his blood, reveling in it, in her.

His cock strained against the confines of his trousers.

Oberon leaned down, placing one hand on the slope of her neck. "Say it again." His mouth brushed against hers as he spoke.

Her voice was breathy. "Your Majesty."

He closed the remaining distance between them, their mouths fusing in a fiery kiss. Her lips parted, and he took advantage, his tongue flicking against hers in an intimate caress. His hand slid from her neck, gliding down over her shoulder.

Titian pulled away on a moan, then raised her hand and licked his blood from her fingers. By rowan and ash, that was sexier than he'd thought it could be. He took a step forward, only to slam into an invisible barrier, his forehead aching from the blow.

Startled, he raised his hands, only to find them land against a smooth wall. One that he could not see. One that kept him from his mate.

"What—?"

Titian smiled, that coy, cunning smile that turned him on like nothing else. "Oh, Oberon, you honestly didn't think we were going to live happily ever after, did you?"

He stared at her.

She laughed, the sound like tinkling bells.

What is going on? He stepped backwards, only to slam into another barrier. Worried, he tried to escape the invisible cage, but there was no crack in the walls. He was caught in a three-foot wide prison.

"It's a ward. You won't be able to escape." She pointed at the ceiling.

Looking up, he saw an intricate design carved into the plaster. A spell. But it wasn't like any he'd seen before. He frowned. *What was that symbol?*

"You don't have the magic to do this." He stood with his arms loose by his sides, feet apart. Ready to fight—even though he wasn't sure there was anything to *fight*. When it came to raw magical strength, she was no match for him.

"No." She shook her head, her eyes alight and glowing with pride and...malevolence. "But I have money. And access to power."

The bathroom door opened and a man strode into the room, an aura of dark energy clinging to him. Brown haired, and with skin the color of bronze, he was close to seven feet tall. The stranger's leather clothing was unusual, nothing like the fashions on Avalon, and it was covered in mystical symbols. His eyes burned red with raw power, while the irises had a peculiar yellow ring around the edge.

What is he?

Better yet, *who* was he?

The man came to a stop behind Titian and wrapped powerful arms around her shoulders and across her chest in an embrace that spoke of prior intimacy. He then kissed her neck, right where her pulse beat, right where Oberon loved to lick and suck, his red and yellow gaze locked on Oberon's face.

Rage at the sight nearly short-circuited his mind.

Titian leaned into the male's kiss, titling her head to the side, her eyelashes fluttering shut. The foreigner's hand swept up, cupping her right breast and stroking her nipple through the thin fabric. She let out a little mewl of pleasure and then turned, her lips meeting his while she pressed her body firmly against the other male's. One of his large hands cupped her ass, and Oberon's eyes closed at the sight. He tried to block out the image that had etched onto the inside of his eyelids, block out the sounds of her soft cries and the stranger's low groans.

Was this a test? Was this—

The sound of ruffling fabric and movement had him opening his eyes against his will. Nausea roiled in his gut at the sight before him: Titian on her knees, her blonde hair tangled in the man's large fist. They'd moved, deliberately positioning themselves so that he could see them clearly as the red-eyed male guided her mouth back and forth over his cock, the hard length glistening. Wet sounds reached him as she took the male as deep as she could, choking as the tip hit the back of her throat, her cheeks hollowed as she sucked on him.

She'd never gotten on her knees for him, saying that she would kneel for no man.

Something within him broke at the sight, at the utter betrayal. Bile rose up the back of his throat and his vision hazed with red as he called on his power. He'd blow the entire palace to pieces before he stood there for another second. Destroy half the entire fucking planet if he had to.

But when he called on that power, nothing happened. No magic filled his veins, raced through his body. In shock, he looked at the ward and saw it flare red, before magic funneled down the sides of the transparent walls to beneath his feet, where it began to swirl in a vortex.

No.

No, this is not happening—

The male soon had Titian's hair clenched in both hands and began slamming his cock between her lips, over and over, fucking her mouth with pure abandon. Oberon watched, unable to look away, horrified and sickened by the sight. Titian slid a hand down her body, her fingers disappearing between her thighs as she gagged on the man's erection, tears running down her cheeks. But she didn't look sad. No, her cheeks grew flushed as her fingers moved, rapidly stroking her pussy, and she groaned low, her lips circling his cock. The male suddenly stilled, his body bowing, before he began jerking his hips uncontrollably. Titian's gaze focused on Oberon as her cheeks bulged from the man's come, and she moaned long and hard while her fingers brought her to the edge of orgasm.

Her mouth worked frantically, trying to suck him dry, when she suddenly bucked against her own hand, coming, her throat arching as she swallowed every drop of his seed.

The few times she'd been willing to take him in her mouth, she'd spat Oberon's out.

Without thinking, he reached again for his magic, only for the ward to flare brightly once more, the vortex at his feet growing stronger.

Titian opened her eyes and levelled Oberon with a cold stare, one filled with revulsion. He wanted to think her expression was fueled by what she'd just done, but he knew that it was aimed at him. She let the man's erection slip from her mouth, running her tongue over her lips like she missed the taste already. She stood, the silk slip half dangling from one shoulder, exposing the mound of her breast, while between her thighs, it stuck to the dampness of her pussy.

The sight would have once gotten him so hard he could barely think. Now...now he just felt rage, cold and dark and endless. The emotions filled him to the brim, so that he could barely breathe.

She shook her head as she stepped closer to him. "You were so stupid. Thinking that a mate bond would erase all the travesties your family has done to mine over the centuries. That I would be content by *your* side."

"You accepted the bond." He barely recognized his voice, so low and guttural.

"I wanted to be queen. I would have done anything for that."

Oberon sneered, feeling disconnected from her, from the situation, from himself. "So I see."

"You were so easy to trick. So willing to believe in our matehood." She continued to approach the ward. Something inside their bond twisted, and he felt her disdain, her hatred, her revulsion—of him. Somehow, she'd been able to hide her true emotions from him, tricked even the primal magic of the bond.

Pain wrenched through him. He hadn't known. How could he have not known?

Pureblooded fae can't lie.

Frantic, he recalled their conversations, their planning for the future. She'd never said she loved *him*. Not explicitly. Just that she'd loved their bond, being *his* mate, that she couldn't wait for the future. Not *their* future.

"Every time you touched me, I would picture Helios in my mind. That it was his hands, his mouth, his cock. Every time I came, it was for him. Never you." She was on the edge of the ward now.

Helios.

That was the name of a god.

Oberon looked over Titian's shoulder at the red-eyed man. Disdain and satisfaction lined the male's face. Avalon had a portal to the god realm. But he hadn't even known that a deity had come through, let alone fucked his mate.

"Helios is a sun god, so was able to prepare this ward. It's really quite clever. Activated by your blood, it is keyed only to you. Once started, it begins to siphon your power and slowly build a portal. If you use your magic, it draws the power away and feeds the portal all the more quickly."

She was going to send Oberon somewhere? Remove him from *his* world?

"There is nowhere you can send me that I won't come back." Fury coated each word.

"That is where you are wrong." It was the first time the god had spoken, and the words raked over Oberon's senses like hot coals. "There is a world that is almost impossible to escape from, even if you are as powerful as a god."

Which Oberon was. It wasn't hubris, it was just fact.

"We hadn't planned to do this so soon after the coronation, but since you were able to defeat the crown's magic so quickly, I knew we couldn't risk you settling into the throne." Titian almost looked...apologetic. "I had originally planned on waiting until we had conceived a child, but I can't take the risk that you wouldn't betray me first."

"Betray you?" Oberon barked out a laugh that bordered on hysteria. "You would have failed the trial without me. I *helped* you pass the crown's test."

Her green eyes flashed. "Liar. No one can interfere with the test. I did it on my own."

"I shared some of my power with you through our mate bond." His tone turned taunting. "Surely you felt the sudden boost near the end?"

She slashed her hand through the air, fury replacing any attempt she'd made at earnestness. Stepping through the ward, she stood within arm's reach. Brave of her, since his magic was now useless. She stank of sex, of another man, of betrayal.

He held his breath, unable to tolerate the reek.

"*I* am the High Queen. My family have hunted the Ó hUainín to near extinction. And we have whittled your kin down to weaklings. You were my only threat." Her mouth tightened, lips pursing. "I accepted the mate bond to win the throne, even though I wanted you dead. But my family, and even Helios, convinced me that it would be the best way. Even if it means I can't kill you, since I don't want to risk going insane." Her beauty morphed into a mask of cruelty. "But that doesn't mean I have to keep you here, either. You will be exiled. Forever."

Wind began to swirl at Oberon's feet, the vortex coalescing. He didn't have much time. And he had no idea how to break the spell, since using his magic only seemed to strengthen it.

One moment, he'd had everything in his grasp.

Now, he had nothing.

Less than nothing.

He'd been tricked, fooled into a mate bond that should never have been. His hand clenched on the handle of his iron dagger, rage pouring through him, a cleansing fire. Titian had betrayed him over and over, and he hadn't realized it—he'd been blind to it, and her. By rowan and ash, he'd even *loved* her. He, who had loved nothing more than power since he'd come to understand what it meant.

But Oberon wasn't going to let her win.

No.

If he couldn't have the throne, then neither could she.

Oberon leaned forward, breathing through his mouth so he wouldn't have to smell her, smell *them*. "You really should have killed me."

A portal had formed at his feet, its center dull and dark.

Where were they sending him?

She frowned at him, confused. She thought she was safe. That he wouldn't risk harming her because of the bond she had violated.

Quicker than lightning, he slammed his dagger into her cruel, empty heart. Warm blood spurted over his fingers as Titian screamed, the sound high and broken. She scrabbled at the dagger, at his hands.

"What—" Blood dribbled from her mouth, mixed with white swirls of her lover's come.

He leaned down and whispered, "Death is beautiful on you."

Fear clouded her gaze, and he twisted the blade, the sound of snapping cartilage and her anguish music to his ears. He jerked the iron dagger free, then kicked her body away from him. Titian fell limply at Helios's feet, blood pooling over her chest, dripping onto her lover.

The portal flared to life.

Oberon met the god's irate gaze and bared his teeth in a mockery of a smile. "Until we meet again."

Helios's bellow of rage followed Oberon as he was sucked into the portal. He lost all sense of up from down, left from right, and night from day as he was pulled through space and time before being unceremoniously dumped out the other end. The mate bond broke as he slammed into the ground, hard, his shoulder protesting the impact in a starburst of pain. The jolt knocked the bloodied dagger from his hand, and he groped blindly for it in the darkness. He wouldn't be defenseless, not here, not in this unknown world. Fingers closing on the cool metal, he lay panting on the frozen earth, his head ringing from the landing and the snapping of the mating bond.

I'm alive.

At least severing the bond hadn't killed him outright.

An ache lay deep in his mind where the bond had been, but it wasn't torturous. *No risk of insanity—at least not yet.* Maybe it came on slowly.

Light trickled into his vision bit by bit, the evening sky above him barely visible due to a layer of dense fog. He sat up, staring at the stony ground and the mist-covered landscape, one hand clutching his shoulder, which objected to the change in position. The stench of sulfur was thick in the air, while water lapped against a nearby—but shrouded—shoreline.

As he leaned forward, trying to see through the haze, the crown fell off his head, clattering to the ground next to him. Grimacing, he picked it up, something wrenching deep inside him. Was he still High King? Had the crown rejected him?

The metal warmed in his hands, almost in response to his thoughts. Then it...shrank?

Seconds later, the High King's crown was so small it fit easily in the palm of his hand. What was he going to do with it now? Wear it as jewelry?

Wait.

He could wear it as a ring—it was small enough. And he wouldn't have to try and hide the crown in this new world. A world which probably wouldn't take kindly to deposed kings.

Sliding the crown onto his right ring finger, he was pleased to find it fit snugly. One problem solved. Now on to his biggest issue—where was he?

The sound of footsteps on gravel had him looking up, and a woman emerged out of the fog. She came to a stop before him, her black hair tied back from her striking face, body swathed in fighting leathers. She crossed her arms over her chest and stared down at him, face a cold mask. Then she smirked, the expression almost wry.

"Welcome to Hell."

CHAPTER 3
OBERON

TARTARUS, THREE MONTHS AGO...

F*ive thousand years.*

Five thousand years he'd been trapped in Tartarus, a realm that never saw a flicker of daylight or felt the change of seasons. The planet was a nomad—discarded and adrift in the universe, with no solar system to welcome it home.

Much like Oberon.

But he hadn't given up, and he wouldn't—not until the crown was back on his head, and he had destroyed Titian's legacy and bloodline for good. The panther within him stretched, agreeing with the sentiment.

Vengeance, Styx often told him, wouldn't repair the damage that had been done. But it sure would make him feel better. The kelpie had found him by her river the day he'd been dumped out of the portal onto Tartarus. She'd wanted to kill him—hell, she'd been murdering any man stupid enough to come near her river for over a hundred years—but something about him had made her pause.

She said it was the betrayal she'd sensed around him.

He said it was because he was too handsome to kill.

They had agreed to disagree.

It was strange how it took being exiled for him to finally create a family, of sorts. Caius, Styx, Pollux, Abyssian, and Legion, they were his best friends. Hell, they were probably his only friends. Although, he'd never really taken to Abyssian; there was just something about the other man that grated. Perhaps it was because the male was supposedly a minor fae deity—one that Oberon had never even heard of, let alone worshipped.

Magic exploded outward from Caius, the god's power ricocheting through the castle chamber, blinding in its intensity. Oberon squinted through the pain, his mouth going dry at the sight of the portal forming, the swirling vortex a shock to the system.

"Let's go," Caius said, eyes locked on the newly formed portal as its edges sparked with power.

Styx grinned. "Finally."

Oberon nodded, indicating he was ready. He wasn't eager, like Caius, having never been to Earth. But he could understand the feeling —if Avalon had been on the other side of this portal, he would have already gone through it. He admired the god's restraint.

Caius strode through the portal, Oberon and Styx following closely behind. A second later, they were on the other side. Huh. That hadn't been what he'd expected. Sure, his last inter-world portal trip had been five millennia ago, but it had been a hell of a lot more disorientating than that.

At least I don't have a dislocated shoulder this time.

Hell, he hadn't even rolled an ankle.

His panther huffed in either amusement or disdain; Oberon couldn't tell.

Frowning, he looked back over his shoulder at the swirling vortex behind him. It hovered like a black hole over the remains of a broken fountain. Beyond it, a large building with a cracked dome arched toward the sky, the waning moon visible in the star-laden expanse above.

Power flooded through him as his magic reached down and out at the same time. On Tartarus, he'd been able to access his magic, but not having a nearby star or other astral bodies meant his powers were limited; he'd been able to draw from the planet and its moons, and not much else. Here, they were in a solar system, his senses told him. This planet had a single moon, and it orbited a yellow dwarf star. There were seven other planets, with four being gas giants.

So many celestial bodies to pull from.

So many different types of power.

He felt giddy, drunk on magic.

Ahead, Caius stood quiet and still, staring at the world around him like he would a long-lost lover. Oberon came up beside him, Styx on Caius's other side. "Of course we'd come here at night. Haven't seen the sun in five thousand years. What's another day?" the kelpie muttered.

He looked up at the night sky and awe left him breathless. The sky... it was familiar. Not identical to Avalon, but the constellations were achingly similar. Above him, three stars clustered together in a straight line—it was part of Nuada, the first ever fae to be crowned High King in Avalon legend. He spun around; there, on the far horizon, was Queen Méabh, the first High Queen and progenitor of the Ó Duibh bloodline.

Earth couldn't be far from Avalon if they shared constellations...

Oberon breathed in deeply, the air rich with the scent of magic, life, water, and dust. "Gods...we're actually here." Magic sizzled through his veins; he needed an outlet. Something to fight. "Which direction?"

Caius lurched forward, like he was about to topple over, and Oberon leaped after in case his friend needed help. But the god righted himself. "That way, apparently."

"You feel your soul calling to you?" Styx asked, skeptical. But Oberon understood, at least partially. He may not have had his soul stolen, but he'd been mated, had his soul tied to another. He'd been able to sense Titian, know her whereabouts.

Too bad he hadn't been able to sense her betrayal.

His panther snarled at the memory—one they didn't share, but one his shadow shifter half knew was fundamental in making Oberon who he was today.

Caius nodded, as if words failed him. Then he started running.

Oberon kept pace as they sped over a grass-covered knoll, their footsteps loud in the quiet of the night. The silence, it was strange, Oberon thought as they ran along a stone path, which connected them to a series of streets that transitioned from tall buildings to single-story houses constructed of wooden panels, covered in peeling paint. Even on

Tartarus, a place of perpetual night, the sound of animals and people were rich and ever-present.

Here, it was as if even the rodents were afraid of the dark.

"What in the..." Styx slowed. "Are those what houses look like now?"

"It would appear so," Caius replied.

Oberon kept quiet. He had no idea what the houses had appeared like before. Compared to Avalon, however, these properties looked like hovels.

A scream tore through the silent night, pain filled. Caius snarled in response and pointed at a house on a nearby street corner. "There."

Oberon's brows knitted. The place was dark, the windows closed tight against the night. Then again, with magic this thick in the air, it could be an illusion, designed to make people think no one was home. "I'm in first," he said, eager to use his magic, test his renewed strength.

Taking the lead, Oberon sprinted for the house. Moments before he reached the door, he called on power from the molten core of the planet, forming a small ball of fire. He threw it at the door, causing the panel to explode in a mess of wooden fragments.

He burst through the entry, coming to a stop before a group of people. Surprised screams met his entrance, and he quickly took stock of the situation as he unsheathed his short sword.

Way too many people crammed into one small space, that was his first thought.

But it all seemed centered around one woman—the guardian of Caius's soul?—who lay face down on the ground in the middle of the room. She was being pinned by a youth with shaggy brown hair and a woman with dark, shoulder-length hair. Another woman—one with glowing hands—knelt nearby while a large male shifter leaned over the guardian, holding a knife in one hand. Finally, a middle-aged woman hovered next to the group, a small boy in front of her, watching everything with a keen gaze.

The stench of blood and rot permeated the air, and it seemed to come from the prostrate guardian.

The young dark-haired woman looked up, her pale gaze skimming over Caius and Styx to land on him. She glowered.

Oberon's gaze locked on her.

Pale, pale blue eyes watched him as she stood up slowly, her beauty almost a slap to the face. Her hair was dark as a crow's wing, glimmering in the flickering light. It slid behind her shoulder as she moved, exposing the arched ears of a fae. She wore a plain black top and pants that were covered in splattered paint.

Time slowed.

Caius's voice boomed through the room. "Stop."

Oberon halted but remained alert. Everyone seemed to be focused on the guardian and the shifter with the knife, and Caius, but that wasn't where the threat lay. No. The fae with the pale eyes. There was something about her...something not right. She was a danger.

His panther growled low in his mind.

"The guardian..." Caius murmured, his words barely audible. Styx reached for the two spikes she wore in her bun, but Caius's hand shot out, grabbing the kelpie's wrist. "No."

"What?" Styx's voice betrayed her shock at the command.

"No. She's...my mate."

Oberon almost jerked at the statement, at the word "mate." *Of course, the guardian is his fucking mate.* He shook his head. If there was one thing he'd learned over the years, it was that fate had a wicked sense of humor—or irony.

"Well, I didn't see that coming," Oberon muttered, and then sheathed his sword with a twirl. He wasn't about to lay a single damned finger on Caius's mate. Nor go anywhere near her. He'd spent millennia watching shadow shifters go crazy once their mate was within their sight—he could only imagine what a god with a shadow form would be like.

Lucky for Oberon, he had already found—and killed—his before turning into a shadow shifter. No mate bond to deal with. Better still, his panther was quite pleased by the fact.

"Hey! Get out of here!" The shaggy-haired boy's voice was so high-pitched it made Oberon's ears hurt. Thankfully, the woman with the glowing hands shushed him.

Then she turned her attention to them, her voice filled with power. "What do you want?"

Oberon almost laughed. The woman was a witch—a fairly powerful one, at that—but she was trying to use magic on a god.

Caius's eyes narrowed. "Ask your questions, witch, but your magic won't work on me."

"I can see that. I know The Crossroads is a bit different from the rest of No Man's Land, and you're obviously not from around here, so I'd highly suggest you get out before someone kills you." Then she added, "And the name is Clara, asshole."

"I think not," Caius replied.

Verbose as always, Oberon thought.

Caius's mate twisted on the ground, moaning in pain. Next to her, the large shifter turned the knife around in his palm.

"Tío, I'm not so sure that's a good idea." Clara shook her head.

Caius came to a decision. "Hold them back."

Styx muttered something under her breath, then followed Oberon as he rushed forward. The shaggy-haired youth tried to throw himself over the prone woman, to protect the guardian. But Clara shoved him aside. The two fought, but Oberon tuned it out, his attention split between the blue-eyed fae and the large shifter with the knife. As Caius approached the guardian, the shifter lunged forward, and Oberon pinned the man against the wall, while Styx tackled the fae woman.

Teeth snapped the air near Oberon's face, rage filling the shifter's eyes. "Get your hands off her!"

Damn it, the man was an alpha. Oberon growled back at the shifter, refusing to budge. He couldn't, even if he wanted to. His panther was also an alpha, but a loner. And alphas only respected one thing—strength. His panther didn't care for a pack, but he'd never back down from a challenge.

Oberon was about to unsheathe his dagger when Caius's words stopped him. "Knock him out if you must, but keep him alive."

You've got to be fucking kidding me.

Oberon felt like he'd been dumped into a house full of crazy. One moment they were on their way for murder and mayhem, the next, they were pinning down a crazed alpha shifter, an outraged fae, and saving the guardian's life.

It took most of Oberon's concentration to help subdue the shifter, but he never lost track of the fae woman. She watched the scene in front of them like a hawk, her focus on the injured woman, even though Styx had her immobilized. When Caius approached the guardian, Oberon started to feel a horribly familiar—but also unfamiliar—power building in the room.

A young boy's shout tore through the room, and old, old magic rose up, almost choking in its intensity. "Raegan!"

The alpha shifter struggled anew, and Oberon shoved him back down with a grunt. He then leaned forward and hissed in a whisper, "Quit moving, or you'll be unconscious for the next month."

Oberon's focus remained solely on the alpha shifter and the fae woman. If the male shifter got away, there'd be blood spilled, and Oberon had the feeling that Caius would be pissed if that happened. As for the fae woman—she was using her magic to draw on power she shouldn't be able to reach.

Caius approached the alpha Oberon had overpowered. "You're related. Who are you?"

The shifter's voice was a low growl. "Her father."

Caius's chin dipped as he looked at Oberon and then Styx.

As one, they stepped back, letting the shifter and fae go. The alpha's body shook with barely contained rage, but he stepped forward, coming toe-to-toe with Caius. While he did that, Oberon backed away, putting himself closer to the door—closer to the fae woman.

The god's voice was level. "I imagine you have questions."

"You could say that, starting with who the hell are you?" His voice was low, rough with rage.

"I'll answer yours if you answer mine," Caius replied.

Oberon took note of the conversation flowing around him, but he didn't participate in it. No, his job here was to protect Caius, since killing the guardian was now out of the picture. At least, for the moment.

His new spot also placed him in a better position to watch the fae girl, who was still slowly drawing power, her gaze locked on Reagan's unconscious body. After finishing his discussion with the alpha, Caius picked up Reagan, holding her limp form.

It was...strange.

Five thousand years they'd spent plotting the destruction of the guardians of Caius's soul. And here he was, cradling the latest as if she were the most precious thing on the planet.

Reagan came to, appearing dazed at first. Then she froze, before scrambling off Caius's lap like he was diseased. Fear was thick in the air, and that seemed to be the catalyst for the fae woman. She stepped forward, placing herself between Caius and Reagan. The temperature in the room plummeted.

Oberon's breath emerged as a puff of mist. But no one else seemed to notice the chill.

"Sin, don't..." Reagan's voice was low, thready.

Sin.

Her name was Sin.

"No," she replied, her voice reminding him of cold graves and death.

A death dealer? *Here*?

Death fae were rare, even on Avalon.

But that wasn't right. Not quite.

No death fae he'd ever known could affect the temperature of a room.

His breath fogged in the air when he exhaled again. His panther paced within his mind, fascinated by the fae woman. Frost formed on the windows, and it crept along the ceiling, leaving intricate patterns behind. It was a cold so deep, so dark, most people would assume it was the icy touch of death.

But Oberon knew better.

This was the cold of nothing.

Of everything.

Of space.

"He doesn't get to just barge in here and claim he's your mate." Sin's face was a cold mask.

Caius didn't even look at her as he replied, "Step aside."

Power rose swiftly, cresting, and it was so familiar Oberon's chest ached.

"I will not. We know what you are."

"Then you know what I'm capable of."

"Try me—"

Before the fae could release her magic, she was flung sideways, slamming into the back of a couch. She was then held there by Caius's will. The sense of power being pulled reached him again, and Oberon's mouth went dry as realization kicked in.

This Sin, she wasn't just any kind of fae.

She was a Celestial.

CHAPTER 4
SIN

THE CROSSROADS, TWO WEEKS LATER

Nog was up to something.

To be fair, Sin thought, Nog was *always* up to something. Normally, however, her sister, Reagan—along with their *prima*, Clara—would ensure that Nog escaped his latest stunt with his head still attached to his neck. But both Reagan and Clara were in hell.

Literal hell.

So now it was Sin's job to ensure that Nog didn't succeed in one of his harebrained schemes. And there was plenty of scheming going on. Sin had been trailing him—at a distance—all day. It had proven to be a tad bit difficult, considering he was trapped in his new shadow shifter form, which was a knee-high corgi. He was jet black in color; his coat so dark that the light was just absorbed by his fur. And even though his eyes glowed orange, he would've been beyond cute, if it weren't for the slightly maniacal stare from said puppy dog eyes.

Sin wasn't sure how much of Nog himself remained when he was stuck in his shifter state, but she hoped that there was a bit of human sensibility present. Not that he had much sense to begin with, but some was better than none.

Sin crept closer to the buildings that lined the edge of the Old Kiener Plaza, watching as Nog trotted along the pathway toward the broken fountain and its new inter-world portal.

He had Ben Flowers with him.

Sin's eyes narrowed as she looked at the tall, broad-shouldered shifter her sister had been casually dating. Reagan said their relationship was a "friends with benefits" type of situation; their cousin Clara said he was Reagan's "fuck buddy." Sin called him a distraction. Ben was cute, if you went for that sort of thing, which Sin didn't. He was too, well, *boring* for her. And that was the point, she realized. Reagan wasn't attracted to someone exciting, to someone dangerous, or even to someone fun. No, she wanted somebody who was like plain toast. You'd eat it and survive, but you wouldn't really enjoy it.

Too bad Ben hadn't realized that before he attempted to mark Reagan.

Sin's hands curled into fists. Oh, how she would love to give the guy a black eye and then some for daring to try that shit on her sister. But Reagan had already punched him, and if Sin sprang out at him now, she would give away the fact she was stalking—uh, following—Nog.

As the shifter and dog approached the portal, Sin wondered why the hell Nog was even with Ben. He'd been just as pissed as Sin and Clara when he learned what Ben had attempted. And why was Ben chatting to the dog and waiting for Nog to bark in answer?

Suddenly, it clicked.

Ben could talk to dogs.

Sin barely refrained from hitting herself on the forehead. Ben—and Nog—would hear her if she did that. Instead, she inched into another shadow, this one cast by a tree on the edge of the plaza.

The duo wasn't exactly being subtle. They walked confidently along the cracked pavement, like they didn't have a care in the world. Sin glanced toward the portal, which hung suspended over the broken fountain. Thankfully, the black tendrils of death magic that had spewed from the portal when it first opened were gone. Now, it simply hovered in the air akin to a small black hole, except there was no time dilation or increased gravity. Darkness was all she could see from this side of the portal.

And to be fair, black hole or not, Sin worried about it and what it meant for her family.

Her sister and cousin were stuck on the other side of that portal, and it was guarded twenty-four seven. Clara had been kidnapped by the Soulless One, an ancient primeval god, and Reagan had followed soon after, determined to free their *prima*.

The fool.

The stupid, beyond brave, fool.

But right now, Sin just wanted to get her back.

Sin—and the whole family—had been coming to the portal to get news about Clara and Reagan, but the guards had told them nada. And one fae guard in particular...Sin preferred not to think about him at all.

Sin knew that her sister and Clara could handle themselves. Clara, their *prima*, was a witch with soul magic—magic that meant she and Sin had more in common than Sin did with anyone else in the family. And Nog...Sin knew he was desperate to get his sister and Reagan back. Nog and Clara fought like literal cats and dogs, but if you dared to look at one of them funny, the other would come after you.

Ben and the corgi shifter were only around two hundred yards from the portal now. There were three guards on watch; the blond-haired fae who normally oversaw the operation wasn't there. And neither was the fae woman who wore spikes in her hair.

Sin faded back into the shadows, scanning the area around her, trying to see if the fae—Oberon—was behind the portal or lurking somewhere else nearby.

Because the man liked to lurk.

And he liked to stare.

At her.

She didn't know why, but something about that asshole pissed her off whenever she saw him. Maybe it was because he'd pinned her father —an alpha shifter—effortlessly against the wall of their living room, so the Soulless One could kill Reagan. Maybe it was because he stared at her like she was a strange critter that had wandered in uninvited. Or maybe it was just because he was so damn handsome it made her teeth ache.

No, scratch that.

He wasn't even that hot.

Yeah, yeah, lie to yourself some more.

But he *was* the leader of the Soulless One's portal guards, and right now, he was conspicuously absent. Especially when Nog and Ben were now mere feet from said portal. At that moment, Ben slung a backpack off his broad shoulders, pulling out random jars and lining them on the pavement next to his feet. What were those two idiots up to?

Nog began to bark, the sound high pitched and frantic. Then he was running, like a deranged, well, corgi. Yapping and dodging in glee, he quickly had the guards chasing him around the portal in a madcap game of tag. Ben, on the other hand, began throwing the jars—which turned out to be magical Molotov cocktails—at those same guards. Explosions rent the air, and Sin realized what they were doing.

Creating a diversion.

Nog's plan was clear to Sin now: use Ben as bait so that they could distract the guards enough for the corgi to sneak through.

Although Nog hadn't yet succeeded in giving them the slip.

She stepped forward, hoping this would be her chance to sneak through—

"So, why are you lurking in the bushes?" The dark voice rolled over the back of Sin's neck, making the tiny hairs stand on end and her skin prickle.

She froze. She hadn't even heard him approaching.

Turning slightly, her mouth thinned as she realized the tall fae male was *right next to her*. Her stomach did an uncomfortable flip-flop as she took in the white-blond hair that was brushed back from his face, his jaw clean-cut and rock-hard. Dark eyebrows arched over midnight-colored eyes, his mouth curved in a wicked grin. All in all, he was ridiculously handsome.

No, she didn't just think that. He was nothing more than a giant oaf. Broad-shouldered and well over six feet in height, he'd put her on her ass five times in the last two weeks. Just because she'd tried to go through the portal. There was *nothing* about him to admire.

Okay...fine. The blond jerk was an exceptionally good fighter. And whatever magic she used, even if she tried to use the gifts she normally fought to suppress, he seemed easily able to counter them, too. She had absolutely no idea what kind of fae he was.

"Well?" His eyebrows rose even higher.

She tapped her fingers on her thigh. "I was just out for a midnight stroll."

"Because the views are so excellent at this time of evening." He waved a strong hand in a graceful arc.

"They are." Sin looked up, taking note of Orion, Gemini, and Leo. The views were actually quite good this time of year, especially when there wasn't any cloud cover. Pollux and Castor, Betelgeuse and Arcturus...the stars were bright, glimmering overhead. Too bad it wasn't one of her sleepless nights, where she watched the stars as an escape from life. Now wasn't the time to revel in her connection to the cold, dark, endlessness of space, or to wonder why she could feel the glowing specks of dying and distant suns.

The barking morphed into a continual growl and Sin glanced at the portal. Nog had somehow managed to find a rope and had tied up one of the guard's legs by running laps around him. The corgi was trying to drag the rope—which was clamped in his jaws—away from the portal, while the guard frantically attempted to extricate himself. Ben, on the other hand, was fighting a different guard, dodging and punching with the ferocity of a wolf in human form. The third sentry lay semiconscious on the ground in front of the portal.

"Aren't you going help them?" Sin asked, gesturing toward the chaos.

Oberon gave her an amused look. "Why would I do that, when the biggest threat is right here?"

"I don't know what you're talking about." Sin crossed her arms over her chest, inadvertently pushing her breasts up against the square neck of her tank top.

Oberon's eyes dropped down and a wall of heat slammed into her, her mouth going dry in response. For a moment, she thought he had pressed his body against hers. But no, they were still half a foot apart. He was just so big that he took up all the air in the space between them.

He leaned down. "You wouldn't happen to be thinking of trying to get through that portal again, would you?" His breath fanned across her face, and she could almost taste the cedarwood and citrus scent of him.

She ran her tongue over her lower lip, wetting it. "Would it matter if I was?"

An evil smile curved his lips. "It would."

"That's a shame."

His gaze dropped down to her mouth, and for a moment, she wondered if he wanted her. If that was why he was always so horrid. Like a schoolboy in the yard, pulling on the hair of the girl he crushed on.

No, don't be an idiot.

Oberon was a grown-ass man. But...she wondered. And considered how she could possibly use that to her advantage. Sin began pulling energy up through the Earth, feeling her body warm as power flooded her senses.

She needed to get away from him, and she needed to get away from him fast. But she didn't want to hurt him—not too badly, at any rate. Sin didn't want Reagan or Clara to suffer the Soulless One's wrath for her actions. So, she had to distract him while she gathered enough power...

Without giving herself a chance to second-guess her hasty—and stupid—plan, she acted. Moving forward, she closed the distance between them, twining her arms around his neck, pressing herself against his body. Fuck. He was like a furnace. And his chest...her breasts ached where they met the wall of muscle. Touching him like this—it was wrong. He was keeping her away from her sister; he was preventing her family from helping their own.

But why did it feel so good?

Gods, he was tall, she realized, as she stared up at him through her lashes. He'd frozen in response, dark eyes wide with surprise, his arms splayed out to the side, as if he was unsure what to do with them.

"Sin, what are you—" His hands came up to rest on her shoulders as a muscle ticked in his jaw. He was going to push her away, she realized.

Damnit. She'd misjudged the situation. But that was okay. In for a penny, in for a pound. There was no going back now. Standing on her tiptoes, she pressed her lips to his, shock sizzling through her at the contact. At first, he didn't respond, standing still as a statue, and she figured she was going to have to just smash him with her magic, even though it wasn't quite ready. But after the most awkward three seconds of her life, he groaned, his mouth moving against hers.

Holy shit, he was kissing her back. Rational thought fled when Oberon tilted her head to the side with a firm hand, his tongue invading her mouth like it had every right to do so.

The cedarwood and citrus smell of him grew intoxicating as she dueled with him, her tongue clashing with his, fighting for control. He deepened the kiss, demanding she give in, but she refused, matching his passion with her own. His large hands slid down her body to clamp on her hips, his fingers digging into her soft flesh as he tugged her even closer. Her thighs clenched as her belly pressed up against the hard length of him. He pulled on her hips, grinding her body into his; in response, she nipped his bottom lip, wanting to tease him...torment him for what he was doing to her. For how he was making her body come alive, for *him*.

He jerked away, raising a hand to his mouth, dark eyes wild. "You bit me!"

A drop of blood swelled on his lower lip, and for some crazy reason, she was tempted to lick it away.

The thought was like a cold bucket of water being poured over her head. She had kissed him to distract him while she built up power—and here she was *enjoying* it. She'd even bitten him, for gods' sakes!

What the fuck was wrong with her?

Without warning, she shoved her hands out, palms first, across his chest. He blinked in surprise at the touch, his dark gaze heating. He reached out, his hands gently cupping her shoulders. "Sin, maybe we should slow things down—"

She shoved the energy into him, the magic blasting through her palms in a wave of electricity. Oberon let out an *oof* of surprise and shot back through the air, slamming to a stop when his back rammed into the trunk of a distant tree. He slid down the bark, but she didn't stop to watch him hit the ground.

Sin sprinted, running faster than she ever had in her entire life, trying to get to that damned portal. Nog had somehow taken down the guard he'd tangled in rope, and Ben had just felled the soldier he'd been sparring with. The third and final soldier was still out for the count.

She had to get through.

Accelerating, Sin was three quarters of the way there when she was suddenly hoisted into the air, and then dumped unceremoniously onto the ground. Hard. Air whooshed out of her lungs, and she gasped like a landed fish, trying to catch her breath.

She hadn't even heard him behind her.

Rolling onto her side, Sin glared up at Oberon as he closed the distance between them, his anger like a dark storm cloud around him. He'd used magic to toss her around like a doll. Turning to the portal, still trying to take a full breath, she watched as Nog darted through, Ben close behind.

Fuck.

Her head fell back against the cold ground.

Oberon squatted next to her, his expression dark. "Nice trick." He tugged on the material of his T-shirt while he wiped the back of his other hand across his mouth. Something within her chest ached at his clear repudiation of her. "I liked that shirt." Her handprints had burned away the fabric, so that she could see his skin through the two holes.

Sin didn't know how to respond to that. She struggled into a sitting position, her shoulder and hip aching from their date with the ground. "Aren't you going to chase them?"

Oberon pivoted toward the portal, and strangely, he smirked. It was a slightly cruel expression, though, complete with smeared blood from her bite. "Did you really think Caius was stupid enough to only guard one side of the portal? If Nog and the wolf shifter got through, they're going to have to deal with the soldiers on Tartarus. Not only that, but the portal opens onto a garden with carnivorous tendencies. If they manage to make it past that, then they'll deal with Caius himself."

Oberon didn't look concerned at all.

Sin clambered to her feet, and the fae male slowly shook his head at her. "You need to give up. I'm not letting you through that portal."

"Never going to happen." She drew her chin up.

"I thought you might say that." He stood, and the next thing Sin knew, she was upside down and over his shoulder, stomach pressing into his collar bone.

Sin froze, trying to process exactly how she'd ended up in this position. She inhaled his scent—that infuriating scent—with every breath. Gods, it was *worse* now that she knew what he tasted like.

"Put me down! Now!"

"Oh, I'll do that. When you're home and out of my godsdamned hair." He started walking away from the portal, but she could hear the rage in his voice, even with the blood rushing to her head.

"*What*?"

"I swear, you were born to annoy me. Did you escape from the circus, or is this your natural state?" He rubbed his face against the side of her hip, catlike.

She spluttered. She annoyed *him*? And had he just likened her to a clown? He was such a *prick*. "Were you just sniffing my leg?"

She *felt* him chuckle. Sin started squirming then, and he grunted as his hand closed like a band of iron around the back of her thighs. She started pummeling his back with her fists, and then reared up until she was upright, trying to shove her way out of his grip. "Put. Me. Down!"

He glared at her, his dark eyes flashing. "Do that again and I will spank your ass."

"You wouldn't dare." She tried to buck away.

He stopped walking and used both of his arms to pin the back of her thighs to his chest. Somehow—she really wasn't sure how, when both his hands were on her legs—he pushed on her back until her stomach muscles couldn't withstand the pressure, and she ended up back over his shoulder.

Then Oberon smacked her on the ass.

Once.

Twice.

She barely even felt the sting through the blood rushing into her head. Red hazed over her vision, and she drew power into her hand, letting it sizzle there. How fucking *dare* he? She slapped her hand on *his* ass, hard, letting her magic taser him.

But he didn't even flinch.

No, the jerkface just burst out laughing. "Is that the best you got?"

Fury had her hissing, and she dug her nails into the firm muscle of his ass.

He started walking again.

Why hadn't that worked? Most people would be crying in pain right now. "Not even close," she hissed through gritted teeth.

"Next time, use some real magic."

"'Use some real magic,'" she mimicked. "Put me *down*!"

He adjusted her on his shoulder, and she felt him shake his head, his hair brushing against the top of her hip. "Not a chance."

CHAPTER 5
SIN

THE CROSSROADS, NOW-ISH

If Sin had to hear Oberon's jerk-ass voice one more time, she was either going to vomit or scream.

She hadn't decided which.

She grabbed her keys out of her leather pack before slinging it over her shoulder. Taking a deep breath, she stared at the door to the small house she shared with Reagan and Clara and counted to ten. She hadn't been home in six days, and if she strode inside with rage heating the air, she'd have to explain, and that, she didn't want to do.

Fumbling with her keys, she cursed as they slipped through her fingers, the clatter as they hit the dirt ground sharp in the otherwise quiet.

Gods, he was just *so damned frustrating*.

Not just because he'd carried her home over his shoulder like she was a sack of potatoes—more than once. And he'd spanked her, *spanked her*, like she was a fucking child. He'd also prevented her from getting through that damned portal and finding her sister more times than she could count. And he'd done it by putting her on her ass, which was just plain embarrassing. Sin may not have been a natural fighter like her dad, but she could hold her own in a brawl. And her magic was normally enough to even the odds.

Just not when it came to Oberon.

He'd also never let anyone else fight her—not the kelpie woman, or any of Caius's other lackeys. No, Oberon toyed with her, before turning her away. Like a giant blond cat with a mouse.

Sin didn't like it. She didn't like *him*.

Sighing, Sin bent down and retrieved the keys.

Gods, she could almost *smell* the bastard—cedarwood, citrus, and the faintest hint of something that spoke of the skies. It wasn't fair that he smelled so good, not when he was rotten to the core. She sniffed, growling low in her throat. His scent clung to the air, polluting it.

She kicked the door.

"What did that door ever do to you?" The dark, sensual voice wrapped around her in a deeply unpleasant way.

Sin froze, hand outstretched toward the house and safety. Well... relative safety.

No, she'd just hallucinated Oberon's voice. She hadn't slept in forever. He wouldn't have followed her home from the portal. Not when he'd actually been off guard duty for the first time in weeks.

Shaking her head, she shoved her key in the lock, and was about to chant a spell to neutralize the wards when a muscled arm moved in front of her face, blocking her.

Gods. The *smell*.

She breathed through her mouth, before turning to glare at the owner of the arm.

Oberon.

He was standing right in front of her house, his white-blond mane swept back from his nearly perfect face, the tips of his pointed ears hidden by the fall of hair. He was dressed in dark pants and a leather jacket, with a short sword belted to his hip, and at least three visible daggers in sheaths on his hip and arms.

Scream or puke, she thought.

She opened her mouth to scream, then reconsidered. Her family was nearby—those that weren't currently on Tartarus—as well as her friends. They'd come running, ready for blood, and she didn't want to have to explain to them her response to a member of Caius's inner circle. Mostly because that meant she would have to explain it to Reagan, which she was reluctant to do. They'd only just made up; she didn't want to add any tension to her sister's sort-of honeymoon. Plus, Sin was meant to be the most level-headed one in the family, aside from Jo, who'd been the calmest nine-year-old on the entire planet. Her heart ached at the thought of her *primito*.

"Uh, hello?" Oberon waved his arm again. His accent was strange, almost British, but with an unusual lilt to it. She tried not to look at his too-perfect face. "Earth to Sin."

She bared her teeth in the pretense of a smile. "Fuck off." Then she muttered, "*Que te folle un pez.*" She didn't think he knew Spanish—at least, she hoped not.

The prick just crossed his arms and leaned against her door. "Come now, is that any way to talk to your brother-in-law's best friend?"

She gave him a flat glare. He was touching her house. Without her permission. "You aren't anybody's friend. And stop touching my house."

"Don't project your own situation onto me." He leaned forward, and it took all of her self-control to stay in place, to refrain from clawing out his amazing—no, disturbing—eyes. Gods, why was he so *big*? He wasn't massive like Caius, but Oberon was over six feet two inches, with wide shoulders and tons of lean muscle. He overshadowed her.

Sin spluttered. "I have friends."

Yes, that didn't sound overly defensive at all. Or like a fifth grader.

"Family doesn't count." He moved back, using her door as a prop again, apparently satisfied he'd gotten under her skin.

"I wasn't talking about family."

"Sure, you weren't." Those midnight eyes seemed to look right through her.

Sure, *most* of her friends were family, but not all. And while Reagan was her best friend, so was Kasha. They just had a different relationship. One that didn't mean Sin had had to lie by omission for Kasha's safety. At least, she didn't have to keep secrets about Kasha to protect Kasha from herself.

Sin rubbed her forehead.

She withdrew the key and pocketed it. If she didn't disarm the warding spell soon, the house would take defensive action against a potential intruder. Her *prima*, Clara, had some interesting curses up her sleeve. "Why are you here? To blow up another part of my house?"

And while she would dearly love to see what her magical security system did to Oberon, she didn't want to have to explain to Reagan—or Caius—why the fae was injured on her doorstep. Although, Clara had installed the magical system *because* Oberon had blown their door apart the day Caius had come for Reagan.

His expression turned serene. "I couldn't just be coming to check on Reagan's sister?"

Sin stared at him.

Pureblooded fae couldn't lie—she knew all about that—but it seemed like Oberon had mastered obfuscation.

He rubbed a hand over his chin, the skin scraping over dark stubble. The flicker of light on shimmery gold caught her attention, and her gaze locked on a ring she had never noticed before. He wasn't exactly a jewelry kind of guy; his ornamentation seemed to favor weapons. The ring's design was intricate, almost too intricate for the size of the band. And it looked almost like a—

"Like what you're looking at?" He smirked, and while the expression would have normally made her brain stutter in abject horror, she reached out, trying to grab his hand. She wanted—no, she *needed*—to have a better look at his ring.

He weaved away, somehow slithering away from her with cat-quick reflexes. "Whoa! Hands off the merchandise."

Sin jerked, distracted from her need to see the ring in better detail. "Merchandise?"

A piece of his white hair settled over his forehead, contrasting with his black eyebrows. His expression was almost innocent as he spoke, "What? I've adapted to the native language."

She snorted, amused despite herself.

Now it was his turn to sound defensive. "I was stuck here for almost three months."

Yeah, keeping her out of Tartarus. Preventing her from helping Reagan.

"Poor baby." She gave him a sympathetic pout. "It must have been so hard for you."

His gaze swept over her body, scalding her skin. "You have no idea." But when she dared a glance at his black gaze, it wasn't the fake leer she'd expected. No, it was something else, something she was better off not thinking about too much.

Sin was done with whatever game he was playing. "Say your piece and leave."

"Aren't you going to invite me inside?"

She narrowed her eyes. "No."

"Well, guess we'll have to see who is the most stubborn then. I am not saying my piece out in the middle of the street."

"Because there are so many people around to overhear." Sin swept an arm behind her at the thankfully empty road. Since the new portal had opened in The Crossroads, their part of No Man's Land had suddenly become a lot busier. Not from people traveling in and out of the portal—Caius had that well controlled. No, people flocked to the new portal to see if their magic would change as a result, or to see where it led. And in the case of the Houses, they came here to establish embassies.

Oberon shrugged and continued to lean against the door.

Sin began tapping her foot, thinking. Was she really going to do this? Was she really going to stand here and argue about inviting Oberon into her house?

Yes. Yes, she was.

Because it wasn't just about her not wanting him in her personal space, putting his scent all over her things. It was the fact that she didn't like *him*, and she didn't trust him at all. Inviting him inside meant that he could kill her, and no one would know.

No one who could do anything about it, anyway.

Banging—the sound of pots slamming against her kitchen counter most likely—could be heard, ever so faintly, from inside the house. Her time was up. Oberon turned slightly to stare at her door, a quizzical look on his face.

"I thought you lived alone since Reagan moved to Tartarus, and Clara began spending most of her time annoying—uh, visiting us."

Her eyes narrowed. "Why would you know anything about my living arrangements?"

"I make it a priority to understand everything about a potential enemy." He frowned. "Was that glass breaking?"

Gods, I hope not, Sin thought. She only owned one set of drinking cups.

"Me? A potential enemy?" One of Sin's eyebrows rose.

"You tried to attack Caius. It's not something I take lightly."

Sin's expression turned dark. "He swatted me like a godsdamn fly. I'm not the threat you claim I am."

That had been humbling. Even knowing Caius was a god, it had still been a shock to be so easily overpowered. Sin had spent most of her life *downplaying* her abilities, to the point where she suspected she may have broken her magic. And even then, she was normally more powerful than most of the people around her.

A corner of Oberon's mouth lifted. "You may not be a threat to him —or me—but that doesn't mean you aren't a threat to Reagan, or anyone else in Tartarus."

Sin's vision hazed with red. Had he just claimed she was a danger to her own sister? To her family? "Caius blackmailed my sister into going into Tartarus."

"Your sister is happy in Tartarus."

"Now she is, but not then."

His head dipped. "True." Then he leaned down slightly, his breath hot as it fanned over her cheek, making her blood heat. "Now, invite me inside."

She bit the inside of her cheek, hating how her body reacted to his. She should never have kissed the jerk, even though it had been nothing more than a distraction tactic. "I didn't know fae needed an invitation into someone's home. Do you have some kind of curse, like the old-school legends about vampires?"

Oberon looked at her like she'd lost her mind. And maybe she had—she was still talking to the prick, after all. "Your house is warded. I can't break the ward without destroying your house, and whoever is inside breaking your shit."

The sound of cracking wood was suddenly deafening.

Damnit.

Shoving Oberon aside, she ignored the heat the contact always generated, and quickly chanted the spell to deactivate the ward under her breath as fast as she could. The lock glowed bright blue before dimming, and she pushed the door open, only to come to an abrupt stop just inside the doorway.

Mouth ajar, Sin gaped at the chaos inside her home.

The petite side table she'd had near the door was lying on the floor, one of the legs snapped off, and the ornaments that she'd painstakingly placed on it were broken on the ground, shattered pieces of glass and ceramic strewn over the hardwood floorboards. Through the internal doorway, Sin could see the kitchen, where half the sage-colored cupboard doors hung open—some almost pulled off their hinges—and Reagan's copper pots and pans were strewn over the floor.

She did not leave the house looking like this.

Oberon's breath tickled the shell of her ear as he leaned down and looked over her shoulder to take in the scene before her. "Seems like your mysterious roommate didn't like you staying out past curfew."

She elbowed him. Hard.

He let out an *oomph* and stepped back, rubbing his stomach. "You play dirty." He eyed her arm. "And why are your elbows so pointy?"

"My elbows are not 'pointy'! And I am *not* 'playing' anything with you."

He grumbled something about her elbows in response, which she chose to ignore. Her elbows were perfectly normal.

"*¡Un hada! ¡Has estado ahí parada hablando con un hada!*" *A fae! You've been standing there talking to a fae!* Sin automatically translated. Her mother appeared in the hallway, semi-transparent and fueled by rage. She waved the broken table leg in her hand like a spear, her pale pink eyes crazed.

Sin sighed.

She should have expected something like this to happen.

"Why is there a table leg floating in the air?" Oberon asked, his voice strangely neutral.

"Because there's a ghost holding it."

The back of her head burned under his stare.

"Why did you ruin the house?" Sin asked her mother, stepping forward gingerly. There was the body of the small glass cat statue she'd salvaged from an "antique" store, and to the left of her booted foot was a fragment of the mother-of-pearl box she'd scavenged from a former client's grave.

"I didn't—" Oberon began, but shut his jaw with a snap when he presumably realized she was asking the ghost.

"You said you'd only be gone a day or two. It's been a week!" Her mother, Dianthe, shouted.

"So, that meant you could destroy the house?" Sin made a point of looking at the carnage at her feet.

"Well...no." Her mother lowered the table leg. "But I could sense you were here, but you wouldn't come inside. Now I see it was because you were talking to a fae. He had better not be your mate."

Sin's cheeks flamed red. Thankfully Oberon didn't appear to have the powers of a death fae—he didn't seem to be able to see or hear ghosts.

"He isn't and he wouldn't leave," Sin replied.

Why *wouldn't* he leave?

Her mother shifted her focus to Oberon, and her expression went from dark to deadly. That wasn't a good sign. Then again, Sin felt much the same about the asshole.

"Are you going to break more of my things?" Sin asked her mother, distracting her.

Dianthe dropped the table leg and it clattered on the floor. "*Ahora no.*" *Not now.*

That was about as good an answer as she was going to get, Sin figured. Sin's mother had been dead for almost twenty-eight years. Ghosts typically weren't meant to linger on Earth; doing so drove them insane. Add in the fact that Dianthe had already been psychologically unstable prior to her demise, and well, it meant that she was one hell of an unpredictable entity.

More poltergeist than ghost. But Sin wasn't stupid enough to say that out loud. Her mother's mood swings would have made Jekyll and Hyde look rational in comparison.

"Watch your step," Sin said, realizing that Oberon was going to follow her inside, whether or not she—or her mother—liked it.

Careful to avoid stepping on any of her broken ornaments—she might be able to repair some of them—Sin made her way into the house. Thankfully, her mother hadn't decided to destroy the whole room. An antique TV was nestled near the window, with a navy sofa in the center of the room, and a sage-colored sitting chair to the side. Oberon stepped inside and shut the door behind him. Sin took the chair, while Oberon sprawled over her entire sofa, making the three-seater look tiny.

She glared at him.

"So, why do you have a ghost in your house?" He withdrew one of his daggers—this one looked to be made from pure iron—and began twirling it through his hands.

"What do you want?" Sin ignored his question as her mother rubbed the side of her transparent face and muttered something unintelligible.

Having conversations with more than one person at a time was exhausting.

Dianthe floated over next to her, dressed as she was the day she died: in a white hospital gown covered in blood. Her stomach protruded slightly against the gown, her pale silvery hair hung lankly down her back, and her translucent skin was waxen. Dianthe had died hours after Sin was born.

Oberon leaned forward. "I want you to come with me to Avalon."

Sin rubbed her ears, thinking she'd misheard him. "You want me to go with you to the fae home world? Is this some kind of joke?"

He glowered at her. "It's not a joke."

"You don't even like me—"

He spread his hands out. "What's not to like about a prickly and stubborn woman who won't listen to reason?"

She glared at him. "—and I can't stand you."

"Wow, tell me how you really feel." He placed a hand over his heart.

"Why?" Sin demanded. "Why should I go with *you* to Avalon?"

"Because I asked?" He winced, clearly realizing that was not the argument to win her over.

She settled back against her chair. "Not a chance in hell."

"Avalon?" Her mother's screech had Sin rubbing her right ear in pain.

Most fae on Earth had come through the Avalon portal when it opened in Ireland four hundred years ago, but Dianthe's family had been here far longer than that, having come to Earth via a different route. At least, that was the story Sin's mother had told her during one of Dianthe's saner moments.

Sin preferred not to think about her biological father or his family at all if she had the choice.

"Come now, it would be an adventure." Oberon spread his arms out and smiled, the picture of magnanimity.

"The answer is still no."

"*No puedes ir a Avalon,*" her mother announced.

"Why can't I go to Avalon?" Sin asked. Not that she wanted to—at all—but her mother had never cared where Sin went, as long as she came home within a couple of days. Which wasn't always possible.

"Because I said so," her mother snapped. She must have taken note of Sin's expression, because she went on to say, "The fae there will want you dead. Especially the High King or Queen."

"*What?*" Sin wasn't sure she'd heard right. She didn't know much about the fae world, but she knew it was ruled by the High King or Queen, and that all the other fae courts answered to them. And that not just anyone could be crowned High Queen—there was some mystical test that had to be passed.

Why would they want Sin dead?

Dianthe floated over to the boarded-up window and stared at the wood panels as if she was looking into the sky. "It's going to rain later."

Right. Sin had thought for a moment that her mother was rational, but that was clearly not the case.

In a sing-song voice, Dianthe crooned: "On a bright summer's day / The cursed king made his way / To be crowned this night / Through magic and might / He rose to power / Only to lose his lover / So was the cursed king of the fae / Lost and never finding his way."

She had *no* idea what her mother was talking about.

"What's the ghost saying?" Oberon demanded, the dagger in his hands stilling.

Sin turned to him. "A poem about a cursed fae king."

Oberon didn't laugh at her statement.

In fact, it just made him frown. In that moment, Sin realized she'd never seen him just be...him.

And it was startling just how appealing that was.

CHAPTER 6
SIN

"Who is this ghost? And where did they come from?" Oberon asked.

Sin's mouth clamped shut. She didn't want to tell him. *Reagan has probably already told Caius about my unique...circumstances...* But that didn't mean Caius had told—or would ever tell—Oberon about Sin.

Caius protected Reagan with everything he had.

But that didn't mean he'd protect Sin. Not when he seemed to think she was as much a liability as she was a sister.

He might tell Oberon, if he asks...

Damnit.

Sin was a private person by nature. She'd had to be. Raised by shifters and witches, she was the odd one out, even in her family. Sin couldn't lie, so they'd told everyone Sin and Reagan had different mothers so that people would assume they were biological sisters. But Sin was a foundling; adopted by Alvaro Santiago a few years after her birth, he'd brought her home and raised her as his own. He'd been searching for Reagan at the time, but he hadn't been able to leave her with the foster family who'd been terrified of her.

Most people thought Sin was half death fae, half latent shifter. But she was pure fae, although she had no idea what her non-death fae bloodline was. She didn't have a name for it, but she could feel power flowing *into* her at times, power that came from an outside source. Originally, she'd been worried she was draining it from those around her, from her family. It had been Jo who had finally calmed that fear. He'd told her that she didn't take it from people, she just took it from the planet.

Which still made absolutely no sense at all to her.

Gods, how she missed him—the kind, old soul who had been part of her family for too short a time.

Fae magic was often tied to the elements: fire, water, air, the earth. But that didn't mean they drew power from those, just that they could manipulate them. One of the exceptions were the death fae, who manipulated life itself. Her biological father had been able to raise armies of the dead—a true necromancer. Sin couldn't do that, but she could hold a soul to a body, preventing them from death. And she could see and talk to ghosts, as well as cast death magic at living beings.

"Who. Is. The. Ghost?" Oberon ground out each word, shocking Sin back to reality.

The fae was standing in front of her, leaning down to put his hands on the armrests of her chair, his upper body inches from hers. His scent was like a physical slap, and she felt tiny and insignificant in the face of his irritation.

Close. He was way too close.

The dagger he'd been playing with was nowhere to be seen and his grip on the chair was punishing, his knuckles white as the bone pushed up against his skin as he trapped her. His black brows were drawn tight, and his dark eyes bored into hers. He was clearly pissed.

You idiot, she thought. She'd been so lost in her head she hadn't even heard—or seen—the fae move. She'd been worried about him killing her, and she'd given him the perfect opportunity.

Only he hadn't taken it.

Sin shoved at his arms, hating how her palms tingled at the contact, even though his leather jacket meant she was nowhere near touching his skin. It had to be his magic. She didn't react like that to other men. "Get out of my face."

"You're distracted today." He didn't move for a full minute, making it clear her attempts to shove him away were pointless.

"And you're a prick." Yeah, she was not having a good day.

He barked out a laugh as he stood slowly, showing her that he was in control of the situation; that he'd moved only because *he'd* wanted to. "At least you're honest."

"What other choice do I have?" Sin grumbled.

"If you were half-shifter, you could lie to me as much as you wanted. And I know you would dearly, dearly love to lie to me." One of his dark eyebrows lifted, and a small smile played at the corners of his lips.

Fucking hell.

Sin's stomach dropped while her heartbeat pounded in her ears. "I'm failing to see your point here."

His voice was low, almost a purr. He picked up a piece of her hair, his eyes flashing orange as he played with it between his fingers. It made her stomach do an awkward flip flop. "Only pureblooded fae can't lie. You're meant to be half-sisters with Reagan. Unless you're the one who has been cursed?"

Sin slapped his hand away, not bothering to reply.

"Mmhmm." He moved next to the couch, dropping onto it with the causal grace of a hunting cat, one leg stretched out before him. "So, who is the ghost?"

"You don't have to tell the fae anything," Dianthe said, her eyes locked on Oberon.

Which was true.

But Sin was tired. Bone tired. Sick of hiding who she was—*what* she was. And at the end of the day, Oberon wasn't going to stick around and make her life more of a hell than it already was. Not once he finally got it through his thick head that she wasn't going *anywhere* with him, let alone Avalon.

"The ghost is my mother," Sin said with a sigh, leaning back into the chair.

Oberon's eyes narrowed. "Your mother? But you were a baby when..." His voice trailed off.

"I may have died, but I wasn't going to abandon my only child." Dianthe's voice was eerily calm.

"She never left me," Sin said quietly.

No, Dianthe may have been struggling with the concept of sanity when Sin had been born, but she hadn't wanted to abandon her daughter. But complications from the birth had led to her mother bleeding to death while the doctors and healers had tried to save her. Sin wasn't sure if her death magic, even as a baby, had inadvertently tied her mother to the world.

He began tapping his knee, the movement attracting her gaze. "Fae souls are meant to return to the Host when they die."

"Mamá didn't." That was all Sin could really say to that. *What the hell was the Host?* she wondered. Some death fae were able to herd souls into the afterlife, which was meant to sit next to their reality—the death plane, some called it—but she lacked that ability. She would have encouraged her mother to move on a decade ago, otherwise.

"Was your mother born on Earth?" Oberon asked, fingers still tapping a rather unrhythmic beat on his knee. Two taps, stop, one tap, stop, five taps, stop, three taps, stop. But the tapping didn't seem to repeat.

It bothered her.

Sin bit the inside of her cheek. "Does it matter?"

"Yes."

"Well, then. You can't expect me to give you those answers for free." She smoothed her palms over the arms of her chair, fighting the urge to slap his hand and its ridiculous out-of-sync tapping.

His eyebrows shot up. "You want me to *pay* you?"

"Information is power. You expect me to just hand it to you?"

From the look on Oberon's face, he expected just that. "What kind of payment were you after? And please note that I won't be accepting sexual favors if offered. I've been burned by you before. Literally." He ran a hand over his intact shirt, as if remembering what she'd done back at the portal.

"Sexual—" She gagged. "No, you pervert. Payment in kind."

He stared at her. "You're the one who kissed me!"

"Come on, it was a distraction." She rolled her eyes. "And you fell for it."

"You leapt on me like a starving woman."

Sin wondered if she could set him on fire, just through the power of her gaze. She needed to change the topic, before she decided to strangle him. "You ask me a question, and I ask you a question in return."

Sin was ninety-nine percent sure that Oberon was a full-blooded fae; he was far too powerful not to be. So that meant he couldn't lie to her, either. Not that she was foolish enough to take anything he said at face value.

"About me?" he asked, surprise lacing his tone.

She scoffed. "No. There isn't *anything* about you I want to know."

No, she wanted to know more about Tartarus, about Reagan's future.

Sin had no idea what lay in store for her, but she wanted to ensure her sister would be okay. They'd spent their whole lives frightened, worried the cult that had taken Reagan's mother and raised her until she gave birth to Reagan, would find her and kill her. A bright future filled with life and joy wasn't something Sin had ever expected for Reagan.

Had she hoped for it? Absolutely.

Daydreamed about it millions of times? Yes.

But had she believed it would actually happen? No.

That was something she'd thought of as pure fantasy.

As for Sin, all she wanted for herself was an unremarkable, boring future. Fame, fortune—or hell, even being noticed by anyone with a smidgeon of power—held little to no interest for her. She just wanted to live. She'd consider her life successful if she managed to be content; not happy, just content. Helping her family in their business, and assisting her dad in saving children, those were her goals. She wanted to make a small difference in this world, and hopefully go unnoticed while doing so.

Oberon's fingers stopped their incessant tapping and his expression morphed, his mouth tightening. "Why *wouldn't* you want to know more about me?"

Sin waved a hand in his general direction. "Because you're...you."

He sat up, looking like an affronted cat. "What is wrong with me?"

"I don't have time to list all of your many and varied faults," Sin said, rolling her eyes again. "My questions relate to Reagan and Tartarus. Do we have a deal?"

Sin's fingers clenched tightly on the armrest of her chair while she waited for his response. If he didn't agree, she'd kick him out of her house. She had no idea *how* she would manage to accomplish that feat, since he was as immovable as a mountain, but she'd give it her best effort.

Oberon glowered at her. "I'm not going to answer anything that compromises the safety of my friends."

"Fine." Sin shrugged. She wouldn't have thought he would. "Do we have a deal?"

"We have a deal."

A tingle of power sizzled up through the earth, zapping the soles of her shoes, before crackling through her. She sucked in a surprised breath. Had that deal been sealed by magic?

"So, was your mother born on Earth?" Oberon asked, either immune, oblivious, or unfazed by the magic. She had no idea which of the three it could be. And she wasn't going to waste one of her precious questions asking him.

"Yes, she was," Sin replied. "My turn. Does Caius control the portal to hell, and can the portal be closed without his approval?"

"Caius controls the portal. Only he can open it, and only he can close it." Oberon tilted his head to the side. "When did your mother's family come to Earth?"

Sin turned to her mother's ghost. "Mamá?"

Dianthe looked at Sin, her figure flickering in the dim light. "Our family has a lot of legends. But my grandmother said that we here before the Giant's Causeway portal opened."

The Giant's Causeway portal was in Ireland, and it had opened around four hundred years ago. How much of the family lore could be preserved over that length of time? Especially when they'd had to hide from humans before the Portland portal opened, and the world changed forever.

Sin repeated her mother's answer.

"The rumors I've heard said that the gate in Ireland opened less than half a millennia ago," Oberon said, voice thoughtful. He withdrew the iron dagger again, twirling it through his fingers. At least these movements seemed to have a pattern to them.

Sin didn't bother to respond. He hadn't asked a question. "Is Reagan safe on Tartarus?"

"As safe as I can imagine," Oberon replied. Then he looked at her, the movement strangely catlike. "It's not like I can guarantee her safety."

"I'm not asking for a guarantee. I'm asking if she's safe. Caius's own brother tried to murder her. Are there any more dissenters in the ranks?"

"That's two questions," Oberon said, voice irritatingly prim. "Reagan is safe as far as I can tell. How did your family get here if they didn't come through the Giant's Causeway portal?"

Sin wanted to strangle him. Why did he care so much about her family? Surely no one would blame her if she killed him just a tiny bit?

They wouldn't if they know him.

Dianthe spoke, her attention focused on Oberon, even though he couldn't hear her response. "Family legend has it that they left through one of Avalon's portals. They then traveled through a few different worlds before finding Earth. They wanted a place that didn't have a portal that would open directly onto Avalon, so they'd be safe."

Sin relayed what her mother had said.

His eyebrows rose. "Your family fled?"

"You didn't answer my second question." Sin crossed her arms over her chest.

Oberon released a slow breath. "As far as I'm aware, there are no other people who are discontent with Caius and who want to overthrow him. However, I've spent most of the last three months on Earth." His lips quirked. "Kicking your ass."

Sin refused to rise to the bait.

He sat back. "So, your family fled Avalon?"

Dianthe shrugged. "'Lost and never finding his way.'"

Sin rubbed her forehead. "Mamá hasn't got an answer for that."

"What did she say?"

"A line from that poem about a cursed fairy king," Sin replied.

His eyebrows drew together. "Does it say which king?"

Sin spread her hands wide.

"I see. Can you repeat the poem?"

Dianthe floated into the other room, her gaze focused on something Sin couldn't see, so Sin attempted to reproduce it from memory.

Something dark flickered over Oberon's expression. His firm jaw tightened in response and the room dropped in temperature until Sin's breath turned to mist in the air. She froze.

Had she done this?

No, she realized. The cold wasn't coming from her, it was coming from *him*.

Shock rooted her to the spot. She'd never met another fae who could drop a room's temperature like that—so that the world felt like death was hovering on the horizon.

Was Oberon's magic similar to hers?

But he couldn't see Mamá.

"Come with me to Avalon." He lurched forward, as if to grab her hand. She jerked away. The room's temperature rose quickly in response.

"No."

"Why not?"

"Better yet, why would I?"

"Don't you want to know what kind of fae you are?" He stood, the movement barely contained fury.

Sin got to her feet. "I know what kind of fae I am."

He looked at her in disbelief. "You just lied to me."

"No, I didn't."

"You said—"

Sin glared at him. "I *know* what kind of fae I am: I'm a death fae. My father was a death fae. His father was a death fae. And *his* father was a death fae."

And so was her half-brother, but she didn't want to think about him.

"But what about your mother?" Oberon asked.

Sin glanced at Dianthe's transparent form, her mother floating through the kitchen in seeming surprise at its state. Reagan was going to be pissed. "What about her?"

"You are not just a death fae." Oberon stepped forward until he was almost chest to chest with her. His scent was overpoweringly masculine, heady. And she hated it. Hated that he made her feel small, like she needed protection from the big bad wolf.

You're an alpha, Sin. Act like it.

Technically, she wasn't an alpha in the truest sense, but she'd grown up around shifters—they responded to her like they did her father. She was powerful, strong, and cunning. And she could take on this alpha shifter and win.

"I've played your game; I've answered your questions." Sin glared at him. "Go away."

"You're the one who demanded we play twenty questions."

He was blaming *her*?

Rage burned through her at that. She was just so damned sick of him. "Leave."

He leaned down slightly, so that his breath mingled with hers, his eyes flashing orange in a blatant challenge, and said, "Make me."

Her body reacted instinctively to the dare. She tilted her head like she was thinking, then kicked him low and hard, right on the shin with the pointed toe of her reinforced boots. Exhilaration rushed through her.

Oberon's dark eyes widened, and he let out a surprised grunt. The fae leaned down to grab his shin, and wobbled backwards, hopping on one leg. "You kicked me!" Outrage laced his every word. "In the shin!"

She stared at the image of the fae hopping through her living area like a deranged kangaroo. It was the best thing she'd seen all year.

He stopped to scowl at her. "Are you smiling?"

Sin grinned.

"It's like that, then." He stood, gingerly placing his weight on his left leg. Then he stared at her feet. Creep. "What the fuck are your boots made out of, anyway? Dragon hide?"

"Go away."

"Fine." Oberon limped to the door. Gods, how the sight gave her joy. "I have to go see Nog, anyway."

Weariness swept through her. "What for?"

"None of your business." He made it to her front door.

"My family is my business." Nog had a knack for getting himself into trouble. And Oberon was nothing but trouble.

"Then you can ask Nog after I'm done." He strode through the door, his gait improving with every step, and onto the street. He turned back to her and gave her a mocking bow. "Until next time."

She slammed the door shut in his face.

CHAPTER 7
OBERON

Oberon walked down the dusty street, away from Sin's house, then turned the corner so that he was out of sight. This part of The Crossroads was still largely quiet, even though the sun was just beginning to drop below the horizon, painting the sky in a torrent of peaches, oranges, and reds. Then again, it was almost nighttime, and that's when it was the least safe to be out on the streets. Unless you were a fae—*and panther*, he added quickly, when his shadow half bared their teeth—who could take care of himself.

He turned down another street and kept walking toward the portal. Toward his home.

Gods. That woman was *beyond* frustrating. If he didn't need her—

He spotted a large rock in his path and kicked it.

It exploded into a thousand fragments.

"Fuck." He hadn't even realized he was channeling magic.

She kicked me in the shin.

And he let her.

No, scratch that. His *panther* had let her.

It had wanted to see what she would do when challenged. It had been highly amused by the bruise Sin had left on his ass after he'd spanked her, and it wanted to test her, see how she responded. Even though she was fae, his panther recognized that she also understood and respected shifters. And that she had no problem meeting his gaze—which most people, shifters or not, struggled to do.

A stare from an alpha, even a lone alpha, was difficult for anyone to match. Not unless they were another alpha—or they had a death wish.

What the fuck was wrong with him?

You're trying to convince her to leave everything behind and go through a portal to a world she's never seen, his conscience drawled. *You could have tried to be a bit more charming.* Why did that sound strangely like Caius?

Maybe because Caius did the same thing?

Except, rather than waste time trying to convince Reagan to go to Tartarus, Caius had just kidnapped her cousin. The emotional—and physical—blackmail had worked like a charm.

Oberon groaned and started walking again.

It wasn't that he *wanted* Sin to come with him—far from it. He didn't trust her an inch, even if his panther thought she was a worthy opponent. She was infuriating, headstrong, rude, and dismissive. If he didn't suspect she was a Celestial, he would have left her here to rot in The Crossroads.

But suspect, he did.

Which was insane.

Because for all intents and purposes, she *couldn't* be a Celestial.

That line of fae had only ever been born to the three royal bloodlines. And Oberon couldn't see how the fae rulers would have let a member of one of the royal families slip through a portal to another world. Not without being monitored. And there was no one monitoring Sin, he knew.

He'd been watching her.

Now you sound like a stalker.

That mental voice sounded like Pol. The fucker.

But it wasn't wrong.

Sin was his ticket to getting back into Avalon.

Why can't we just go back without her? The thought came from his panther, who didn't usually bother to articulate his thoughts in words. It preferred to communicate through images of body language and emotions.

Who is going to believe I am the High King from over five millennia ago? Oberon asked his other half. *Especially since I am now also a shadow shifter.* Fae were not—normally—shifters.

His panther licked its paw in response.

Typical.

Still, it didn't change the fact Oberon needed a reason to travel through the portal into Avalon. Since the portals were controlled by the Houses, he needed a legitimate excuse. "Returning to take revenge and steal back the throne" probably wasn't a checkbox on the immigration documentation. He needed a reason, and possibly a fake identity.

So, Oberon had developed a plan: Sin would hire him to act as her "protection." She would claim that she wanted to journey to Avalon to learn more about her heritage. Death fae were rare, so she would most likely be approved despite the fact she didn't have a House affiliation—and him along with her. However, if he couldn't get Sin to agree, he had a backup plan. But that involved a lot more conflict and destruction, which would inevitably piss off the eight Houses who ruled over the world. Oberon didn't need a price on his head—especially not when there was an entire House dedicated to the mercenary arts, and their renown for hunting down their targets had reached even The Crossroads.

Once on Avalon, Sin also would serve as a bargaining chip. She was either the result of a new—and unknown—royal bloodline, or she was the descendent of the Ó Duibh, the Geals, or the Ó hUainín. Considering Titian claimed to have eradicated the Ó hUainín, Sin would be very valuable to the royal families. As new breeding stock, if nothing else.

His panther hissed in disapproval.

Oberon shrugged as he walked east toward the portal and the cracked arch he could see from over a mile away. It wasn't like *he* would use her for that. Gods, the thought sent a shudder down his spine. She'd probably castrate him for daring to touch her. The fact she'd kissed him as a distraction showed just how desperate she was to get through the damned gateway.

Oberon headed down what was once a large road, toward the portal and its half-demolished fountain. People had begun to roam the streets more freely, this close to the heart of the former city. What had once been manicured parklands to his left were now wild and overrun by thorny plants and towering trees. The houses to his right were the larger type, with more multi-story buildings. Some of the passersby were vaguely familiar from his time spent at the portal. Some even waved hello.

He nodded in response and kept walking, dust swirling around his boots as he strode over the uneven surface. He hadn't really been planning on finding Nog until he'd blurted it out—mostly because the kid annoyed the hell out of him. But he'd known that telling Sin he was off to see her cousin would infuriate her. And since he couldn't lie, well, he would go find the boy so that his magic wouldn't decide to turn back on him.

It was worth it, though, to see her squirm.

She is protective, his panther said.

Why are you suddenly so chatty? Oberon asked, not used to feeling like they were two separate beings. Normally his panther felt like just another facet of his personality—not like someone distinct with separate thoughts.

The panther swatted at him.

Fine, be like that.

Oberon was barely two hundred yards from the portal when a familiar figure came jogging toward him over the cracked pavement filled with brown weeds. "Hey, Oberon, my dude!" Nog waved at him, before turning back and flipping the current portal guard the bird.

Pol must be on duty.

Oberon closed the distance quickly, his long stride compensating for Nog's gait.

"Fuck you, puppy!" Pol shouted, his shaved head glinting in the evening light. But there was no heat to it. For some bizarre reason, Pol liked Nog.

Maybe because they are both...strange. That was the panther again.

His shadow half certainly wasn't wrong, though.

"Nog." Oberon looked down at the youth. His shaggy brown hair was messy, and his T-shirt looked like it may have been put on backwards. Oberon assumed he had done it to piss off his sister, Clara. Then again, this was Nog. The youth might have simply gotten dressed in the dark and not bothered to check after he was done.

"What are you doing?" Nog asked, coming to a stop next to Oberon. The newly created shadow shifter was almost bouncing on his toes, the broken head of a statue lying behind him.

"Walking." Plotting Nog's cousin's downfall was probably a more accurate description, but he wasn't about to share that with the boy. He didn't need to be nipped in the heels by a pissed-off corgi shifter. Mostly because Oberon wasn't entirely sure that his panther wouldn't try to eat Nog if that happened.

"So, are you going back to Tartarus?" Nog asked, giving in and bouncing up and down on his toes beside Oberon.

"Yeah, are you going back through? Already?" Pol called, his voice taunting.

Oberon shot Pol a quelling look and closed the distance between them. "You just come back through the portal?" he asked the bouncy shifter. Not that he was particularly interested in the response, but he wasn't a stranger to making polite conversation.

"Yeah," Nog said. "Think I've got things under control now."

"True, you are in your human form. I'd say that's a step in the right direction," Oberon said dryly.

"Caius helped me again." Nog rocked back on his heels. "Dunno why I keep getting stuck."

Oberon decided it was best not to provide advice on that particular topic. Nog had been a latent shifter, much to his frustration—frustration which Nog had described to Oberon in unnerving and unwanted detail—and had only transformed because he hadn't been able to resist touching the shadow magic that had emerged from the portal when Caius had first opened it.

Clearly, the boy lacked common sense.

And the ability to look with his eyes, not his fingers.

"I don't know why you persist in shifting when you know you can't turn back," Oberon said.

"Because shifting is like breathing. It's essential to my existence." Nog was all earnest eyes and puppyish enthusiasm.

Both Oberon and his panther wanted to roll their eyes.

"Self-control is an important part of being a shifter." Gods, who would have ever thought Oberon would be giving advice to youths with no impulse control? And sounding like a pompous ass while doing it?

"Because you are a bastion of self-control," Pollux drawled.

Oberon shot a stream of energy at the other man. Pol gave a startled grunt, and Oberon tried to hide his snicker as Pol's leather vest smoked, like he'd just been zapped by electricity.

"Yeah, but there are just so many things to do as a shifter. You just wanna get out there, be your animal, feel the rawness. The power," Nog said.

Oberon stared at Nog. "You're a *dog*. A tiny dog."

The kid wasn't even a wolf.

"Yeah—I'm a predator. I can't just be cooped up like some pampered housecat all day." Nog was waving his arms around, like he was trying to explain his feelings through interpretative dance.

Oberon's panther hissed.

Pol let out a laugh that ended in a choked snort.

Oberon shot the other man a glare. Then he turned back to the shaggy-haired youth. "You're a *corgi*. You literally *are* a pampered house pet."

"Pet? Seriously? You wouldn't believe how much I can eat in that form. And the smells..."

"I would prefer not to think about the smells," Oberon said wryly.

"You're missing out." Nog shook his head.

Oberon decided he had a headache. He rubbed his temple slowly. Then he noticed that Nog was wearing a backpack. "Where are you off to?"

"Just checking in on Mom."

Both Pol and Oberon studied Nog. He shifted from foot to foot before blurting, "I've got a job to do."

A job?

"Where's your sister?" Oberon asked. Pol was frowning as well.

"She's back on Tartarus." Nog shifted from side to side. "She knows about the gig."

Clara did not know about the gig. Oberon would bet a year's supply of Reagan's homemade moonshine on that.

"Does Reagan know?" Oberon asked.

"Ye—yeah." Nog's gaze darted from Pol to Oberon and back.

Oberon looked at Pol, who raised one eyebrow and glanced down at the kid. Oberon sighed.

Godsdamnit.

He wanted to go back and continue plotting out how he was going to convince Sin to come with him to Avalon so he could use her as a hostage—uh, as a motivating factor. Now he was going to have to babysit a reckless baby shadow shifter.

Oberon pulled out his favorite dagger and began twirling it through his fingers. "What's the job?"

CHAPTER 8
OBERON

Oberon wasn't sure he'd heard Nog right.

"Your job is to what now?" He shoved the dagger into its sheath and started walking east. Or rather, following the corgi shifter east out of Old Kiener Plaza.

They crossed over what was once the I-44 and into a large park. It had been a wide, grassed expanse, locals told him, before magic took over the world. Now it was overgrown with self-seeded trees and tangled looking shrubs. The pathways through the park were still there, although the vegetation had encroached, turning the former wide walking tracks into narrow trails.

Nog looked at Oberon over his shoulder. "To dig up a grave."

"Why do you need to 'dig up' a grave?" Oberon's headache from earlier was definitely setting in to stay—in the form of a lanky corgi shifter.

Nog shrugged as he walked, dodging spiked branches. "To reunite a family with their lost belongings."

Oberon frowned. Raegan had said the family business was unusual, but he hadn't ever thought to ask about it in detail. It was foolish of him not to have asked. "What are the 'belongings?'"

Herding cats would be easier than directing this conversation.

"A thigh bone, and an heirloom." Nog hooked his fingers around the backpack's straps as they walked by the base of a giant archway—the Gateway Arch, so he was told—turning northward.

"Somebody lost a femur?" Oberon's eyebrow rose as he tried to picture that scenario.

"Well, I mean, they lost the person who owned the leg bone." Nog gave him a look of pure innocence under the shagginess of his hair.

"They somehow lost the person, but you just so happen to know where the grave is?" *Skepticism, thy name is Oberon.*

Nog didn't answer.

"Grave robbing. That's quite the family business." Oberon ran a hand through his hair. He'd done his share of killing over the years before he got to Tartarus, and then after. Pilfering the dead, however, just didn't sit right with him.

His panther shrugged. Dead was dead.

That was the animal for you.

"If your cemeteries are anything like they are on Tartarus, then they're usually full of curses and spells." They walked past a lake that was lined with tree plantings; although they had been filled in with strange, straggly-looking bushes. The water was green and murky; it was no doubt the perfect home for something unsavory.

Nog shrugged. "Yeah, it's pretty common here, too."

They reached a set of damaged stairs, which Nog bounded up without hesitation. Oberon walked more sedately, taking in the scene. At the top of the stairs, they came to a large, paved area that overlooked the Mississippi River and Eads Bridge, which cut across the river in a curve of metal and stone.

Nog hurried toward the bridge, which had four stone arches built over a roadway, with several other smaller, filled arches along its embankment. *What is it with humans and arches?* Oberon wondered. They were everywhere.

An elevated railway led northward under the bridge—clearly added later, since it appeared shoehorned into the bridge structure, and was framed in gray stone and steel, rather than the surrounding yellowed sandstone.

He stared at the boy's shaggy head. "You can't do magic."

"So?"

"How are you going to counter a curse or spell if you have no magic?" Oberon asked, fighting the urge to strangle the youth. How Nog had survived this long, he had no idea.

"I've been doing this work for years. I know my way around a grave or two. Come on, or we'll be late for the train." Nog started jogging.

"Train?" Oberon echoed. He'd watched a bit—okay, a lot—of TV since arriving in The Crossroads (he may have appropriated an old television he'd found during his off time). He'd wanted to learn as much as he could about the world, so he'd spent a lot of time viewing old TV shows. When he wasn't doing that, he'd been haunting the local bars and pubs, trying to learn about how Earth society worked.

He'd thought that since trains were technology based, they hadn't kept functioning after the Portland portal had opened. He should have realized that wasn't the case—cars were still around, after all. Cars that ran on magic, but they were still cars, nonetheless.

On the northern side of the bridge's embankment, what appeared to be a train platform had been built out of a pile of debris. It rose over fourteen feet high, meeting the edge of the railway bridge. Stairs had been added to the side of the debris platform, made from scavenged brick. Oberon climbed the staircase next to Nog, careful to ensure he didn't roll an ankle on the unorthodox structure. The platform was leveled at the top, and a small sign had been erected on it that read Laclede's Landing 2.

"This doesn't look like a legitimate train station," Oberon muttered. The sign wasn't even one of the old, printed ones—it was handwritten.

"The original Laclede's Landing station is that way." Nog pointed east, down the bridge embankment. "The light rail headed inland from the Mississippi, but there was nothing heading north. So, some enterprising shifters decided to acquire the former freight line," Nog said.

Less than a minute after Oberon had decided that catching this train would probably result in death or dismemberment, a small carriage appeared on the tracks, gliding closer to them. It didn't look like a train —at least, not like the ones on TV—and it didn't appear to be powered by an engine or motor of any kind. It seemed more like a tramcar, but there were no overhead powerlines.

The carriage slowed to a stop and the doors opened with a strange whooshing sound. A bald shifter stuck his head out the door and shouted, "Tickets!"

Nog hurried over and handed the man something that did *not* look like a ticket. The taller shifter nodded and stepped back, allowing Oberon and Nog entry. But the shifter's gaze was cold and hard as he surveyed the fae.

"Are you Oberon? From Tartarus?" The shifter's mouth pinched, like he'd bitten into something sour.

"Yes. Are you from the Blackwell Pack?" Oberon replied, voice mild. Styx was currently being unwillingly pursued by Corbin Blackwell, the shifter steadily taking over the various factions of The Crossroads. Oberon found it hilarious, but was clever enough to not mention this fact to Styx.

He met the bald man's glare and let his panther creep into his eyes. The other shifter looked away, unable to meet the stare of an alpha. He might belong to the Blackwell Pack, but Oberon didn't want the man to be confused about who was more powerful in this carriage.

"Sure am. Why are you with the puppy?" The bald man flicked a somewhat disapproving—but slightly friendly—look at Nog.

"Babysitting," Oberon muttered.

The shifter barked out a laugh.

Nog shot Oberon a look that stirred something almost like guilt in the depths of his frozen heart. "I don't need babysitting." His chin jutted out.

Oberon didn't answer—mostly because he couldn't without lying. The carriage had about forty seats, plus a lot of standing room. Currently, it only had about twenty occupants. "Busy," he commented instead.

They stood in the central part of the carriage, near a pole that he could grip if he lost his balance, and a large window he could shatter if they needed to make a quick exit. The carriage tooted a horn as the doors closed and it took off northwards, the movement jerky.

"It's not the most popular form of travel in town," Nog muttered under his breath.

"No?"

"Their version of security is to kill first and not bother asking questions later." Nog's normally cheerful tone had dimmed.

Oberon nodded and decided to keep quiet. Personally, he admired that kind of approach. He knew Styx did, too, even though she wouldn't admit it.

The train stopped twice, letting a handful of passengers on and off each time. Oberon studied the platform signs, but it was difficult to see how they related to the current city—there was no large mound at Big Mound, and Hyde Park was anything but a park.

"This is us." Nog moved toward the doors at the end of the carriage.

They got off under the penetrating stare of the conductor, and Oberon noted the station name, North Riverfront.

Nog cut west across the deserted land surrounding the station, towards a large, tree-lined park. Soon, they came up to a broken wrought iron gate that had once hung between pale sandstone pillars, but now listed pitifully to one side. He imagined that this cemetery had previously been orderly, but now headstones and plots seemed to fight for space in a haphazard arrangement, and flowers and weeds alike grew over the space. Everything from angel and demon to fae burials were here.

Nog roamed the site, heading deeper toward the middle of the cemetery—and the older graves, going by the dates on the gravestones. Finally, they came to a stop near a grave that had a covering of yellowed grass. It was like the ground itself repelled life.

Oberon stared at the plot. "I assume you normally do this with your sister or Reagan."

"Oh, I've taken on a few freelance jobs." Nog slipped his backpack off.

Oberon might not be able to lie, but he was fairly confident that Nog was telling him a massive untruth. He sighed. "How much shit am I going to get in for helping you do this?"

"Shit from who?" Nog gave him a look full of guilelessness.

Oberon snorted. "Does that look work on anyone?"

"Yeah, my mom. Either way, I'm going to be digging up this grave. So, you can help me, or you can go back and tell Reagan that you decided to abandon her cousin in a graveyard while he was trying to exhume a dead body."

Oberon sucked his teeth. He'd just been had, and by a corgi shifter, no less. It was a novel experience, and one that he did not want to repeat.

His panther let out a low snarl, but it didn't hold much heat.

"Where is the shovel?" Oberon asked.

"Here." Nog opened his bag and pulled out a collapsible spade.

"That looks about as useful as a spoon." It certainly was going to take Nog a while to excavate the hole with that tiny tool.

Nog gave him a bashful smile. "Reagan usually did the digging."

"Why am I not surprised?" Oberon mused. He then sat down next to the grave, stretching one long leg out in front of him, and bending the other leg at the knee.

Nog gave him a startled look. "I heard that."

"I intended you to."

Nog started digging, his face turning red as a small pile of dirt began to mound next to the grave.

"So, what is the payment for the job?" Oberon asked. "And when did you get the job? Haven't you mostly been on Tartarus?"

"This one came in a while ago, but I wasn't able to convince Reagan and Clara to do it."

Great. Just great.

The two women in Nog's family who seemed to have common sense, and he'd ignored their advice.

Oberon wondered how it would feel to smash his head against the mausoleum wall a few yards away. Surely, it had to hurt less than this. "Let me get this straight. You're taking on a job that even your witch sister, and Reagan, refused."

"They were just chicken. "

Would I get in a lot of trouble if I knocked him out and dragged him back to Tartarus?

His panther shrugged. Thankfully, it found the whole situation amusing, rather than a precursor to corgi dinner. But there was a fine line between the two.

Another thirty minutes passed while Oberon sat and watched Nog dig. The corgi shifter was panting and sweat covered by the time he paused for a break. "You aren't going to offer to help?"

Oberon looked at him. "No."

"Come on. This is going to take forever if it's just me digging."

Oberon glanced up at the sky, which was beginning to tint with the colors of sunset. Great. He'd wandered around with Nog for over two hours.

"Fine, I'll help."

Nog hopped out of the grave and tried to pass Oberon the shovel. The fae snorted and waved his hand. In response, a large, rectangular block of soil slid upward from the grave and into the air. Oberon deposited the block ten yards from the grave, where it collapsed into a heap.

"You could have done that this whole time!?" Nog stared at the pile of dirt, and then the excavated grave. Then back again.

Oberon gave him a small, wicked smile. "Yes."

"Then why didn't you?"

"You never asked for help."

"I didn't know you could do that. I thought you were a fire fae, not an earth fae!"

Oberon didn't bother to reply that he was neither. He stood up and walked to the edge of the grave and studied the steel coffin within. That was not a good sign. It looked like the coffin was trying to stop something from getting out, rather than stopping people from getting in. "So, what's next?"

CHAPTER 9
SIN

Sin was at Tía Celeste and Tío Amos's place—just to make sure Oberon hadn't maimed Nog—but he wasn't there. If he had come back through the portal not long after Oberon left, then he should've been home by now.

Or was Oberon visiting him on Tartarus?

"*Nog iba a hacer un trabajo*," Tía Celeste said, standing in the doorway of her home. The glow from behind her spilled out onto the stoop in the dim twilight. Tía Celeste lived a few blocks away from Sin's place.

Sin frowned. "He was doing a job? On his own?"

They didn't like Nog working on his own, because, he was... well, Nog.

"I thought he was going with Clara," Tía Celeste replied.

Sin hadn't thought that Clara was coming home anytime soon. She seemed to enjoy it on Tartarus.

"I don't think Clara is back yet," Sin said. That meant Nog was doing the job on his own. She frowned and muttered, "*Tonto del culo.*" *Dumbass.*

"Sin! Don't talk about your *primo* like that."

Sin flashed Tía Celeste an apologetic smile. "*Lo siento, Tía.*"

Her tía nodded in response to Sin's apology. "Want me to go with you to look for him?" Tía Celeste was a witch, but she was also watching Sin's *primo*, Hugo.

"No, it's okay. I'll find him."

"That boy—" Tía Celeste huffed, but fear lurked in her eyes. She was remembering another boy, another son; one who didn't get to come home.

Sin bit her lip, her throat aching. "*Te quiero Tía.*" *I love you.*

"*¡Cruzaré mis dedos por ti!*" *I'll cross my fingers for you.* Celeste shut the door, but her eyes had been dark with concern.

Sin hurried away, heading toward the portal. If Tía Celeste was anxious...worry began to coalesce in Sin's chest, the emotion a gnawing sensation. Had Oberon met with Nog? And if he had, what had he done with her *primo*?

By the time she got to the Old Kiener Plaza, worry had soured to dread in her stomach. She hated this place. She hadn't always, though. No, before the portal opened, it had just been another abandoned square in The Crossroads, a remnant of St. Louis before the world had changed. To be honest, she hadn't ever really thought much about it at all.

Now...now it reminded her of failure.

It didn't matter that everything had worked out in the end. Reagan had almost died here, and Sin hadn't been able to stop it. No, she'd gotten knocked unconscious and left behind, all because she'd hesitated. Because she hadn't wanted to kill, not in front of her sister...

Pol was at the portal, dressed in fighting leathers, as Sin practically sprinted toward the destroyed fountain. The square was lit from the glow cast by magic-powered streetlights. The shadow shifter looked her up and down, a smirk settling on his face. "Hey, Sinner."

She sighed. She had no idea why Pol thought that giving her that nickname was funny. She tried not to react to it, because it would just make him use it more. "Hey, Pollo."

He gave her a flat stare. He hadn't known what the word meant when she first used it—after he'd called her "Sinner." Clara hadn't told him, and she'd been calling him that for weeks, apparently. His name was Pollux, and *pollo* was chicken in Spanish. It just made sense.

"To what do I owe the pleasure of your company, sweet fae?" His smarmy words did not match the cold look in his eye.

She glanced over the top of the portal, past the collapsed dome and the soaring, but unstable Gateway Arch beyond. "I'm looking for Nog."

"He came through here a few hours ago." Pol nodded at the shimmery portal with its black center behind him.

Great.

She was hours behind. Sin shouldn't have tried to clean up the mess her mother had made of the house. But she hadn't been able to tolerate leaving it that way. So, she'd tidied the kitchen as best she could—cleaning the pots and putting them away. Thank the gods Dianthe hadn't decided to mess with Reagan or Clara's rooms. Then again, her mother was terrified of Clara, who'd threatened to stuff her soul into a crochet toy if she didn't behave herself.

Sin had removed the table and collected her broken treasures in a small box so she could sort through them later. Some were beyond fixing, but others she might be able to salvage.

At least her mother seemed to have worn herself out and vanished into her "room"—a locket Clara had spelled to house Dianthe's spirit.

When Pol didn't say anything further, Sin asked, "Where did he go?"

"Toward the river." Pol gave a shrug, but his expression was coolly neutral.

Sin was about to leave when something about that look made her pause. "Was there anyone else with him?"

Pol's expression changed, a dark smile curling over his lips. "Oberon."

Sin hissed. "*Mierda.*"

"Come now, you kiss your father with that mouth?" Pol laughed.

Sin glared. "Since when do you speak Spanish?"

"Since you and your cousin started calling me a damned chicken."

"Fair enough." She would have laughed if worry wasn't clawing at her. "Wait. Was Nog in human form?"

"Yeah, but who knows for how long?" Pol shrugged.

Damnit.

Sin waved a hurried goodbye to the shadow shifter and hurried toward the small bridge above what had been the I-44. She was almost at the edge of the park, near the partially collapsed former courthouse, when goose bumps rose suddenly over her arms. She paused, looking around, trying to see what had caused the reaction.

There, in front of the crumbled dome of the courthouse. As Sin watched, a shimmery oval began to form in the air above the cracked pavement. The edges of the oval crackled, like sparklers on a cake.

A portal.

This one wasn't like Tartarus's gateway, this was a small portal used by people to travel across the world. Temporary, and big enough to fit one person at a time.

Sin looked for cover and spotted a gnarled tree a few feet to her left. The streetlights didn't seem to reach the darkness under its branches, so hopefully she could spy on whoever was arriving through the portal without being noticed. She'd be barely twenty feet away from them, close enough to see and hear their arrival. She hurried over to the tree, hiding behind the wide trunk as the portal began to darken.

A silvery-green field and a dark sky became visible on the other side of the magical doorway. A moment later, the portal gleamed for a heartbeat and a man stepped through. He was soon followed by two women, but Sin couldn't look away from the male.

His back was to her, but there was something familiar about him...

A tall, slender woman came up beside the man, her hair a waterfall of copper. She spun in a small circle, her arms held out from her sides, and Sin bit her lip. The woman was exquisitely beautiful, dressed in a leather jacket, jeans, and practical boots. There was something... magnetic about her. She drew the eye, just by breathing.

The second woman waved a hand, and the doorway vanished. Sin's attention turned to her. A witch. Her long brown hair was partly tied back with a scarf and her eyes were a pale color, striking against her kohl-lined eyes. She wore a long, boho-style dress, and the scent of neroli wafted in the air to Sin.

She froze.

Downwind.

That meant she was downwind.

Thank the gods.

She'd completely forgotten that her scent could give her away—an inexcusable mistake, considering her father and sister were shifters.

The man looked over his shoulder and Sin's breath caught in her lungs. He was well over six feet tall, with shoulder-length black hair swept into a ponytail at the back of his head. His ears were pointed like a fae's, but he was broad-shouldered and thickly muscled—a far cry from the lithe build typical of a fae male. An air of menace clung to the man, and when he spoke, Sin thought she saw a flash of fang.

No.

She swallowed past the sudden dryness in her throat.

He wasn't *here*.

He couldn't be.

It wasn't him. Her imagination was just in overdrive.

"The new portal should just be over there," the witch said and pointed toward where Pol was located.

"Let's go. Uncle Max is due to meet us there in about fifteen minutes." That was from the redheaded woman.

Who was Uncle Max?

"Someone's watching." The male's voice was wrapped in darkness, and Sin imagined she could hear the screams of the dying trapped in his tones.

"Of course, somebody's watching," the redheaded woman replied, stroking a hand down his arm. "We're in No Man's Land."

"Something about it just feels...odd." He looked over his other shoulder, toward where Sin was hiding in the trees. She slid back.

"Kieran, you can't murder everybody who looks at you funny." Sin swore she could hear the woman's eyeroll.

The man sniffed. "Why the fuck not?"

Kieran.

The name slammed through Sin's consciousness like a hammer. Her knees wobbled and her heart pounded, and she tasted nothing but ashes on her tongue. She clutched at the rough bark of the tree to keep upright.

No.

Not in her town.

The trio talked a little longer, and then began walking toward the

Tartarus portal. Sin stared at their backs, trying to convince herself she was hallucinating their appearance. She pinched herself.

Ouch.

No, this wasn't a hallucination.

Sin watched as Kieran bent slightly to listen to something the redheaded woman said, his arm curling protectively around her shoulders before it slid down to her waist. She leaned into the contact.

There was only one fae that Sin knew about who had fangs and was named Kieran. Half-vampire, half death fae, he wasn't meant to exist. And he was mated to the leader of the House of Death and Diamond. Kieran Aspen, mate to Sabrina Fhearchair, step-nephew to the King of Blood and Beryl.

And her half-brother.

Sin bit the inside of her cheek hard enough to draw blood, the iron-rich taste filling her mouth.

I need to tell Reagan and Papá.

No.

She wasn't going to tell them anything. Her dad knew that there was a chance Kieran Aspen would come to The Crossroads. All the Houses were setting up embassies here, after all. Her cousin Danni was even thinking of coming. Sin just hadn't thought there was a chance she'd have to see him.

And Reagan was in Tartarus. She didn't need to deal with Sin's problems.

Kieran's head lifted and he sniffed the air again before turning to look back at the tree Sin was using for shelter. She flattened herself against the trunk, the taste of blood overwhelming in her mouth.

She stayed quiet and still for what felt like an eternity, before she peered out around the tree. The trio were gone.

Sin let out a long breath and turned toward the river. If Nog had been heading this way, he was probably going to catch the train that ran along the riverfront. Hopefully, she'd be able to find someone who had seen him.

What are you going to do about Kieran? she thought to herself as she walked across the bridge above the I-44.

Nothing. I am going to do nothing.

She stepped off the bridge into the chaotic parklands surrounding the Gateway Arch. In the darkness, it was easy to think that there were eyes watching her in the trees. It was unnerving.

Sin hurried toward the end of the park, keeping to the middle of the tracks, her mind whirring. According to her mother, her older half-brother was an abomination. But her mother wasn't an unbiased source; Kieran was the reason Dianthe wasn't sane.

He was the reason her biological father was dead.

And he was the reason she'd been born an orphan.

Kieran had killed Dianthe's mate shortly before Sin had been born. The fact that her mother hadn't died when her biological father had was just a testament to Dianthe's will. The death of a mate usually resulted in the death of both. But her mother had survived three more months to birth Sin, only to die hours later.

And then she'd stayed behind to "raise" her.

Sin heaved a breath of relief when she made it to the stairs near the edge of the park. Away from the trees and vegetation, the moonlight was clearer now, and power seemed to sizzle in her veins in response.

She made it to Eads Bridge, where she climbed up the makeshift train platform. She had no idea what the timetable was, so she peered down the tracks, hoping to see lights. Then she began to pace.

Checking her watch, she saw that only five minutes had passed, but she was about to crawl out of her skin.

Take a deep breath. Calm down.

Sin wasn't one to get rattled like this, but her day had gone from bad to worse. First having to deal with Oberon, then losing Nog, and now finding her half-brother in The Crossroads?

Yeah, it was no wonder she was a tad bit freaked.

The sound of wheels clattering on train tracks drew her attention, and Sin looked back down the platform. The bright, glowing headlight on the train nearly blinded her as it swung around a bend.

Oww.

Rubbing her eyes, she heard the train slow and then come to a stop. Blinking a few times, her vision returned, and she frowned at the carriage. Why were half the passengers crammed up at one end?

She was about to approach when the doors swooshed open and two people stepped off.

"Tickets!" a shifter shouted from behind them, their voice oddly strangled.

But Sin was too busy staring at the disembarking passengers.

Oberon stood with his hand wrapped around the back of Nog's neck, like he was scruffing the youth. A strange, green ooze coated Oberon's white-blond hair, and trickled down the side of his face. His lips were pressed in a grim line, and he looked pissed. Nog was doused in the green muck, as well, and his shoulders were hunched as he tried to shimmy out of Oberon's grip.

"Sin." Oberon said in a tight voice.

"What happened?" Sin demanded. She stepped closer, and then the stench hit her. She gagged and spun around, trying to find a trashcan to heave into. She couldn't find one, but the wind was blowing past her face and dissipated the odor.

Thank the gods.

What the hell is that?

She turned around, careful to maintain a distance between them. "What did you do to him?" Her eyes were watering.

"Oh, I didn't do *anything* to him." The temperature plummeted, and Sin's cheeks stung from the sudden cold. "Nog, care to explain what happened?" Oberon's voice was clipped, each word enunciated carefully.

Sin met his black gaze. It was eerily calm.

She had a feeling he was not just pissed, he was furious.

For some reason, cold rage was way scarier than hot anger.

Nog tried to wriggle away. "No."

Oberon's grip must have tightened, because her *primo* winced.

"Let him go," Sin growled.

"And let him cause more chaos?" Oberon's eyebrow arched.

Gods, she wanted to smack that look off his face.

"I didn't cause chaos!" Nog protested.

"No, you just triggered a spell that ended up with us splattered in decayed and liquified corpse."

Sin stared at the two of them. And then her gaze locked on Nog's backpack. "You actually did a job? Without us?"

Her heart ached.

Nog's chin jutted out.

Her *primo* was so eager to prove himself. Always had been. But since he'd developed a shifter form? He'd gone into overdrive.

"You took the Rhynehart gig, didn't you?" Sin ran a hand over her face. They had decided against that job because Clara had said the grave was boobytrapped to the nth degree.

"...Maybe." Nog looked past Sin's shoulder, unable to meet her gaze.

She sighed.

Nog stomped a foot. "But we got what we needed!"

"Only because I shattered the damned coffin," Oberon muttered. He let go of Nog's neck.

"Yeah, I owe you. Thanks." Nog rubbed his face, smearing the goo.

"No!" She blanched and glared at Oberon. "He doesn't owe you anything."

"Sin—" Nog began.

She spun on her cousin, breathing shallowly to avoid the stench. "You can't say things like that to people like *him*."

"What's that supposed to mean?" Oberon's voice was ominous as it rolled over her.

"One, you're not trustworthy! Two, you're unreliable and secretive. And three, you let Nog walk into danger." She emphasized each point with a raised finger.

A muscle ticked in Oberon's jaw. "Me? *I'm* unreliable and secretive? You don't know *anything* about me, about who I am."

"Sin—" Nog looked at her, his expression pitiful.

"Fine. Then instead of Nog owing you, I do." A surge of magic rushed through her, and she spun away and wretched over the side of the platform.

A vow. She'd just somehow made a vow to Oberon.

She heard the damned fae male approach, and tried to breathe through her mouth, but that didn't help. He stank just as bad as Nog did. Oh, gods. She could *taste* it when she breathed through her mouth.

Oberon settled his black gaze on Sin.

She looked up.

"He's your problem now. I hope you have as much fun as I did." Then Oberon stepped back, his form melting into a pool of shadows. Less than a heartbeat later, a large, magnificent panther with glowing orange eyes stared at her and unfurled massive, ink-dark wings. Her mouth dropped open. The feline pounced, and Sin ducked down, thinking for a moment it was going to attack her. Then she stared in amazement as Oberon's shifter form took to the sky, the creature surprisingly graceful in flight. He clutched something in one of his paws, and Sin thought it looked like a weapons belt.

"Did he just turn into a cat *with wings*?" Nog demanded.

"He did." Her day just got crazier and crazier.

"That's weird, right?" Nog tapped his leg, splattering ooze over the platform.

Sin grimaced at the ground.

This was going to be a painful walk home.

CHAPTER 10
OBERON

TARTARUS

Oberon didn't think he would ever feel clean again.

He'd washed his hair four times and scrubbed his skin so hard it had turned red. But he could still smell the putrid scent of dead body.

It was disgusting.

He stepped out of the shower, his bathroom swathed in steam. Thankfully, his transformation into his shifter form had destroyed most of the evil-smelling sludge, but unfortunately not all of it. He hadn't bothered to even acknowledge Pol as he'd flown back through the portal, but he'd heard the other man gagging as he flew past.

The asshole.

Even the guards on the Tartarus side of the portal had turned rather unflattering shades of green and gray upon his arrival, their hands rising to cover their noses. He was just glad Caius hadn't been there, that would have just added insult to injury.

Oberon stood swathed in steam, naked, and closed his eyes. Next time, if he ever felt the slightest bit inclined toward helping someone, he would remember this moment—this humiliation—and refuse. He'd had to get on a train, covered in dead body, with most of the other passengers being shifters. The smell had been a physical insult to them, and himself. And then...

And then Sin had been standing on that damned platform. Looking ready to take on the world to save her fool cousin, only to be brought to actual nausea by the sight of them.

While Sin infuriated him, he didn't enjoy seeing her bent over, trying to expel whatever food she'd had for the day. In fact, his panther had wanted to swat the corgi shifter for reducing such a strong woman to that.

His afternoon had definitely *not* gone according to plan.

How was he ever going to convince Sin to help him—that he was actually an incredible fighter and tactician—when he couldn't even control her corgi shifter cousin?

It didn't help that she clearly didn't trust him.

He ran a towel over his face, scrubbing his cheeks, feeling the rasp of the soft cloth against his stubble.

You could always try to charm her. That had been Caius's advice the last time Oberon mentioned his plans to the god. Oberon had tried to gut his friend for the suggestion.

Caius found the entire thing all too funny.

There were only a dozen women over the years who'd been immune to Oberon's natural charm—and Sin was one of them. There was no way he was going to even *try* to win her over.

Gods, he could still smell it. The stench.

Looking over to where he'd dumped his daggers, sword, and their sheaths, he sighed. The revolting mess had gotten on everything. If he'd been wearing clothing on his return, he'd have incinerated it upon arrival. As it was, he'd dunked his panther form in a large lake before heading to his quarters, much to his panther's disgust. Felines—especially those with wings—did not like water. The scent must be lingering because it was on his weapons, even though they'd taken a bath along with his shifter form.

Oberon bent and grabbed the sheaths. He then opened the door to the shower and tossed them inside with a clatter. Oberon turned the water on scalding hot and let the flow wash away the mess. He finished drying himself off and dressed in a pair of black pants and a gray T-shirt. He returned to the bathroom, turned the water off, grabbed the weapons, and winced.

The smell was still there.

Annoyance thrummed through his blood. Oberon had carefully engraved a series of intricate fae designs into the hellbeast leather, which was fire resistant and durable. He had spent over a hundred hours working on the sheaths and belt, and he'd been proud of the work, too. But the liquified corpse had soaked in, despite two washes.

He wasn't going to be able to save the sheaths.

He growled low in his throat.

Removing the weapons, he placed the daggers in the bathroom sink and the sword next to it, and then called on the heat of the earth. Starfire would have been better, but there was no sun near Tartarus. Instead, he used the heat from the molten core of the planet to incinerate the leather, until nothing more than sticky ashes coated his hands.

He sent a flicker of power to his daggers and sword, destroying the fabric he had wrapped around the hilts of the weapons. Fabric that he'd dyed and prepared himself.

There goes my afternoon.

He'd have to rewrap all the hilts until he was satisfied with the workmanship. At least he had kept his old sword belt and sheaths; he could use those until he had the time to make new ones. He left the bathroom and entered his main sleeping chamber, heading for the closet. Inside, he kept a trunk full of weapons paraphernalia—there, his old belt and sheaths were tucked in one corner. He grabbed them, an old cloth, and a tin of mineral oil.

At least I didn't let Nog accidentally kill himself.

Surely that alone was worth some of the trouble that had occurred. What was the human saying? Win him some brownie points? Sin was so prickly though, he doubted it. At least she'd vowed that she owed him. It would give him a small advantage in their war of wills.

He threw the old leather pieces on the bed and headed into the bathroom, where he quickly oiled the daggers in the sink, then his short sword. The action helped soothe some of the raw edges that had formed over the afternoon. He was so close to returning to

Avalon, to taking back what was his. But this new world stood in his way.

Sure, he could go through the world of the gods—there was a portal somewhere on Earth in a mountain range that claimed even the most experienced hikers' lives. But he'd still have to go through the Houses to get approval to travel through the portal, and then he'd have to deal with gods. And while he loved Caius like a brother, Oberon had very little time for any other deities. In fact, if he ever saw a particular sun god again, he was going to relish destroying the male.

Oberon emerged from the bathroom and placed the weapons on a side table opposite his bed. Before he could do anything else, there was a firm knock on the door. Oberon strode over and opened it—Caius stood on the other side.

Speak of the devil.

"From the trail of corpse stink that leads from the portal and eventually to your rooms, I gather you weren't able to convince Sin to join you in Avalon?" The god's dark eyes creased as he smiled.

"That wasn't Sin's doing." No, the bruised lump on his shin had been from her.

"Oh?" Caius then crossed his arms over his broad chest and leaned against the doorjamb.

"That was all Nog."

Caius tilted his head to the side. "Why doesn't that surprise me?"

"What happened with Nog?" Like the thought of her cousin had summoned her, Reagan came up next to her mate. Caius wrapped an arm around Reagan's shoulders, his fingers caressing the column of her throat.

Oberon turned back to his room and found a spare pair of boots. Shoving his feet into them he said, "Nog took on a job that apparently you—and the rest of your family—had decided was a no-go. I found him on his way to the cemetery and offered to help." He held up his hand. "I realize my mistake, even as I say it."

"Why didn't you stop him?" Reagan demanded, glaring at him.

Oberon's eyebrows rose. "What is your success rate at stopping Nog from doing something stupid?"

Reagan and Caius exchanged a look.

"So why the smell?" Caius asked, clearly unable to answer the Nog question.

"The grave was boobytrapped," Oberon replied and strode to the door. He shooed them both out of the way. "Nog triggered it."

"Is it too much to ask if Nog is still alive?" Reagan said, worry lining her face.

"He was alive when I left him with Sin, covered in juices from a decaying body. Whether or not he's still alive now, I can't say." Oberon did have to admit that he rather enjoyed the thought of the consequences of Nog's actions coming to find him in the form of Sin.

"You gave him to my *sister*?" Reagan did not look reassured by that scenario.

"I didn't *give* him to her, I just left him in her custody."

Reagan shut her eyes. "We only involve Sin when we have no other option."

"That sounds rather ominous." Oberon shut the door behind him, a spark of humor banishing the sour mood he'd been in. Plus, he couldn't help but feel a little joy that Nog was probably suffering the scolding of his life.

Reagan didn't bother to answer him, walking next to Caius as they headed down the hall.

"But at least Nog and Sin owe me now," Oberon said, running a hand over his still-damp hair. He liked to look at the bright side of life, on the odd occasion.

Reagan glowered at him. "You are not fucking with Nog. Or Sin."

"No fucking will be done with Nog, don't worry about that." Oberon didn't know how he managed to keep his face expressionless, but he did.

Caius smirked at him over the top of Reagan's head.

"On the plus side," Oberon continued, like Reagan wasn't attempting to murder him with her stare, "Nog did stay in his human form throughout the whole ordeal."

Footsteps approached from down the hall, and Oberon glanced up to find Legion striding purposefully toward them. The shadow dragon was the general of Caius'ss forces, and he looked haunted.

"Legion," Oberon greeted. "You look like shit."

"You smell worse." The dark-haired male shot him a look that told him to mind his own business. Which was fine, because Oberon had given him the same look far too many times recently.

"I fucking washed!" Oberon sniffed his armpit, not that that was where the goo had landed.

The general snorted and turned to the god. "Caius, could we talk for a moment?"

"Of course," Caius replied and stepped away with Legion.

Reagan turned to Oberon, not looking particularly mollified. "I told you before, you won't have any luck convincing Sin to go with you. You need to leave Nog out of whatever issue you have with her."

Thinking over Reagan's statement—her certainty that her sister wouldn't give in to Oberon's arguments—he decided to approach the issue from a different angle. An idea surged to life, and he marveled at how simple it was. How easy it would be to achieve.

No, Oberon didn't think he'd be able to *convince* Sin to go with him, even with the vow.

Trick her, however?

That he *could* do.

CHAPTER 11
SIN

THE CROSSROADS

Sin hadn't thought Nog would be able to top the stupidity of the great flying pizza incident, but she was clearly underestimating her *primo's* ability to cause havoc. If she didn't need to—literally—clean up his mess, she might even have admired his ability to terrorize the world simply by existing.

Sin had decided to deliver her stinking, slime-encrusted *primo* to Tía Celeste's house. No way was she bringing him near her place in that condition. Tía Celeste opened the door, hand clutching a wooden spoon, barely even batting an eye at the scene. Sin was breathing through her T-shirt—she'd pulled it up so the neckline covered her mouth and nose—and Nog was dripping gunk on the doormat. They'd had to walk down Market Street, and everyone they'd encountered had visibly turned a different shade or started retching.

Sin had almost—*almost*—started to feel sorry for Nog.

But considering she was stuck next to him with that smell...pity only extended so far.

A cloud of orange colored smoke billowed out from the kitchen into the small living room behind her. She must have been working on some kind of potion before answering the door.

"¡Ay niño mío!" She pointed a slightly trembling finger, her voice gathering strength, *"¡Baño! Ahora."*

"Si, Mami." Nog left a trail of green-tinted sludge through the house as he obeyed his mother's order, going straight for the bathroom, head ducked low. He looked like a dejected puppy after it had been caught gnawing on its master's shoes.

Sin winced.

Tía Celeste stared at her wooden floor and shook her head sadly. *"El que tiene boca se equivoca."*

Whoever has a mouth makes mistakes. Sin wasn't sure if her tía was trying to convince herself or them that nobody was perfect while she studied the slime trail.

"I'll get the cleaning supplies." Sin walked into the kitchen.

"It will take more than that." Tía Celeste clicked her tongue and followed her into the kitchen.

Sin and Celeste went back into the room, her tía's arms filled with small, brightly colored bottles and sachets, while Sin held a mop, a bucket of steaming water, and a towel. Sin looked over at the sofa, still unable to process the fact that Jo was gone. There were other kids living with her tía and tío, but it wasn't the same. Celeste chanted over the pail and then dropped a series of green herbs into it. She then dumped the contents of four sachets onto the footsteps.

Magic made the little hairs on the back of Sin's arms rise as the spells her tía created took form. Sin might have no real connection to witch magic—it was different from fae—but she could still feel when it was being used. Like the power was connected to hers, in some way.

Ten minutes later, the trail of corpse slime was gone, and Sin was finally able to get a deep breath of air. Celeste began taking the supplies back into the kitchen. When she remerged, she eyed Sin. "I take it Clara wasn't with him?"

"No," Sin replied slowly. "He was with Oberon."

Her tía shook her head, her dark hair swinging with the movement. "Then we have the fae to thank that he's alive."

"I don't know if it was that bad," Sin hedged. Mostly because she didn't want to give Oberon credit for anything.

"How did Nog even manage to get the details of the job?" Celeste asked.

"He wouldn't tell me on the way back here." And Sin had asked more than once for that piece of information.

Reagan and Clara handled most of the bookings for the business. The ones that Celeste and Alvaro didn't manage, anyway. Somehow, Nog had gotten into the system and discovered the details for the job. He claimed that the pay was worth it, but Sin wondered how much they'd have to forfeit to Oberon to keep the fae happy.

She also didn't like the fact that Nog said he "owed" Oberon.

"I don't know what we're going to do with him," her tía murmured, voice thick with worry.

Sin bit her lip. "Send him to Tartarus?"

To be honest, she hated that idea. But Nog seemed to do better with Reagan around, and she was living there, rather than here.

"He just needs to find his place in the world," Tío Amos said, coming into the room. He must have been at the other end of the house when they arrived. "Most people do."

Sin just looked at him. "Most people aren't Nog."

He shrugged. "He can shift now. He thinks he's immortal. He needs time."

"He needs a leash," Sin muttered.

"Hey! I heard that." Nog strode into the room, his shaggy hair slicked back from his face and his skin still damp, like he hadn't bothered to dry himself properly with a towel. He wore a T-shirt and shorts, his body all gangly limbs, and had a towel in his hands that he dabbed at his hair. "I got the job done. A job that no one else wanted to take."

Sin turned to face him and looked him up and down. "I think there was a reason no one else wanted it."

"So? It's done." He threw the towel on the back of the sofa, then hurriedly picked it up after his mother glared at the yellow fabric like it was a mortal offense.

"You said you *owed* Oberon." Sin's teeth ground together.

"He's not as bad as you think he is." Nog rolled his eyes.

Sin rubbed her ears, convinced that she'd misheard her *primo*. "He's some trumped-up fae overlord who actually came from the fae home world. That doesn't signal anything good."

"Caius trusts him."

"I don't trust Caius."

Celeste and Nog sighed.

"What?" Sin demanded, aware her tone was too defensive.

"Caius is Reagan's mate," Celeste said. "He won't risk hurting her by hurting her family. That means he wouldn't allow Oberon near us if he thought the male was untrustworthy."

"Plus, the guy's been suffering for thousands of years. I heard he got banished to Tartarus after his mate betrayed him. That's gotta suck." Nog's fingers played with the towel.

Sin stared at him like he'd lost his mind.

Oberon had supposedly been betrayed by his mate?

And Nog thought that Oberon was innocent?

Mates couldn't hurt each other. Not true mates. Sin had heard that there was dark magic that could mimic the mate bond, but she knew what happened to mates when their other halves died. They went insane. Her mother hadn't even loved Sin's biological father, but losing him, losing the bond?

It drove her crazy.

Why would anyone risk betraying their mate when the cost was so high?

There was a reason Sin never wanted to find a mate, and that was it. She wanted to live without caveats, without forfeiting her life. Her mind.

Sin shook her head at her *primo*, realizing she'd been quiet a little too long. "You will believe literally anything."

Nog shook his head. "Look, Oberon's cool, okay?"

Sin clenched her fist so hard her nails bit into her palm, drawing blood. There was so much more Sin wanted to say, but she was tired. Dead tired. The day that wouldn't end just kept throwing punches her way. She didn't want to sit here and listen to Nog praise Oberon—a fae that had some dark, ulterior motive for wanting to return to Avalon. And for wanting to drag her along with him.

Sin stood. "I'm heading home for the night. Try not to cause any more drama while I'm gone." She kissed Nog on the cheek, then hugged her tía and tío.

As she shut the door behind her, she could say with absolute certainty that there was only one good thing about her day: kicking Oberon in the shin. Everything else had been a shitshow.

Thankfully, her house was only a few blocks down from theirs. It would be a short walk in the dark. Surely nothing could go wrong in the five minutes it would take to get there.

Taking a deep breath, she closed her eyes and felt the power of the night touch her—it almost felt like the stars themselves reached down to dust her skin with delicate tendrils of fiery power.

She was halfway across the street when a tall man stepped out of the shadows, coming to stand in her path. His dark hair was tied back, and he wore a leather jacket over a blue shirt with black jeans.

Shock had her feet skidding in the gravel road, her heart pounding in her ears.

Kieran Aspen.

Sin met his arctic gray gaze with her own and felt her blood turn sluggish. How had he found her? Did he know who she was?

Sin went to step around him, and he followed the movement, blocking her.

He gave her a half smile, but there was no mirth to the expression. "So, you were the spy at the portal." He sniffed the air, then pointed to her palm, where she'd cut herself only moments earlier. "I'd recognize that scent anywhere. Your blood has a...unique flavor to it."

That voice. Gods, it was smooth, and dark, and horrific.

As was the sniffing.

And what was wrong with her blood?

Sin straightened her shoulders and met his stare. "I'm no spy. And that's creepy as fuck."

"No? Then you just like to lurk behind trees?" That smile grew, and this time something almost like real amusement was apparent.

"A person can't go for a walk in the woods?" Sin hedged. That was the problem with not being able to lie. Slowly, carefully, she began coaxing wisps of power up through the earth.

"What's a death fae doing in The Crossroads?" Kieran crossed his arms over his broad chest.

"I live here." There was no way he knew who she was.

He shook his head. "Mmm, try again."

"I. Live. Here." She spoke slowly and clearly, her irritation thick in the air.

"Then why were you lurking by the portal?"

Gah. He was like a dog with a bone. "I was heading somewhere else when it opened."

"Then why did you hide?"

"What, you just walk up to portals of unknown origin and introduce yourself to whoever comes through?" Sin glared at her half-brother.

Thank the gods, he genuinely didn't seem to know who she was.

"No. If it was a portal of unknown origin opening in my territory, I'd normally kill whoever comes through, then I'd ask questions of the ghost after."

Sin blinked. *The apple didn't fall far from that tree.*

From all accounts, her biological father had been a psychopath. It appeared that Kieran wasn't much better.

He rolled his gray eyes. "If they haven't gotten approval to open a portal on my land, then they most likely have bad intentions. I don't like bad intentions."

This was the strangest conversation she'd ever had. And she was related to Nog, so that was saying something.

"You're crazy," Sin said, and tried to move around him.

"There may be some truth in that," the fae-vampire hybrid admitted.

Sin closed her hand in a fist, the sting sharp as her nails bit into the already-broken skin.

Kieran stepped forward, closing the distance between them, trying to intimidate her. "If I catch you spying on me or mine again, you won't like the outcome."

"What, you came all this way to give me a warning?" Sin rolled her eyes.

"Yes." Kieran tilted his head. "You can never be too careful when you're consort to a House leader."

"House leader?" Sin made her voice turn shaky, as if she didn't know who he was.

"Oh, how careless of me." He gave her a smile that she was sure others would consider charming. To her, it just showed he had too many sharp teeth. "I'm Kieran Aspen, mate to Sabrina Fhearchair, ruler of the House of Death and Diamond. And you are?"

"None of your business." Sin backed up a step.

His gaze narrowed on her. "You look awfully familiar. Have we met before?"

Sin backed up a step. "No."

"Are you sure?" He once again closed the distance between them.

"I'm sure." She'd never met him, but that didn't mean she didn't know who he was. Or about what he'd done to their biological father.

He stared at her for a handful of heartbeats before he stepped to the side. "Remember what I said. No more spying."

Relief poured through her, so strong she could almost taste it. "Oh, I won't forget."

"Good." Then he vanished, swallowed by the shadows.

Had he moved so fast she couldn't track it? Or was he able to teleport?

Either way, he was gone.

She'd spent most of her life trying to hide from that man, and he'd tracked her down in a matter of hours. What was it about her blood that had piqued his interest? Did she smell...odd?

Taking a deep breath, Sin hurried toward her house, to safety.

Fuck.

What was she going to tell her mother?

She'd just met her half-brother, the man who had brutally murdered her bio father and then strewn his ashes across the Mariana Trench, so there was no way he could be resurrected. And who'd stated that he'd destroy any hint of his sire's legacy. Which meant he'd kill Sin as soon as he knew who she was. What she was to him.

There was a reason she'd never wanted to visit their cousin Danni after she'd mated the king of the House of Blood and Beryl. Her half-brother was the man's damned nephew.

I need to get out of town.

At least until Kieran left.

Until she was safe.

CHAPTER 12
OBERON

Oberon watched from the corner of a nearby unlit house as the man who'd cornered Sin disappeared into the night. The male had smelled like death and blood and moved like an assassin. Oberon had partially shifted in response to the danger the man had represented; now he looked like a damned fallen angel with black feathered wings. But he was far from that. He wrapped his wings around his sides, his panther prowling through his mind.

Should he go after the fae, break the bastard's legs, and demand he divulge what he had wanted with Sin?

No, first he would ensure she returned home safely. She was his ticket back to Avalon, after all. He scowled, watching as Sin stalked toward her house. She was angry, he could tell by her precise, brisk steps, her ramrod posture. The sheer control with which she held herself.

She often looked that way around him.

What had the male said to her?

The stranger had been another death fae—Oberon had been able to feel the man's magic from where he stood. But it had been tainted.

Impure.

He stalked through the darkness before taking to the air, his wingbeats slow and painstaking as he gathered height in order to melt into the midnight hue of the sky. He observed as Sin made it to her door, her body awash in the pale blue glow of her wards. She looked over her shoulder as the door opened, as if she sensed that she was being watched.

He waited until she was inside the house with her poltergeist mother. Hopefully that meant she'd be safer than when she was outside on the streets, although, considering the damage the ghost had done earlier in the day, he couldn't be certain.

But she was behind her wards, and he couldn't break them easily now that Clara had upgraded them after the portal opened.

He flew to the Tartarus gateway, looking for the male.

There.

Striding toward the portal, frustration radiated from the stranger. Oberon glided on updrafts through the sky, closer to edge of the park's treed border. He came to a stop, hovering, hidden in the darkness. Then he glided to the ground. He shifted completely into his panther form, melting into the inky blackness that spread from the tree-lined edges of the park.

Glowing orange eyes locked on the fae male as he reached a redheaded female and a wolf-eyed witch. Surprise shot through him. That was Kieran Aspen, co-leader of the House of Death and Diamond. Half-vampire, half-death fae. A being that shouldn't exist, but somehow did.

And he'd found Sin. Cornered her.

Then scared the shit out of her.

A low growl rumbled in the panther's chest.

No one messed with Sin other than him.

She was *his* ticket to revenge, to freedom.

What had the other fae wanted? Why had he sought out Sin, potentially the only other death fae in The Crossroads? And upset her in the process?

Oberon didn't want to contemplate the possible answers. Sure, the man was mated, but as Oberon knew all too well, that didn't mean much. Mates could betray each other. It was rare, but he'd experienced it himself. Was this man interested in Sin because she was one of his kind?

He didn't like it.

No, he didn't like it at all.

Kieran wrapped an arm around the redhead, nuzzling the woman's neck as Oberon watched from his hiding spot. The woman made the fur on the scruff of his neck stand on end. There was something...unnatural about her. Oberon's ability almost seemed repelled by the woman. He knew what she was; he'd heard the news as much as anyone else in The Crossroads. She was supposedly a phantom—a new race of creatures that had been created by the planet's magic. Whatever she was, his power didn't know how to respond to her, and it normally responded to humans at least a little, since they were the children of stars. Everything on this planet—like Avalon—was created from stardust; the remnants of supernovae.

The trio spoke briefly to Pol, who was still on guard duty. His friend looked bored out of his mind by the encounter. Halfbreed fae, a new species, and a wolf-eyed witch were apparently uninteresting to his friend.

Oberon bared his teeth.

There was something familiar about the shape of the other fae male's jaw, the slope of his nose. Maybe he sprang from a line of fae Oberon had once known? There weren't too many death dealers, after all.

He backed away deeper into the shrub, tucking his wings tightly to his sides so the feathers wouldn't get torn on any jutting branches. Kieran and his mate left soon after, the pale-eyed witch in tow.

He needed to get Sin to leave The Crossroads, sooner rather than later.

He didn't want the complication that Kieran Aspen represented.

Sin was attached to her family, which was going to prove problematic. As was her core of honor. At least he knew she'd refuse any advances from that death fae-vampire hybrid, if the asshole made them. But Oberon didn't want her to have any...distractions.

He needed her.

She was his passage to Avalon, and he wasn't going to lose that because of some whacked-out fae crossbreed.

He needed to accelerate his plan.

Tomorrow, he was going to see a girl about a dog.

CHAPTER 13
SIN

"Coffee with *chocolate*." Kasha handed Sin a ceramic coffee cup, her nose scrunched in distaste. They were at Kasha's place. Sin hadn't liked the fact that Oberon's scent had lingered in her living area, or that her mother had been asking her endless questions about said fae.

She'd needed to get out.

"It's called a mocha." Sin took the cream-colored cup, wrapping two hands around the warm sides.

Kasha looked at the coffee like it was poisoned. "It's called sacrilege."

Sin grunted and took a sip of the chocolate-imbued caffeine. Oh gods, how she needed that. She hadn't slept well last night; not after the day she'd had, or the encounter with her meant-to-be long-lost brother. Oberon had been the rotten icing on that stale cake. Almost literally.

"I heard Oberon was at your place last night." Kasha waggled copper-colored eyebrows.

Oh, how fast the gossip chain was. And there hadn't been a single soul out on the street at the time. That was the problem with living near a group of shifters—they had excellent hearing. Sin stared at her. "Yesterday afternoon."

"And he stayed for a while..." More eyebrow waggling.

Sin almost choked. "He followed me home and wouldn't leave me alone. There is absolutely no need for your eyebrows to be doing *that.*"

"Yes, there is. That guy is so hot he burns." Kasha fanned herself.

"Like a rash," Sin muttered, and took another sip of her drink.

"What is *wrong* with you? You know I'm right." Kasha sighed. "When was the last time you slept with anyone?"

"I don't see how that is relevant." Sin did *not* need the image of Oberon being so hot he burned in her brain. She wondered if there was a magical equivalent to bleaching one's brain.

"Sex is good for you." Her best friend looked at her like she was nuts, her green eyes wide and incredulous. "At least, it is when you have the opportunity. Mine have been too far and too few between as of late."

"Not with *him.*" Sin wasn't exactly one for casual sex. Not when she'd been hiding who she was and what she could do her whole life. And well, male shifters didn't seem to want to partner with a woman who was as much of an alpha as they were—if not more. Not that shifters were her only option. But The Crossroads had more shifters than other kinds of beings.

"You're blind. That is the only explanation."

"I am not blind. I just can't stand the guy." He grated on her nerves. Every last one of them.

Kasha flipped her medium length copper hair over a shoulder. "Hate sex is a thing."

Now it was Sin's turn to scrunch her nose. "You are more than welcome to pursue that line of thinking—for yourself."

Kasha saluted Sin with her coffee cup. "Maybe I already have."

"With Oberon?" Sin hadn't thought Kasha had ever spoken to the guy. She ignored the tiny rush of irritation that sprang up at the idea of her best friend with...*him.*

Kasha choked on a mouthful of espresso. "No." She dabbed at her mouth with the corner of her sleeve. "Not that I'd be against it."

Sin tapped the table with her index finger. "Then who? Spill."

Later that morning, Sin went looking for Nog.

She'd checked in with her tía last night, after she'd gotten home, and spoken to her mother, to ensure that Nog was no worse for wear after his exploding corpse incident. He'd apparently passed out on the sofa not long after she'd left.

Then Sin called her father, Alvaro, and filled him in on the latest Nog adventure. She may have forgotten to mention that her half-brother had hunted her down, thinking she'd been spying on him.

Which she sort of had been. But she hadn't known who was going to come through the portal when she'd decided to stop and hide to get intel. If she'd known it would be *him,* she wouldn't have stuck around to get caught.

At least he doesn't know who I am, Sin reassured herself.

Kieran had destroyed any chance she'd had of being raised by her biological family. Which was probably for the best, to be honest. She loved her family, and she had no regrets that she'd grown up with them. She had the feeling that her biological parents would have provided her with a toxic upbringing, despite being mates, if Dianthe's ghostly personality was an indication of what she'd been like when she was more...alive and sane.

But Sin didn't want to become the latest mark on Kieran's murder board. Not that she knew if he had one or not, but she'd paid attention to the rumors about him, and she knew he'd been a torturer long before he'd killed and dismembered her mother's mate.

"What do you mean he's gone?" Sin asked, staring at Tía Celeste's pinched expression. She was outside in the weak sunlight, and her tía squinted at her from inside the house. She held the door propped open against her body.

"Oberon came by earlier this morning. He needed help purchasing a portal spell. Nog decided to act as a guide."

Sin closed her eyes and counted to ten. Then back to one.

Why couldn't Nog keep himself out of trouble? Was he pathologically unable to make a single sensible decision?

"Nog offered, or Oberon asked?"

"Nog volunteered." Her tía stared at her, as if she could see right through her. Normally, she didn't mind the sensation. She had nothing to hide from her family—not anymore. But today it made her feel uncomfortable.

She decided that she'd wring Nog's neck later. Once she found him.

"Did he say if he they were going to Fluxers or Broomsticks Aplenty?" Both names were terrible, but both magic stores were excellent.

Celeste pursed her lips. "They didn't say. But they're the best options for portal spells."

"They charge through the roof," Sin muttered to herself. The last time she had gone to Fluxers for a spell—one her family couldn't produce—she'd had to cut off an inch of her hair for payment. Apparently, death fae hair was a thing.

Sin wondered what Oberon would've had to give in exchange for a portal spell. They weren't cheap. And sometimes they demanded eyeballs, tongues, or even limbs.

No, scratch that, she didn't want to know.

If he had to lose a limb, so be it. He probably deserved it.

"I'll swing by the market area and see if I can find Nog," Sin said and slowly rubbed a hand over her forearm, over an old burn scar.

"Thank you. I worry about that boy. But Oberon will watch out for him."

Sin sighed, the sound bone-weary. "That's what I'm afraid of."

By the time Sin made it to the market area of The Crossroads, it was already teeming with people. Most of the shoppers were shifters, but there were also fae, witches, and even a few vampires out and about.

This part of town hadn't suffered too badly from the eruption of magic caused by the Portland portal and its fallout, and it was still largely filled with shops. Except they had changed from fashion designers and clothing stores to apothecaries and techno-magical hardware stores.

Sin headed for Fluxers, since they charged more reasonable prices, and were more likely to give Oberon the portal spell. *What does he need a portal spell for anyway?* She wondered. Why couldn't he just get Caius to open one straight to Avalon? From what Sin understood, the god could open a portal to anywhere in the universe from Tartarus.

Sin thought she saw the tell-tale white of Oberon's hair a hundred feet away, near an exotic foods store. She couldn't see his face—just the back of his head. No sign of Nog's brown mop next to him, though. Hurriedly, Sin strode through the crowd of shoppers, using her elbows to help force her way through. Until she smacked into a woman. Without thinking, she grabbed the woman's shoulders to stop her from toppling over.

Sin's magic went crazy.

Her heartbeat pounded in her chest; up and down seemed to lose meaning. It felt like she was deep underground, entombed in the earth, while she flew through space with nothing but the cold of the void to keep her company. Her skin was chilled but electrified, the tiny hairs on her arms standing on end.

She'd never felt like this before.

Blinking the haze from her eyes, she took in the person in front of her.

It was the redheaded woman from the portal. She was dressed in a pair of black jeans and a brown leather jacket, which she had buttoned up against the brisk air.

Kieran's mate. Sabrina.

She seemed to flicker—one moment flesh, the next transparent, like a ghost. Almost in time to the pulsating of Sin's magic. The other half of Sin's power, the part that felt connected to everything, recoiled at the contact.

Sin let go with a jerk.

"That was—wh—what are you?" Sin gaped at her hands, then the woman.

Stupid. Stupid. Stupid.

Everyone knew what Sabrina Fhearchair was. Even if they didn't understand it.

Bright blue eyes stared back at her. "What kind of fae are you?"

They both stood there, a foot apart, not saying anything in response to the other's question.

"You're a death fae," the redheaded woman finally blurted. She rubbed her biceps, like she had a chill. Sin echoed the movement.

Sin didn't know what to say in response. For some reason, she felt like confirming what she was would be giving away too much information. Even though both Sabrina and Kieran had seemed to know she was a death fae, despite there being no physical clue to tell them as much. There was no obvious characteristic that marked a death fae from any other kind, but fae just seemed to always know.

"My name's Sabrina. I'm a phantom." Sabrina gave her a bright smile.

She didn't add her title: Ruler of the House of Death and Diamond. Interesting how she kept that quiet, when most House leaders wouldn't be caught alone out on the street, let alone introducing themselves to random Houseless women. Plus, assassination was a real risk. Maybe that was why she'd dropped the title.

Sin took a step back. "That's nice."

Sabrina's grin grew wider, but her blue gaze was assessing. A small crowd of people had gathered around them, and Sin didn't like it. Sabrina might not fear being killed by an assassin, but Sin didn't much want to be caught in the crossfire.

A tall, dark-haired male shoved himself through the crowd to come up beside Sabrina, complaints following in his wake. Kieran. He stood behind his mate, completely dressed in black, wrapping his arms around her waist and tucking her head under his chin. His gaze was icy as he stared at Sin over his mate's hair.

"Still following us?" Kieran asked.

Sin crossed her arms over her chest. "No."

He was the *last* person she wanted to bump into. Sabrina had probably been the second to last, purely because if she was around, he surely wasn't far from her side.

His gaze surveyed the surrounding onlookers. "Fuck off."

They scattered. It was amazing how quickly they found something else to occupy their attention.

Sabrina rolled her eyes and leaned back against Kieran's chest. "Do you remember that concept we spoke of? Manners?" But her voice was light, teasing.

He nipped her ear. "Manners are like cookies. They're a 'sometimes' thing."

Sabrina turned a flat look his way. "Biscuits are an 'all the time' thing."

Sin wasn't sure that Sabrina's definition of biscuits matched hers.

But then, the woman was Scottish. And either way, she wasn't about to wade into their argument.

"Do you know who your parents are?" Sabrina asked suddenly, twisting to stare at Sin.

Sin blinked. "...Yes."

"And...?"

Sin started backing away. "And what?"

Sabrina stepped forward, Kieran following closely behind. "Who were they?"

"I don't see why you need to know. I'm not in a House." Sin backed up until her back hit a wall. A hard, warm wall. Odd. Then the scent hit her. Cedarwood, citrus, and something undefinable. How she was coming to loathe the combination.

Oberon.

She almost groaned. In relief or annoyance, she couldn't say.

Annoyance, she decided a moment later. Definitely annoyance. An arm wrapped around her shoulders, Oberon's hand settling on her left shoulder. She froze. His forearm rested against her collarbone. It was a possessive hold. One that declared she was now off-limits to other males.

Blood rushed to her head as rage flared through her.

She was *not* his.

Sin was about to stomp on his foot when a small black corgi wove between her legs and sat down on her boot. Nog turned to look up at her, his orange eyes almost glowing against his dark fur. His shadow shifter form was ridiculously cute. Her anger lowered a notch, and she took a small, calming breath.

But then there was the scent.

She growled low in her throat.

"Are they bothering you?" Oberon asked, his voice knife sharp.

"Are *we* bothering her? Looks like *you're* the one annoying her," Kieran said, eyes taking in Oberon's arm and Sin's clenched fists.

She hadn't even realized she'd done that.

It took concentration, but she relaxed her hands, although she left them by her sides. No way was she going to encourage Oberon and whatever insanity he was engaging with.

"You need to keep your mate on a leash," Oberon said, directing his words at Sabrina.

Oh no, he didn't just say that.

"A leash?" Kieran sniffed. "You're the kitty cat."

Sin almost choked on her own saliva. Oh, how she wished she could see the expression on Oberon's face...

Oberon's voice was dry when he said, "Meow."

Laughter bubbled up in Sin's chest. She hadn't known Oberon could be...funny.

Kieran shrugged. "If I wanted a tame housecat, then I would have just gotten a pet."

Oberon's arm tightened slightly, and then he let her go. Sweet, sweet relief swept through her at the break in contact. "We have somewhere to be." He then grabbed her forearm and dragged her away from Kieran and Sabrina. Nog trotted along beside them.

What the fuck was happening?

She frowned. Oberon was wearing his usual ensemble—leather jacket, shirt, dark pants, and weapons—but he also had on a backpack that looked like it had been packed for a long road trip. Was it full of spells?

Sin glanced back over her shoulder and Sabrina hopped on her tiptoes and waved. "Bye!"

She's not quite sane, is she? Sin thought. *How could she be? Mated to a torturer.*

While Sin did appreciate the escape, she did not appreciate the hand on her arm. Or how he had held her. "Let me go." Her voice was a low snarl.

He snorted. "You have a death wish?"

She narrowed her eyes as he dragged her away. She growled low in her throat. Normally, the sound would be enough to make even the most stubborn shifter step away. It only made Oberon's hand grasp her tighter. They turned down a side street, and he tugged her into a small alley between buildings. There was no one else near them, but that didn't mean someone wasn't watching. Or listening.

He spun to face her. "Are you an idiot?" His voice was low, angry.

Angry?

What right did he have to be angry with *her*?

Sin gave in to temptation and stomped on his foot. He didn't even flinch. Damnit. She wanted that to hurt. "*Me*? You're the one groping me in public!"

"I didn't grope you." He leaned forward, all dark menace and fire.

Sin put her hands on her hips. "Oh, so putting your hands on me—without permission—isn't groping?"

"I'd say, no, it isn't." He leaned down, his voice lowering. "I didn't touch any part of your body that your family wouldn't."

True, but her family wouldn't have touched her like *that*.

Possessive.

Like he owned her.

Fury threatened to swallow her again.

No one owned her.

Not now.

Not ever.

Nog whined at Sin's feet. Glowering at the fae male before her, she squatted down and patted the corgi's head. "It's okay, Nog. I'll only kill him a little."

Oberon's eyebrow rose. "You could try."

"Oh, I'd be happy to." And she would love every damned minute of it. This asshole just seemed to love complicating her life.

His expression shifted, turning cagey. "But you owe me. So, another day, maybe."

He swept out a hand, throwing a pungent orange powder into the air in front of him. It landed in an eerily perfect line on the cracked pavement at their feet. Then he rolled up the sleeve of his jacket, exposing the sinewy strength of his forearm. He withdrew the dull gray knife from its sheath, then dragged the tip along the inside of his arm, his jaw clenching as blood fell onto the powder. It sizzled.

Oberon whispered the words to a spell in a language Sin didn't recognize; power surged around them, a wave of hot air blasting through the alley. Sin's hair was blown back against her face, and she had to shove it away from her eyes. Nog crowded against Sin, and she rested a protective hand over his side.

Three heartbeats later, a vortex sprung up from the powder. It glimmered in a dizzying array of colors before settling on a cool silver, like the surface of a mirror. It was tall enough to fit a grown adult, and wide enough for one to squeeze through. Slowly, an image coalesced in the center—a dark and fractured track winding toward the sea, with a cliff arching up toward the sky on one side, and dark rocks on the other.

"Come with me." Oberon turned to look at her, his expression almost...earnest.

She shook her head. "No way."

He began walking backward until he was a hairsbreadth from the portal. He stepped through, one leg on either side. "You made a vow..." He smirked at her, like he'd won.

Sin snorted and stood, dusting off her hands. "I said I owed you one. Not that I'd go through to another world with you."

There was no way in hell she was going through that portal with him. He had offered her nothing she wanted. Plus, she couldn't leave her family. He could go to Avalon and do whatever it was he needed to do. Without her.

Oberon glanced down at Nog, who wagged his tail at the fae. Sin frowned. Then her *primo* turned wide orange eyes toward her, his gaze beseeching, tongue lolling out the side of his mouth.

"Oberon's a big boy, he can take care of himself," she told him.

Nog sneezed.

Oberon hooked a hand around one of the straps on his backpack. Then he smiled at her, and fuck, it was like a punch to the chest. Beautiful. Dangerous. Triumphant. A small whine emerged from Nog, then he was darting away from her as Oberon fully stepped through the portal. The fae's hair was windswept, and he was grinning as Nog emerged next to him on the dirt road.

Wait. What?

No.

No.

Sin lurched forward, throwing herself at the portal, only to land on the ground knees first. Hard. Something whizzed over her head. She shoved to her feet and looked around, but the portal was gone, and she was covered in stinking orange dust. Was that an arrow on the ground behind where the portal had been?

Standing, she looked around, but she was alone in the alley.

Fuck.

Nog had just gone through the portal. To Ireland. To the Avalon portal.

She was going to *kill* him.

And after that, she was going to murder Oberon.

Slowly.

CHAPTER 14
OBERON

GIANT'S CAUSEWAY, IRELAND

Oberon made it through the portal and smirked as Nog bounded by to land at his feet. The air here smelled different; briny, with a thick layer of woodsmoke and something else. Almost like magic—if it had a scent.

He turned to look back at the temporary portal, about to raise an eyebrow and goad Sin into stepping through, when the portal snapped shut.

Fuck.

That had been quicker than he'd anticipated.

The dark-haired witch who had sold them the spell had assured him it would last for at least five to ten minutes. It had barely lasted four. He was just thankful that it hadn't closed while he—or Nog—was halfway through.

That's what you get for buying cheap spells.

Then again, the portal spell had been exorbitantly priced. Not for him, since he'd only had to part with six of his shifter form's feathers. Which, to be fair to the witch he'd bartered with, she hadn't known they were feathers Oberon's panther had shed. Bastets were rare on

Tartarus—they were apparently damn near mythical on Earth, with one of his feathers being worth six archangel feathers on the black market. So, in reality, that spell had cost the equivalent of thirty-six archangel feathers. Not fun trying to come by that amount of plumage legally.

It was a good thing his panther had let him collect last year's molt. Sometimes it liked to play with them and tear them up.

He studied Nog, who was rolling around in the dirt, and sighed. His plan had not gone...well, according to plan.

Then again, he hadn't been blessed with luck in a *very* long time.

Staring at the space where the temporary portal had been, he shook his head. Clearly, he didn't buy the best of the best when it came to bartered magics. But it had gotten him to Ireland, within a couple hundred feet of the fae portal at the Giant's Causeway. Which meant that he had been at least partially successful.

Take the win where you can.

Oberon glanced down at Nog, who had stopped rolling and was now sitting on the cracked road, tail wagging happily, plumes of dust wafting around his small form. The shifter's tongue lolled out the side of his mouth as his orange gaze darted over the landscape.

Oberon squatted so that he was almost eye level with the corgi. "Thank you for coming with me."

Nog gave a small yip, and his tail wagged faster.

Legend on Earth had it that the fae never said thank you because it indebted them to whoever they were speaking to. That concept hadn't been a thing when he'd been on Avalon. Maybe things had changed. Either way, he'd manipulated the boy into coming with him, knowing that Sin would never willingly leave The Crossroads on her own. If this worked, he owed Nog more than a mere "thanks."

He stood. To be fair, he hadn't anticipated that Nog would be coming to Giant's Causeway in his shifted form, but he should have factored that in. The boy struggled to keep his human body, and apparently being flirted with by a young witch with smokey eyes had been a little too much. Oberon had offered to take Nog back through to Tartarus when it first happened—he had no idea where that magnanimous suggestion had come from—but the youth just shook his head.

Nog stood and twirled in a circle, while Oberon focused on the dusty road, which meandered along the shoreline.

It was quiet, almost eerily so.

He had no idea if that was the norm for a portal, but The Crossroads was always busy. Oberon spun in a slow circle on his heel. The road had once been bitumen, but it had cracked and been repaired so many times, it was a patchwork of lines and gravel. A cliff rose toward the sky on his right, the surface covered in a mishmash of grass and rocky extrusions. To his left, the path dropped into the steel-colored ocean, jagged columns of basalt emerging to form an uneven shoreline. The strange, hexagonal rocks spread out toward a peninsula-like point where a cluster of guards stood.

A small building was perched over the rocks on wooden stilts, and it appeared to be no more than ten feet by ten feet in size. It had a small chimney and a large window on one side with a ledge. It had been built about twenty feet in front of the portal, which was actually in the sky, hovering over the water. It looked wide enough to fit at least ten people side by side, but it seemed like the guards weren't particularly worried about an incursion. Hell, half of them appeared to be more interested in talking than watching their backs.

But Oberon wasn't foolish enough to think that they would let him approach and enter without a fight.

Turning back toward the curving path, he started walking along the uneven road, Nog following. Small buildings hunched near the shoreline; the hillside cut away to accommodate them. Most bore crests that indicated they belonged to one of the ruling Houses. There was one structure with sharp lines and graceful curves that reminded him of Avalon, and another that was under construction. He wondered what would happen if there was a high tide. Would the buildings be flooded? Or did they have wards to prevent it?

The path transitioned from sealed to a dirt surface, then became a mere walking track on the side of the cliff. A steep rock face climbed upward to their right, while the ground dropped away to their left. Oberon and Nog were heading east, only to come to a point in the track that had them doing a complete one-hundred-and-eighty-degree turn, before they began walking west, back in the direction they had come—

just a hundred feet or so higher than before. The path continued to slope upward and they wove their way around the side of the cliff, which was now on their right, coming to the top of the escarpment. It seemed this once may have been a lookout, as the track ended at the cliff's edge. That, or the cliff had collapsed into the ocean.

Oberon turned back and looked down at the portal, shimmering in the air above the sea. The nine and a half structures along the shoreline were the only buildings aside from the guardhouse visible on the peninsula-like point. He assumed the half-constructed building belonged to the new House—something to do with destiny and dragons, or was it dragomir?

The buildings were new(ish), anyway. When the portal had first opened, humans hadn't known of it. Apparently, Giant's Causeway had been a tourism destination; hundreds of thousands of people had come here and never realized the fae world was a mere handful of steps away. It had been cloaked with magic originally, but it was also in a remote part of Ireland, according to the intel he'd been able to gather.

Oh, there'd been legends, of course. Like that the rocky outcrop itself had been built by Fionn mac Cumhaill, so that he could fight a giant named Benandonner, only for it to be destroyed. Neither of those names were familiar to Oberon, but that didn't mean there wasn't some truth to the fable. He'd been gone for millennia—much could have changed in that time back on Avalon.

At the top of the escarpment, an undulating plateau spread out for miles. Fields of grass and orange wildflowers fanned out from either side of the path for a few hundred feet before houses began to line the southern side of the path, their front doors a handful of feet from the path and cliff's edge. The structures were a mottled assortment of stone, brick, and timber, and had the look of shanties that had somehow become permanent dwellings.

Oberon's hands tingled as he stared at the shore and the portal, the ring on his finger warming. Startled, he looked down at his hand. The crown had been inert since it had changed form five thousand years ago; was it finally awakening?

Like calls to like.

He hadn't needed confirmation that returning to Avalon was the right choice—he was going regardless. But the feel of his magic stretching, reaching toward the portal? And the warming of his crown-slashring? They were signs he couldn't have ignored, even if he'd wanted to.

He and Nog continued walking west until the track veered south. There, in the distance, he could make out the roofs of larger structures. The small houses continued to cluster to their left, alongside the path. Nog and Oberon paused as they came to the top of a small rise, the landscape dipping down in front of them. The sounds of life finally reached them, along with a stronger scent of woodsmoke. Before them, the undulating plateau had been filled with snaking roads and buildings—this must be the heart of the portal town.

Oberon walked toward a large, white structure. It was one of the biggest buildings and also looked the cleanest. It had a charcoal roof, dark accents, and was two stories tall, with at least five chimneys that he could see. Causeway Hotel was written in block letters along one side of the building, and stables had been built out of the local dark volcanic rock in what appeared to have once been a large, paved allotment. Several other outbuildings were associated with the hotel; some appeared to be of the same age as the building, and others were newer, like the stables.

Probably from when the world changed.

He'd heard there'd been a radical shift from technology to magic, and that life had regressed in many ways. Avalon had never been much interested in technology when he'd been there—he couldn't help but wonder if that had changed. Then, they'd used magic to power most things.

Several horses and motorbikes were stationed in front of the hotel, and it had the appearance of being a popular place.

This was it, then.

Gravel crunched under his feet as he walked toward the hotel, Nog trotting along happily in his wake. He wasn't sure how long he was going to have to wait for Sin to come after her cousin, but he doubted it would be long. Sure, his plan could backfire—and considering his luck so far, that was a real possibility—but he knew she would want to come for Nog herself. The real risk was if she brought Reagan, or her father, Alvaro.

The alpha shifter wasn't Oberon's biggest fan, and Raegan would no doubt expose his plan. But it was a risk he had to take.

As he approached the hotel, his magic began to thrum against his skin. Weird. It was almost as if he could feel the power of the Earth itself flowing directly under his feet, and out back towards the cliff, toward the portal. He'd never felt anything similar to this at The Crossroads, and there was a portal there, too.

Oberon gave the horses a width berth—he didn't want one of them to kick Nog, who had decided to sniff everything in sight—and then walked up the steps to the inn. Noise broke through the doors as he opened them, the sound of laughter rich in the air. A bustling taproom met Nog and Oberon as they stepped inside, filled with a wide variety of beings, although the population swayed more toward fae rather than shifter, unlike in The Crossroads.

Hotel staff wove through the crowd, serving drinks, food, and gods knew what else to patrons. Oberon walked up to the bar, ignoring the curious stares which seemed to focus equally on him and Nog. Jet-black corgis with orange eyes must be an oddity around here.

Oberon tapped his fingers on the polished wood countertop of the bar. Nog sat down practically on top of his boots. The kid was wary, even though he looked carefree, with his tongue lolling while he panted. But his small body was rigid as he leaned against Oberon's calves.

Oberon simply waited.

A bare two minutes later, a large fae male working behind the bar made his way over to Oberon. The man's hair was navy, and his dark skin contrasted with the white shirt and apron. Delicately pointed ears were covered in piercings, while white tattoos wove over the male's hands. Power radiated from the other fae, and Oberon kept his expression bland. The male was an elemental—common enough. But they usually only had power over one element; Oberon had a suspicion this male was intimately acquainted with at least two.

Pale gold eyes locked on Oberon's face while he held a dishtowel tightly in one hand. "You're new."

It wasn't a question, so Oberon didn't bother to respond.

"What do you want? Food, beverage, a room?" The fae's voice was deep, like coiled thunder. It also had a lilt, which was quite different from how the people at The Crossroads sounded.

Oberon gave him a quick smile, but the expression didn't reach his eyes. "How about all three?"

The fae grunted. "We only have one room available. And your dog can't stay inside the inn. No pets allowed in the rooms."

"He isn't a dog."

The fae frowned and leaned over the counter to take a better look at Nog. The corgi blinked innocently in response.

The bartender made an odd coughing sound, then whipped his gaze back to Oberon. "Is that a hellhound?"

"Have you ever seen a hellhound that looks like a corgi?" Oberon asked, tone mild.

"I ain't never seen a hellhound before, not until that new portal opened. But pictures have been circulating." The bartender pointed to a newspaper a few feet away on the counter.

"Hellhounds do tend to be limited to hell."

And possibly Soleil, the demon world. But they were technically a different species, even if they were called the same thing.

The fae's golden gaze narrowed. "But I also ain't ever seen a corgi with glowing orange eyes."

"He's a shadow shifter," Oberon said. He figured there would be no harm in admitting what Nog was.

The bartender frowned. "Ain't that the kind of new shifter that came through that hell portal?"

"It is." Oberon had to admit, he was surprised. He hadn't thought that news of Tartarus would have spread to such remote places in the three months the portal had been open. But it made sense that the other portal towns would learn about the new interdimensional doorway as soon as they could.

The fae made a sound between a grunt and an exhale in response to Oberon's acknowledgement.

"So, Nog can stay in the hotel?"

"Not in his dog form. There're a few patrons here that would consider him a good...snack. And we have a policy about it for allergies.

He can stay in the room, provided he turns into a human. But as I said, there's only one available."

Oberon gave the other fae a flat stare. "He would prefer to stay in his shifted form." He wasn't about to admit that Nog wouldn't be *able* to shift back into his human form.

"He can stay in the stables, then. There're protection spells there for the animals."

One eyebrow rose. "You have one for the stables and not the inn itself?"

"Those spells are costly. Better to keep the protection in one place."

Oberon wasn't sure he bought the excuse, but he was willing to leave it. "You happy with that?" he asked Nog.

The corgi nodded.

"During the day, he's with me."

The bartender shrugged. "If you think you can protect him, then sure."

"I think I can manage that." Oberon turned to glare at a female vampire who'd come a little too close to them while they'd been talking. She had a short bob and wore dark sunglasses—even though they were inside—and she was beautiful. The kind of beauty that emerged after living for far too long—it refined the face.

The blood drinker gave him a toothy smile.

"St. Claire, don't try and scare my patrons." The bartender's voice was dry, almost amused.

The female vampire sniffed. "I wouldn't do anything so crass. I'm just here to buy a drink."

The other fae rolled his eyes. "Because you don't have booze down at the embassy."

"Not any worth drinking." She flicked a hand in dismissal. There, on her middle finger, was a ring with a pinkish stone. What was the name of that House again? Blood and something that started with a *B*?

"I don't sell blood here."

"I'm not looking for blood. Not right now, anyway." She darted a glance down at the corgi. "I'm after a Bushmills 30."

Nog pressed himself so hard against Oberon's legs, the fae thought the boy was trying to become one with his shin bones.

"Neat or with ice?" the bartender asked.

"Neat."

"You got it." The fae hustled off to grab a dusty bottle of amber-colored liquid from a shelf high above his head.

"So, you're from the new portal." St. Claire's gaze tried to bore through Oberon.

"What makes you say that?"

She sniffed delicately. "You smell weird."

Oberon choked a little on his own saliva. "I just came through a temporary portal. It could be that." There had been that peculiar orange powder, after all.

She shot him what he thought was a sidelong glance—hard to tell with the dark sunglasses. "It could be, but it isn't."

Nog's tail began to thump against Oberon's shins.

The bartender returned and slid a glass toward St. Claire. "Put it on your tab?"

"Yes."

Then he turned to Oberon. "What drink do you want?"

"Got a beer?"

The fae stared at Oberon like he was missing a few brain cells. "This is a pub. In Ireland. And you're asking if we have beer?"

"Yeah, you definitely come from the other side of a portal." The female vampire snickered.

"Well, do you?"

The bartender clutched his heart as if shot, while Nog put his paws over his eyes.

The vampire shook her head with exaggerated slowness. "Oh, you poor, sweet summer child."

CHAPTER 15
SIN

THE CROSSROADS

Sin rubbed her hands against each other, trying to loosen the sticky—and gross-smelling—orange powder from her palms. Sadly, it wasn't going anywhere. She would have to try and convince her tía to make a remedy so Sin could eat without the risk of poisoning herself—which might be a bit difficult considering she had allowed Celeste's son to leap through a portal to gods-knew-where.

Damnit.

Had that arrow been there before Oberon opened the portal? She couldn't remember. She spun around again in a small circle, but she still didn't see anyone. And using her ability to sense if there were any souls nearby would be pointless—they were in a city. Of course, there would be souls.

Sin scuffed her foot against the ground, anger pulsing through her anew at the memory of Nog jumping through that portal. What the hell had Oberon promised her *primo* to get him to do that?

Adventure? Fame? Fortune?

Gods, it wouldn't even have to be all three. One would be enough to lure Nog, considering how desperate he was to prove himself to the family. Not that he had to, but that was youth for you.

Sin was about to leave the crime scene—well, where Oberon had committed his latest crime against her, anyway—when the crunch of a heeled boot against broken glass had her glancing up. Sabrina, Kieran, and the brown-haired witch who had come through the portal with them emerged from around the corner, coming to a stop at the mouth of the alley.

Sabrina was flanked by her mate and the witch, whose pale blue eyes reminded Sin of a wolf. They took in the scene—Sin standing there, *alone*, a line of smelly mandarin-colored powder spread out on the ground behind her. A dumpster was to her left, and a pile of trash to her right. It was a glamorous place to be found.

She groaned.

She hadn't thought her day could get any worse, but she'd been wrong.

You should know better than to tempt fate.

Sin settled into a loose stance. Her fighting skills had improved a lot over the last three months. She met the cold gray gaze of her half-brother who had moved behind his mate. *Yeah, you'll hold your own for the entire ten seconds it takes Kieran to rip your throat out.*

"You were the one who accused *me* of stalking." Sin met Kieran's gaze over the top of Sabrina's head.

Her attention was brought back to Kieran's mate when she said, "It didn't look like you were all that willing when Mr. Blond Hotness grabbed your arm. So, we decided to follow."

Kieran made a choking sound. "'Blond Hotness'?"

Sabrina flicked a sidelong look at her mate. "Not as hot as you, obviously."

"Clearly. I would have said the Blond Prick or even the Blond Princeling, but hey, whatever floats your boat."

"You float my boat." Sabrina let out a low "grrr" and pretended to claw Kieran's chest.

Sin did *not* need that image seared into her retinas. Were detoxes for the brain a thing? And if so, where could she get one? She figured detoxes were probably more practical than the magical bleach she'd hoped for before.

"She decided to follow you. I followed her." Kieran crossed his arms over his chest.

"...And I followed them, because I didn't know where they were going." That was from the witch, her expression amused, as she pointed at them with her thumb.

Sin had the strongest urge to rub her forehead.

"As you can see, I'm perfectly fine. You can go do the things House rulers do." Sin made a shooing motion with her hands. She *really* needed to get home, see her tía and explain what had happened to Nog, and then procure a portal spell. Maybe even drop by to see Reagan so she could fill her sister in. And ask Caius to kick Oberon's ass.

"Or we could—" Sabrina began. Kieran groaned and the phantom hit him gently in the stomach with the back of her hand. It didn't seem to bother him. "—just find out what the hell is going on."

Kieran leaned closer to his mate's ear. "Didn't we talk about not getting involved in other peoples' business?"

"I'm the leader of a House, other peoples' business is *literally* my business."

Kieran huffed.

Giving into the urge, Sin rubbed her forehead. "I'm going home."

She was going to lock herself in her room, activate the anti-ghost ward, and just sit in blessed silence while she processed the day. Then she'd tackle her to-do list.

"Why don't we walk you there?" Sabrina gave her a bright smile.

Sin shot her a sidelong glance. "I know my way, it's fine."

Kieran's voice was low. "Sabrina, remember what we talked about? We only help people who *want* to be helped."

Sin hadn't thought she'd ever have a reason to be thankful for her half-brother—but today, she was. If he could convince his mate to leave her alone, yes, that would be great.

The witch tilted her chin slightly and her nostrils flared as she... sniffed? "There was a portal here."

She could *smell* portals? What kind of witch was she?

"Tamsin?" Sabrina's brow furrowed—but not in annoyance, Sin realized. The phantom was thinking.

The witch—Tamsin—strode past Sin, careful not to touch her, and came to a stop next to the line of powder. "Yes, there was." Bells jingled as the witch squatted down, and Sin realized they were braided into her hair, along with bones, feathers, and...rocks. "Where did it open to?"

Sin took a careful step back—she didn't want to accidentally get the powder or trash on her boots. "I'm not one hundred percent sure, but I can guess."

Tamsin reached out a hand and touched the orange gunk.

"I wouldn't—" Sin frowned and snapped her jaw shut.

Tamsin rubbed her fingers together, the substance falling away, as if it were nothing more than dust.

Sin looked at her stained hands. *Great. Just great.*

The witch stood, the sound of cloth sliding against itself and stones chinking against each other accompanying the movement. "The spell wasn't particularly good."

"Barely lasted four minutes," Sin said, her voice deadpan.

"That's what she said," Kieran snickered. Sabrina elbowed him in the stomach. He shot his mate an indecipherable glance and rubbed his abdomen. "Why did you wake up today of all days and choose violence?"

Sabrina just rolled her eyes.

"If you need to burn out some angst—"

"That blond guy was a fae," Tamsin said quickly, cutting the vampire hybrid off, like she was used to interrupting him.

Thank the gods.

"Yes, he was." Sin nodded.

"And he purchased a portal spell to go somewhere?" Tamsin's lip curled in disdain.

"Yes."

"Interesting."

Sin hoped it wasn't interesting to a witch who seemed to think one of Fluxers' portal spells was cheap and nasty. That kind of magic was difficult to produce and procure—so how powerful was this witch?

"Know why there's an arrow on the ground that looks like it was aimed at the portal?" Tamsin tapped her foot.

"No."

Kieran frowned.

"I need to get going. It was...ah...an experience seeing you again." Sin couldn't even lie and say it had been nice. Because it hadn't been. She began to edge around the trio.

"To go buy another shitty portal spell?" Tamsin's pale gaze narrowed as she turned to look at Sin. She then pointed at Sin's stained hands.

"What does it matter if I do?" Sin asked, meeting Tamsin's stare, challenging the witch.

"It could snap closed on you when you're only halfway through..." Tamsin ran a finger along her throat.

Yeah, Sin didn't need the hand movement to decipher that she'd meet a grisly end if that happened.

"How about we make a deal?" Sabrina said suddenly, bouncing on her toes, reminding Sin of Nog, unfortunately.

"Nope, we are not going to make a deal with her." Kieran shoved himself between Sabrina and Sin.

"Why not?" Sabrina demanded, trying to look around her mate's back.

Kieran pivoted and the two mates stared at each other for what felt like a handful of minutes, the silence growing awkward. Sin tried to sidle away, but Tamsin grabbed her wrist. She wrenched her arm, but the witch had a surprisingly strong grip. Thankfully, there was no disconcerting experience like there had been with Sabrina, just pressure and irritation at being touched against her will.

Tamsin leaned closer. "They are telepathing each other."

"Cute." Sin tugged harder. "Now let go of me."

The witch ignored her. "What kind of fae are you?"

"None of your business."

"Hm." But she let go of Sin.

She massaged her wrist.

Tamsin flicked a glance down at where Sin was rubbing her forearm. "I don't have germs."

That was when Sin realized that the orange coating on her palms was flaking off. Huh.

Sabrina flicked her hair over a shoulder and turned to face Sin and Tamsin. "We can get you a portal spell, one that won't self-combust."

Sin rocked back slightly on her heels. "That's a big promise."

"We know a witch." The redhead smirked.

Tamsin's lips quirked in a small, smug smile. Yeah, they knew a witch, all right.

"And what will this amazing spell cost me?" No one did anything out of the kindness of their heart, least of all a House ruler.

Sabrina's expression turned suspiciously bland. "A sample of your blood."

Sin froze in surprise, then she narrowed her eyes. "Why do you want my blood?"

"Curiosity." Sabrina gave her another bright smile.

Did the phantom think grinning like the Cheshire cat would lesson Sin's concern?

"It killed the cat, you know. Curiosity." Sin's tone was drier than the Sahara. Then she backed away.

Sabrina followed her. "And satisfaction brought it back." The redhead tapped her chin, as if in thought. "Although death isn't really a hindrance. At least, not to me."

Sin stopped and stared at the phantom.

Sabrina hooked her fingers in her coat pockets. "I'm pretty much immortal."

Kieran groaned, like the words physically pained him.

"The whole dead-but-not-dead thing, right?" Sin didn't know why she'd opened her mouth, but she had, and then the words had just spilled out.

"Comes with being a phantom. But I was a ghost before that."

Kieran slapped a hand over his eyes.

And suddenly it made sense. Her half-brother who was part death fae. "Ohhh. You see ghosts, too."

He shot her a look she chose not to interpret. "Not all death fae do."

"How can you stand touching her?" Sin blurted at him. Great, her mouth was just on a rampage this morning.

His eyebrows rose. "I find it rather enjoyable."

Sabrina swatted at him.

He looked aggrieved, but not murderous. So maybe he was infatuated with his mate, after all. "More violence? If you've got an itch—"

Tamsin made a gagging sound. "I think I just puked in my mouth."

"I don't turn incorporeal when he touches me," Sabrina said, ignoring her mate and the witch, responding to the question Sin hadn't asked.

"Just for me, then."

"So far. But I don't tend, or plan, to go around touching death fae."

Sin found herself nodding. "Probably advisable."

Tamsin snapped her fingers. "Death fae. Of course."

This was one of the weirdest conversations she'd ever had the displeasure of experiencing. And considering how many conversations with Oberon she'd had to endure, that was saying something.

"So, why do you want my blood?" Sin asked again, trying to get things back on track.

"Just to see if there's anything different about it," Sabrina hedged.

Sin wasn't convinced.

Kieran's magic supposedly tended toward the dark—being death fae and a vampire had apparently resulted in some oddities when it came to his abilities. But Sin figured she wasn't meant to know that; she only did because she'd researched all the ways he may decide to kill her if he ever learned about her existence.

Playing with fire, literally.

"How much blood?" Sin asked.

Why are you even entertaining this?

Because she needed to get to the Giant's Causeway, and this might be the quickest—and cheapest—way.

"Just a tiny vial." Sabrina held her thumb and index finger about half an inch apart.

"You can't do blood magic with it." Sin crossed her arms over her chest.

Kieran glowered at her.

Sabrina gave her that megawatt smile. "Sure."

"Fine. A vial of my blood in exchange for a portal spell to Giant's Causeway. No blood magic."

Sabrina nodded. "Deal."

CHAPTER 16
SIN

"That's it?" Sin asked, frowning at Tamsin's apparent lack of preparation.

The witch might be happy to risk her own life, Sin thought, but she wasn't. Willing to risk her own life, that is.

They stood in the downstairs "office" of the new House of Death and Diamond embassy. It was less of an office, and more of a room that housed a bunch of boxes, but that's what Tamsin called it. There was a table, at least, but it was comprised of a plank of unsanded timber perched across two stacks of boxes.

The embassy itself was considerably smaller than some of the buildings that had been acquired by a few of the other Houses, such as Gold and Garnet, and Sea and Serpentine. Although Sea and Serpentine's was closer to the Mississippi—but not too close. One of Caius's inner circle had apparently been seen near the river, and Styx wasn't known for playing well with others.

Sin liked how Styx operated, not that she'd admit that to the other woman. Sin still held a grudge for the kelpie pinning her against a wall.

"That's it." Tamsin nodded.

"Portal spells normally require more blood, eye plucking, or the creation of bodily wounds." Sin mimicked cutting her arm open with a pretend knife. "Not that." She pointed at the single white feather in Tamsin's hand.

"I don't need it."

Sin wasn't convinced.

Tamsin sighed. "Magic is usually tied to something."

"Yes, like an element, or a thing, like souls." She knew how it worked. She might be a fae and her magic had a different rule system, but her tía and *prima* were witches. Sin shifted one of the straps of her backpack so it rested more comfortably over her shoulders.

"Right." Tamsin gave her a strange look. "My magic is associated with space and time. Portals warp both."

Sin just looked at her.

"You kind of need to understand the concept of general relativity to get it."

That was not something she'd ever been guilty of. She liked astronomy, but she'd never studied astrophysics.

"Because they teach physics nowadays in No Man's Land." Schools weren't really a thing, not formal ones. Not anymore, not here.

"I happen to know a former physics professor, if you're interested." Sabrina said as she walked into the room, a smudge of dust on one pale cheek.

Sin didn't think she'd have to reply, but the phantom was looking at her like she expected an answer. "Ah, no thanks."

"Are you ready?" Tamsin asked.

Sin sucked on her teeth as she looked around. She'd said her goodbyes to Tía Celeste, although Tío Amos hadn't been there. And her dad, well, she'd sent him a text message. Cowardly, yes. Absolutely. But she didn't want to have to tell her father where she was going, or—more importantly—who she was going to visit. He didn't like Oberon at the best of times, considering the man had pinned him down when Caius had first come for Reagan. Alphas didn't tend to forget when a more powerful alpha bested them.

As for Reagan, Sin would let her know what happened—after it had happened. She didn't want to worry her sister; Reagan was living a new life, in a new world, with a new mate. This was just a simple retrieval task, anyway. But she'd left a note with Kasha, just in case.

Her plan was simple: Get Nog, get home.

She was *not* going to get embroiled in any more of Oberon's schemes.

There was only one downside to her plan: her mother wanted to tag along. When Sin had gone home to pack, Dianthe had asked where Sin was going—and why. Plus, she'd been having one of her saner moments. Rather than leave her behind to destroy the house, Sin had decided to take the locket and necklace that Clara had bespelled to act as a genie lamp for her mother's soul and that would allow her to travel. The locket had been gifted to Sin at birth, and it had been Dianthe's before she died.

"So, uh, what's with the ghost in the other room?" Kieran came through the door then, dressed in black on black on blue. Did he ever wear anything approaching a vibrant color?

"What ghost?" Sabrina asked, then stuck her head out the door. The phantom frowned. "When did Uncle Fergus get here?"

"He followed Max," Tamsin replied.

Sin frowned and joined Sabrina at the door. Her mother was in the front room, which resembled a construction zone, and she was talking animatedly with another ghost. This one wore a bright purple suit that was paired with a tartan tie. It clashed horribly with the male ghost's faded orange hair.

Her mother spotted her. "Sin! I just met the most interesting gentleman."

"I bet you did," Sin muttered.

Dianthe floated over the sawdust and building debris as she closed the distance to them. Sin stepped through the doorway to meet her in the room.

"Lass, ye are too kind." That was from the purple suited ghost.

"Uncle Fergus—" Sabrina said.

"Ach, lassie. Let yer uncle have some fun, aye? It's not often I get to meet bonnie ghost ladies who aren't related to me."

Sin really didn't want to think about what that meant.

"Uncle Fergus is one of the oldest phantoms," Sabrina whispered to Sin.

"My mom is dead. Like, properly dead. She isn't a phantom."

"I prefer the term 'life challenged.'" Fergus swept forward, grasped Dianthe's fingers, and pressed a kiss to her transparent hand.

Sin rubbed the bridge of her nose.

The last thing she needed to deal with now was a ghostly romance.

"Don't forget payment," Kieran said, gaze locked on Sin's mother and the male phantom.

Sin rolled her eyes. "Got a vial?" She slid the backpack's strap off her shoulder and shrugged it around so she could access the front pocket. She unzipped it and pulled out a small knife.

Tamsin reached into her flowing dress and withdrew a small glass jar with a cork top.

Sin pulled up her jacket sleeve and nicked the skin on the back of her forearm, squeezing the skin until blood welled. She then took the vial from Tamsin, uncorked it with her thumb, and scooped a few drops of crimson fluid into the glass container. She handed the uncorked jar back to Tamsin.

The witch looked at the floor where the cork had fallen. "I swear all you death fae are the same. "

"Hey!" Sin and Kieran both protested at the same time.

"Damnit," Sin said, while Kieran muttered a low, "Fuck."

Tamsin watched them, her head turning back and forth, like she was watching some kind of sporting match. "Interesting."

"No, it isn't." Sin muttered. "You've got the blood, you're ready to make the portal. Let's do this."

Dianthe clapped her hands together soundlessly, like an excited child.

Tamsin bent down and picked up the cork, stoppering the vial. It then disappeared into one of the folds of the witch's dress. When her hand emerged, she was holding a pink lighter. Tamsin flicked open the lid and activated the lighter with one hand. She then held the flame up to the white feather in her other hand, chanting quietly as the feather caught fire. They watched as it curled, withering from the heat of the flame.

Once it was little more than ash on her fingers, the witch waved an arm in the air in a circular pattern. As her hand moved, sparks ricocheted out from her palm, the glow forming the edges of a portal.

That is cool.

Way more impressive than gross powder.

The portal formed once Tamsin's hand reached its starting point. The sparks met, and the surface of the portal changed, a scene growing visible in its center. It wasn't the same landscape as the one in Oberon's portal: there was no grassy plateau or windswept beach.

No, it looked like the portal opened into the middle of a town. A large white building was visible in the background, with small wood and stone structures scattered in the foreground.

Sin frowned. "I thought the portal would open at the Giant's Causeway."

Tamsin nodded. "This is the portal town. If I dumped you at the portal, you would have a long hike back up to the top of the escarpment, and it's a shit walk."

"Oberon's portal opened at the actual portal." At least, that's where Sin assumed it had opened.

"Then he's gone through, or he's at the town. No one sticks around the actual portal."

Sin stared at Tamsin.

Kieran snorted. "It's windy as fuck."

"...Okay." Sin wasn't exactly happy about the change in destination, but it was still close enough that it shouldn't matter. And she doubted Oberon had gone through the portal already. He'd wanted Sin to help him cross; while he could use Nog for the same purpose, she somewhat doubted he had. At least, not right away. He had to know she'd follow.

"Let us know when you need a ride back to The Crossroads. I'll give you my cell number," Tamsin said.

Both of Sin's eyebrows rose.

"We should do coffee," Sabrina added.

Sin bit the inside of her cheek. "I have no idea why you guys want to hang around with somebody like me."

Sabrina dusted off her hands, not that they were dusty. "What do you mean by that?"

"I'm nobody, and you are the ruler of a House. And you can open a portal with a wave of your hand."

Sin wasn't one to downplay her abilities. She was a death fae who could throw literal balls of death magic. But she was just her, and they were three of the most powerful people in the world.

"Everybody is somebody," Sabrina said.

Sin couldn't really argue with that statement, because there was a certain logic to it.

"But not everybody is somebody worth knowing," Kieran muttered.

Wasn't that the truth.

"Plus, I have a thing about people who are overlooked." Sabrina met Sin's gaze. She had the feeling that there was something personal there. A story to be told.

"I hate to say it," Sin said, "but Kieran's right, not everybody is worth knowing."

She grabbed the chain and locket that hung around her neck and closed the distance to the portal. Without saying goodbye, she stepped through, her grip on the necklace dragging Dianthe with her.

There was a dizzying moment as her magic interacted with that of the portal, and then she was on the other side. A brisk wind buffeted her, causing strands of her hair to tickle her face, the scent of woodsmoke and salt water thick in the air.

She turned back to the portal.

Tamsin pulled out the little vial of blood and handed it to Kieran. He smirked at Sin as Tamsin waved her hand, and the portal disappeared.

Damnit. Sabrina had agreed not to do blood magic with it, but Sin hadn't gotten Kieran to promise the same.

It's too late now to worry about it.

She was at the Giant's Causeway.

It was time to find Nog.

And kick Oberon's ass.

CHAPTER 17

OBERON

GIANT'S CAUSEWAY, IRELAND

Oberon was in the Causeway Inn's stables.

As he stared at the beautifully appointed structure, he wasn't sure that the term "stable" was accurate. The stone-walled building was almost as large as the inn itself, plus it was more modern. The center aisle was paved with dark gray cobblestones, the edges lined in a cream-colored tile. The stalls themselves were built out of wood and blackened metal, with wall sconces between each stall. Looking up, Oberon realized that there was a second floor. And a mezzanine level continued above, with at least four walkways spanning the gap between each side of the building.

At the opposite end of the aisle, a long ramp led from the ground up—so that four-legged guests could reach the second level, he assumed. Studying the stalls that were visible, it became apparent that horses weren't kept on that upper level. Instead, there were various types of creatures up there, and many seemed to have more than four legs. Some of them looked achingly familiar. It had been over five thousand years since he'd last been on Avalon, but he swore that he could see a water-bull—an amphibious cow-like creature that was native to the northern continent—in one stall, and a myrmecoleon—an ant-lion beast—in another.

Nog let a low huff. The shifter stood to Oberon's left, his midnight fur coated in a shower of gray dust, making him look almost silvery. His pink tongue lolled out of the side of his mouth as he panted, his tail wagging happily. He seemed completely at ease in the current situation, which was probably a good thing. Hopefully, he wouldn't notice the rather large spider—it was bigger than Nog—silently dropping from a web that arched over the timber roof on a spool of silk.

"Anyone here?" Oberon called out. He'd come here looking for the stablemaster. The bartender had told him that he had to get their approval for Nog to stay here: no agreement, no stay. It didn't matter what he offered for payment, the stablemaster had the first and last say.

"It's not just our guests' animals here." A woman emerged out of the end stall, her accent unusual. She wore a pair of denim overalls and a loose tan-colored button-up shirt underneath. She wore rain boots rather than regular riding footwear. "We host some of the local towns-folks' beasts, as well as some from the House embassies."

The woman closed the distance between them, the torches glinting over her multi-hued hair, which he could only describe as the color of autumn. It started as a dark brown at her roots and then faded into shades of orange, burnt umber, and then yellow at the end. It wasn't a dye job either, Oberon thought. This woman was fae, with pointed ears clearly on display. A series of piercings ran over the top part of the arch of her left ear, whereas the right only had two simple earrings: one a crescent moon and the other a charm in the form of a chimera. She was pretty in the way of the fae, but she wasn't as interesting to look at as Sin.

Nope, he did not think that.

There was nothing interesting about Sin. She was an aggravating means to a long-awaited end. That was it.

If only he didn't know how she tasted...

The woman came to a stop in front of Oberon and Nog. "Name's Dana. I'm the stablemaster." She held out a hand to shake, which Oberon didn't take. Not when he saw she had red eyes ringed in burnt umber—because he'd only ever met one other being with irises similar.

But Nog put his paw up, and she dipped down to complete the gesture with the corgi.

Oberon reappraised her, frustrated with himself that he'd dismissed her because she was fae and seemingly friendly. A portal inn's stablemaster was no simple job, especially since most of the occupants didn't appear to even be from Earth.

"You didn't come through the Causeway portal recently, did you?" the woman asked, her gaze raking over him and Nog.

"No, I never came through the Giant's Causeway portal." He didn't know why he elaborated, considering he could've just said no and still been telling the truth.

"So, you're a fae who never came through the Giant's Causeway portal," the woman mused. "Avalon has a portal through to the gods' world, and one to a demon realm. Did you come through one of those?"

Oberon frowned. When he'd been on Avalon, the second portal had opened to a witch world which he'd heard referred to as the Old Country. He didn't think portals just...closed. He also didn't appreciate the stablemaster's interrogation. Or perhaps, it was mere curiosity. Either way, he didn't enjoy being the one questioned, as opposed to being the one doing the questioning.

"Does it matter which portal I came through?" he asked, voice mild.

"Not really. But the fae who come here don't seem to come to Earth via other worlds. If they go other places, they don't tend to make it here."

He ran a hand over his chin, which was prickly with stubble. "And you would know so much about that?"

"I end up meeting most of the fae when they come through the portal here. And I've seen plenty of animals from the other worlds, but they're rarely accompanied by the fae, unless they come from Avalon."

"This is all very interesting." His tone made it clear he didn't find it interesting at all.

The fae gave him a slight smile, like she was amused by his desire to escape the small talk. "I think so. Especially because of your 'dog.'" She made air quotes with her fingers around the last word.

Two could play this game. "So, were you born here, or did you come through the portal?" Normally Oberon wouldn't have bothered asking at all—but there was something odd about this fae woman, and it wasn't just the fact she liked playing twenty questions with strangers.

"I wasn't born here. But I wasn't born on Avalon, either. Living this close to the Causeway portal, it tends to feel like you're almost on Avalon, though."

Oberon snorted. That, he didn't believe. His magic might feel more familiar on Earth than it did on Tartarus, but that was only because this planet was in a solar system, and one that seemed to be close to Avalon's, based on the night sky constellations. But back on Avalon, it had felt like there was nothing his magic couldn't do.

Except detect the lies of my mate.

He didn't need to go there. Really, he didn't.

Funny how little I've thought of Titian in the last millennia. Before that, especially when he'd been new to Tartarus, fury at her betrayal had consumed him. Every waking moment for *years*, he'd tormented himself, rehashing their relationship, her every remembered word, every look, every moan and sigh. And still, he doubted he would have ever picked up on her subterfuge. She'd be dust now, anyway. Humans had a saying he'd discovered: "Revenge was a dish best served cold." But there was no point in serving it if the diner was dead.

No, what he wanted was his throne.

Dana looked him up and down. Her eyes had slit pupils. Unusual, even for a fae. "You were born there, I'm guessing."

"A very, very long time ago," he muttered.

She gave a small laugh. "You make it sound like it was thousands of years ago."

If only.

"Where's your beastie, then?" Dana looked behind him, as if trying to find the horse that wasn't there.

Oberon shook his head. "No beastie, just the dog."

The fae glanced down at the dust-stained corgi, who in turn took the opportunity to sit on Oberon's foot. He glanced at the shifter, who returned the look with soulful eyes. "Nog, remember what we said about personal boundaries?"

To be honest, it had been less of a conversation and more of Oberon telling the shifter that he didn't want to be the dog's equivalent of a cat tree.

Nog farted in response.

"Nog!" Oberon grimaced.

Dana let out a strange squeaking sound, and when he shot a glare her way, she had a hand slapped over her mouth and was breathing in an alarming pattern. He decided to ignore the other fae.

It had only been half a day, but he was looking forward to Sin coming and collecting her wayward cousin. Convincing Nog to join him here really hadn't been his smartest move.

"Just a 'dog.'" Dana squatted down so that she was nearly at eye level with Nog. She blinked once, twice, and then bit her lip as she considered the creature before her. "He is as much of a dog as that is a spider." The stablemaster pointed up at the ceiling, where the oversized arachnid had been steadily working its way down toward them.

Nog looked up and froze, his little body locking up at the sight of the descending eight-legged monster.

Oberon slid his boot out from under the shifter's butt. He did *not* want the corgi to piss himself in fear on his shoe. "So, if that's not a spider..."

Dana stood and made a series of clicking sounds at the arachnid who chittered in response, then began working its way back up the spider silk thread, its movements appearing aggrieved. "It's a *tsuchigumo*."

He blinked.

"It's a Japanese *yōkai*."

"I don't know what either of the last two words mean." He didn't like admitting ignorance, but he also couldn't pretend he understood what she meant, either.

"How recently did you come through from one of those 'other' portals?" She didn't bother to wait for his answer. "Japan was a country made up of an archipelago before the Portland portal opened. Now it's in Sea and Serpentine's territory. *Yōkai* is the Japanese word for demons, monsters, and supernatural creatures or spirits."

Right.

He would file that information away under "never to be used again."

"So, since Yamagumo is not a spider, and this is not a dog..." Dana frowned at Nog, who watched the *tsuchigumo* with wide orange eyes. "Then he's a shifter."

"You are correct."

"I've never seen a shifter with eyes that glow orange and with fur that is completely jet black." She tilted her head to the side, birdlike. "Well, that I think is meant to be totally black."

Dana then squatted again and extended her right hand. Nog crept forward and gave the tips of her fingers a delicate sniff, then ran his tongue along the outside of her hand.

"Nog, what did we say about licking?" Oberon crossed his arms over his chest. What had he become? A damn dog-sitter?

Nog whined.

"Yes, yes, I'm sure she smells lovely. But you can't go around licking people." Now that he thought about it, he hadn't detected a scent from the other fae. Which was peculiar.

"He's a dog. Sort of." Dana's eyes glimmered with amusement. "He didn't mean anything by it."

Oberon looked at the *pretty* female fae. "In his human form, he's a nineteen-year-old boy."

Dana stood and dusted off a scattering of hay from her overalls. "I figured as much."

Oberon glowered at the corgi. "Nog, no more flirting with the stablemaster." The kid should really just refrain from flirting, full stop, since he'd gotten stuck in his shifter form as a result of the last instance.

If Pollux and Caius could see Oberon now, they'd be rolling around on the ground, gripping their sides from the force of their laughter.

Nog made a rude-sounding huff.

Oberon decided to be the bigger person and ignore the dog's sass. "I'm not allowed to keep him inside the inn, apparently. I was hoping that he could be housed here while we wait for our...companion to join us. The barkeeper said there's some kind of protection spell for animals here."

Dana walked over to a wall sconce and tapped it, fire bursting to life in the light fixture. Oberon narrowed his eyes. He wouldn't have figured she was a fire fae. They didn't tend to surround themselves with wooden structures, for one.

"Despite this being the Avalon portal's town—or maybe because of it—there's plenty of beings here who think dogs or cats," she gave him a penetrating look, "are appealing treats. But not on my watch. The stable is warded against violence toward animals. So provided he stays in his dog form, he'll be fine. Once he steps outside the stables, though, I can't guarantee anything."

Oberon leaned down. "Hear that? Stay here and you'll be safe."

Nog nodded, his orange eyes solemn for a moment before they glinted with wickedness. Oberon shut his eyes. Why did he think that Nog was going to cause more mischief than the stablemaster would tolerate?

"Why doesn't he just turn back into a human form?" Dana asked.

"His shifting ability only came out recently. He tends to get...stuck." He didn't think there was any harm in admitting that.

"Learning to shift can be a difficult time."

"And you know that because...?"

Dana walked over to another sconce and lit it with her magic. "I may be able to shift myself."

"There're only a handful of fae that can shift, and you're not a kelpie or selkie."

"There are more fae shifters than those. You should know that."

"True." He let the panther gleam in his eyes. Her gaze sharpened, and he swore another alpha stared back at him from behind her red-and-umber gaze.

With effort, she broke his stare and turned to Nog. "You are not a regular shifter."

Oberon hid his surprise. Alphas were rarely able to back away from a challenge. She hadn't submitted, which meant she was able to put aside the urge to dominate. What the hell kind of shifter was she?

"No," Oberon relayed on behalf of Nog. "He's a shadow shifter."

"I've heard of that term." She tapped her chin as she thought. "From the new portal from that hell world."

"Yes."

A whicker interrupted, and then a horse poked its head through the top of a nearby stall. Dana walked over and patted the beast on its head, her hand moving slowly up and down its brown forehead, the sound of her hand scraping against the fur reaching them. She gave it a couple of last pets and then moved away.

"How much will it cost for Nog to stay here?" Oberon asked.

"If he's willing to be my assistant while he's here, we'll call it even." She put her hands on her hips. "But if he eats all the food and doesn't help, then it will be pricey."

Nog gave a small yip, his rapidly wagging tail causing a swell of dust to rise in the air behind him, coating his fur anew. Oberon took that to be assent. "I think we can come to a deal."

"Excellent."

Oberon turned at the sound of footsteps approaching, the stride hurried but decisive. The delicate—and familiar—scent of lavender and lemon reached him. His eyes widened as he spotted Sin storming toward him, her dark hair a nimbus surrounding her face, which was lined in fury. Her hands were fisted at her sides, and she was wearing a dark gray padded jacket, a pair of blue jeans, and tan boots. Backpack straps were visible over her shoulders. She was obviously dressed for travel.

"You!" She pointed a finger at him, and then thrust out her right hand, a ball of shining pale blue light slamming toward him.

Oberon ducked to the side, barely avoiding the orb of magic. "What the fuck?!"

He looked behind him at the wood of the vacant stall, now scorched from her magic. As he watched, the wood began to wither and rot. He whipped his head toward Sin. "You threw *death* at me?"

"That's the least you deserve." Her pale eyes were furious as they raked over him.

"Good thing I ducked, then."

Sin closed the distance between them, coming almost toe to toe. This close, her expression was regal, bloodthirsty.

His cock suddenly got *very* interested in the situation.

No, stop, he told himself sternly. He did *not* find her anger attractive in the least.

"What the hell did you do to my stable?" Dana's voice was like a whip as she stared at the deteriorating timber.

Sin glanced at the other fae. Then did a double take. He wondered what she saw... "Sorry. I was aiming for his head."

He tried to tell himself that she was lying, but he'd never caught her in one. And the steel in her eyes—no, the hatred—meant she really had been trying to kill him.

She was *beyond* pissed.

"That still doesn't explain *that.*" Dana pointed at the skeletal wood.

They ignored the stablemaster.

Oberon raised both his hands. "Nog jumped through that portal willingly."

"Nog is nineteen years old and recently shifted. Do you really think he was capable of thinking clearly?"

Nog produced a sound that was a cross between a whine and an affronted huff.

Sin looked down at the corgi, who had sidled closer to Dana, like the stablemaster was going to help him. "Don't even get me started on you."

"He's come to no harm," Oberon said, not sure why he was opening his mouth. "I was just arranging safe accommodation for him."

"Oh, how magnanimous of you." Sarcasm dripped from every word.

Dana's eyes began to glow. "Will someone *please* explain what she just did to my stables?"

Sin rolled her neck. "It was death magic."

The stablemaster frowned. "But the timber was already felled..."

"My magic causes the rapid deterioration of cells. It destroys life. All life."

"That is..." Dana seemed at a loss for words.

"Scary as fuck," Ysabeau St. Claire said from the doorway.

CHAPTER 18
SIN

Ysabeau St. Claire was standing in front of Sin.

The second-most powerful woman in the House of Blood and Beryl was standing in front of Sin.

And now the woman was looking directly *at* Sin.

Fuck my life.

Sin had never met her before, but most people on the damned planet had heard of her. She was the nightmare you warned your kids about.

To make matters worse, Kieran and Ysabeau had worked together for decades. They were probably friends—assuming her psychopath of a half-sibling knew how to make friends.

You know, you really sound like a stalker when you think about him.

Yeah, Sin had probably taken the concept of "knowledge equals power" a little too far. She'd learned everything she could about Kieran—especially after their cousin, Danni, had mated the king of Blood and Beryl.

But the fates obviously didn't care about her preparation or plans, because they seemed to take great joy in fucking her over.

"Me? 'Scary as fuck'?' I don't think you're one to cast aspersions." Sin crossed her arms over her chest, mostly because she didn't want to give in to temptation and throw another orb of death magic. And she was still far, far too angry at the damned fae male before her to be rational.

She'd arrived here intent on taking her frustration out on Oberon and convincing Nog to go home with her. Now she had to fear for her damned life because she'd been stupid enough to use her magic in front of the wrong person.

You know, Caius is more dangerous than this vampire.

But Caius was her brother-in-law now. That reduced the scare factor a significant amount.

Ysabeau raised a dark eyebrow in response to Sin's tart comment. She wore a black power suit and dark sunglasses. Her hair was cut in a sleek bob, and her mouth was generously proportioned, but her lips were just a little *too* red. She was a vampire that had seen more than one millennium, if one were to believe the rumors. Which Sin did.

"I don't think we've met previously, so I'm not sure how you could say that I was casting aspersions. Maybe I was talking in admiration." Ysabeau's voice was cool, but Sin could detect the slight mocking edge.

"Does one have to formally meet the second-in-command of the House of Blood and Beryl to know who they are?" Sin asked, pretending to examine her fingernails. In reality, she was watching the vampire in front of her, while trying to track Oberon and the other fae in her peripheral vision.

Nog was standing near the fae woman in overalls.

Traitor.

"Second-in-command?" Oberon asked, voice deceptively mild. Sin shot him a look. While he sounded mildly surprised, his expression was utterly calm. Amused almost.

Nog took the opportunity to bound over next to Sin, pressing his side against her right calf. She would have squatted down to pet him if he hadn't made her travel halfway around the world to drag his sorry ass home. Apparently the stablemaster and Oberon McJerkface were no longer suitably capable of protecting him.

"It's not an official title," Ysabeau murmured.

"You may not have the title, but that's what you are. Everybody knows it. Even people from No Man's Land." Sin lowered her arms to her sides. She wished she could see the vampire's eyes—she felt like she'd be able to read the situation better if she could. But the sunglasses prevented that.

"Who I work for has little bearing on this conversation. I'm not the one throwing literal balls of death." Ysabeau stepped into the stables and waved an arm in a strangely liquid movement.

A weird, tingling sensation licked over Sin's skin, almost like her magical ability was reaching out and tasting the other woman. A being who had defied death for longer than some civilizations had lasted. It left her feeling...hollow.

"It was a *ball* of death. Singular," Sin said. "And I'm a death fae."

"It's...unusual. And very useful." Those red lips curled in a smile then. One that had a shiver running down Sin's spine. No, she decided, she did not want to be able to see Ysabeau's eyes—she didn't want to see her own mortality in that stare.

"Is the pissing contest over?" the other fae asked. Sin assumed the fae woman was the stablemaster, since she was wearing work clothes that fit with the job title. She also had hair the colors of deep autumn, and the kind of beauty that drew the eye. Beauty that had apparently drawn McJerkface's eye—from the way he'd been interacting with her when Sin arrived.

"For now," Ysabeau replied, her tone dry.

The stablemaster looked back and forth between Ysabeau, Oberon, and Sin, finally settling on Sin, like she was the biggest threat. Which was laughable. Ysabeau was a thousand-something-year-old vampire with the associated speed and reflexes. Sin wouldn't even have the time it took to blink before she was killed, if Ysabeau decided Sin needed to die. And Oberon was an annoying prick, but that didn't change the fact that he'd put Sin on her ass more times than she could count. He was dangerous. And she didn't know what kind of fae he was, either. But he could create orbs of fire, she knew that, at least. And drop the temperature in a room. It was why she'd struck first. She needed every advantage she could get.

"Good. Then you can leave my stables." The stablemaster pointed at the wall which had taken the brunt of Sin's magic. "I would prefer the rest of the building avoid that fate."

The wood was now nothing more than a few strands of cellulose, barely holding itself together.

Her stomach felt like it did an uncomfortable flip-flop in her abdomen. She rarely used her magic for harm, and this was why. Imagine if an innocent had been behind Oberon, or an animal...

No, she'd prefer to not imagine that scenario. She carried enough guilt as it was.

"I'm sorry. If Jerkface over here hadn't moved, your stable would still be intact."

Oberon's mouth thinned. "Excuse me?"

Nog chuffed.

"You're excused." Sin wasn't sure if he'd taken affront to the nickname she'd used, or the fact she was blaming the damage on him.

"*You* threw the magic. I just ducked. And I'd be nothing more than bones if I hadn't."

Sin rubbed a hand over the back of her neck. "Bones would be an optimistic outcome."

Nog bit her leg, gently. She hissed at him.

"He's from Tartarus," she explained to her *primo*. "He became a shadow shifter after being exposed to death magic. He could have been immune."

Yeah, she had no idea if that was true or not. But...it technically wasn't a lie. Plus, Sin hadn't really been thinking all that clearly when she'd come into the barn. She'd been so worried about Nog that when she'd seen her cousin hale and whole, and Oberon attempting to charm the beautiful stablemaster... Sin had let her rage take over.

"So...?" The stablemaster didn't finish her sentence, but Sin got the message.

She strode down the length of the cobblestone aisle, and then stepped through two massive black doors, into the weak sunshine outside the barn. A wash of magic spread over her, and she belatedly realized the stable had a warding spell. One she hadn't sensed when she'd first arrived, probably because of her heightened emotions.

Where has my famous control gone?

She blamed her lapse on Oberon. He had a way of getting under her skin unlike anyone else she'd ever met.

Sin took a deep breath, then turned around so that she was facing the stables. Oberon had followed her and was standing just inside the barn next to Nog, who hadn't joined Sin outside. Damn. She rubbed her chest. Still picking the damned fae over her?

She frowned. "Nog?"

"Nog is safe if he stays in the stables," Oberon explained. "Once he leaves them, the protection spell ends."

The stablemaster approached them slowly, like Sin was a wild animal that needed taming, while Ysabeau walked in the opposite direction, farther into the stables. Sin realized the vampire had made a beeline for the wood Sin's magic had destroyed. Ysabeau studied it for a full minute, nobody speaking while she did so. Then the vampire turned and prowled her way back to them, her movements so fluid it was jarring.

"Protection spell? Is that the ward I felt?" Sin asked.

"You felt that?" The stablemaster's brow furrowed in thought. "Yes. The spell protects the animals within the stables."

"He's half-animal." Sin pointed at Oberon.

"Hey!"

"You are!"

"Yeah, but you don't have to go around announcing it." He glowered at her.

"As if we couldn't smell it," the stablemaster muttered. "Plus, he wasn't in his animal form, and I hadn't extended the spell for him."

So, it was manually controlled. Interesting. Clara would love to study the ward.

"So, why were you throwing balls of death at Blondie over here?" Ysabeau asked, gesturing toward Oberon.

Sin scrunched her nose. "It's personal."

Oberon coughed.

"Not *that* kind of personal." Sin shuddered at the idea. "It relates to family." She gave Nog a pointed look.

"Hmm." Sin wasn't sure if the vampire or the stablemaster made the noncommittal sound.

"Why is the second-in-command of the House of Blood and Beryl hanging around the stables of a No Man's Land inn, anyway?" Sin asked. Better to be on the offensive, she figured.

"You're a suspicious little thing, aren't you?" the vampire asked.

"Yes; it's kept me alive so far." Sin's voice was droll.

Ysabeau sighed. "Not that it's any of your business, but our House has an excellent seer. She said that a cursed king would be stopping by the Giant's Causeway around now." She made a show of looking at her wrist, as if she was reading the time on a watch, when her wrist was bare of any ornamentation.

"A cursed king." Sin felt a bubble of laughter rise up. Wouldn't that fit her lucky streak?

Then she realized that Ysabeau was staring at Oberon.

Him?

No.

Sin whirled on him. "*You?*"

Oberon held up both of his hands. "I wouldn't say I'm *cursed*."

"What are you king of? Nothing?" Sin taunted, unable to stop herself.

Nog made a sound that was a bit like a whistle, if a dog could do such a thing.

Oberon's dark brows lowered, his gaze burning as he met her glare. "Because me being a king is so hard to believe?" He shoved his hands into the pockets of his jacket.

Sin made a show of looking him up and down. Damn, why did he have to be so beautiful? "Yeah, it's that hard to believe."

But now his insistence on going to Avalon made sense. If he'd been kicked out and lost his throne, he'd want it back. Even after being trapped on Tartarus for millennia.

Not my circus, not my monkeys.

"Come on, Nog, let's go."

Nog looked back and forth between Oberon and Sin, then his head dipped, and his tail drooped.

Sin frowned.

Oberon closed the distance between them, coming to stand next to her. She hated that he was so close. That she could feel the heat his large body produced. It sent warning messages down the entire right-hand side of her body.

"Nog!" Sin stepped back toward her *primo*, away from the damned fae.

Oberon snapped out a hand, grabbing her wrist in a vise-like grip. She could feel her bones moving in protest, and she spun toward him with a low snarl. She raised her left hand to strike him, but his other hand moved quicker than she could track, and the sound of metal clicking had her arm jolting in response. Something golden flickered around her wrist—*a handcuff?*—for three heartbeats before it vanished.

Molten heat scorched her wrist where the flicker had been, like she'd stuck her hand into the furnaces of hell. She hissed as the scalding sensation spread, and kept spreading, until her whole arm *burned*. Her muscles locked as she fought the pain, her magic trying to eject the spell taking root.

She didn't know how long she stood there, fighting the enchantment and the pain, but eventually, a ribbon of the foreign magic slipped through and spread like wildfire through her body. She couldn't tell where the agony finished and she began. She was blood, and bones, and heart, and nothing and everything, all at once.

Then it just...stopped.

Gone as if it had never been. Oberon let go of her wrist with a jerk. Panting, Sin grimaced at the red mark that wrapped around her wrist. It looked like a healed burn, the flesh raised and bumpy.

"What the fuck was that?" she demanded, shaking her hand, as if that might make the mark disappear. She then ran careful fingers over the welt, but it didn't hurt. And she couldn't feel the metal cuff. Just her raised skin.

"A binding spell."

No.

No, she hadn't heard him right. Couldn't have. That kind of magic was so expensive as to be nigh impossible to procure. She tried to protest, her throat worked, but no sound came out.

"It means where I go, you go." Oberon leaned down, his height allowing him to tower over her. "We're now bound."

"I had made you a vow—you didn't need this, too." For the first time in a long time, she felt truly small.

Weak.

"You refused to come through the portal, *despite* your vow. This is insurance."

He'd *trapped* her?

Fury had a red haze descending over her vision. She wanted him to feel like her, weak, powerless. Lost. Instead, she slapped him hard. His face lurched to the side, and a red palmprint bloomed on his left cheek.

Her hand stung, but she reveled in the pain.

Oberon slowly turned back to look at her, his black eyes devoid of the usual white speckles. He ran a hand over his now clenched jaw. "I'll let you have that one. Try it again, and I'll spank your ass."

The temperature around them plummeted. "Try it and die."

He leaned down again, his face hovering above hers, so close she could taste his breath. Oranges and whiskey. "Don't tempt me." In response, Sin held out a hand, letting an orb of death magic form over her palm. Oberon's lips quirked in wickedness. "You might want to rethink doing that."

Her voice was flat. "Really."

"Really." He smiled, triumph, arrogance, and pure masculine pride evident. "I die, you die."

"No." Disbelief had her hold on the death magic weakening, and the orb vanished.

"Yes."

What the fuck kind of magic had he done?

"Remove the spell," she ground out.

"No." He crossed his arms over his chest, smug.

The bastard.

Sin's hand formed a fist, her fingernails biting into the skin of her palm. "Remove. The. Spell."

"No."

Without conscious thought, she struck out with her fist, aiming for whatever body part she could reach. He ducked easily and swept her legs out from under her in a smooth, easy movement. Before her brain could process it, she was on her ass on the dirt ground. Air exploded from her in a whoosh, and she lay there, butt and head aching while she desperately tried to fill her lungs.

He shook his head slowly. "I would have thought you'd have learned by now."

Wishing he would just drop dead, Sin rolled to her side and scissor-kicked his legs. He dropped to the ground, but unlike her, he actually broke his fall. "Remove the spell."

He rolled smoothly to his feet. "Eventually."

Gods, why was he so damned pigheaded!

She stood. "Now."

"If you had just agreed..." He held out his hands, palms up.

She stabbed a finger against his chest. Fuck. That hurt her finger. Was he made out of rock or something? "Oh no, you are not blaming your psychopathy on me."

Oberon smirked. "Please, save the flattery for when we're alone."

Could he just kill her already?

She pinched the bridge of her nose.

Oberon held out a hand, as if to guide her away from the stables. "Come. Let's get you settled in, and we can talk over the details of our new...partnership."

She didn't even have the energy left to protest. She had to get this spell removed. So, if that meant playing along for a little while, then she'd do it.

She looked around the asshole fae toward her *primo*. He was sitting on the ground near the stablemaster and Ysabeau, his gaze puppy dog sad. "Nog? You'll be okay?"

He gave a small woof, which she took to mean *yes*.

But she wasn't about to abandon Nog with strangers—at least, not totally. She unhooked her mother's silver locket from her neck and walked over to Nog, her boots crunching against the gravel. She squatted down next to him. She met his stare and held up the necklace. She saw the recognition in his gaze as he took in the chain. "Nog, I'm going to put this on as a collar."

"Wait." The stablemaster held out a hand. She reached into an overall pocket and withdrew a red dog collar. "Use this and attach the locket to that. It will be safer for him."

Sin wasn't going to ask why the woman had a spare collar on her person. She simply nodded, taking the collar and fastening it around Nog's neck. He sat patiently while she did so, his tail wagging slowly. Then she hooked on the locket. "My mother will watch over you."

Sin muttered the incantation Clara had set, and Dianthe emerged from the locket in a cloud of muted smoke. She formed next to Sin and looked around the stable with wide eyes. "You didn't get Nog and go straight back home?"

"No," Sin replied. Dianthe had had a mild tantrum when she'd realized Sin had gone through the portal to Ireland. Hence why Sin had locked her back in the locket. She hadn't intended to let her out for a few days, but had decided that spying on Nog would be a good use of her mother's time.

She could feel the curious gazes of the stablemaster and Ysabeau St. Claire. Then the vampire muttered something about death fae and ghosts.

Her mother turned more transparent. "You can't go to Avalon."

"Don't worry, Mamá. Can you watch Nog? I need to go and get settled for the night."

"Where's Nog?" The ghost frowned and looked down at the corgi. "Who is the dog?"

"Nog."

"Isn't he a boy?"

Great. Her mother's grip on sanity had once again become tenuous.

"He's both," Sin replied.

Sin wasn't sure that Dianthe would understand, but the ghost gave an elegant shrug. "He always was an odd boy."

Oberon sighed. "I think I officially moved into the next century while waiting."

Sin glared at the blond fae before her. She ran her hand over Nog's head and ruffled his ears before standing.

She was ready.

"Fine. Let's go...talk."

And if she accidentally killed Oberon...well, it would be worth it. Even if it cost her own life.

CHAPTER 19
SIN

Strangely, the inn wasn't as ornate as the stables.

Despite that, it was an exceptionally nice establishment, especially for a portal town in No Man's Land on the edge of the Atlantic Ocean. The outside was painted white with black timber features, and it stood two stories high, surrounded by stone pavement.

Reluctantly, Sin followed Oberon through the foyer. She wanted to go home, but Nog clearly wasn't ready to leave yet. She had no idea what was going on in that doggy brain of his, but when he eventually shifted back into his human form, she was going to give him an earful.

Was he there when Oberon bought that binding spell? Had Nog known that the asshole fae was planning to use it on *her*?

Sin tamped down that line of thinking. It would only end in her getting angry at Nog, and even though he might deserve it, she needed to try and keep a rational mind. Nog usually had a reason—even if the reason made sense to no one but himself—for why he did the things he did. Plus, her magic responded to heightened emotion, and she'd already lost her temper at Oberon more times in the past week than she had with anyone else in the entire year prior.

Oberon entered the inn's taproom, which was full of patrons. She followed, the scent of tobacco smoke, alcohol, and garlic hitting her. She wouldn't have expected it to be so busy, but then, this might be the only pub in town. She looked around the room, memorizing the layout. The bar was positioned to her left and took up almost the entire length of one wall. It was made from some kind of dark wood—walnut, maybe? —and had an interesting array of alcoholic and magical beverages stashed behind it on glass shelves. Two servers worked behind the bar, steadily taking orders. The male server was fae, with midnight-colored skin and dark blue hair—he was handsome, with an aura of power that made Sin categorize him as a potential threat. The female bartender was also fae, her hair the color of a warm flame, and her skin a pale gray. Her ears tapered into steep points that almost rose to the crown of her head. Sin had no idea what kind of fae she was.

Sweeping her gaze away from the bar, Sin took in the remainder of the taproom. The floor was covered in a dark green carpet that held a patchwork of stains. Wooden tables were scattered throughout the room, the timber matching that of the counter. Booths lined the back and side wall, upholstered in what appeared to be green leather. Overhead, stained-glass lights shone down, the red and orange panes reflecting warm light on the crowd.

A pool table was to her right, and it seemed popular, with people milling around while a female vampire played against a male shapeshifter. There were two doorways—not including the one she'd just arrived through—one which was next to the bar, and the other on the opposite wall, leading into what appeared to be a darkened corridor. She assumed the one near the bar led to the kitchen, since that was where the scent of garlic seemed to originate.

"This way." Oberon's tone was low and lacked the taunting edge that it usually held. He put a hand on her lower back, and she shimmied forward, breaking the contact.

"Don't touch me." She didn't even bother to look back at him when she said it. Gods, she felt repulsed by him. Absently, she ran a hand over the raised mark on her wrist.

"Fine. Follow me." Oberon strode around her, leading the way through the taproom.

She could feel the curious stairs of the patrons, some letting their gaze linger a little too long on her as she moved through the crowd.

Her skin itched in response. A particularly large fae male was watching her with a dark gleam in his eyes. As if sensing her unease, Oberon turned to glare at the closest offender, then stopped, waiting for her to come up next to him. He placed an arm around her waist. She wanted to protest, but he wasn't actually touching her. It just looked like he was. She could feel his arm brushing the fabric of her jacket, and he slipped his hand in her pocket, but he wasn't touching her body.

The large male who'd begun to close the distance between them stopped, then looked away in a hurry when Oberon directed a flat glare his way. Huh. She didn't want to say she was grateful to the asshole fae for anything, but that was impressive.

Together, they walked the remainder of the taproom. Once they were in the corridor opposite the bar, he slid his hand out from her jacket pocket and stepped away from her. Instantly, she felt cold, like his body heat had been warding off the chilly air.

You're being ridiculous.

The hallway seemed to wrap around part of the building, and she was able to see doors opening off of it, each with their own number. They walked down the hallway, reaching a set of wooden stairs that led up.

"This way." Oberon strode up the stairs before her, and Sin realized that he didn't believe she was a threat to him at all. He let her follow him, his back exposed to her.

You never exposed your back to an enemy.

Even though I can throw literal balls of death, he doesn't fear me.

She would like to say that it was because he was an idiot. But he was powerful, and his fighting skills far surpassed her own. She might have once been the most powerful member of her family, but to Oberon or Caius, she was about as scary as a butterfly.

It was humiliating.

Sin was a damned death fae, and this man didn't give two fucks about it. Was it hubris? Or was he really that confident that she couldn't—or wouldn't—hurt him?

You've proven that you're more than willing to hurt him.

Yes, but he'd walked away with a red cheek that had already healed, a burned shirt, and a temporarily sore shin. She'd never actually done any lasting damage.

What kind of fae *was* he?

If she understood that, maybe she'd then understand how powerful he was. And what she'd have to do to escape him.

She reached the top of the stairs a couple of steps behind Oberon. He didn't even bother to check if she was following him. Sin gritted her teeth. She watched as he turned left and headed down another hallway before she followed. He stopped outside a green door labelled 209.

His deep voice rumbled through the hall. "This is us."

"Us?"

He unlocked the door and stepped inside.

Sin didn't follow. "I'm not staying with you."

"I just told you that we can't be separated. This spell has a limit on the distance we can be apart."

"How about we put it to the test?" Sin turned and marched back along the carpeted hall. "I'm not staying with you."

She didn't even get to the top of the stairwell before a sharp pain sliced through her head. It was like a sudden onset migraine, leaving little to no space for thought, just acute agony, almost as intense as when the binding spell activated. Nausea roiled in her stomach, and she tried to move, but her muscles locked in protest.

Sin stood there shaking while she tried to process the pain, to *think* past it. Almost as suddenly as it began, it receded, leaving Sin shivering in the aftermath. Perhaps she had been able to overcome it?

A wall of heat scorched her back, and the scent of cedarwood and citrus hit her. No, she hadn't gotten used to it. Oberon had just gotten closer.

Fuck.

As she went to move, she realized her hand was clutching the side of her head. Lowering it, she turned slowly to glare at the blond fae, her body still not entirely convinced that the pain was gone. She expected him to be smirking at her, pleased with his victory, but his mouth was pressed in a thin line, and his eyes were like lit coals. "I'd say that gives us about twenty feet, wouldn't you?"

"I could still get a room next door." Sharing a room with Oberon was like her personal version of hell.

"Yes, except my room was the last room available, apparently." And...there was the smirk.

Asshole.

"Fine." She didn't believe him, even though he supposedly couldn't lie. But she would check at the bar when they went down later. Because there was no way she was going to stay trapped in a room with him for the next few hours.

Or for the night.

Sin swept past Oberon and stalked down the hall back to the room, going inside. She came to a rather sudden stop in the middle of the room—if you could call it that. Sure, there was a bed which took up the majority of the space, and a wooden wardrobe that was stained to a dark mahogany color. There was even an attached bathroom, although it was the tiniest one she'd ever seen; a shower, toilet, and a sink were crammed into a mere six by three-foot space. It was even smaller than a damned grave.

She chuckled to herself.

"What's so funny?" Oberon shut the door with a decisive click.

"Just a family joke."

"Oh?"

"I'm not going to tell you about it."

His dark gaze narrowed, but he seemed to decide to let it go. "This will be our base for a couple of days before we go through the portal."

Sin crossed her arms over her chest. "I'm not going through the portal."

"Oh, you're going through it, even if I have to carry you over my shoulder."

"I'd like to see you try." Her hands formed fists by her sides.

He shrugged. "Been there, done that. Even got the T-shirt for it."

She would prefer to *not* be reminded of that night. "This time, I won't hold back."

That infuriating smell of his seemed to fill the space, and she breathed shallowly through her mouth, trying to dilute it.

"How did you ever make it to adulthood without somebody strangling you first?" Oberon shrugged out of his leather jacket, then threw it on the bed.

"Lucky, I guess." Sin looked at him through her eyelashes, wondering if she could get away with kicking him in the shin again. It wouldn't hurt him much, but it might make her feel better.

"I see violence in your eyes. I'd recommend keeping that impulse in check."

Sin rolled her eyes and took off her backpack, dropping it in the corner of the room. "I get the bed."

"I am not sleeping on the floor. I'd barely fit."

Sin looked at the narrow space around the bed, then at his six foot plus frame. Yeah, it would be a tight fit, especially considering he was covered in a stupid amount of lithe muscle. "Not my problem."

"I paid for the room. I get the bed."

"You put a *binding spell* on me. I get the bed. You get the floor."

He growled low, then shoved a hand through his shoulder-length blond hair. "Let's sort this out later."

Like there was anything to sort. She wasn't going to be sleeping on the floor, and he was an asshole. That meant that he was going to be the one getting the sore back, not her. Her stomach took that moment to let out a loud rumble, and she nearly groaned in embarrassment.

"You're hungry." His lips quirked in something like a genuine smile, and Sin quickly looked away. He was devastatingly handsome when he did that, and she didn't like it.

"I haven't eaten since this morning," she admitted. Ireland was about five hours ahead of The Crossroads and it was past dinner time.

"We'll get room service."

No way was Sin going to tolerate being trapped in the room with Oberon while they ate dinner. Where would they eat; have a picnic on the bed?

No, thank you.

"I want to go check on Nog."

"We're not leaving this room. Not before we eat. Plus, didn't you leave your mother's ghost to watch over him? Shouldn't that be enough?"

"You saw what my mother did to my house."

"So? It means she's got a good arm."

"I don't know why I thought you'd understand. You don't have a family." That was low, Sin admitted, even for her.

"Oh, you really do try and aim for the balls, don't you?"

"I don't want anything to do with your balls. Now or ever." Gods, why did she say that? Her gaze kept wanting to drop to his groin—to visually confirm he had said balls? She didn't know—but she was able to stay focused on his chest. Barely.

He snorted.

She chose to take that as agreement.

Oberon walked over to a wall-mounted phone and picked up the receiver. It was old-school; it even had a cord and a number pad. He dialed zero and put in an order for a roast dinner. He then pulled the phone aside, placing his hand over the receiver. "What would you like to eat?"

Why did that feel strangely intimate? "I don't even know what they've got."

She could hear another voice talking on the other end of the phone, and Oberon listened as they rattled off a series of menu items that she couldn't quite make out. "There's roast of the day, pasta of the day, or fish and chips."

She'd heard of fish and chips before—and at least that meant she didn't have to wonder what the roast or pasta might include. "Fish and chips."

He relayed the order and then hung up the phone.

Sin stood awkwardly, not sure what to do. She scratched at a patch of dirt on her pants. That decided for her. Grabbing her backpack, she marched toward the bathroom. "I'm taking a shower and I'm locking the door. If you break in, I will kill you."

"You have nothing to fear. Believe it or not, I have more worthwhile activities to occupy my time than barging in on contrary females."

Sin shrugged. "You're the 'Cursed King.' Maybe you got cursed because you were a pervert."

Something dark flashed across his face, but he didn't rise to the bait. "Bathroom is all yours." Then he sat on the edge of the bed.

She didn't need the image of Oberon on a bed engraved into her retinas, so she quickly slid through the door, shutting it behind her. She locked it, the sound of brass mechanisms echoing through the tiny room.

She dropped her pack on the ground, wincing at the clank of buckles against the bottle-green tiled floor. She hunted for a towel, finding one in the small wood cupboard under the sink. It was green. What a surprise. She then turned the shower on to let the water heat, figuring a place as old as this might have ancient pipework. To her surprise, steam soon filled the bathroom.

Methodically, she stripped off her dust-stained clothes, feeling weary to her bones, yet worried at the same time. She was worried that Oberon wouldn't respect her boundaries and would break down the door just to piss her off, and tired because she couldn't remember the last time she'd slept through the night. She kept half an eye on the door while she undid her sports bra. To be fair, she didn't have a reason to think Oberon would be inappropriate. The man was hot enough that he could pretty much ask anyone for sex, and they'd probably agree. He didn't need to resort to force. And while she hated him, she didn't think he was evil in *that* way. But it didn't mean she trusted him.

Stepping into the shower, she almost groaned as the hot water hit her cold and goose bump-covered body. She held her breath and lowered her face under the spray, thinking about where she was, why she was here.

Gods, how she missed her family.

Sure, her mother was with Nog, but Dianthe wasn't exactly excellent company at the best of times. Reagan and Clara were on Tartarus, and although Alvaro often travelled between Reagan's new home and The Crossroads, he rarely stayed in The Crossroads for long. He struggled to stay still, and would hit the road, off to save disadvantaged children.

And Jo...

Tears mixed with the water trickling down her cheeks. She scrubbed her face, trying to distract herself from thoughts of her lost *primito*.

Ever since Sin and Reagan had become adults, their dad had gone away more and more. He had a mission in life, Sin understood that. But that didn't mean she missed him any less. He'd saved her and raised her as one of his own. She couldn't ask for a better father. It didn't change the fact that she felt...alone.

You're feeling sorry for yourself.

In a way, Sin had always been alone. Born to a dying mother, and then fostered by a fae family who had apparently been terrified of her as a baby. Found by her dad, and then brought back to The Crossroads to his large and extended family. Rather than give her up to Tía Celeste, he'd raised her as best he could by himself, all while hunting for Reagan.

And then he'd found her. The child he'd lost from his mate who'd been brutally murdered. And Sin had a little sister. But Reagan hadn't been right when she'd come home. There had been nightmares, and she'd been so powerful, her magic out of control. Sin looked down at the raised scar on her right arm that spread from the middle of her forearm to her elbow. It had been bigger when she was a child, but as she'd grown, it had remained the same size. It was a souvenir from when Reagan had almost burned Sin to death while suffering a nightmare. Sin had tried to wake her sister up, and Reagan had set the room on fire, and then Sin.

Their dad had lied to Reagan for years about its origin—Sin still hadn't told her sister the truth, either. She wasn't sure she ever wanted to.

Sin lifted her head up and wiped the water from her eyes. She grabbed one of the tiny courtesy shampoo bottles that had been left on a rack that hung from the showerhead. She rubbed her hands together until suds flowed over her palms, bubbling against her skin. As she washed her hair, her mind went back to the aftermath of Reagan's magical outburst. She'd been lucky—she'd lost her eyebrows and a chunk of her hair had been singed off; she'd also had minor burns over twenty percent of her body. Thankfully, her tía healed most of the damage, and what she couldn't, other witches in the family had repaired. She was only left with that single scar.

But it was that night that had driven their father to make a terrible decision: lock away Reagan's magic. Sin had been recovering from her burns when Alvaro had done it—but she'd known about it, and she hadn't told her sister. Sin had carried the secret for well over a decade, and it had eaten away at her as she'd watched her sister struggle in a world that ran on magic. But Reagan hadn't been ready. At least, Sin hadn't thought she was.

She understood what it was like to have a magical power that nobody else did. To have a burden that nobody else seemed to carry. She was a death fae, but she'd never heard of one who could literally throw orbs of death magic. And then there was her other ability, the one where she drew power from the Earth. Sometimes, it even felt like her power came from the stars themselves. Not only that, but she could manipulate it, transforming it to an extent. But she'd never embraced it fully because she was afraid of being caught. Afraid that if people knew where her magic came from, it would make people ostracize her more than they already did.

Her family and Kasha loved her, but the other people in The Crossroads? They tolerated her because they knew Reagan and Clara would get pissy if they didn't. She wasn't exactly Miss Popular.

"Now is not the time for a pity party," she muttered to herself.

"Did you say something?" Oberon shouted through the door.

"Fuck off!"

"Got it." There was a pause. Then his voice dropped an octave. "You enjoy that 'me' time."

Sin blinked rapidly as water dripped down through her lashes.

'Me time'?

Oh, no, he's not thinking that I'm...

No. He was just trying to mess with her.

And what did it matter if she was enjoying some quality orgasmic time? Not that she would with him right there listening—although she did wonder what he'd do if he really heard her come...

No. She didn't want to know that at all.

Stupid Kasha, putting the concept of hate sex in her mind.

She finished washing her dark hair, then spread conditioner through it. While she let it soak, she scrubbed herself clean. The water was still warm when she turned the faucet off and stepped out of the shower. She dried herself off with the green towel and dressed in a pair of blue tracksuit pants and a T-shirt from her backpack. She unlocked the door and stepped into the room, a cloud of steam following her.

"Use all the hot water?" Oberon asked, standing. He stretched his long limbs and rolled his neck, the sound of cracking joints loud in the room.

"I'm sure there's a drop or two left." Sin gave him a small smile.

Oberon walked into the bathroom, shutting the door behind him. He didn't bother to lock it, and she knew he was mocking her. She heard the shower turn on, then the rustling of clothing. She stared at the door, wondering if she should open it just to shock him.

But then you might see him naked...

She didn't need that vision in her mind. She shook her head at herself, and then climbed on the bed. She sat on it, legs crossed lotus style. The mattress was surprisingly comfortable.

A bare five minutes later, Oberon emerged from the bathroom. He wasn't wearing a shirt, his bare chest glistening in the light of the inn room. He wore a pair of jeans without a belt, the waistband hanging low, exposing the sharp planes of his hipbones and the dark trail that ran from his belly button down. *Fuck.* Sin's mouth turned dry.

She tried not to stare.

She *really* tried not to stare.

But the man had muscle upon muscle, and it was really *not* fair.

"Like what you see?" His gaze taunted her.

"You look better when I can't see you." Because her imagination was filling in all the gaps, and it was a damned fine mental view. Plus, imaginary Oberon didn't talk. That took him from an eleven out of ten to a twenty.

"I'm sure that was *meant* to be an insult," Oberon muttered.

Sin glowered at the fae.

Someone knocked on the room door. Oberon opened it, then spoke to the server, who handed the fae a tray with two plates covered by cloches. Oberon placed them on the bed with a flourish and kicked the door shut behind him.

"Dinner is served."

Sin grabbed the fish and chips. Her stomach growled again, and her cheeks flushed red. Strangely, Oberon didn't tease her for the sound, but merely picked up his plate, sat on the bed, and began eating with meticulous manners.

Sin demolished her food in less than ten minutes. She was wiping her mouth with a napkin when she caught Oberon staring at her.

"What?" she demanded.

"I didn't realize that people attacked their food, rather than eating it."

Sin's blush darkened. "I hadn't eaten since breakfast."

He put his cutlery down and stared at her. She waited for a snarky response. It didn't come.

"Here." He offered her the dinner roll that had come with his roast. Sin stared at his hand like it was a viper about to strike. He shrugged, and it looked strangely awkward. "If you're still hungry."

He's just being nice.

The realization made her feel...off balance. She was so used to their adversarial relationship, she hadn't even considered that he might try and do something kind. She ran her fingers over the raised mark left by the binding spell and his gaze dropped to follow the movement. Something almost like regret flashed across his face, so fast she figured she'd imagined it.

His hand slowly began to retreat.

Her stomach feeling heavy, she reached out and solemnly took the roll. Accepting his peace offering. "Thank you."

CHAPTER 20
OBERON

It felt strange, sitting on the bed with Sin—sharing such a small space with her—and it not being, well, difficult.

Oberon finished eating the roasted meat while Sin devoured the small roll he'd offered her. The worst part of this mess was that he actually kind of liked her. She was sharp-witted, passionate, and clever. She was beautiful, too, but he'd long ago learned his lesson about valuing someone's appearance more than their heart or their mind. Her whole family spoke highly of her, when they weren't muttering about how they didn't involve her in drama unless they had to.

Sin was a means to an end, he kept telling himself. But he was also going to inevitably fuck her life up. And he hadn't even warned her about what was to come.

Guilt began to gnaw at him.

The emotion had been easy to ignore when Sin acted prickly, contentious, and angry. He figured she hated him enough that one more black mark against his name wasn't going to change the situation for either of them. But that was when he viewed her as nothing more than a tool to get what he wanted.

And until an hour ago, he'd still been able to convince himself of that.

But now? Now he was seeing the real Sin, and the guilt was harder to sideline.

"You and Reagan don't look much alike." Oberon didn't know where the thought came from, but he'd just blurted it out.

"We tend to tell people we've got different mothers." Sin's plump lips thinned. Gods, he really wished he didn't know what they felt like under his—or what she'd tasted like. Sure, she'd only kissed him that one time to distract him, but it had been one hell of a distraction.

"That's pretty obvious," Oberon replied, tone dry. Reagan's mother had been murdered by a cult, and Reagan had never mentioned the fact that her mom haunted Sin.

Wait.

"You 'tend to tell people'?"

"I wondered if you'd catch that." Sin gave him a half smile, and damn him, his response was instant—and physical. He bit back a groan at his cock's sudden interest, and tried to think about anything other than the way her lips moved when she was amused.

What if they were wrapped around your—

No. He wasn't going to go there.

But it was difficult to push the thought away, knowing that *he* was able to get a reaction out of her, when to the rest of the world, she was eerily calm and collected. If he was honest with himself, he *liked* that he was able to get her to discard her vaunted control. And he wondered—for the briefest, stupidest second of his life—what it would be like to watch her completely lose that control. With him. While he was sheathed inside her, driving them both insane with pleasure. Seeing that quiet power of hers, her confidence, focused on him—

"I'm adopted."

Her voice broke through his daydream, and he shifted uncomfortably on the bed. Damnit. He'd really let himself get lost in the vision. Thankfully, she was too busy picking at a napkin and tearing it into a thousand pieces to notice the raging hard-on that was trying to poke over the top of his jeans. He shifted his plate so that it hid his lap a bit more.

"It makes sense," he replied, startled at the gravelly nature of his voice. But she didn't seem to notice, thankfully.

Her being adopted didn't really surprise him. She had dark hair like Reagan and Alvaro, but Sin was tall and lean, whereas Reagan was shorter. She was generously proportioned—he'd felt her breasts pressed against his chest and had cupped her hips in his hands during that one fateful kiss they'd shared—and she didn't seem to have a shifter side. His panther would have noticed if she did. If Alvaro was her father, she should have been half-shifter.

Then there was the added fact that Sin also didn't really look much like her extended family. From what he understood, they were either foundlings or only partially related to each other, anyway. So the fact she'd looked different hadn't really mattered. But he'd suspected she was a full-blooded fae from the moment he'd laid eyes on her.

He'd never heard of a Celestial who wasn't.

He shifted the plate around, trying to better hide his erection. "How old were you when your family found you?" He shouldn't be asking these questions. He shouldn't be trying to get to know her at all.

But gods, how he wanted to.

He wanted to know what made her tick, wanted to know why she was so adamant that she couldn't go to Avalon. Why she seemed to hate him so much; why she thought he was untrustworthy, when he'd done nothing but keep her and her family out of harm's way.

Her sister was on Tartarus, and from what he'd heard, Sin had only come to visit Reagan twice since the Santiagos had been granted permission to travel back and forth at will. He wanted to know why. Because it was clear to see that Sin and Reagan loved each other. There wasn't any rivalry or angst. He could tell that Sin loved Reagan with an absolute purity of the soul.

But Sin was also hiding from her.

And that, he didn't understand.

Then again, he'd never experienced that kind of devotion from a single person.

He'd been born into a family that had seen him as the tool he was, a way to take over the throne. He was one of the most powerful Celestials born in generations. He'd been a pawn in a millennia-old chess game. And when he'd been exiled to Tartarus—which he now realized was a blessing, rather than a curse—he'd found his true family. He never would've really understood how to be a good leader if he hadn't stood next to Caius while he'd transformed Tartarus into the thriving society it now was.

Oberon couldn't remember the last time a High King—or Queen—had actually been liked by the people of Avalon. He doubted he would have been an exception to that pattern, especially if he'd stayed mated to Titian.

"We think I was about three."

Her response startled him. He'd almost forgotten he'd asked a question, so lost he was in thought. "Think?"

"My mother's recounting of events is not exactly...how do I put this...reliable. And the foster family who cared for me after I left the hospital couldn't hand me off fast enough. Dad had a bit of trouble getting dates out of them. He spent years trying to relocate them, but they vanished."

"You were a baby, why did they run afterwards?"

"They were frightened of me." Her voice was low as she stared down at her lap.

His earlier arousal vanished. "Frightened of a baby?" He let scorn coat his words.

She flicked him a glance. "Yeah. They were supposedly death fae themselves, but I was scary, even for them. Guess I must have been able to cast death magic even then."

Death dealers had been rare, even on Avalon, so he was surprised that they would've rejected Sin. Especially when she could've brought a new bloodline into the mix. It was callous thinking, but that's how the fae thought. Bloodlines, power, prestige. The fae he'd met on Earth weren't any different. Unless you mated, you married for political reasons.

"Why didn't your biological father look for you?"

"He was dead." Her voice went flat; an emotional void. It made his skin feel itchy, tight. His panther prowled in his mind, not liking how she sounded.

"You were an orphan. No other family ever tried to find you?" Yes, he may have had an ulterior motive in asking that question, but he would've asked it anyway. It was strange to hear of a fae who'd been abandoned by her family—especially when they carried the blood of a Celestial in their veins, like Sin did.

She made a noncommittal sound.

Oberon interpreted it to mean there was potentially other family, but she didn't want to talk about them. Since she couldn't lie, she simply chose to remain silent.

Wait a minute...

He thought back to Kieran Aspen, and how the man had been trailing Sin. How the hybrid had confronted her near her house, and then again in town. Oberon winced, remembering his own actions; how he'd grabbed her in the possessive hold of a dominant male shifter, warning others away. When he'd seen the fae male hovering over Sin, something in his hindbrain had snapped. He wanted to blame it on the panther half of himself, but he couldn't entirely.

Because he'd placed his hand around her shoulders before his brain had caught up with his body. In all honesty, Oberon was surprised that Sin hadn't tried to rip his balls off then and there for daring to do so. She wasn't a shifter, but she was raised by and lived with an alpha. And that told him she was more worried about Kieran and his mate than she was about Oberon's public claim.

He mentally compared the Death and Diamond leader to Sin. The shape of his nose, the tilt of his eyes...the color of his hair. If you put them side by side, they looked like brother and sister.

"Who is he? An uncle? A brother?" Oberon mused aloud.

Sin's brows knitted. "Who's my uncle? What are you talking about?"

"Kieran Aspen."

"...Why would you ask about him?" Sin's expression closed off, but her eyes flashed.

"Because he followed you home. And then he cornered you in the street. And I'm guessing he helped you get a portal here, since I could smell him and his mate on you. And that witch."

Sin nibbled on her lower lip. Then she glared at him. "Followed me home? How do you know about that?"

Oberon shrugged, deciding it was probably better not to answer the question.

"Let's move on from the fact that you were stalking me." She shot him a sidelong glance, then sighed. "He's my half-brother."

Oberon set his plate back on the tray. His erection was well and truly gone, thankfully. "You don't sound remotely happy about that."

Then again, the half-fae, half-vampire seemed like a jackass.

"Would you be happy if you found out you were related to the guy who murdered your biological father?" Her voice was bitter. "Not only that, but he also burned his corpse and spread his ashes in the Mariana Trench."

"I don't know what this Mariana Trench is, but I'm assuming it's somewhere inhospitable," Oberon replied, deliberately keeping his tone mild. He gathered Sin's plate—empty except for the shredded napkin—and added it to the tray, then replaced the stainless-steel cloches.

"It's at the bottom of the Pacific Ocean. It's the deepest place on Earth," Sin muttered. "Cremating the corpse of a death fae is anathema."

Even Oberon knew that.

He picked up the tray and took it to the door, where he left it on the floor outside their room. "How do you know about what Kieran did to your father?" he asked, closing the door behind him and leaning against it.

"My mother told me. She also told me he swore to wipe out my father's line."

His gut tightened in response.

No. He wouldn't allow it.

But...Sin didn't know Oberon would protect her, even though he already had. There was a reason he'd prevented her from fighting Styx, from going through that portal. Because she would have done anything to save her sister, and he hadn't wanted to see her hurt.

Oberon studied Sin as she sat on the bed. Her hair was a dark cloud around her face, and her shirt and sweatpants covered far too much of her delectable skin, while simultaneously revealing far too much of her body for his comfort.

"From how he interacted with you, I assume he doesn't know you're related, right?" He crossed his arms over his chest. He may have positioned them so that his biceps were on display.

He caught Sin peeking and it caused heat to pool low in his belly.

"He didn't know before I left. But I think they suspected something."

"How—"

"I had to give them my blood to pay for the portal."

Oberon closed the distance to the bed, leaning down over Sin before his brain caught up with his body. "You *what*?"

"Aren't you going to put a shirt on?" Sin asked, derailing his outrage.

His panther stalked through his mind, rubbing against the edges of his skin. It was pleased that Sin appeared to find his human form attractive. Oberon swatted the bastet away in his mind. "Shirt? That's so last century."

Sin shook her head. "You're as bad as the Earth shifters. And it's not like I haven't seen them change a thousand times before. But you could poke an eye out with those things." She pointed at his chest.

His nipples were a bit...pokey.

He walked over to the closet where he'd put his things and pulled out a shirt from his bag, slipping it on. Oberon flexed as many of his back muscles as he could while he did so. He thought he heard a sharp intake of breath and smiled against the fabric of his shirt as it slid down over his face. Then her words sank in. "Wait a minute. What do you mean you've seen a shifter shift a thousand times?"

Sin slipped off the bed with a smirk. "The Crossroads is a shifter town, remember?" She then slid her feet into her boots.

He wasn't mollified by her answer.

How many men had she seen naked?

Better yet, why did he care?

"What are you doing?"

"I need a drink." She stalked toward the door.

Oberon leaned against the green wallpaper. "Remember the spell?"

"And that's why you're coming." She stood at the door, palm hovering over the brass handle as she waited.

Oberon let out a slow breath. His panther nudged him toward the door. Fine. They could get a drink.

A few minutes later, they were back down in the taproom. It was still busy, but not quite as popular as earlier. The bartender from before was still working, but the pool players had changed. It was getting close to midnight now—surely people would go to sleep soon?

Oberon found a table near the bar. "I'll get us some drinks."

Sin shook her head at him. "I want to see what they've got."

"Be my guest." He waved a hand through the air and sat down at the table. Leaning back against the chair, he put one elbow on the sticky tabletop and took stock of the room.

Sin gave a little huff, which his cat delighted in, and then strode the additional nine feet to the bar. The bartender acknowledged Sin's approach with a nod, then chatted with her for a few minutes while he got her order ready. She was leaning forward, her forearms on the counter, listening intently to the fae male. Oberon glowered in their direction.

It didn't take long before other men in the room took notice of Sin's arrival. Before he knew it, there were three or four males sniffing around her. Plus a couple of fae females. Was it her beauty that attracted them? Or her quiet aura of power?

Her admirers weren't too obvious at first, but he could see them leaning in or edging closer, trying to hear what she was saying to the bartender. She hadn't even bothered to get changed and was still wearing the T-shirt and tracksuit pants from earlier. But her hair was unbound, and it just begged for a man to take it in his fist...

Don't even think about it.

One male decided to approach her. Oberon felt his lip curl in a sneer. The man wasn't as tall as Oberon, but was stocky and well built. His hair was a russet color, and he moved like a shifter. He supposed the male was attractive, and for some reason, that made Oberon clench his teeth. The stranger smiled, the expression a clear attempt to charm. Sin was soon thoroughly engrossed in what appeared to be small talk with the male, and she turned partly to the side to face him while she waited for her drink.

Oberon watched her, waiting to see if she needed help extricating herself from the situation. But she seemed calm and at ease—completely unlike how she was with him. His hand closed into a fist on the table. The man said something quietly to her, leaning down and whispering in her ear, and she laughed.

Sin actually laughed.

His fingernails dug into the table as the sound washed over him. Gods, he wanted to hear her laugh again. His panther wanted to hear her laugh all the time.

She's not our mate. You shouldn't even be thinking about it like that.

The panther flicked its tail and pressed one ear back at him.

Oberon sent back an image of a raised middle finger.

Sin glanced back at Oberon and her eyes widened when she registered his expression. He tried to smooth over the irritation, and in response, she returned her attention to the male and smiled widely at the shifter. What the hell was she playing at?

His panther wanted to rip the male's head off.

Oberon went to stand, but a hand clamped down on his shoulder, pushing him back against the chair. It was surprisingly strong. He could break the hold, but he wasn't sure he wanted to when he realized it was Ysabeau St. Claire pinning him down.

"I wouldn't do that if I was you," Ysabeau warned. She let go of his shoulder and slid into the seat opposite him.

He sat up straight and opened his fist, pressing his palm against the tabletop, feeling the scratches he'd made in the surface. "I don't know what you mean."

"Don't play coy. From what I can gather, you and she are not together." The vampire inclined her head and gestured toward Sin. Then she nodded at the raised mark on his wrist.

"He's manhandling her," Oberon gritted out. Sure enough, the male touched Sin's arm lightly. And she didn't brush it away.

He couldn't see St. Claire's eyes behind the sunglasses, but her nose scrunched ever so slightly. "A man touching her arm is not manhandling her. She can look after herself. Plus, he's a member of the House of Gold and Garnet. You try to kill him, and half the room will come after you."

Oberon didn't particularly care. "Who said anything about killing?" He felt offended she thought he'd try. He'd succeed.

"You're an alpha shifter." As if that explained it all.

And normally it would. But shadow shifter males weren't like Earth shifters. They only tended to go crazy when they'd met their mate. And his panther was *not* crazy. And Sin wasn't his mate—she couldn't be.

"She's not yours," St. Claire said, as if trying to drill the message in. "Once you remove that binding spell, she's got people here who'll take care of her."

Oberon turned to face the vampire. "What is that supposed to mean? "

"I had an interesting phone call from a former colleague." St. Claire adjusted her glasses. "He knows about her."

His heart wanted to beat right damned out of his chest at those words, but considering there was a vampire sitting in front of him, he focused on keeping it steady. Plus, who was this former colleague? And what did he know, exactly? That Sin was a Celestial? He doubted that. Oberon had never even heard the term linked with the fae on Earth. And he'd been asking plenty of questions since his arrival.

Sin walked back to the table with two drinks in her hands and then sat, placing a huge glass mug in front of him. It was filled with a pale ale. She'd chosen to sit next to him, he noticed, rather than St. Claire.

"What's got you looking like you're sucking on a lemon?" Sin asked.

Oberon raised an eyebrow. "St. Claire was just telling me that she had an interesting phone call from a former colleague."

The color drained from Sin's normally tan skin. Her eyes shot to St. Claire's face. "Which former colleague?"

The vampire's mouth formed a tiny smile, seemingly amused by the entire thing. "I believe you're acquainted with Kieran Aspen."

"Aye, what's this I hear about my son-in-law?" Another damned redheaded male approached Sin and sat down at their table next to St. Claire.

What was it with the gingers?

Oberon glared at the stranger. But since the male didn't seem terrified of St. Claire, he decided he wasn't going to protest. At least, not right away. Instead, Oberon shifted a few inches closer to Sin, turning his torso toward her.

"Your son-in-law?" Sin's expression was carefully blank.

"Aye, the arsehole's married to my daughter."

Sin choked on a mouthful of beer. "Asshole?"

It was a rather unique way to describe one's son-in-law, Oberon thought.

"The bastard tortured me for a wee bit. Then he went off and mated my sweet lass."

St. Claire shook her head, dark hair swishing around her face. "Water under the bridge, Douglas, water under the bridge."

"Ye weren't the one being tortured." The man settled a disgruntled look on the vampire.

Oberon figured that he was not going to touch that conversation with a ten-foot pole. "So why is he interested in Sin?"

St. Claire sniffed. "He has a family claim."

Sin appeared utterly composed, but he could feel the tension radiating from her. He reached down under the table and gave her leg a squeeze. She didn't seem to notice.

"She's his daughter?" Douglas looked uneasy at the thought.

Sin shook her head in protest. "No."

"Shall I tell them, or will you?" St. Claire asked.

Sin's shoulders drooped. Oberon wanted to pick her up and carry her back to their room. She clearly didn't want to be having this conversation, and he didn't particularly enjoy seeing her unhappy. His panther lashed its tail, wanting to slice at St. Claire for upsetting Sin.

Douglas was looking between Sin and St. Claire, clearly waiting for one of them to talk.

"He's my half-brother."

CHAPTER 21
SIN

Sin had wanted nothing more than to escape the hotel room earlier, because it had been feeling a little bit *too* intimate with Oberon. Like they were friends. Companions.

If someone had asked her three hours ago if she'd willingly open up to Oberon about how she was related to Kieran, she'd have asked if they'd been smoking anything interesting lately. Not that it would've mattered if Oberon learned the truth. The fae wasn't even from Earth, after all. But Kieran was the co-leader of the House of Death and Diamond, and Oberon was Caius's right-hand man. And Caius was interested in making alliances with the Earth rulers. Reagan had told Sin that Caius had already received a letter from their cousin, Danni, about engaging with Tartarus at an official level. So, it made sense that Oberon would know who Kieran was, and potentially understood the ramifications of Sin being related to him. But he hadn't *needed* to know. Yet she'd told him anyway.

Worst of all, there had been compassion in his gaze while she'd spoken about her past. To be fair, she didn't hate Kieran for killing their biological father. From everything she'd learned from her mother, he'd been a piece of work. But that didn't change the fact that Kieran had promised to wipe their father's line from the Earth, and Sin was her father's line.

The fact that Oberon had guessed he was her brother...well, she'd realized that the truth was going to come out eventually. Now she just had to wait and see if Kieran would follow through on his promise.

As for now, Sin couldn't wait to finish her drink and get the hell out of the taproom. The only fun part of the evening had been when the fox shifter had flirted with her. He'd been utterly charming and had made her laugh. Originally, she'd only allowed him to start a conversation to irritate Oberon. But the shifter had made her feel carefree, and she couldn't remember feeling that way—ever.

And then she'd turned to see Oberon glaring murder at the shifter. She'd hurried back over to the table, only to learn that Ysabeau knew who she was. And that Sabrina's damned father was also here. The man barely looked older than thirty, even though he had one or two very fine gray strands in his thick hair. *What kind of water are they drinking in that House?*

Then again, defying death would keep a person young.

Sin glanced at the hulking fae lord who lounged in the chair next to her, his legs stretched out in front of him. Oberon had angled himself toward her, which she was of two minds about. Was it because he wanted to protect her? Or was it another display of ownership because of the binding spell?

She noticed his pint was empty, while hers was still half full. And he was tapping his fingers against the table, impatient. He and Ysabeau spoke quietly amongst themselves, while Douglas interrogated Sin in a way so subtle he probably thought she didn't realize what he was doing.

She'd also realized he, too, was a phantom.

It had become apparent soon after he'd sat down at the table. Her reaction to him hadn't been as strong as it was to Sabrina, but it was unnerving, nonetheless. She had no idea how Kieran tolerated being surrounded by phantoms all day, every day. But then, he was half-vampire, so that probably changed the way he reacted to the sort-of dead.

Sin pushed her pint in circles on the tabletop. She didn't want to finish it. Hell, she didn't want to be in the taproom pretending to make friends. She just wanted to be alone with her thoughts. Better yet, she wished she could go and give Nog a hug, but she had a feeling Oberon's patience was wearing thin.

She shoved the pint away from her.

Oberon caught the movement. "Are you done?"

She nodded.

"Let's go."

Sin would have liked to protest, but only because Oberon had given her an order. She really did want to leave. She stood, and the fae male followed suit, rising to his full height.

"If you want that binding spell removed any time soon, you come talk to me," Ysabeau said to Sin.

"Thank you." She had every intention of getting rid of the binding spell, but she still hoped that Oberon would do it himself. And if not, she had a cousin or three who could probably remove it for free. She didn't need to be in debt to Ysabeau St. Claire.

Douglas's eyebrows rose, and he looked at Ysabeau. "Binding spell?"

Sin chose that moment to make her escape. She slid around Oberon and then headed for the door at the back of the taproom. She could almost taste the freedom when the fox shifter—Akseli—hooked his arm through hers and pulled her toward his table.

"Come and meet my friends." He began towing her toward a table that held two other people, one a woman who made Sin's magic itch, and another shifter.

"I was just leaving," Sin protested. Akseli was handsome, really handsome, and if she hadn't been literally bound to Oberon, she probably would have taken him up on his unspoken offer of a good time—mostly so she could annoy said fae—but Oberon's temper had been on edge all evening. She wasn't willing to risk someone's life so she could have a bit of fun.

"My friends are keen to meet you, though." He gave her a disarming smile. "Gold and Garnet really is a great place for death fae."

As soon as he'd worked out what she was, he'd been eager for her to meet his friends, Ayla and Edvin. Apparently, Ayla came from the Outcast Coven, which specialized in death magic.

"Now isn't the time."

"If you need help—" Warm brown eyes met hers, before his expression hardened as he looked over her shoulder.

Oberon's heat was almost a physical wall against her back. She stepped out of Akseli's grip, but it was too late. Oberon had the fox shifter by the throat and was holding him in the air.

Holy shit.

"Touch her again, and I'll kill you." Oberon's face was a cold mask as his hand tightened. The fox shifter had started trying to kick out at the fae. His friends stood, clearly ready to intervene.

Sin shoved her way in front of Oberon. "Put him down."

"No." He only moved the shifter to the side, still holding him by the throat like the male wasn't almost six feet tall.

"Put. Him. Down."

Oberon turned to look at her, his eyes flickering between orange and black. Shit. His shifter side was fighting for control. That meant it was the alpha part of him reacting to the other man.

"I'm tired. I'm leaving." She turned and walked away. She could hear the hissed intake of air as onlookers watched her leave, but she knew a thing or two about male shifters. And alphas. If Oberon was protective of her—for gods knew what reason—then he'd drop the man and trail her.

Well, he'd either kill the man or drop him. She hoped for the latter.

She didn't pause when she exited the taproom, heading straight down the hallway and then up the stairs to the second level. She could feel Oberon keeping pace just a couple of steps behind her. But when she got to the door of their room, she stood aside, since she didn't have a key.

Oberon let them in and locked the door behind him, his expression thunderous.

Sin strode into the middle of the room, which meant she came to a stop at the foot of the bed. She had a feeling that if she said the wrong thing, he'd pounce on her faster than she could blink. The alphahole. "Wow. You really nailed the caveman chic vibe. Did you leave your club and loincloth at home?"

He blinked slowly at her, but she could tell when the fae side of him regained control. "I'm glad you noticed. I decided to go for a modern interpretation. Less fur, more fashion."

"And here I was, thinking you were just into the violence of it all."

"That's definitely part of the appeal."

"Did you kill him?" She crossed her arms over her chest.

"No."

"Good."

His eyes narrowed. "Your approval has me swooning with joy."

"You groped me under the table." Sin was pretty sure that wasn't what she'd planned on saying, but she'd blurted it out before her brain caught up to her mouth.

He drew back, shoulders pressing against the door. "I was trying to offer comfort."

"By grabbing my thigh." Sin didn't know why she was picking a fight about this, considering she had barely even felt the touch, it had been so light. But picking a fight with Oberon was something that she excelled at, and she felt angsty, like there was too much energy trapped inside her.

Possibly because she'd just stopped him from killing poor Akseli.

And she didn't want him to go back and finish the job.

Oberon closed the distance between them. She tilted her head back, meeting his gaze. "There was no groping." His eyes flashed. "Plus, you're the one with a history of groping. Remember how you threw yourself at me previously?"

Sin's jaw dropped. "I didn't *throw* myself at you."

"Oh, so it was more of an accidental collision of your mouth against mine, then?" Oberon leaned forward, crowding Sin until her back pressed against the wall. He placed his hand above her head, leaning on the wall behind her.

Sin glared at him. "It was a distraction, in case you forgot."

"Don't tell me you didn't love every second of it."

"Why, because you did?"

Oberon snorted. "It was an endearing effort."

Embarrassment had Sin's cheeks reddening. No. He was provoking her, trying to push her buttons. And she'd fallen for it, like she did every other time. "Only endearing? If that's all it takes for you to start humping a woman, I feel sorry for your past lovers."

His jaw ticked. "I did not hump you."

"Oh? We must have different memories, then." Admittedly, it had been more grinding than humping, but it was close enough to the truth that she could get away with the statement. Sin tapped her chin in pretend thought.

Something sinister flashed across Oberon's expression. She wasn't sure she should keep teasing him. Her body was mere inches away from his. He leaned down slightly, his nostrils flaring as he sniffed the air near her. "You stink of him."

She wanted to sniff herself, but refrained. Barely. The alpha side of him was still riding him hard, though. He was going to stay like this while Akseli's scent lingered on her. She could either take another shower—which meant he might go and finish killing the shifter—or get *his* scent on her. Which left her feeling all kinds of uneasy, but if it would get him out of this mood...

"How about tit for tat, then?"

"Tit for tat?" His voice was almost a growl.

They'd played this game before—only previously it was for information.

Before Sin lost her nerve, she reached out and ran a hand along his upper thigh. Just a light caress, a quick movement. But his muscle locked under her palm, and his expression darkened as he looked down at her. Her fingers tingled.

His voice was low as he snarled, "Just because you're pissed, doesn't mean you have to take it out on me."

Oh, because her touch was a punishment. Right.

Stupid asshole didn't realize what she was doing. Which was probably a good thing.

"You're the entire reason I'm even here." Sin's voice rose, on the edge of shouting, distracting him with her anger. "You're the entire reason I had to give my blood to my half-brother, who I've been trying to hide from my entire fucking life!"

Oberon reared back like she slapped him. But then his eyes focused on her mouth. "I see."

She had *no* idea what he saw.

He lowered his free hand to her neck, sweeping it down and over onto her collarbone, leaving a line of goose bumps in its wake. His gaze was locked on his hand's movements, and his throat bobbed while his palm rested on the skin of her shoulder, before he slid a finger down along her arm.

Sin stood still, reeling from the delicacy of his touch, from the way her heartbeat galloped in her chest and how her skin felt electrified.

"What? Are we not playing this game anymore?" His words echoed her thoughts from earlier and Sin almost flinched at the mocking edge to his voice.

But she wasn't going to back down from the challenge. No. He didn't get to keep messing with her. Not without suffering, too. She repeated his sweeping movement, starting on his neck, just below his ear, and gliding her hand down over his exposed skin and onto his shoulder. Except when she did it, she let a little magic spill, causing angry kisses of energy to nip at him as she moved. Gods, his skin felt smooth under her fingertips. And his *smell*. She swore the rich cedarwood and citrus scent of his was increasing.

He hissed as her magic teased him, but he threw his head back, closing his eyes as he exposed more of his neck to her. Sin bit her lip, stunned he was willing to do that. Alpha shifters didn't expose their neck to anyone. Was this his way of apologizing? Of showing her she could trust him?

She hadn't realized his eyes had opened until she felt his gaze on her. He swept his tongue along his lips, the movement quick. Sin almost groaned. What the hell was she doing?

She was playing with fire, considering she didn't even like him. But her body didn't care. Her blood was heating, and her heartbeat was pounding in her chest at the temptation, the challenge of him.

"If I kiss you, will you bite me?" His voice was low, rough, and his eyes were focused on her lips.

Sin wasn't sure she'd heard him right. She looked at him, confused.

"Last time, you bit me."

She didn't know what wickedness took hold of her, but she slowly shook her head, her fingers sweeping from his shoulder down over his chest. "Cross my heart and hope to...who am I kidding? I don't hope for anything."

He looked ready to break away, but something dark settled across his face when she said she didn't hope for anything. And then her fingers were dancing just above his jeans. His hand shot out, pinning her palm to his stomach. Her skin heated at the contact. Before she could ask what was wrong, Oberon's mouth crashed down on hers, his restraint snapping. Her body responded instantly; under the shock, the electric sizzle of the contact, she felt giddy. His lips and tongue clashed with hers, and the cedarwood and citrus taste of him made warmth pool between her legs.

He cupped the side of her neck, and she whimpered against his mouth, her fingers splaying out over his chest, trying to feel as much of him as she could. His hand tightened on her neck before sweeping down and curving over her collarbone and down to cup her breast. Light danced behind her closed eyes as the warmth from his hand branded her. Her nipples hardened in response, and she arched against him, seeking more. Gods, she didn't think getting to second base had ever felt so good.

She pulled away, gasping, only to lick a slow and torturous path from his neck to his collarbone. Gods, his *taste*. His hand left her, and she wanted to grab it in response, but he pinned both her arms above her head.

"What are you playing at, Sin?" Oberon's black gaze was heated, his chest heaving with each breath, as if he'd run a marathon.

She jerked against his hold, pressing her breasts against his chest. "Not playing."

No, it felt like her whole body was on fire, and the only way to quench it would be to have Oberon all over her. In her.

What the hell is wrong with me?

But she couldn't seem to care that this wasn't right. That she shouldn't be making out with him. Wanting him. Needing him.

He crowded her, pushing one leg forward so that his thigh parted hers, and then pressed hard against her core. She gasped in shock at the pleasure that jolted through her at the contact.

Oberon's hand tangled in her hair while his other hand cupped her hip, urging her to move against his hard muscle. She pressed forward, and the surge of bliss made her moan, her eyes fluttering closed. Gods, it felt so good. She tried to arch against him, knowing that just a bit more pressure would be mind-blowing. But his hand tightened in her hair and the sting had her opening her eyes, her hips still sliding back and forth over his thigh, her panties growing soaked.

His jaw worked, and he was breathing fast. "Gods, I can smell your arousal, Sin."

She should feel embarrassed, but the friction from his leg was too good, and she was getting closer—

"Get on your knees." He pulled his thigh away, and Sin almost toppled forward.

"What?" She looked at him, startled.

His mouth was tight, his gaze dark and almost angry. "Get on your knees."

Something wasn't right, she realized. But her blood was scorching through her veins, and her clit was throbbing in protest at the loss of his leg. Slowly, her gaze locked on his as she kneeled on the floor, his hand still tangled in her hair. He was so tall her face came to just under his belly button, and her eyes widened at the sight of his swollen cock, which poked above his waistband. He'd gone commando.

The idea of it had her stomach clenching.

Oberon undid the button on his jeans, followed quickly by the zipper, his erection springing free from the confines of his pants. She grabbed the base of his shaft before she could talk herself out of it, her hand barely able to close around his girth. It was so smooth, like silken steel, and Sin wet her lips, imagining how it would feel to slide her tongue over his cock, to taste the bead of moisture that had gathered at his tip. To have him at her mercy.

"Gods, Sin, are you just going to stare at it? Or will you just suck my damned cock."

She slid her hand up and down the shaft, her pussy throbbing as she watched the head darken. "I didn't hear a 'please.'"

Oberon cursed, and both his hands fisted in her hair. She looked up at him, her mouth a bare whisper away from the tip of his cock. His jaw was a harsh line, his erection bucking in her hand while she waited. "*Sin.*"

He snarled when she just slid her hand up and down, up and down. "Please." The word sounded torn from him.

She grinned, then leaned forward, licking the darkened tip and moaning as she tasted the sweet saltiness of his pre-come. He shuddered in response, and her hand moved back and forth along his length while she swirled her tongue over the slit, savoring the taste, savoring *him*. She closed her lips over the end of his hard length and hummed, before grazing the sensitive tip with her teeth. His breath sawed through his chest, making her own enjoyment spiral out of control. She found she wanted to give him pleasure, to banish the darkness that rode him.

Sin pulled away, and Oberon's hands tightened in her hair in protest. She met his gaze while she laved her tongue over the tip. "I love how you taste."

Then she closed her mouth over him, sucking him in deeply, taking as much of him as she could, until her lips bumped into her hand around the base of his cock.

"Fuck." Oberon threw his head back, his hips bucking against her. "You look so good with your lips wrapped around my cock."

Her core clenched at his words.

She slid her head back slightly, then pushed forward, trying to take him as deep as she could, before easing back again. She kept stroking him in one hand while she used the other to massage his balls. His hips were jerking against her, and his gaze burned as he watched her take him in her mouth, her cheeks hollowed out while she sucked on him as hard as she could.

His expression turned wild, predatory. "Sin! Keep doing that and I'm going to come in that pretty mouth of yours." He tried to pull away.

Her right hand clamped down on the base of his cock, and her other grabbed his jeans, holding him in place. She urged him to move, feeling his cock hit the back of her throat as his hips jerked uncontrollably. She fought the urge to gag, and opened her mouth as wide as she could, taking him deeper with every thrust.

"Sin!" His voice broke on her name, his cock swelling in her mouth.

She hummed and sucked hard, wanting him to feel pleasure, wanting him to know that *she* had caused it. His breath turned jerky, and she pressed her thighs together tightly to ease the growing ache between them as he exploded between her lips. He growled low in his throat as his cock jerked in her mouth, and she swallowed over and over as he came. She felt powerful, knowing she'd shattered his control.

His hands loosened their hold in her hair, and she let him pull back, his cock sliding out of her mouth with a pop. "Damn, Sin. You're too damned good at that."

She stayed on her knees, panting, struggling to process what had happened. To keep her own arousal under control. But with every heartbeat it seemed to grow, to flood her body with need.

Oberon squatted down next to her. He cradled her cheek carefully. "Sin? Are you okay?"

She squirmed, trying to clench her thighs even tighter. Her need was turning savage. "It hurts."

He breathed in deeply and his palm froze against her cheek. "Fuck." His pupils dilated as he looked at her aching nipples, at her clenched thighs. His hands were on her hips and then she was moving, somehow ending up on the bed, her sweatpants and underwear gone. She hadn't even felt them disappear.

"*Sin.*"

She looked up and saw Oberon kneeling between her splayed legs, his gaze locked on her pussy. Gods, she was so wet, so needy there. And while she was desperate for him, she also didn't want to totally lose control. She propped herself on her elbows. "Why do you keep saying my name like it's a curse?"

"Gods, woman, do you ever stop talking?" He surged up her body, his mouth descending on hers to silence it. She met his passion, her lower body writhing against him. Gods, she needed to come so bad. Releasing her lips, he slid down her body, ripping her T-shirt in half to expose her breasts. He cupped the mounds in both hands, then flicked his tongue out, grazing one of the hardened peaks before wrapping his lips around it and sucking. Sin arched into the caress, one of her hands snaking down her body, toward her core, desperate for relief.

Oberon's head snapped up as her fingers grazed the top of her pussy. He grabbed her hand. "What are you doing?"

"I need to come." Her hips bucked in response, at the denied chance.

"I was getting there," he growled.

"*Now*."

"Patience—"

Sin's magic flared out without her conscious control, but Oberon countered it with a curse. Shocked eyes met hers. "You used magic—"

"I can't help it!" Sin wailed, her head thrashing from side to side.

"It's okay, Sin. I'll take care of you." Oberon released her hand, but pushed it away when she tried to shove it between her legs, his own fingers sliding over her mound to cup her. She hissed at the insane pleasure his touch gave her. "Fuck, you're so wet."

His fingers eased down, slipping inside her inner folds to circle her entrance. Sin moaned, tossing her head restlessly against the mattress. His touch was featherlight as he ran his fingers up and down the center of her, coming close to—but not touching—her aching clit. She arched, whimpering.

"Tell me what you want." His dark voice washed over her, sinking into her.

"I need to come."

"With my fingers?" He spread her open, then slid a fingertip inside her pussy, his thumb putting pressure on her sensitive clit before gently stroking it with a teasing touch. She almost bucked them both off the bed.

Her hands came up to grip his shoulder. "That feels—"

"Or with my tongue?" He withdrew his hand, and Sin thought she was going to murder him right then and there. But then he put his mouth on her, and she screamed, curving against him. He held her down with one palm while he spread her legs apart with his other. Then he swept his tongue over her, and pleasure short-circuited her brain, her hands gripping the bed sheets as she writhed.

He pulled away, only to breathe a stream of hot air against her aching pussy. "You taste fucking amazing." Then he was sucking her clit, simultaneously flicking it with his tongue. She rocked her hips, needing more. Needing him. Tingles spread upwards from her toes, racing through her, but it wasn't enough. She needed more.

"I-I need—"

He slid a finger inside her, and her body exploded, her inner walls clamping down as she came viciously around him. "Oberon!"

Ecstasy pulsed through her as he pumped his finger in and out, while still sucking on her clit. Her orgasm tore through her, and pleasure unlike any she had ever experienced before had her gasping, her core clenching over and over. She had no idea how long he coaxed her through it, but eventually she lay still, skin slick with sweat, her body thrumming in bliss.

Slowly, she opened her eyes, staring at the ceiling.

"Sin?" He withdrew his finger from her, and an involuntary whimper escaped her lips. He watched her, concern etched into his features. "Are you okay?"

She met his gaze, embarrassed. She'd lost control. Lost total and utter control. She'd never done that before during sex—never even gotten close to unleashing her magic. She'd all but begged him to fuck her—and he hadn't. He'd pleasured her, but he hadn't been close to losing control like she had when she'd held him deep in her throat.

He was staring at her, his dark gaze almost...tender.

"I don't know." She looked away, and strangely, tears pricked her eyes.

"Sin—"

A sob racked her, and then another. Curling into a ball, she lay on her side as tears threatened to obliterate who she was. Oberon growled and scooped her into his arms, cradling her as she cried and cried. She had no idea why she was doing this, why she was so out of control. But he held her anyway, murmuring soft words in a language she didn't understand, his hand gently stroking over her head and arms. She cried until there were no more tears left, only darkness.

CHAPTER 22
OBERON

Oberon lay on the green bedspread, holding Sin in his arms while she slept. He tucked her head under his chin, the lemon and lavender scent of her sinking into his pores. He cursed himself for a fool.

He'd been too rough, too demanding.

He had no idea what had come over him when he'd ordered Sin to get on her knees. No, that was a lie, he told himself—he knew what he'd been doing. It had been over five thousand years since Titian had betrayed him. And Sin was nothing like her. *Nothing.* But something had been riding him, and he'd needed to know that Sin was different. That Sin would bend when he needed it, just like he'd do whatever he needed to satisfy her.

He still had no idea what exactly had triggered it, though; they'd both kind of gone a little crazy.

Was it the binding spell? he wondered.

His panther swatted at him.

No. It wasn't the spell.

It was almost like the heat had come over her, although just temporarily, and he'd responded like any alpha male would. But he'd never responded like that to other females before. And Sin wasn't a shifter of any kind—nor had she turned into a shadow shifter like Nog had. Hell, it wasn't even the full moon—and it didn't affect him here like it did other shifters. But it was like hormones had overridden his sense of control.

Worse, Sin had been in almost physical pain after he'd come in that beautiful mouth of hers. He cursed himself because he hadn't even realized. Too intent on reaching his own pleasure, he hadn't recognized that she was suffering. And then she'd been too impatient, unable to wait for him to pleasure her properly. He'd wanted to take his time, to savor her, to revel in the sounds she made, to enjoy the way her breathing hitched when his fingers skated near her clit. To relish how she tasted when he pressed his tongue against her in the most intimate of kisses.

His cock grew hard at the memory.

Godsdamnit.

He shifted uncomfortably on the bed and Sin muttered a sleepy protest. He rolled onto his back, his arm under her head. He was about to work himself free when she followed him, snuggling into his side and throwing a leg over his hips. Possessive little thing.

His lips curled in a smile and he shifted a little, trying to get his erection out from under her thigh. Miraculously, she didn't wake, just made a ridiculously cute snuffling sound against his shoulder.

You are in trouble, he thought to himself.

His panther snorted. It thought they'd done a rather good job.

Oh, so *now* it decided to voice its opinion.

Oberon shook his head at himself. He wasn't any good for Sin, he told the panther. He'd barely even known what to do when she'd broken down. He might not have been the one crying, but he felt hollowed out, empty.

It didn't make any damned sense.

He and Sin weren't mated. There was no bond. But it felt almost like that, almost like what he'd lost once could be replaced again. But if she was his second-chance mate, the bond would be there. He'd know.

The truth was, he'd murdered Titian. There would be no second-chance mate for him.

And Sin deserved better than him, anyway.

Because he was going to take her through to Avalon. Now though...

now it wasn't just about him and getting his throne back. It wasn't just about revenge. This was now also about Sin.

She was a Celestial. Untrained, untried, but a Celestial, nonetheless. It was her birthright to go to Avalon and win the throne. Or, at least, try to win it. And if that meant he had to share the throne with her, well, he was willing to do it. For her.

Who knew if the crown would even accept him anymore, for all that the ring was still on his finger. When he got to Avalon it might fall off and refuse to be placed back on his head. And there could have been another Celestial born in the last five thousand years who was good, and just. Although all the intel he'd gleaned from St. Claire seemed to point at civil unrest in the fae world.

If the crown accepted Sin, she'd be a good queen, he knew that. She had an inner core of steel, a will that he admired. She was kind, she was (usually) patient, and she had been able to handle the shenanigans of her family for well over two decades. If she could handle Nog's bullshit, she could handle the fae courts.

You are such an idiot. You're getting attached to her.

His panther flicked its tail at him.

Oberon admitted that over the last few hours, he might have fallen a tiny bit in love with her. But it didn't matter. Because Sin wasn't going to choose somebody like him, she'd made that perfectly clear.

Not wanting to leave her, but unable to lie there so close, Oberon shimmied out from under her. She made a small grumbling sound of protest, and he quickly stripped off his pants and shirt. Then he shifted in a swirl of darkness.

Now in his bastet form, he sprang onto the bed and settled next to Sin, curling up beside her. He rested one of his wings over her, so she wouldn't get cold. Then he laid his head on his paws and purred.

Oberon woke to the feel of fingers in his fur. His panther half rolled on his side, exposing his belly for more rubs.

"You are a shameless hussy," Sin said, her voice low and quiet, but amused.

Oberon opened an eye and squinted at her. Then he batted at her playfully. She looked different from this angle. He let out a huffing sound.

"Yes, yes. You are very beautiful in this form." One of her hands stroked gently over his head, while the other scratched his belly.

She should pat us more, his panther said to him.

She's patting us right now.

She's ours. Show her.

Then the panther shoved, forcing the shift. Surprised, Oberon didn't fight it. A moment later, his form was encased in shadows. When they cleared, he was lying naked on his side, Sin's hand buried in his hair, while her other palm stroked his abdomen.

"What the—" She startled, pulling her hands away.

Good work, he told the panther.

Give her pats. Then she will pat us again.

His panther was trying to be sneaky. *Why do you want pats so much?*

It didn't respond.

"Morning. Is it morning?" He stretched, flexing his muscles a little more than he needed to. The scent of her grew stronger, making his mouth water.

"It's still dark outside."

It was winter and they were pretty far north, so it might be morning. "If it's still dark, I'm not getting up." He put a hand over his eyes, while his panther snarled in his mind.

I can't just pounce on her.

The cat didn't understand why not.

"Are you okay?" Sin asked, her voice uncertain.

"My panther is bugging me."

"About what?"

"You."

"Me?" Her voice was a squeak. "Should I not have touched him?"

He lowered his arm, taking in the view of Sin sitting on the bed, wearing one of his T-shirts. Both man and panther liked that. "No. I mean, yes. He liked it."

She looked confused.

Oberon sighed and raised his gaze to the ceiling. "He wanted you to pet us more."

"Oh. But you're human now."

Oberon tilted his head to look at her. Her cheeks flushed a dull red as realization sank in, and she glanced down at her hands, which were twisted in her lap. "I, uh, well—"

"Please, don't jump at the opportunity." He propped himself up on one elbow.

Sin's brows lowered and she looked at his groin, which wasn't exactly standing at attention. "There's an opportunity?"

"Hey! It has feelings, you know." He covered his groin with his hands, flopping onto his back.

Sin laughed.

Something inside his heart clenched at the sound, about how *right* it was that she was here. That they were arguing, but having fun while doing so.

Sin surprised him and lay down next to him. "Spoon me."

"What?"

"You do understand the concept of spooning?"

He grumbled under his breath, but turned on his side, tucking her to him. Her curves pressed against him, her firm ass wriggling as she tried to get comfortable. And damn if that didn't get a certain body part standing at attention. Sin gave a small huff of laughter. "You're poking me."

Oberon ran a lazy hand down her arm, smiling as her skin pebbled in the wake of his touch. "You're wriggling."

She stopped moving. Which was a shame.

"Oberon, about last night—"

"If you're about to tell me it was a mistake and we shouldn't do it again, I'm going to spank you."

Sin half turned and bit him on the chin. He reared back, but his panther was delighted. "Hey!"

"That was for threatening me." She turned back.

He smoothed her hair down and propped his abused chin on her head. "You're feisty when you're riled."

"Not normally." Her voice was thoughtful.

He took the opportunity to resume his earlier exploration. His hand roamed over her shoulder and down her arm, then back up along the arch of her back. She gave a little breathy moan, and it went straight to his cock.

He inhaled, the scent of her arousal making him want to bite her. "You're already wet."

She tensed slightly, then shook her head. "Damn shifters."

"It's only fair."

"Fair?" He could *hear* her frown. It was fucking adorable.

He pressed his hips and hard cock against her ass. She hissed. "That's different."

"How?"

"I don't know."

He grinned against the back of her head. He pushed her hair to the side and began kissing her neck, reveling in the way her breath hitched when he laved her skin before pressing his mouth to her sensitized flesh. His hand snaked down her body to cup between her legs. Gods, the *feel* of her.

He shut his eyes as her pussy grew impossibly hotter, wetness spreading to coat his fingers. Gods, he had to feel her—

"Oberon—"

"Unless you're about to say, 'please finger me until I come,' I don't want to hear it."

Sin's breath hitched, and one of her legs moved slightly, granting him better access. Oberon growled low in his throat while his fingers danced over the outside of her core. She whimpered into her fist, while his tongue fluttered against the tender spot between her neck and shoulder. He nipped her, the shifter part of him wanting to bite down hard, marking her as his. He resisted.

The feel of her soft flesh against his fingers had his cock aching in response. Pleasure pierced him, going straight from his mouth and hand to his groin. He wished he could see her face as his fingers parted her inner folds, as he stroked the hard bundle of nerves at the apex of her thighs. He wanted to see her pleasure, taste it. He withdrew his hand at the thought, bringing his fingers to his lips.

"What are you—"

She looked over her shoulder but her words died as she watched him suck on his fingers, licking every drop of her arousal from his skin. Her cheeks flushed a deep rose color.

"Oh gods, you really need to fuck me."

His hand froze, and Sin snarled, rolling her hips.

Oberon shook his head. It was one thing to play like this, but it was another thing entirely to slide deep within her, to feel her surrounding him, holding him in the most intimate of ways. "What did you say? I think I hallucinated."

Her voice was a low growl, "I said, 'you really need to fuck me.'" Then she lifted her leg and reached between her thighs to take hold of his erection. His hips jerked in response to the feel of her grasping him. Then she guided his cock to her soaking pussy.

Oberon groaned, his head falling back against the pillows. "*Sin.* Haven't you heard of foreplay?"

"I thought you'd be all about yourself when it came to sex. But you always have to do the opposite of what I expect." Her voice was grumpy.

"I will try to ignore the insult considering where you've just put my cock."

She let go. "Foreplay later."

He almost wept in frustration. But then she lowered her thigh and positioned herself so that his cock was encased in her heat. He wasn't inside her, no. But he was between her legs, sliding between the folds of her pussy, the tip of his cock rubbing against her hard clit with each stroke, making him crazy.

"Oh, fuck." She felt so amazing that he could come from this alone.

"Not quite," Sin muttered.

Oberon chuckled, and she stilled. Then she turned her upper half to look over her shoulder at him again. "You laughed." Her expression was amazed.

"It happens from time to time." Then he continued moving his hips, drugged by the feel of her heat. At how wet she was. If he just changed his angle ever so slightly—

He didn't know if it was him or her who did it.

One moment he was gliding through her slick wetness, and the next, his cock was sliding deep inside her pussy, stretching her as he found his way home. They gasped together. *Holy fuck.* His brain lost the ability to think. He could only feel Sin.

"You're so fucking tight," he gritted as he tried to hold still, to buy time before he lost all restraint.

But she didn't give him any time to adjust. She began rolling her hips against him, and he reached a hand around to her front, pinching the nipples he had wanted to spend time worshipping. Her inner muscles gripped him greedily as she moved, her breaths growing jerky as her thrusts got wilder.

He didn't want her to come like this. Not looking away from him. He wanted to watch her, to see her come, knowing it was him who caused it, not some faceless male she could try and forget after.

He pulled out, and she whimpered in protest. "Oberon?"

He rolled onto his back. "Ride me."

He wasn't sure she would acquiesce, but a heartbeat later, she settled over him, his damned T-shirt hiding her body. She lifted herself up slightly and positioned his cock at her entrance before sliding down in one agonizing glide to heaven. Fuck. It was like she'd been made to take his cock. He closed his eyes in pleasure, but then realized he was missing out on seeing Sin's face. He watched as she slid up and down, glacially slow, taking him to the hilt in her body, then releasing him.

She had to be punishing him for all his crimes against her.

And it was fantastic.

Unable to stay still, his hands grabbed her hips, and he began to thrust upward to meet her downward slides, increasing the pace of their joining. He let one hand curve away from her hip to where they joined, pressing his thumb to her clit. Her hips bucked wildly in response.

His head fell back as Sin rode his body to her pleasure.

To their pleasure.

He watched her from under hooded eyes. "I want to feel you come around my cock." He thought he might die if she did so, but it would be one hell of a way to go.

Sin shuddered at his words, and he teased his thumb over her nub. Once, twice. She tensed, her gaze turning dreamy, her mouth falling open as she silently screamed her pleasure. Her pussy clamped down on his cock, squeezing him so tightly that all thoughts of control vanished. He began thrusting like a madman, pleasure exploding from the base of his cock through to his balls, and he came hard, driving deep within her core.

He'd never felt pleasure like this before. Not even when she'd sucked him dry.

No, it felt like his whole world rocked on its axis, then righted, and his universe had a new center of gravity.

"Sin."

CHAPTER 23
SIN

Sin woke a few hours later. And she was sore. Really sore. But the kind of sore that meant she'd had the best sex of her damned life.

I really need to let Kasha know she was right about hate sex.

...Not that she hated Oberon quite as much anymore. The fact that the man had given her several mind-blowing orgasms had tempered her emotions toward him. She turned on her side, and to her shock, he was still asleep.

He almost looked...innocent. The tension that usually lined his features had disappeared now that he was shed of all guards and pretenses. He looked young. Sin propped her head up on an elbow. You wouldn't believe that he was a millennia-old fae lord. Most of the time, Sin forgot he was older than her. He'd been alive long enough to see literal empires fall, and yet, right here, right now, he was just a man.

A very sexy, very arrogant man, but a man—well, mostly—nonetheless. She smiled as she took in the sheets tangled around his legs and waist—he was a bed hog, which was totally not surprising. It was unfortunate that the sheets covered the lower half of his body. With daylight streaming around the closed curtains, she thought she may get a better view of all his...assets.

"I can feel you watching me," Oberon said, his voice low and rough, even though his eyes were still closed.

Heat rushed into Sin's cheeks. "You look kind of peaceful when you sleep."

"Peace is relative." Oberon opened his eyes. The darkness of his irises was decorated with the tiny pinpricks of white that were occasionally visible. But his mouth softened as he returned her stare, something like tenderness touching his expression.

Sin had a feeling that his eye color meant something, but she just wasn't sure what it was.

"I was thinking that I'd grab Nog once we're ready, and then I'll arrange to head home."

Oberon let out a slow breath. "I'm still going through that portal."

Her heart felt heavy. "That doesn't mean I need to go with you."

He held up his branded wrist, and then pointed to her own. Disappointment welled within her. He wasn't going to remove the binding spell.

A dark emotion flashed across his face. "You didn't sleep with me just to get the binding spell removed, did you?" Oberon's voice was damn near gravelly.

"Who wouldn't want to have mind-blowing sex for a chance to lift hexes?" If stares packed punches, Sin would have been knocked out cold by Oberon's look. "No, you idiot, I did it because I had a moment of insanity."

Why did she think that their being intimate would change anything? That he'd actually *want* to do the right thing?

He looked like a pissed-off cat who'd been taken on a date to the river with a shopping bag and a brick. "A moment of insanity, how very flattering."

"You forgot I said 'mind-blowing.'"

"A moment of *mind-blowing* insanity, be still my beating heart." He held a hand over said organ. Who knew hand gestures could be sarcastic?

Sin tapped her lip. "Two. It was two moments of *mind-blowing* insanity."

Oberon gave her a flat glare.

She bent down and nipped him on the lip. Hard.

He hissed in response, his eyes flashing orange for a heartbeat. "You. Bit. Me."

Sin tapped him on the nose, delighted that his shifter form had emerged. "Play nice, kitty."

Oberon grabbed her arm. "Mine."

Shock had Sin wobbling on the bed. Oberon steadied her and shook his head, his eyes returning to their normal hue. "Sorry about that."

"Sorry?" Sin hadn't known her voice could get that high. "You just said—"

"That was the panther."

"...The panther." Sin said each word slowly.

His cheeks subtly flushed. "He thinks you're ours. And he's pissed there's no bond."

"Bond?" Her voice could definitely reach pitches she'd never known before.

Oberon shoved a hand through his hair. "He apparently decided last night that you are ours. *Even though there is no mating bond.*"

Sin flinched. But she had a feeling the last sentence had been more for his panther's benefit than hers.

"Fuck." Oberon reached out a hand, but she pulled away. "I'm sorry, this is—"

"I don't want a mate!" Sin didn't realize she'd shouted the words until he drew back from her.

"What?"

She spoke more evenly. "I don't want a mate."

"But—"

"My mother died because my biological father was murdered. She managed to make it until she gave birth to me, but then she just...died. Most mates can't survive the death of another. And my biological father—he was an asshole. I don't know how bad he really was. But he was bad. I don't want to be trapped with someone I might hate. And not be able to walk away." She slashed a hand through the air. "I don't want to be trapped. I don't want to die."

Sin sat up, tugging the sheet up so that it covered her chest. "I'm sorry your panther is annoyed. But I would say no, even if you were my mate. I'd reject you."

She couldn't explain it, but she *felt* his panther's hurt. Like she'd betrayed something that didn't even exist. But for a mating bond to survive, they both had to accept it—or have sex.

"Sin—" He reached for her shoulder, and she shrugged out of his grip.

She tasted saltiness, and realized tears were dripping down her cheeks. She angrily rubbed them away. "Don't mock me."

"I wasn't going to."

She shot him a disbelieving look.

His expression was filled with concern. "For what it's worth, I believe you."

"That I'd reject you?"

"Yes. And I wouldn't blame you."

She did a strange little laugh. "Sure, because most sane women reject their mates."

His expression turned dark. "Maybe they should."

Sin wrapped her arms around her legs and rested her chin on her knees, keeping her eyes forward.

"I wasn't always a shifter, so my panther wasn't with me when I first mated." Sin's stomach did a strange somersault. He'd been mated? Was he still mated? "So, it doesn't know what can happen when the bond turns bad."

Sin turned to look at him. His face was expressionless, and that made her heart clench all the more. "Turned bad?"

She had a feeling she didn't want to hear this story.

"The day I got crowned High King of the fae was the day I was betrayed by my mate and exiled from Avalon. She sent me through a portal to Tartarus, thinking I'd never get free. "

A lump formed in the back of Sin's throat as she studied his expression. Nog had been right. Oberon had been betrayed. He didn't even look angry anymore, just...empty.

"Mates aren't meant to be able to betray each other," she protested.

"That's what they'd like you to believe. And for most people, that's probably true. But I was lucky enough to mate a lying, conniving schemer. So, there's that."

Sin bit her lip. "So, she could still be there?"

Oberon barked a sound that was meant to be a laugh, but it was too bitter to ever be confused with mirth. "No."

"She died while you were in Tartarus?" Good riddance, Sin thought.

"No. The last thing I did was kill her before I got sucked into the portal."

Goose bumps broke out over Sin's body.

He'd killed his own mate.

He looked at her. "Worried about me now? If I could kill a mate, what else am I capable of?"

Yes. Yes, to all of it. But...

"Caius trusted you. "

"Coming from you, that's not exactly a compliment." He raised one eyebrow.

Sin tilted her head in acknowledgement. "No, but Reagan trusts him." And she trusted Reagan.

"She cheated on me."

Oberon's gaze flicked towards her, making brief eye contact. Sin's mouth suddenly tasted like ashes. "And before you ask, yes, she really did. Because she did it in front of me."

Fury, pure and true, burned through her, shocking her with its intensity. Because Oberon couldn't lie. "How is that even possible? "

"First, you get Stick A and put it into Slot B..." On one hand, he formed a circle with a finger and a thumb, and then poked his other index finger through it.

Sin rolled her eyes. She didn't know how or why, but he'd managed to somehow lighten the mood. "Thank you for the terrible anatomy lesson. What I mean is, how could a mate do that to another mate? I thought you didn't even want to *look* at another lover."

"It turns out that she was able to trick the mating bond; I don't know how. Maybe it was because her lover was a god. Either way, she face-fucked Helios in front of me. And she never even bothered to kneel for me."

She saw the moment he regretted saying the last sentence. But his demand for her to kneel last night, his distance...it had been a test, even if he hadn't meant to do it.

He reached out a hand in appeal. "Sin—"

"I'm not like her." She looked him directly in the eye. "I may not want a mate, but it doesn't matter if I did. Because I would never betray someone like that, bond or no."

"I know you're not like her." He looked angry she'd even suggested it.

"Plus," Sin said, a sly smile blooming, "she was a fool if she didn't love the way you felt hitting the back of her throat, how you lose control as you come—"

Oberon slapped a hand over her mouth. "Godsdamnit, woman."

Sin bit his palm.

"Ow! That's fucking it!" He grabbed her, and they wrestled on the bed. She had a slight advantage because he was still caught in the bedsheets, but soon enough, he had her pinned beneath him. And he was rock hard.

"Mmmm." She rolled her hips.

"Sin Santiago, stop that."

He knew her surname. She grinned at him, loving the fact he looked flustered, and that his hair was a mess around his head. He growled, "You are shameless."

"Am not." She rocked her hips into his.

"Are too."

"Not."

He bit her.

Right where her neck and shoulder met. Sin froze. She hadn't thought he would try to mark her without her consent—

He gave a warning growl then let go. His eyes were orange, but his teeth were still human. He hadn't marked her. Just given her a bruise that would be damned obvious to anyone who looked at her.

"You almost—" She looked at him with shocked eyes.

"Never." The voice was that of the panther. His eyes glowed orange. "Bit naughty, mate."

"I am not your mate."

"Bit naughty...lover."

She had a feeling the damned panther was more stubborn than Oberon. And the cat had decided she was his mate. Without a mating bond!

The orange eyes narrowed, like he could sense her train of thought.

She huffed. "I will play nice."

He snuffled her. It was strange, she wasn't going to lie. Interacting with a human-shaped panther.

"For now."

He snorted.

A heartbeat later, Oberon was back to himself. He looked at the bite mark on her shoulder, then rubbed a thumb over it. "He wouldn't mark you without your consent."

"I didn't think shifters normally felt separate from their human half." Her sister had, but Reagan's situation had been...unusual.

He dropped a kiss to her nose then pushed himself off her. "I was fae a long time before I became a shifter. And in this, we disagree. I've had a mate, so I know what it's like. The panther hasn't. But he thinks he's chosen."

Sin didn't really know what to think. But she knew that the problem of the panther and its conviction would be an argument for a different time. "We need to talk about what's happening next."

"We go through the portal."

"No. I need to take Nog home. You got covered in corpse juices the last time you went on a job with him. He can't go through that portal."

Oberon lay back on the bed. "He *is* a walking disaster."

"You can see why I need to get him home. Why he can't come."

"There was no way he was ever going through that portal."

Something in Sin's gut unclenched. At least she knew he wasn't planning on using Nog any further. *No, he'd just used Nog as bait to get me here.*

"Explain to me why you need me to go with you. You know Ysabeau St. Claire now. She probably can get you through."

Oberon flicked his hands, and the outside noise—sound she hadn't really noticed until it was completely absent—disappeared. "What—?"

"I don't have any Earth papers. And I probably shouldn't be travelling under my real name."

"Because that's not remotely ominous." How had he done that sound-blocking spell?

"I don't know who rules the fae now. Or even if there is a High King or High Queen. News of the fae home world isn't exactly easy to come by. From what I can understand though, there is civil unrest."

"And?"

"I don't know what stories have been told about me, if any have been. But if I just waltz into Avalon and tell them I'm their dispossessed High King, it probably won't go down well."

"And how is my presence going to change that?" He was a damned High King. She was just... her. No one would care about her compared to him.

"You are not a regular death fae."

"Excuse me?"

"You are a death fae," he held up a hand when she went to interrupt him, "but you are also more than that. Correct?"

Sin bit the inside of her cheek.

"You can draw power from the Earth. From the stars and moon and sun. Correct?"

"How do you know that?"

"The first night, when I broke into your house, I sensed you drawing the power."

Sin blanched. He'd known from *the first night?* And he'd never said anything?

"How did you—"

Then it clicked.

"You know what kind of fae I am." Something almost like betrayal hit her. He'd known and he hadn't said anything.

"I do."

"Because you're one, too."

"Yes."

Sin shut her eyes. "And it's special, isn't it?"

"Yes."

"Are you going to tell me or leave me hanging in suspense?"

"We're called Celestials. There are only three known fae royal bloodlines that produce the Celestial ability."

Nausea churned in Sin's stomach. "We could be related? Wait—I'm royalty?"

"If we are, then it would be barely. It would have been from a cousin of mine, over five thousand years ago."

Yeah, that didn't really help.

"So, I'm one of these bloodlines." Sin played with the sheet.

"Probably an Ó hUainín."

"Is that your family?" Sin's brow furrowed.

"No. My former mate said she'd wiped the Ó hUainín from Avalon. But some might have escaped."

Sin had the sudden realization that Oberon had forgotten to tell her one very important piece of information about his mate. "She was a Celestial, too, wasn't she?"

"She was." Then he sniffed. "But she was weak."

Sin wasn't weak—but she was no match for Oberon.

"I can tell what you're thinking. And you're stronger than she was. Even untried, untrained, you've got more ability than she ever had. You will probably equal me, when trained."

"How long were you planning on using me to get to Avalon?"

He didn't answer.

"So did you sleep with me because you—"

His expression turned menacing. "Do. Not. Finish. That. Sentence."

"You asked me—"

He put a finger over her lips. "I was an idiot. But don't ever doubt that whatever *mind-blowing* insanity you suffered, I had it, too."

She wanted to bite his finger, but she didn't want to get nipped again by his panther. "You used me."

"You knew I was using you." He pulled away, smug.

"How does that make it better?"

"It doesn't?" He raised his eyebrows.

"No. Yes. Maybe." She rubbed a hand over her face. Gods, the man was infuriating. "Say I go with you to Avalon. What happens to me?"

"If there's no High Queen, you undergo the test."

"What?"

"You're a Celestial. It's your right." He shrugged. Like it was no big deal.

"But—but—I don't want to be High Queen of Avalon!" she wailed. She was pretty sure that counted as a wail, anyway.

"Then don't do the test."

"But if they know I'm a Celestial, and I don't do the test...will they let me leave?"

Oberon reached out and took her hand in his. He ran his fingers over the inside of her palm, and her fingers curled at the sensation. "Once you know how to use your magic, they won't be able to stop you."

CHAPTER 24
OBERON

Oberon stood near the edge of the cliff, looking at the escarpment below. Steel-colored waves slammed against the basalt shore, and the skies overhead were overcast, full of rain-laden clouds. Fog shrouded the landscape behind them, its cool, wispy fingers disintegrating as they reached the cliff's edge.

They stood in a curve of the rocky cliff, protected on one side from the gusts scoring the shoreline. But even then, the wind still had a bite to it.

"Can you feel the power?" Oberon asked Sin, who stood at his side. She was wearing a clean pair of jeans, his T-shirt—which she chose to not take off—and a sweater. She'd then layered a jacket over the top and added a scarf, which she'd wrapped around her neck and pulled up to cover her mouth and nose. She looked damned beautiful, even with half her face obscured, and her hair slicked back in a braid.

She glowered at him. "I feel cold."

"You can warm yourself up, you know." He shook his head.

"I wasn't aware you were into exhibitionism."

His stomach clenched at the idea of Sin slipping her hand into her jeans and touching herself right here, right now. Fuck. Nobody would probably even see, the fog behind them was so dense. He almost begged her to do it. But they weren't here for sex, unfortunately. No, he was trying to teach her about her power.

His panther prowled through his mind, annoyed at the denial.

"We can discuss my sexual proclivities another time." But he closed the distance between them, crowding her, forcing her to acknowledge his dominance. She tipped her chin up, meeting his gaze with her own. Her scent washed over him, through him, settling deep under his skin. "But I can't wait to watch you touching yourself until you're on the edge of orgasm."

Her lips parted as she hissed in a breath. But she didn't drop his stare. If she'd been a shifter, she'd have been an alpha, no doubt about it. Instead of sending his panther into a craze, it actually pleased the damn contrary animal.

Her gaze narrowed. "You're trying to distract me."

He nipped her lip. "You're the one using all the innuendo. I'm here to teach."

"Hey!" She raised a hand to her mouth.

"Turnabout is fair play. Now. Can you feel the power?"

Sin muttered something in Spanish—he assumed it was something rather unflattering—but closed her eyes. He waited next to her, feeling the magic in the earth flow toward the portal. Ley lines, someone had called them. The mystical web that ran over the world. He could draw from them, but also from the molten core of the planet as well.

Sin seemed to reach for the ley lines without even realizing it was what she was doing. "I can feel it."

"Go deeper."

She opened one eye. "That's what she said."

He raised an eyebrow. "No, it's what I said."

She snorted and shook her head. "It's an Earth saying."

"Focus." He tapped her on her scarf-covered nose, as if she were a naughty kitten.

"What do you mean, 'deeper'?'" She frowned.

"To the heart of the planet. To the core."

She blinked at him. "What?"

"Your magic can tap into the core of the planet."

"Maybe yours can. But mine—"

"You can do it." He believed in her.

"This feels like a terrible pep talk. What if I do it, and I take too much? What happens to the planet?" She was rubbing her hands together, warming them.

"You won't be able to. You're not a god, so your body would never be able to channel that much magic." He reached out and took hold of her hands.

"Fuck, you're so damned warm." She looked startled.

He gave her a sly smile; one he knew would irritate her. "I'm warm because I'm using magic to heat the air around me." He did it almost subconsciously nowadays. It had been damnably cold on Tartarus, and he'd hated wearing layer upon layer of clothing, as it restricted movement.

She blew out a slow breath. "Fine." She didn't close her eyes this time, but he could tell her attention turned inward. It took barely a minute and then the temperature around her began to warm noticeably.

She was a natural.

"GET DOWN!"

Out of reflex, he threw himself to the ground, dragging Sin with him. He had no idea who'd shouted the warning. But he didn't care. He tucked Sin under him, protecting her. An arrow whistled through the air, shattering against the rock wall behind them. Oberon's head snapped up and he surveyed the area, trying to find the archer.

It was a bad idea.

Three other arrows flew toward him, from three different directions. Using quick bursts of magic, he incinerated them in the air.

"You're squashing me!" Sin protested.

He stood up slowly, but he couldn't see a damned thing. Their attackers were positioned behind them, in the fog. *So how are they seeing us?* He drew on the power of the sun, creating a starblade in his left hand.

"What the fuck?" Sin was looking at the shattered arrow next to them. "There was an arrow at the portal—the one you used to come here." A moment later, a pale blue orb hovered over her hand. Death magic.

A shudder rolled through him.

He'd seen what that pale orb could do to sawn timber...he didn't want to know what it would do to flesh and blood.

"Wait. There was an arrow?"

"I didn't see or hear the archer, but Tamsin thought it had been aimed at the portal." At Oberon.

"Someone is hunting us." He tried to crowd her behind him, but she kept moving to his side.

The fox shifter from the evening prior sprinted toward them, emerging from the fog. A witch following closely behind. Where was their third friend?

A low growl rose up from Oberon's chest at the sight of the other shifter. Were they the attackers? He should have killed the bastard last night for daring to touch Sin.

The fox shifter hung back at the sight of Oberon, the witch coming to a stop in front of them. She was wearing black clothes, her olive skin glowing in the weak light. Her dark gaze surveyed them, and she all but rolled her eyes. "Compare dick sizes later. You're the target of an assassin."

"And you would know that because...?" Oberon's voice was dry.

"We've been tracking him."

"How convenient."

"Hey, if you don't want our help..." The witch held up a hand.

A fireball the size of a bus shot toward them from the fog.

"Holy fuck!"

"Run!"

But there wasn't time.

Throwing out his free hand, he shoved a wall of frigid power at the magic-made meteor. He'd pulled the power from space itself, and the flames vanished as they met a cold so deep, it went well beyond freezing.

"What the fuck kind of fae are you?" the fox shifter demanded.

"A rare one," Oberon muttered.

"Thank the gods for small mercies," the witch murmured.

"I'm not staying here to be a target," Sin said, her expression resolute. Good. She was going to go back to the inn, maybe get some help. "If I concentrate, I can feel their souls. I'll try and find them."

He stared at her in shock, convinced he'd misheard.

"Over my dead body," Oberon snapped. His panther was in agreement.

"It might come to that." She took a step forward.

The witch looked at Sin. "Can you see their aura, too?"

The death fae shook her head. "No. I just know there's a soul there."

A witch who saw a soul's aura. That was something he'd never expected to hear in his very long life.

"I can track them," the witch added. "We were trailing one assassin, but there's at least five people here, other than us."

Gunshots rang out over the wind. Oberon shoved Sin to the side. She sprawled on the wet grass, her magic flickering out, then scrambled to her feet. He growled low as a bullet caught him in the arm while he shoved her back down. Fuck. That *hurt.* Blood welled from the wound, but he paused when he saw Sin's blue eyes turn flat. She looked at the injury on his arm, and then she turned toward the fog. "They're dead."

He stepped back. "They will be." He lifted his starblade. It would stop a bullet in its tracks, and end whoever had been shooting at them. Provided Sin didn't get in the bullet's way first.

She touched his arm where his blood welled. When she pulled her fingers away, they were stained crimson. "They hurt you."

"It will heal."

Crazed barking ricochetted through the air, and Oberon swore. A small black shape sprinted through the mists and launched itself at the partially visible leg of an attacker, about a hundred yards away.

Nog.

That fucking idiot—

Oberon gripped his starblade. "Stay here. I'll get Nog."

But Sin lowered her bloodstained hand like she hadn't heard him and walked straight toward the assassins.

"Sin!"

Motherfucker.

The witch tried to grab her arm, but Sin shrugged out of her grip. "You track the others. That one is mine." Something in the death fae's voice must have registered, because the witch took off into the fog, the fox shifter following.

Oberon caught up with her. “Sin, you’re not trained—”

She raised both of her hands, pale blue orbs flaring to life above her palms. “I don’t need to be trained. I just need to be able to aim.”

And then she started sprinting. Oberon kept pace with her, blood trickling down his arm, leaving a trail for anyone to follow. He was debating throwing her over his shoulder when the fog cleared, and chaos came into view.

Nog was tearing at the leg of a mercenary warlock who was throwing spells at the shifter. The warlock wore army fatigues, his face covered in a mask with only his pale green eyes visible.

Nearby, a vampire mercenary was struggling with the fox shifter, while a fire fae tangled with the witch. That explained the fireball. Oberon threw up a wall of blue flame at his back as he heard another mercenary circle behind them. Fuck. They’d just run into the proverbial lion’s den.

Nog let out a high-pitched squeal as a mercenary snap-kicked the small dog across the clearing. Sin leapt at the warlock, who turned startled eyes in her direction just as she slammed an orb of death magic into his torso. The warlock stumbled back a step, and Sin spun away.

Sin didn’t even check to make sure her magic worked.

Instead, she threw the second orb of death magic straight at his head. He whipped to the side, shock sizzling through him. He hadn’t thought she would—

A piercing cry shattered the silence next to him.

Between one heartbeat and the next, the air shimmered, and a fae appeared, the skin shriveling on their gray face as Sin’s magic leeched the life from them. He watched, stunned, as his formerly hidden attacker collapsed next to him, nothing more than a pile of rotting bones.

Bile rose at the back of his throat.

Sin rushed to Nog, scooping the corgi up in her arms. She looked down at her cousin, the pain etched on her face scarring his frozen heart.

Rage unlike he’d ever known eclipsed his mind at the sight of her anguish. He should have protected her, protected Nog. And now, the young shadow shifter was hurt. Maybe even dead.

He drew power from the moon and sun both, reforming his star-blade into a shimmering sunwhip, before coating his iron dagger with moonlight.

Then he attacked.

He sprinted toward the two camouflaged mercenaries, dodging balls of burning plasma from the fire fae, who was also attacking the aura-reading witch. Lashing out with his whip, he sliced the mercenary clean in two. Between one breath and the next, the fire fae split in half, his torso sliding away from his pelvis to land in two separate heaps on the wet ground.

He whirled, his movements smooth and flowing, as he and his panther fought as one. He threw the dagger, aiming it at the vampire. The blade lodged in the vampire's eye, and the bloodsucker dropped with a grunt. But it wouldn't be enough, not if they were old.

Oberon closed the distance to the fallen vampire, who clawed at him, crazed. But the leech was weakened from the injury, and Oberon used his sunwhip like a garrote. The vampire's head came off clean, the wound cauterized by the laser-like whip. He retrieved his dagger, wiping it clean on the vampire's shirt before he kicked the head to the side, where it rolled over toward the dead fire fae.

Four down.

Sin had taken two; he'd killed the other two.

Where was the fifth?

A deafening howl ripped through the heavens.

Oberon looked up, and then wondered if he'd gotten a concussion without noticing. The cloud cover melted away to expose a lion-headed chimera folding its dragon wings to dive, its serpent tail whipping behind it. It hit a white-winged angel with the force of a thunderclap, latching its paws on to the angel's exposed back. The assassin had been aiming a bow and arrow at Oberon, but it dropped the weapon to desperately claw at the chimera, throwing bolts of energy at the immense creature. Despite that, the angel didn't do any serious damage.

Thank the gods that creature appears to be on our side, Oberon thought as the chimera bit down on the back of the assassin's neck. Blood rained from the sky as the lion's teeth tore through muscle and sinew. The angel struggled weakly, until it suddenly went limp in the chimera's grip. The beast let go, and the mercenary fell into the sea, swallowed by the depths of the cold waters. He half expected the arm of a kraken to emerge, searching for another meal.

"Did you just see—" The fox shifter stared in awe at the chimera, who spiraled down to land delicately on the grassy clearing.

"I've never seen a flesh-and-blood chimera before," Sin whispered.

Wait. Did that mean she'd seen some other kind of chimera—

The creature's form disappeared in a burst of sunlight that had Oberon blinking, and then Dana stood there, naked. He snapped his gaze up to her red-and-umber eyes. She met his expression without blinking.

"I followed Nog here," the stablemaster said, oblivious or uncaring of the fact she was naked, had blood dripping down her chin, and that it was cold.

"Here." The fox shifter pulled off his jacket and offered it to the chimera shifter.

"Thanks." She accepted it, shrugging into the garment. It hung to her mid-thigh.

Oberon hurried over to Sin, who was cradling the corgi in her arms. Nog was breathing. Thank the gods.

Dana came up on Sin's other side and reached out a hand. Sin stepped away from the stablemaster.

"I can help," Dana said.

Reluctantly, Sin allowed the stablemaster to press a gentle hand to Nog's back. The redheaded fae closed her eyes, doing whatever her help was, then she withdrew her hand. "He'll be okay. A couple of bruised ribs. He's lucky."

Sin exhaled, her lower lip trembling. "*Eres un tonto, primo estúpido. Pero te amo de todos modos.*"

He figured she'd just called Nog stupid, since he recognized that word, at least.

"Thank you for following him," Sin said to the stablemaster.

"He's got a big heart." Dana's gaze softened slightly. "No sense of self-preservation, but a big heart."

Oberon looked at Sin, and he had a feeling that Dana's words applied to more than just Nog.

The stablemaster's focus turned to Oberon. "Any idea why Houseless assassins were after you?"

"Not a clue." As far as he knew, all his enemies had died over five millennia ago. And he'd barely had time to make new ones since arriving on Earth.

"We'd been tracking them for about a week," the witch said. "They were in The Crossroads before this."

The fox shifter sighed. "Ayla, that's confidential information."

She shrugged in response. "Come on, Aks. The target is dead."

The Gold and Garnet trackers started heading back toward the inn, bickering about NDAs and gods knew what else.

"Do you know why they were hunting Oberon?" Sin called to Ayla.

The aura-reading witch shook her head. "No, I just hunt them. But we were hired by someone in Death and Diamond."

He frowned.

Sin followed the duo, keen to ask more questions, and Oberon moved to keep pace, but Dana stepped in his path. "If you really have to return to Avalon, you might want to dye your hair."

He paused. Sin slowed, as if she sensed he wasn't behind her, ensuring that she was never more than ten feet away.

"Dye my hair?"

Dana started walking. "The blond is pretty distinctive."

His brow furrowed as he moved to catch up to Sin. "It's been a long time, but I swear I've never met you before in my life."

The chimera gave a shallow chuckle, but it wasn't a happy sound. "I know who you are, Oberon Ó Duibh. The Cursed King, former High King of Avalon, and Titian Geal's former mate."

He stopped walking, surprise and shock making his legs suddenly unsteady. His panther stalked toward Dana in his mind.

Sin spun, as if she sensed his unease. He met her gaze, and whatever she saw in his had her closing the distance between them. "What?"

"She knows my name." Then he studied the stablemaster anew. "*How* do you know my name?"

"My father hated you. And your images were all over the palace. It took years for Titian to remove them."

Oberon's heartbeat drowned out all other sound. "Wait—what?"

Dana kicked at the ground, then met his gaze. "Helios is my father."

"And Titian—" Gods, he could barely choke out his former mate's name. Had Dana been the product of their affair?

"No, she wasn't my mother. I was born about a year after your exile."

Sin stared at the two of them.

"You're half-fae." His voice was flat, but his mind was speeding at a million miles an hour.

Dana chuckled. "You're observant, aren't you?" Then she shook her head. "Helios never could keep it in his pants. Even though he had Titian brought back from the dead, he still couldn't remain loyal to her."

There was a strange ringing sound in his ears.

"His former mate is still alive?" Sin blurted.

"I don't know. I fled their fucked-up bullshit a long time ago. But they were still together around a thousand years ago. I've heard Avalon has a new High King. But that wasn't enough to tempt me to go back."

"You look good for someone pushing a thousand," Sin muttered.

Dana laughed. "Multiply that by two. But I'm a demigod, so defying age is in the genes."

Oberon was talking to the child of the man who'd helped betray him. Who'd fucked his mate whenever Oberon's back was turned. He should hate her. Want to destroy her. But as he walked, he realized he just...didn't care.

Blood didn't define anything—except, in his case, power.

"Wait. Did you say two thousand years ago?" Oberon asked, frowning.

"Yes."

"And you were born the year after I left?"

"Yes."

The math didn't math.

"I've been gone for five thousand years." He rubbed his hand over his chin, thinking. Time dilation was a thing, and Tartarus was a nomadic planet.

Dana shook her head, her autumn hair swaying with the movement. "It's only been two thousand since you left."

But...what if the portal had fucked up and spewed him out on Tartarus *in the past*? Rather than instant travel between worlds, it had somehow dumped him out three thousand years earlier—when the portal could actually connect to the planet, before the primordials had locked it down.

Sin clutched Nog in her arms. "We're going to need to find a dog sitter. And I need to chat with my...brother."

CHAPTER 25
OBERON

Oberon and Sin had decided to check on Nog, who'd been asleep in the stables for far longer than was healthy. At least, that was what Sin had been telling him for the past hour. He scratched his head, annoyed at the persistent itchy feeling that came from the dye they'd used to color his hair brown.

"How has he been?" Sin asked.

Oberon had just assumed she was asking Dana, but then he realized she was talking to the vacant space next to the stablemaster. Dana herself was frowning, but not in a concerned way, more like she was trying to overhear the second half of the one-sided conversation that was taking place next to her.

Sin rolled her eyes. "I asked you to look after him, not spy on all inhabitants of the barn."

Oberon had the feeling that Sin's mother hadn't exactly been the best guard dog, for the, err, dog. Especially considering Nog had made his way to an assassination attempt.

"Here." Dana handed Sin the collar that had been around Nog's neck.

The death fae took it, turning the locket over in her hands. "Why did you take it off? Did he pull it off?"

"Go have a look and you'll see why."

Sin shoved the locket in her jeans pocket, then strode toward the closed doors of the barn's office, muttering something to herself. Or maybe to her mother. Oberon wasn't entirely sure.

He kept an eye on her progress, making sure that she didn't step beyond the twenty-foot limit.

"Nog?" Sin's voice was raised in alarm.

Oberon closed the distance between them, peering over the top of her head at the naked human teen lying on the floor of the office. His head was resting on the tiled ground, and a horse blanket had been thrown over his torso. He was sound asleep, hugging a teddy bear.

"Nog! Wake up."

"Sin?" The teen blinked open sleepy eyes. "Go away. It's too early."

"Nog!"

"What? Argh. I'm awake." He rolled over on the floor and stretched out his arms and legs. Then he sat up, blinking in confusion.

"Sin? Why are you staring like that?" He patted his bruised chest and his face. "Yes!" Nog punched a fist into the air, and it made the blanket slide uncomfortably low around his waist.

"Gods, Nog. Why don't you put some clothes on? I don't need to see you naked this early in the morning. Or, well, ever." Sin put a hand over her eyes.

"You've seen him hump a crocheted doll," Oberon pointed out. "Him naked is really much less unpleasant."

The edges of Sin's mouth creased. "I could have lived my whole life without seeing that."

"What?" Nog stood, holding the blanket around his waist. "The fucker had it coming."

"Literally," Oberon snorted.

"Oberon!" Sin shoved at his arm.

"What?"

"Let's give him some privacy to get dressed." Sin pushed Oberon out of the room. Not that he wanted to hang around and see the kid get changed, anyway.

"There's spare clothes in the chest by the desk!" Dana called from the other side of the aisle.

Nog emerged a few minutes later, wearing a stained gray shirt, sweatpants, and a pair of socks. Then he threw himself at Sin, hugging her as if his life depended on it. Which it very well might, considering she was going to be pissed at him for not only following Oberon, but also running out into a field of assassins.

Oberon *almost* felt sorry for the kid.

Nog inhaled deeply, then pulled away from Sin, frowning. "Sin?" The corgi shifter's voice was pure innocence.

Uh-oh.

She looked at her cousin warily. "Yes?"

"Why do you smell like you've had sex with Oberon?"

Sin's face turned a fascinating shade of pink. Oberon shoved his hands in his pockets and rocked back on his heels. He wasn't going to get involved in this conversation, no way, no how.

"You must have hit your head," Sin said.

"My ribs were the only thing that got kicked in. Not my head." Nog plucked up a strand of Sin's hair and sniffed it.

"Hey!" She snatched her hair back.

"I'm not the one who stinks!"

"Stinks?" Oberon demanded. Damnit, he was meant to be keeping out of this conversation.

Nog scrunched up his nose. "Dude, you smell like you dumped yourself in cologne."

"I don't even own any cologne," Oberon protested.

Dana frowned and stepped forward, sniffing the air near Sin as well. "Huh."

"What does that mean?" Sin asked. She grabbed her hair and sniffed it. "I don't smell anything other than shampoo."

"You stink like Oberon." Nog stomped his socked foot.

"No, I don't—"

"Look, just admit you did the nasty with him, and we can move on—"

Sin threw her arms up in the air. "I don't know why I have to admit to anything."

"Explain why you smell like him, then."

"I don't have to!"

"Have you been rubbing your scent on her or something?" Nog asked, eying Oberon like he was disturbed. "Is it a flying cat thing?"

Oberon's panther hissed. It wanted to swat the corgi for its impudence. "It's called a bastet, and no." Something wicked had him adding, "But she's wearing my T-shirt."

Nog's eyes went wide. "You're what?"

Sin shot him a look that spoke of murder.

"You never wear guy's clothes. Come to think of it, I can't remember the last time you got lucky." Nog was rubbing his chin.

"Because it isn't any of your damned business, *primito*."

"Please. We used to annoy Clara and Reagan about their sex lives all the time."

Sin's foot started tapping. "That was you."

"You smell like him because his bastet's claimed you," Dana said, interjecting into the conversation.

Oberon winced.

"*What*?" Nog and Sin shouted that at the same time.

Nog grabbed her by the shoulders. "You let him *claim* you?"

"*No*." She brushed her cousin away.

"You slept with him." It wasn't a question this time, and Nog crossed his arms over his chest.

"It was a moment of insanity; we really don't need to talk about it anymore," Sin muttered. But she was glaring at Oberon.

"Uh, I believe 'mind-blowing insanity' was the term used," Oberon corrected.

Sin spoke through gritted teeth. "Not helping."

Nog turned a little green.

"What does she mean, your bastet claimed me?" Sin demanded, and poked Oberon in the chest.

He caught her finger and lifted her hand, kissing the inside of her wrist, which earned him a grumpy glare. He grinned. "I told you, the panther thinks you're his."

"I didn't consent—"

"You're wearing his scent," Dana said. "That can only happen if you accept it."

Sin's mouth snapped closed.

His panther licked its paw, smug.

He would have preferred to not have this conversation in front of witnesses, but at least she hadn't thrown another death orb at his head. It was the small victories in life.

St. Claire strode into the barn.

Oberon sighed and let go of Sin's hand.

The vampire seemed to study them all, but her focus was on Dana. "Why does it smell like there were four dead bodies on the path down to the portal?" She tapped her chin. "And yet, there are no corpses."

The chimera shrugged. "Because there were four dead bodies there."

"And where are they now?"

"Gone."

St. Claire's mouth thinned ever so slightly.

"What? I have hungry creatures here." Dana pointed, and the large not-spider above their heads wiggled in its web, its abdomen noticeably larger. "Why waste perfectly good meat?"

Sin turned an interesting shade of green, while Nog waved cheerily at the *tsuchigumo*. Oberon decided he did *not* want to know when the corgi and the not-spider became friendly.

A few moments later, Douglas Fhearchair arrived. He was rubbing his hands together, in glee or from the cold, Oberon couldn't tell. "I just had a verra interesting phone call with my sweet lass."

Sin didn't look pleased with the phantom's arrival.

"Straight to business, Douglas? Not even a greeting?" St. Claire asked the male.

"I didna knew ye cared, Ysabeau." Douglas gave the vampire a smile that was no doubt meant to be charming but came across as slightly threatening. "Sabrina says she will provide you both with papers, if you want to go through the Giant's Causeway portal."

"What's the catch?" St. Claire asked, seemingly assumed.

Because there was always a catch.

"Full membership of the House of Death and Diamond."

"How intriguing," Sin replied. But she didn't accept the offer.

Sin had spent a lifetime hiding from her half-brother, and here he was, offering her House membership. Was he friend or foe? And had he sent the assassins to take Oberon out, so he could get access to his sister?

"I can get the papers prepared—"

"She didn't agree, Douglas," St. Claire interrupted. "And why would she join the House of Death and Diamond when her cousin is the queen of the House of Blood and Beryl?"

"She's what?" The phantom looked surprised.

"Dannika is my cousin," Sin admitted, but she didn't seem happy to share the information.

"You mean you're related to *Adora*?" Douglas looked distinctly *un*happy now. He began stretching out a finger on his right hand, as if testing it was working properly. Strange.

"She's also my cousin," Sin said. "Could you pass a message onto Sabrina and Kieran, though?"

"Don't you mean she's *our* cousin?" Nog demanded.

"Ours, yours, mine. What does it matter?" Sin asked.

"By that logic, Oberon is my fuckboy, too, and that ain't ever going to happen." Nog sniffed.

Now that was a thought he really hadn't wanted to contemplate. Ever.

"You could only dare dream of the bliss you would find in my arms," Oberon said, voice smooth as silk.

Nog yanked on the collar of his shirt. "That was kinda hot. Maybe he *is* our—"

Sin slapped a hand over Nog's mouth. "Don't even try to finish that sentence."

St. Claire picked off a piece of invisible lint from her immaculate pant suit. "Danni says she will give you papers to cross over to Avalon—but on one condition."

The death fae raised an eyebrow. "And that is?"

"You have to call her first."

CHAPTER 26
OBERON

Oberon had been told he had to wait outside the barn office, while Sin called the queen of the House of Blood and Beryl. He had the feeling if it weren't for the binding spell, he'd have been told to take a hike. But since he could only be twenty feet away from Sin without her getting a crushing headache...

Well, there were benefits to the spell.

At least for him.

Although, there were also disadvantages. Namely, that Nog had decided to hang out around Oberon, and the fae couldn't escape.

"I knew you had a thing for Sin," Nog said.

Oberon crossed his arms over his chest. "Really."

Because Oberon himself hadn't known he had a 'thing' for the damned death fae. He'd just wanted to use her.

You still do.

But at least his motives were a little less self-serving this time.

Nog rubbed his chin. "Although, I am surprised she let you even touch her, considering how many times I've caught her cursing your name."

Wasn't that fun to learn?

The office door opened with a creak, and Sin stepped out. She blinked owlishly, the light from the stable apparently brighter than that of the office. "The paperwork is all sorted."

Oberon figured that he should be pleased Sin had finally agreed to go to Avalon with him. But her change of mind left him uneasy. Maybe because his conscience had finally caught up to him. Or because he was waiting for the other shoe to drop. He didn't know which.

"What did your cousin want to know?" Oberon asked as Sin came to stand beside him. He inhaled, pleased to find his scent still layered over her unique lemon and lavender smell. His panther flicked its tail.

"Danni wanted to confirm that I wasn't being dragged to Avalon against my will." Sin met his stare, hers full of mischief.

He swallowed, suddenly desperate to see her look at him the same way, but when they were both naked. "I see."

"I told her that I was going there of my own volition...although I did have a binding spell on me, which limited my choices." The corner of her mouth lifted almost imperceptibly, and he realized that she was teasing him.

His stomach clenched.

Nog made a gagging sound. "Get a room, you two."

"We're in a room." Sin waved a hand, indicating the entire barn they stood in.

"I already told you, I'm not a babysitter." St. Claire's voice was stern as she stepped through the doorway of the office. She was still on the phone. She had taken off her sunglasses—they hung forgotten in her free hand—and she appeared...harried.

Oberon turned to Sin, who looked at Nog.

Nog looked at both of them. "Why are you staring at me?"

"I have better things to do with my time." St. Claire's voice was a borderline growl as she spoke into the phone, her fingers tightening on the arm of her sunglasses.

Oberon couldn't hear what was being said on the other end of the call, mostly because whoever it was spoke super quietly. Like they knew there might be shifters lurking in the background with excellent hearing.

"Fine." St. Claire ended the call. She glanced up at Nog, her expression that of a predator sighting prey. She slid her sunglasses back on. "You're with me." The vampire pointed a finger at the shadow shifter.

Nog took a step back. "Who? *Me*?" His voice squeaked.

"You."

"I'm not so sure that's a good idea—" Dark shadows swarmed over the youth. Two heartbeats later, Nog's clothing fell to the ground, and a small form wiggled within the pile of material.

He'd shifted again.

"Does he do that often?" St. Claire asked, inspecting the pile of clothing.

"Whenever he gets nervous, or scared, or happy, or, uh, any kind of heightened emotion, really," Sin said, her voice suspiciously sunny.

St. Claire did not seem particularly impressed by that statement.

"So how come Ysabeau is on Nog duty? Not that I'm against it," Oberon asked.

"My queen demands it." The vampire's tone was drier than the sands of a desert.

"I told Danni that I'm going through the portal, and that I wasn't going to let Nog come with me. But I didn't have anyone who could make a portal to send Nog home before I left. So, we agreed he should be...supervised." Sin was smiling now, as if she enjoyed St. Claire's discomfort.

He liked this side of her.

He'd thought her mean side was reserved for him and him alone.

"I am more than pleased to fulfill my queen's wishes." He had the distinct impression that in this instance, the vampire was far from pleased.

Oberon clapped his hands together, once. "Well, we had best get moving before Nog finds his way out of his clothing."

Sin took a deep breath and nodded slowly. "Okay."

They were almost at the door when Dana stepped in front of them. She was dressed once again in overalls, the fox shifter's jacket long gone. "If Helios is still on Avalon—and if you're unlucky enough to see him—please don't mention you saw me."

Oberon met the stablemaster's crimson gaze and nodded. "I will try. But I can't lie if asked a direct question."

Dana smiled, the expression genuine. "Being only half-fae, I thankfully never had that problem."

"There are pros and cons to being full-blooded," Oberon said.

Dana shoved her hand in a pocket. "You might want to change your name."

"Already done," Sin said.

Surprise wrenched through him. "What?"

"We had to give you a name for the paperwork. So, I said it was Beron Black." She shrugged.

"What?" He felt like a broken record.

"Beron is just your name, minus the *O*, and Dana told me that your surname means black, so there we go. It's technically not a lie, just a... nickname, you might say. And a translation into English."

Sin was sneaky, he realized. His panther appreciated the logic.

"Beron Black. It has a ring to it," Dana said, her tone consoling.

"It has alliteration," Oberon muttered.

"You're also listed as being Oberon's great-grandson," Sin added.

"What? When did I have a son?"

"I hate to interrupt the banter, but you might want to get going before Nog catches up with you." Dana nodded in the shadow shifter's direction. He had somehow managed to stick his head out the sleeve of the T-shirt, but the rest of his body was thankfully still trapped.

Sin chuckled softly. The sound soothed the jagged edges inside of him, jagged edges that had been part of him for so long he had forgotten when they'd formed.

"Thank you for helping us earlier," Oberon said and held out his hand.

Dana stared at it for a few seconds, before shaking it. "I'll try to help Ysabeau look after Nog, but I can't guarantee anything."

"Thank you," Sin replied. "Hopefully we'll return soon, and I can take him home."

Dana chuckled. "Please do."

They left the stables before Nog could wriggle free of his clothing, and headed straight for their room at the inn. Oberon's pack was ready to go, Sin having just finished loading hers, when there was a knock on the door.

He glowered at it when the scent of the fox shifter reached him. "Don't answer it."

"I know you're in there!" That was the witch, Ayla.

Sin sent him a sidelong glance and closed the meager distance to the door. She opened it wide enough so that Oberon could see Aks and Ayla clearly over Sin's head.

"Here." The witch shoved a strange, glittery rock at Sin.

"Uh, thank you?" The death fae took the stone, and nearly dropped it. Oberon darted forward and plucked the rock from Sin's fingers. It felt chilly, but otherwise inert. He handed it back. Her fingers closed around it, hesitantly.

"You can feel its magic?" Ayla asked, brushing dark hair out of her eyes.

"Yes."

"Good. This will help you reach my family's death plane."

"Your what?" Sin's mouth dropped open.

"The death plane sits adjacent to ours, but my family has their own...version, you could say. Being a death fae, you could potentially reach the regular plane, but not ours. So, this will help you do it. But only use it if you really need help, because your spirit will travel to the plane, leaving your body vulnerable."

Oberon didn't like the sound of that. At all.

"It's like a...calling card?" Sin asked.

"Sort of."

Sin turned the rock over in her hands. "Then this must be very...precious."

"It is."

The death fae tried to hand it back. "I don't think I'm the right person—"

"There are assassins out after you—or him. And you're about to go to a world where you won't have anyone to protect your back. If you need help, use this. We will come find you."

"Why are you offering this?" Oberon asked. In his experience, nothing came for free. And it wasn't like the two women had known each other long enough to become acquaintances, let alone friends.

Ayla's expression turned troubled, and the fox shifter behind her looked uncomfortable. "Because I wish I'd had someone to help me, and the women in my family, not too long ago. Sin is bound to you, and you seem to have a target on your back. She needs all the help she can get."

He bit the inside of his cheek, unable to argue with the logic. And he didn't want to begrudge Sin even a burgeoning friendship, although he would prefer the damned fox shifter was as far away from Sin as possible.

Not that she'd ever really looked at the other male. But he'd looked at her plenty. Still was.

"Thank you." Sin slipped the shimmery rock into her pack.

"See you on the other side," Ayla said with a smirk. She and the shifter then stepped away from the doorway and disappeared down the stairs.

"Shall we go?" Oberon asked. He shrugged his pack on.

Sin nodded, then stepped slowly into the hallway. "I think I've lost my mind. But let's go."

He wanted to comfort her, but what could he say?

She wouldn't have agreed to go through that portal if he had lifted the binding spell. And he should do it, he really should. But as they walked out of the inn, and down the track toward the portal, he just couldn't convince himself to break the spell. He needed her power. Her abilities.

He needed *her*.

And he was afraid that without the magic, she wouldn't come. She'd turn her back, and he'd be forced to go through the portal alone.

His panther growled in his mind at the thought.

It didn't approve of the spell, but it understood Oberon's need to keep Sin close. If she chose to leave them—no, *when* she chose to leave them, it would destroy the panther. And possibly Oberon, too.

He wanted to delay that happening for as long as possible.

They didn't talk as they walked down the gravel path toward the shoreline. Sure enough, the bodies of the assassins were gone, although trails of blood and burnt patches of grass and rock indicated a battle had taken place.

"What did you ask Douglas to pass on to Sabrina and Kieran?"

"I wanted to know who in Death and Diamond hired Ayla to hunt down the assassins. And why."

"Did he have an answer?"

"Not yet."

"Was that the first time you've killed?" Oberon asked after they'd cleared the field.

She was quiet for so long, he didn't think she was going to answer, but eventually she said, "No."

He watched her out the corner of his eye—her expression was resolute. "Your family says they don't involve you unless they absolutely have to. Is it because you do the wet work?"

Sin's stride jerked, before she evened it out. "They just don't want to hear the lecture after. If they wanted someone dead, they didn't need to just go to me. Dad's an alpha—you think he'd sit by and watch someone hurt his family?"

"No. No true—or halfway decent—alpha could." Alvaro had desperately wanted to kill Oberon—and Caius—the first time they'd met.

The scent of blood swirled through the air. He turned to Sin; she was biting the inside of her cheek. "People were looking for Reagan over the years. And Dad wasn't always around to stop them. Even when he was..." She turned haunted blue eyes toward him "When I killed them, nothing remained. All organic matter decomposes. I never had to hide a body. Dad did."

He read between the lines.

Sin could kill and no one would ever know.

A female guard approached as Sin and Oberon closed the distance to the portal. This close, he could feel Avalon's magic reaching out, tasting him. The portal's edges glittered like a prism, and the inside shimmered like a mirage. They moved over the uneven, rocky ground, their steps sure.

The female vampire was dressed in the Portal Guard's uniform, with no sign of a House allegiance. He was familiar with the uniform as a small contingent of them had been sent to start learning about the Tartarus portal and what it would take to guard it. Each member of the guard had come from one of the Houses originally; he wondered if they truly dropped their prior associations.

As they drew in line with the small timber building perched near the edge of the rocky shore, he noticed there was also a small contingent of white-clad Avalon guards.

The approaching vampire had bronze skin, and her hair was a riot of dark curls. Her eyes were tilted at the corners, and her cheekbones were sharp enough to cut glass. She was attractive, in the way most human-shaped predators were. "My name is Mei. You looking to travel today?"

They nodded.

"Papers?"

"Here." Sin handed the vampire a clear quartz crystal.

Mei held it in her hand, then tapped it with a pink stone he thought might be beryl. "All seems in order." But her gaze was curious as it took in Sin, then trailed to Oberon. Mei's nose wrinkled when she noticed his brown hair.

He didn't think it looked that bad. Then again, he hadn't entirely been able to wash away the chemical smell of the dye.

She handed Sin the crystal back. "You're free to go."

When they'd said paperwork, Oberon had assumed that meant literal pieces of paper. It was a good thing he hadn't attempted to forge anything himself.

"Just so you know..." the guard's voice trailed off.

"So we know what?" Sin prompted.

Mei slowly exhaled. "Death fae only ever come out of this portal. None have gone back, not in the four hundred years it's been open."

Sin accepted the quartz crystal and tucked it away in a jacket pocket. "None have ever gone back? Not even the ones born on Earth?"

The guard opened her mouth to answer, but snapped it shut when an Avalon guard approached. Their uniform was a conspicuous white decorated with silver thread. Titian's colors—or more accurately, the Geal family colors.

The new High King must be a relative of hers.

"What's the hold up?" The guard's voice was accented, and even though he spoke in English, it sat uncomfortably on his tongue. He still managed to sound pompous, though.

Mei shook her head and looked down her nose at the fae—which was an impressive feat, considering the Avalon guard was taller than the vampire. "Leave them be, Easton. We were just finalizing everything."

"Then—" The white-clad guard froze when he noticed Sin by Oberon's side. "You're a death fae." His gaze filled with malice.

Sin flicked her braid over her shoulder. "And you're an ass."

Easton blinked, his face turning an interesting shade of puce.

Oberon let out a startled laugh.

Sin pursed her lips, but he could tell she was amused. "Sorry, I thought we were just stating the obvious."

The fae guard drew himself up to his full height, which was a little over six feet. Still shorter than Oberon. "Death fae are prohibited from entering Avalon."

"Since when?" Mei asked.

"Since always."

"News to me. Where's the proclamation?" The vampire crossed her arms over her chest.

Their argument drew the other portal and Avalon guards closer.

"There's no proclamation, but everyone knows—"

"Clearly, they don't," Oberon helpfully interjected.

The fae turned a contemptuous stare on him. Then his skin turned ashen. "Your eyes—"

"What about them?" Oberon kept his voice neutral.

"What kind of fae does it say he is?" Easton's voice was slightly panicked.

Oberon and Sin were soon surrounded. The portal guards stayed close to Mei, while the Avalon ones hung near Easton.

"It just said he's a fae and shadow shifter," Mei answered. "They don't need to say what kind of fae they are for a short trip."

"What is a shadow shifter?" The Avalon guard looked at Oberon in disbelief. "Short trip. You applied for a short trip?"

"I don't see what all the fuss is about." Mei seemed frustrated. "Their paperwork is in order. There is no official proclamation about death fae. Let them through."

"That man is a descendent of the Ó Duibh, who are the enemy of our High King. No other fae in our world has eyes like that." The guard's voice rose on the word enemy.

"Easton, the Ó Duibh are gone. The former High Queen wiped them out for their treachery. So are the Ó hUainín. You're being ridiculous." The speaker was another white-clad guard, but their skin was the stone gray of the Trows, one of the Wild Fae. They studied Oberon without malice.

Interesting. Oberon hadn't thought the Wild Fae would be interested in something so mundane as guard duty.

"The Cursed King was sent to Tartarus. You've all heard the rumors that the newest portal on Earth comes from that prison world." Easton pointed at Oberon. "Explain his eyes."

The Avalon fae crowded closer, and suddenly, Oberon understood what it felt like to be a museum exhibit.

The Trow slashed a hand through the air. "Ever heard of a coincidence?"

"The Cursed King was exiled over two thousand years ago," another guard muttered, this one with hair the color of sunshine. "It could be his bloodline."

"Give me the crystal." Easton held out his hand.

Sin turned to Oberon, then Mei, who nodded reluctantly. She withdrew it and passed it over. The Avalon guard tapped it with a milky white rock. "It says his name is Beron Black, and that he's from Tartarus. And that his grandsire was called Oberon."

"Ó Duibh means 'black,'" another guard muttered, but he couldn't tell which one.

Easton's yellow eyes narrowed. "You're a relation of the Cursed King."

"What was his name?" Oberon asked, toying with them. Sin leaned into his side, her pointy elbow digging slightly into his ribs. He took the warning for what it was.

"Oberon Ó Duibh," the Trow replied.

Oberon shrugged. "Cool name."

"Are you a relation of the Cursed King?"

"You could say that." Oberon was definitely related to, well, himself.

"One moment." The Avalon guards huddled together.

Mei shook her head. "You put the cat amongst the canaries."

His panther snickered.

A shifter Portal Guard spoke, his voice low and barely above a whisper. "They're trying to work out if they'll get executed for allowing a descendent of the Cursed King through the portal. Along with a death fae."

Probably another damned fox shifter of some kind, to have hearing that good, Oberon thought.

"Would it help them to know we're both Celestials?" Sin asked. His stomach plummeted to somewhere under the ocean floor.

The Avalon guards froze.

"What's a Celestial?" Mei asked.

"The only kind of fae allowed to rule as High King or Queen on Avalon," Oberon answered. "And a closely guarded secret of the fae," he added.

Easton turned slowly, his movements almost pained. "Prove it."

Oberon formed a starblade in his right hand, the light flickering white due to the nature of the Earth's sun.

"The Moonlight Wraith can form a blade out of moonlight, and he's not a Celestial," Easton said. "That doesn't mean anything."

Oberon had no idea who this Moonlight Wraith was, but if all they could do was harness the light reflected from the moon, then they weren't a Celestial.

"This is formed from the power of a star, not the moon," Oberon said.

They didn't appear convinced.

"What can a Celestial even do?" Mei asked.

"Harness the power of the universe," the Trow replied hesitantly.

Oberon sighed. Fancy light blades clearly weren't going to be enough.

Time for a somewhat pointless, but obvious, trick.

He negated gravity.

Just for the area immediately surrounding them, but it was enough. All the guards around them began to float, their hair flying away from their faces, their clothes lifting where they weren't pinned or tucked down.

"What the fuck—?"

"This is crazy!"

"Put us down!"

Sin's eyes went wide as her feet rose from the basalt rock, too. Only Oberon stayed firmly planted on the ground, unaffected by the magic. It took two heartbeats before Sin's amazement vanished, and she returned to the earth with a thump. Pride welled within him—she'd worked out how to counter his magic on her own.

"I think they've had enough," Sin muttered.

Oberon turned back to the guards, biting back a smirk at seeing that some had begun floating upside down. He flicked his hand—more for show than anything else—and they dropped back to the ground. Hard.

Easton landed on his head.

His panther licked its paw.

"I think I'd prefer it if they went through the portal now," Mei said quietly. "I've had enough of the demonstrations."

"Let them through." Easton's jaw was clenched so tight Oberon wondered how the words emerged.

"Finally," Oberon grumbled.

The Avalon guards were shocked—but some appeared...pleased by his display. Others simply seemed worried.

He took a deep breath and held out his hand to Sin. His mind buzzed with the thousands of possibilities that awaited them on the other side. He was about to go home, for the first time in five thousand years. But... he only wanted to do it if Sin was by his side.

As if sensing his inner turmoil, she slipped her hand into his, squeezing his palm with her fingers. Then they closed the distance to the portal.

This close, he could see through to the other side. It was daytime, the grass was an impossible green, and the skies overhead were a blue much darker than Earth's.

"Ready?" he asked.

"No." Sin said. "Let's go."

Oberon stepped through, Sin's hand in his. The portal's magic whipped around him, a maelstrom of energy, his hair buffeting his face in a wind that didn't exist. So very different from the Tartarus portal—the Avalon one singed his nerves, but also fed magic into his very being at the same time. His fingers slipped from Sin's. Between one breath and the next, he was through.

But Sin wasn't next to him.

Turning back, his heart aching in his chest, he saw Sin on the Earth side of the portal, her mouth parted as she faced him.

Unable to look away, he stared at the death fae who had captured his panther's heart. Was she willing to risk the binding spell, and leave them?

Or would she step through?

CHAPTER 27
SIN

Sin's mouth dropped open in awe as the sky behind Oberon transformed. Streams of obsidian spread out from above the fae, flaring across the sky until the deep blue expanse became eerily dark. Then, one by one, pinpricks of light burst to life on the ebony background—but they weren't stars.

It was like looking into Oberon's eyes.

But he wasn't watching the magical outburst above him—no, his gaze was locked on her, standing on the Earth side of the portal.

"You shouldn't go through," Dianthe said, for the thousandth time.

"Why not?" Sin asked.

Her mother's form flickered next to her. "Nothing but death awaits you there."

Seemed her mother was definitely in a doomsday mood. "Everyone dies. Eventually."

Her mother didn't respond, pensive.

She muttered the spell that Clara had devised to trap her mother in the locket. She had no idea what travelling through a portal would do to a ghost.

"I'm going," she said to herself.

Not just because she had a binding spell that would no doubt be triggered the moment Oberon stepped away from the portal—no, she was going because she'd said she would. And Sin's word meant something; maybe not to anyone else, but it did to her. Plus, she had a vow to keep.

Oberon hadn't dared look away from her, as if he was worried that she'd bolt.

Taking a deep breath, the air whistled as she stepped through the portal.

She'd been through the Tartarus portal multiple times now. This felt nothing like it. She had no idea how long she spent hovering in between worlds, but her body felt as if it was stretched taut, itchy, while her cells were being dissolved and rebuilt, until all she could feel was Avalon's magic tasting, testing her.

Rebuilding her.

By the time she stepped through, she felt exhausted, but also energized, new.

Her hands trembled, and she shoved them into her jacket pockets. "You should look at the sky," Sin said to Oberon.

She didn't love the brown hair. Oh, it suited him. He was the kind of handsome that any color would look good on. But the brown just... wasn't him.

Sin waited for him to look up, but instead, he crushed her to him in a hug that was so tight, her bones ground together. The side of her head was pressed against his chest, and his heartbeat thundered against her ear. She breathed in deeply, and his scent flooded her senses while her body acclimatized to the new world, and whatever it was the portal had done.

"You're squeezing me," Sin mumbled, when it became clear he wasn't going to let go anytime soon.

"There was another arrow. I destroyed it." Oberon shifted, sliding her away but keeping his hands on her upper arms.

Sin looked back through the portal, at the guards who appeared to be combing the area, looking for a hidden attacker.

"But we killed the angel."

"There must have been another assassin."

Oberon let go of her shoulders. "I thought you were going to run."

"Then you don't know me as well as you think," Sin replied. "Look up."

Oberon tilted his head, then hissed out a breath. "It looks like my eyes."

"Vain much?" she asked. But she was teasing. Because that was exactly what it looked like.

His hand stroked up and down her arm, and she shivered in response. Power began to slowly flood her senses, and the cells that had been rebuilt by the portal became bloated with magic. The feeling was heady, and warmth spread throughout her body, pooling low in her stomach.

Gods, it felt like she was on fire.

"What's that?" Oberon asked, staring at the skyline.

Shimmering green light swelled up from the horizon to dance across the dark sky. The sight...it reminded her of emerald ribbons weaving across a darkened tapestry, sewing a story amongst the stars.

"An aurora," Sin replied, her magic coiling within her.

She'd seen aurorae before at The Crossroads, rare though they were. But on Earth, the green light would fade into shades of burgundy and purple, whereas here, all she could see were varying shades of green.

"I think our presence has been announced." Oberon tucked her against his side, wrapping one arm around her shoulders. "And it looks like you're an Ó hUainín. Their name means 'green.'"

Unhappy with the limited contact, she slid off her pack and stood in front of him, pressing her back against his front. He moved his arm, so that it rested on her collarbones, across her throat. The hold of a possessive alpha.

But right now, she didn't care.

The amazing heat of him sunk into her body, and the warmth in her stomach grew hotter, more needy.

"When I came from Tartarus to Earth, I nearly collapsed onto my knees at the feeling of the magic." Oberon's voice was low, his breath tickling the shell of her ear.

"Oh?" How did her voice get that breathless?

He tilted his hips slightly, and his hard length pressed against her backside.

Gods.

Her throat went dry.

"It's like a whole-body arousal, feeling so much magic. At least, it does for me."

"It's wrong to have sex right here, isn't it?" Sin asked.

Oberon growled low in his throat, and bit down on her neck. Not hard enough to pierce the skin, but it had Sin's panties soaking wet. She groaned in response, and he tightened his hold on her, his cock pressing firmly against her. She wanted to feel him inside her, stroking them both to ecstasy while the magic burned in their veins.

His teeth released her, then he laved the tender skin of her neck. "We really need to talk about this exhibitionist streak you seem to have."

She tilted her head to look at him, but he was smiling, his expression wicked. Then reality set in.

She'd all but asked him to fuck her on the steps of a portal.

Glancing over her shoulder, she could see a handful of guards peering at them from the Earth side, their gazes darting from the black-and-green sky to Sin and Oberon. The others were still combing the area for signs of intruders.

"Oh gods." She covered her face with her palms.

Oberon tilted her chin up. "Look."

The green slowly faded from the sky, and the starry black vastness receded in streamers of obsidian, until five minutes later, the sky had returned to its former deep blue hue. A bright sun, similar to Earth's, dipped toward a line of trees, and she gasped, when she noticed the second sun, which was much smaller and a slightly different color.

It looked to her like they were in a temple of sorts; the floor was crafted from black marble, and white pillars with green veins supported a timber roof. It was open to the air, but steps led down toward a grassy lawn in front of the portal.

That was the grass she could see from the other side. It wasn't quite as blue-green as it had looked from Earth, but it was definitely not the same shade of green she'd have expected.

"Avalon is in a binary star system?" Sin asked.

Oberon nodded, his chin moving against the back of her head. "Yes.

I don't think it's too far from Earth, either. For the six months of the year when Avalon actually has a true night, some of the constellations look the same."

Sin marveled at the information. She loved astronomy; stargazing had been her one hobby. She'd felt a connection to the sky, to the tiny pinpricks of light that told stories of other worlds, other suns, other places.

And now here she was, on another planet in a binary solar system.

"You're more powerful here, aren't you?" Sin asked.

His mouth dipped, until it was next to her cheek. "Incredibly so."

She bit her lip, her breath hitching at his low words. "I am, too, I think."

She could throw orbs of death before—what could she do now?

What could Oberon do now?

Guards emerged from the line of trees, striding toward them. Every so often, one would look at the sky, then toward the two of them standing on the marble pavilion.

They wore white uniforms similar to those the Avalon guards wore on Earth. But unlike the asshole senior guard there, these soldiers looked fearful, rather than contemptuous. They each wore weapons belts, with short swords alternating on their left and right hips—she assumed it reflected their hand preference, as opposed to simply being a decorative function.

The guards came to a stop at the bottom of the small staircase, on the edge of the lawn. "Welcome to Avalon. My name is Captain Sorrel." The speaker was a woman with green skin, and long, flowing silver hair. She was beautiful, even with eyes that were completely black. Sin had no idea what kind of fae she was, since the Earthen fae seemed to look more human than not.

"Thank you," Sin replied, stepping away from Oberon and putting her pack back on.

He let her go but still kept close.

"May we see your papers?" Captain Sorrel asked.

"Here." Sin strode down the marble stairs, coming to a stop on the last one. She withdrew the crystal and handed it to the captain.

The green-skinned fae tapped it with what looked like a diamond, its facets throwing a dizzying array of light. "Sinéad Santiago from Earth and Beron Black from...Tartarus." Inky black eyes stared at Sin and Oberon, skepticism causing frown lines to mar the fae's forehead.

Oberon moved around Sin's side and stepped onto the grass. He then bowed low at the waist, the movement smooth and elegant. "I am honored to be welcomed to Avalon by an Undine. I heard tales of the Wild Fae, but did not realize they were now working for the High Court."

Sin studied the fae guards and realized most of them looked like Earthen fae: pointed ears, skin tones ranging from white to darkest black, and hair varying from blue to copper. But the Undine was unique amongst them.

"We are honored to serve our High King," Captain Sorrel replied. But her voice was curiously toneless as she handed Sin back the bespelled crystal. "Please, follow us."

The captain turned and walked back toward the line of trees. The grass was spongy underfoot, and it took Sin a few moments to adjust to the different feel. Or maybe the gravity was slightly different, too.

The guards fell into place along either side of Oberon and Sin, the only sounds that of their footsteps. Not even birdsong reached them. "It's so quiet," Sin murmured.

"The area around the portal is warded," Captain Sorrel replied, not bothering to look over her shoulder at them. "Nothing can go in or out without approval."

"Wards are typically witch or god magic." Oberon's voice was musing, but Sin felt the tension thrumming in his frame. Wards meant something to him, but she wasn't sure what that was.

"Our former King Consort was a god of much power," the Undine replied. "And he taught some of the fae how to craft wards with our own magic. The skill has been passed on."

Was that Helios? Dana's father, and Oberon's mate's lover?

"Is that why the sky turned dark when Beron arrived?" Sin asked.

A couple of the guards jerked slightly at her question, but Captain Sorrel appeared unaffected. She kept walking, face turned toward the tree line. "It is possible."

They passed through the line of tall trees, coming to a stop once they were clear of the sharp branches. In front of them, a road cut across their path, paved with white stones. On the other side of the roadway stood a large building, made from dark wood. The guardhouse, she realized.

"Wait here." The captain walked brusquely across the uneven road, and into the guardhouse. Inside, people shouted, but she couldn't make out the words. Oberon might have been able to with his superior hearing, thanks to being a shadow shifter, but she didn't want to ask in front of the remaining guards.

Captain Sorrel emerged from the timber structure a few minutes later, then waited next to the road.

Sin had no idea what was going on. Oberon was quiet by her side, so she decided to copy his behavior.

Less than five minutes later, what appeared to be a carriage emerged from behind the guardhouse, turning the corner and coming to a stop next to the captain. There was a driver's seat, but there were no horses tethered to the vehicle. A door was mounted in the middle of the carriage, and there were glass windows on either side.

"I have arranged transportation for you," the captain said, walking around the carriage to come to a stop next to the door.

"Where to?" Oberon asked.

The Undine studied them, as if weighing what to share. "It has been an eon since the Ó hUainín and the Ó Duibh bloodlines showed themselves on Avalon. But the sky does not lie."

Tension radiated from the guards on either side of them.

Captain Sorrel's dark eyes met theirs. "I am sending you directly to the High King. I cannot say how welcome the grandson of the Cursed King will be, or a death fae. But the High King will decide your fate."

She opened the door.

Oberon didn't hesitate—he climbed straight into the carriage, then held out a hand to Sin. She wanted to refuse, just out of principle; she didn't want to appear like she *needed* his help. But she understood this was less about an offer of assistance, and more about showing they were allies. So she took his hand.

Once inside, the Undine shut the door behind Sin.

"So, straight to the king, huh?" Sin asked.

"It appears that way."

They dropped their packs on the floor of the carriage. Oberon stared straight ahead, spinning the strange ring around his finger on his right hand. It flickered in the low light of the carriage, like it had a dozen tiny gemstones hidden in its twists of gold. He caught her looking and shoved his hand into his pocket.

"How long will it take?" Sin asked.

The carriage bobbed as someone climbed aboard the driver's seat.

"I have no idea where the portal is. When...Oberon came through to Tartarus, Avalon only had portals to the god world and the Old Country."

It was strange, hearing Oberon speak of himself as a different person. But she understood why he did. The carriage was probably covered in eavesdropping spells.

"I thought the witch's world only had the portal to Earth."

"That's what I heard, too." Oberon reached out with his free hand and picked up hers. He interlaced their fingers, the touch making her heart feel oddly full.

"Nog is going to be so angry we left him behind," Sin said, trying to distract herself.

"I imagine he will be coming through shortly." Oberon leaned his head back against the seat of the carriage.

"What?"

"You were there when he pulled that stunt with the Tartarus portal. Do you honestly think he's going to stay behind?"

Sin frowned. Oberon had carried her over his shoulder and *spanked* her. As if she would ever forget it. "That reminds me—"

He rubbed his thumb over the back of her hand. "Plan your revenge for my past actions another time."

Fine. She would torture him later. Preferably when he was naked and at her mercy. "Ysabeau is going to be so annoyed."

Oberon's lips moved into a slight smile. "It might actually be good for her."

Jealously was like a sharp and unexpected spike. "What do you mean by that?"

"When you've lived as long as I suspect she has, being annoyed can be an invigorating experience." He lifted Sin's hand, again pressing a kiss to the back of her wrist.

She pretended to gag. "Ysabeau eats boys like Nog for breakfast. Literally." The woman was a vampire, after all. She jutted out her chin. "And I'm not that annoying."

Oberon lowered their joined hands, incredulous. "You drove me insane for *months*."

"Me?" Sin pointed a finger at herself. Then she jabbed it toward him. "*You* were the one constantly getting in my way. It seemed like you *lived* to frustrate me."

His gaze dropped to her mouth, and gods, the feeling it gave her when she knew he was thinking of nothing else but her—nothing else compared. "Good thing I was able to ease some of those...frustrations, then."

Wrestling her libido under control, she tried to think of anything other than the way he tasted, or how wild he became when his control finally snapped. Wait. He hadn't denied the fact that he'd deliberately been irritating her. She'd deal with that another time, she decided. Rather than give into the temptation of kissing the jackass, she turned to the window, watching as the countryside of Avalon sped by.

It seemed the carriage could go faster than even a train.

Her brow furrowed as the scenery registered. She hadn't really had any expectations of Avalon, but derelict structures, shanty towns, and a barren landscape had not been it. It looked more like No Man's Land than the mythical world of the fae. The only thing that appeared undamaged in the landscape was the white road. Everything else was... shattered. Even the few fae she spotted were hunched over, as if trying to hide from the very realm that was meant to shelter them.

She turned to Oberon; his body was coiled with tension as he took in the landscape. "It's been destroyed."

"Maybe they should have kept the Cursed King," Sin whispered, her heart aching for the people they saw, the children she imagined. She'd been to Tartarus—she knew it wasn't a hellscape. It had a thriving society, and Oberon had been one of the men responsible for it becoming that way. "Surely he would have done a better job than this."

"I doubt it." Oberon scowled, self-loathing thick in the air. "He was a selfish, cruel man, who thought he was better than everyone but his mate."

Sin looked at him, then squeezed her fingers around his, calling him back to the present. To them. "But you're not that man."

He shook his head, focused on the windows and the truth they told. "No. That man died a long time ago."

CHAPTER 28
OBERON

The closer they got to their destination, the less devastation they saw.

Oberon twisted the ring on his finger, the skin becoming tender. The crown had heated to an almost unbearable temperature when he'd arrived on Avalon, but it hadn't slid off his finger. In fact, it refused to be removed. He'd had to douse the heat with magic before the crown had cooled—like it had tested him for a second time.

He figured that meant he was still High King.

By the time they neared the silver palace gates—several hours later—the surrounding city was in pristine condition. And it was achingly familiar. It was also blindingly white. All the brick and timber buildings had been literally whitewashed, the stucco gleaming in the light of the twin suns. The palace walls had once been decorated in black, green, and white, but now there was only one color.

Titian had erased their history, along with the other royal bloodlines.

What other legacies had she left?

His head craned back as he tried to take in as much of the palace as he could. It hadn't changed much in the supposed two thousand years he'd been gone, but he felt as if he were seeing it anew.

The striking architecture remained, its delicate spires rising like crystalline flowers into the sky, their graceful arcs seeming to defy gravity. The stone walls shimmered as if carved from opal in the light of the setting suns, Grian and Suil. Tendrils of silvery ivy wound around the spires, as if woven by the moonlit hands of Queen Méabh herself, and white blossoms decorated their lengths.

This was the capital of Avalon, Annwn, and where he'd been crowned High King.

The people here were well dressed—the tattered rags of the fae they'd passed were gone. Here, people walked with their heads held high, their clothing clean and intact, and the streets free of trash and waste. And unsurprisingly, most of the fae belonged to the Courts. He didn't see a single Wild Fae.

They'd never really been part of the Court system and had lived largely separate, like the death dealers. But he'd now seen two Wild Fae in the military, which meant that they were being forced into service. He couldn't see how a Trow and an Undine would serve the High King, otherwise.

The carriage slowed as it drew even with the palace gates.

Oberon smoothed his hand over Sin's dark hair, and she woke with a start. She'd been sleeping, her head pillowed on his shoulder, for the past hour or so. Having her tucked against him, trusting him with her safety, had been a humbling moment.

The carriage rolled to a stop.

"We're here," he said quietly.

Sin stared out the window, silent as she took in the beauty of Annwn. "It looks like something from a fairytale."

"Funny, that."

A palace guard, wearing an elaborate uniform with zero functionality, appeared at the window, blocking the view. Sin started in surprise, then returned his curious stare.

The guard's expression turned panicked. "One of them is a death fae!"

"How can they tell just by looking at me?" Sin grumbled.

Oberon chose his words carefully. "There's a...vibe...death fae have that other fae don't."

She gave him an unamused look.

The driver got down from the carriage to argue with the overdressed guard. Oberon recognized the female from the portal. It wasn't Captain Sorrel, but seeing the crowd of fae, he doubted she would have felt safe —or welcome—coming into the city.

"Should we get out?" Sin asked, watching as the guards began shouting at one another.

"No. I don't think we could, even if we wanted to." Oberon tapped the door handle closest to him.

"Magically sealed?"

"It's what I'd do."

She settled back against the seat. "Then I guess we wait."

It took three hours for them to be ushered into the palace.

They were taken in through a side door—one of dozens—and then marched down a series of endless hallways, before being shown into a meeting room. Despite the palace having once been his home, it was like walking through a maze. He wouldn't be able to find the exit quickly, even if he tried.

Then again, the entire building had been designed to confuse and distract would-be invaders.

The room's walls were bare, with a single metal desk sitting at the far end of the room. Chairs were pushed up against the windowless plaster walls, and there was no rug on the stone floor. It looked less like an office and more like a precursor to a prison cell, but then, he wasn't being asked his opinion.

Oberon and Sin were left in the middle of the room while their guide vanished outside, no doubt to summon someone with a bit more authority.

The door had barely closed behind them when it reopened, and three guards marched into the room. They were dressed in leather armor, which had been dyed or painted white, and carried spears. The crest of the Geals was embossed into the breastplate. It confirmed that the High King was a relative—perhaps even a child—of Titian's. He had no idea if she'd been able to birth young after being...revived.

Behind the guards, the High King strode into the room, Titian's silver crown nestled amongst golden curls. Tension spiked in the pit of Oberon's stomach at the sight. The male could have been Titian's twin, he looked so similar; from the sea-green eyes to the golden hair, to the impossible perfection of his face, he was the male version of her. And he wore her arrogance like a shroud. Flanked by two more guards, he came to a stop six feet from Sin and Oberon.

The strain in the air was palpable, as he studied them both, eyes narrowing in a mix of curiosity and suspicion. The king inhaled deeply, his nostrils flaring in response to their scent. The fae's gaze lingered on Sin, his expression shifting, arrogance melting into disbelief as his eyes widened in astonishment. The air of superiority was replaced by a burgeoning uncertainty.

In contrast, Sin's frame tensed beside Oberon, her expression growing shuttered. Where the fae king leaned toward Sin, as if pulled by a lodestone, her hands closed into tight, bloodless fists, her jaw clenching. The temperature in the room plummeted and frost crystals spread over the floor from her feet, expanding outward in a fractal pattern. Oberon's breath misted in the air with each exhalation. She was shaking her head, her dark hair undulating with the motion.

The High King took a step closer, his focus intent on Sin, who turned pale blue eyes toward Oberon, uncertainty—and fear—glimmering in their depths. She was...scared. Worried. But then she turned back to the king, as if her attention was drawn there against her will.

Realization dawned, and a chill raced down his spine.

No. Not Sin. Not now.

His panther roared a denial in his mind, clawing at the restraint Oberon held around it.

"You—" The High King's voice was wondering as he took another step closer to Sin, closing the distance between them.

The death fae stood her ground, tilting her chin up at his approach. Her expression hardened as she met the High King's gaze, her jaw set in the stubborn line Oberon had come to adore. But the temperature in the room remained frigid, her posture speaking of death and destruction.

"No." Sin's voice rang loudly in the silent room.

But the fae kept talking, as if mesmerized by her. "You're my—"

Her voice was a harsh croak. "Don't say it."

"—mate."

Oberon's heart plummeted as the High King's words tore through his mind, the words stabbing into his soul and cutting him to the bone, where he'd thought there could be no further wounds. He was paralyzed, his panther pacing furiously in his mind, wanting to leap out, to rip the High King's head from his shoulders for daring to look at Sin, let alone suggest she was his *mate*. It was all he could do to cage his shadow shifter half; if he lost control, even for a second, he'd shift.

And he'd kill the king.

Seconds later, he would claim Sin with the fury of an alpha denied what it considered his.

Keeping his panther at bay took every ounce of control that he'd developed over his long life. Worse, the part of him that bled from a soul wound he hadn't expected, didn't want to.

The fae king knelt before Sin, looking up at her with eyes filled with the adoration of new matehood.

Ice crystals snaked up the king's knee where it touched the stone ground, spreading to his thigh.

Sin's voice was the cold of deep, endless space. "Stand up."

The High King paused, stunned. "...Pardon?"

The temperature began to rise in the room, the frost crystals shattering on the fae male's clothing. Oberon didn't know if it was Sin gaining control or the king countering the magic. "I said, stand up."

Puzzled, the male stood. "Maybe you do not realize who I am, and what an honor it would be to be my mate."

Gods, did the fool actually think that line would impress a woman like Sin?

"My name is Aodhán Titus Helion Geal. I am the High King of Avalon." He bowed shallowly, a flowery, courtly movement.

Sin didn't reply, but she unclenched her fists.

Sea-green eyes searched Sin's face, as if attempting to memorize her features. "And your name is?" he asked her.

"You expect me to believe you weren't told who we were the minute our papers were checked at the portal?" Sin's voice held a cruel edge.

She hadn't accepted him.

At least, not yet.

His panther conceded the battle between them, settling back to watch the exchange. Oberon inhaled slowly, surprised at the sudden acquiescence.

The panther's voice was a low rasp in his mind. *She does not want him.*

No, it appeared she did not.

But then, Reagan hadn't wanted Caius at first, either.

The panther flicked its tail, and Oberon realized he wasn't helping his situation.

"They said you were called Sinéad Santiago." Aodhán's voice was smooth as silk, seemingly unperturbed by her standoffishness. "And that when you stepped through the portal, the sky was bathed in green light."

"The phenomenon didn't reach this far, then?" Oberon asked, voice mild. He thought it would have covered the entire planet.

The king shot him a withering look, before turning back to Sin. But a heartbeat later, his gaze slammed into Oberon's. Aodhán cursed as he looked Oberon up and down, from his black hellbeast leather jacket to his worn jeans, shitkicker boots, and black T-shirt. "The resemblance is uncanny."

"Resemblance?" His voice was a drawl.

"To the Cursed King. The Ó Duibh bloodline must have once been strong."

There were several veiled insults in that sentence, but Oberon decided to ignore them all.

"You knew Oberon?" Sin asked, her voice neutral.

Aodhán's brows drew together. "No, I was not born then. But Great-Aunt Titian kept a single portrait of his likeness. She always worried he might find a way to return from Tartarus and attempt to usurp the throne again. Even though that hell world has been locked down for millennia." The fae laughed at the absurdity of the idea.

"Tartarus is no longer locked," Oberon murmured.

"I gathered as much, for the Cursed King's spawn to be here." Venom coated each word. "You are not welcome, Beron Black. Go back to your hellhole."

Oberon rubbed the back of his neck, as if abashed. "I'm afraid that isn't possible. Not if you want my companion to remain."

Aodhán clearly wasn't used to being told no. Nor did he like Oberon referring to Sin as his, even if the word he'd used was "companion" and not "lover."

"And why is that?"

"We are magically bound together," Sin explained. "We can only be twenty feet apart before we suffer instant, horrifying pain."

The fae king's expression grew shuttered. "How...unfortunate. For you both."

"It is a...unique predicament," Sin replied.

"There are several experts here who can review this binding spell. We will have it removed as soon as possible. In the meantime, you are both my guests." Aodhán turned to the guards. His lip curled. "Find rooms that enable them to remain within the twenty feet, but that are *separate*. I do not want my mate to be sullied by Ó Duibh blood any more than she already has been."

Then he stepped closer to Sin, morphing from irritated king to fawning mate. "I cannot wait for us to get to know each other better, Sinéad." He spoke her name as if it was a caress.

Bile burned the back of Oberon's throat.

Aodhán picked up Sin's hand, which remained limp. "Until next time." The fae pressed a chaste kiss to her skin, then lowered her arm gently, as if she were formed from blown glass, and not the iron of a planet's core.

The High King swept from the room.

Sin stared at the door, then exhaled slowly. "*Qué pendejo.*"

He didn't know what that meant, but he had a feeling Sin had just insulted Avalon's High King rather soundly. And he fell a little bit more in love with her for it.

We're so screwed.

CHAPTER 29
SIN

Sin gingerly sat on the edge of the fairytale bed, wearing nothing but a warm, fluffy towel, in the room she'd been assigned. She'd desperately tried to wash away the emotions of the last hour, but the reality of her situation clung to her reddened skin.

She'd found her mate.

The man fated to be hers for the rest of her life.

And she didn't want him.

Oh, he was impossibly handsome, and rich, and a damned *king*—but his beauty was nothing but a veneer, and she didn't care about money or power. Arrogance and pride were deeply ingrained in his personality, and he'd ordered her and Oberon around like they were nothing more than chattel.

And how he'd talked about Oberon...

He has been lied to his whole life, the reasonable part of her argued. *He wouldn't know that Oberon was actually the one betrayed.* If Titian had survived Oberon's attack, then she had clearly done her damned best to erase him from the history books—and where she couldn't, she'd lied about him.

Which really was rather remarkable, considering fae couldn't lie.

Or had it been Helios doing the lying?

But Sin couldn't forgive the contempt she'd seen when Aodhán had looked at Oberon. He thought the shadow shifter was nothing more than a usurper.

Oberon was many things, but he wasn't interested in stealing a throne that wasn't his. He'd guarded Caius's back for five thousand years. And he'd been furious to learn of the betrayal that had almost cost Sin's sister her life.

No, he wouldn't have wanted Titian's throne.

He just wanted his own back.

She needed to reject Aodhán, sooner rather than later.

Sin didn't want to lead him on, and she didn't want to have him view Oberon as an obstacle to their future happiness. Because there would be no mated bliss. Not for them.

She would not be tied to a probable narcissist, or a tyrant. And the countryside she'd witnessed on their way into Annwn—no. She was not going to spend the remainder of her life battling to be heard, to be listened to. And she wasn't about to risk her sanity if something were to happen to him.

She climbed from the bed and went over to her pack. She grabbed her mother's locket and opened it, releasing the spell. Dianthe's form slowly coalesced in front of her.

"You actually did it. It feels...different here." Dianthe was staring around her, mouth parted.

She nodded. "I did."

"They don't like death fae on Avalon."

"You could have warned me," Sin muttered.

"I told you not to come here!"

It was true, she had. She'd just never bothered to tell Sin *why*.

"Mother, I just want to prepare you for some...news," Sin began. She suspected her room had enough listening spells to recount her every word for the next decade, but she needed to have this discussion. And she counted on the fact that they would not be good enough to detect her mother's words, considering death fae seemed to no longer be present on Avalon.

Dianthe whirled around to face her. Then she did a double take and pointed an accusatory finger at Sin's neck. "You let that fae claim you!"

"What? No." She glanced down, spotting the fading bruise Oberon had given her.

"Then what?"

"I met my mate today." Each word reverberated in the room with the force of a gunshot. Her mother flinched at the word "mate."

Dianthe wrung transparent hands together. "Have you rejected him?"

"Not yet."

"But you will?"

"I will." She nodded. "Can you do me a favor? Look around the palace?"

"You're in a palace?" Her mother's eyes widened in surprise.

Sin nodded and decided that she wasn't going to announce just *who* her mate was. Not right now.

"I will go now." Her mother zoomed away, passing through the door as if it were nothing more than air.

Sin put the locket away in her pack and then brushed her damp hair over her shoulder. The guard who had delivered her to the door had been extremely apologetic at the quality of her room—which was far more opulent than the bedroom she'd had at home.

Hell, it was fancier than any room she'd ever been in.

The walls were adorned with intricately patterned silver and white wallpaper, which had a raised texture that felt like velvet when stroked. Golden sconces cast a warm, flickering light over the room, and a plush canopy bed took up the middle portion of the space. Its posts were carved with beautiful floral details, and it had been painted white. Fine linens decorated the bed, embroidered with the shield of arms that were on the soldiers' breastplates. A door opposite the bed led to a bathroom that was small but beautifully finished, with golden fittings, white tiles, and a bath that also had a showerhead. Every corner of the room spoke of more wealth and luxury than Sin had seen in her entire lifetime.

Oberon lived in this place.

Not only lived, he'd once been king of it all.

If this was a poor-quality room, she'd hate to see what the rest of the palace looked like.

A tapping sound reached her, causing her to frown. It was coming from the window.

She walked to the lavish velvet curtains and pulled them open. Oberon stood on the other side of the glass, waiting on the small balcony that adorned her room. Hurriedly, she opened the window, and he climbed through, one long leg at a time.

"What are you doing here?" she whispered.

Oberon closed the window and flicked a hand. The room suddenly felt...quiet. Like he'd done another anti-listening spell. "How—?"

He put a finger to her lips. "I'll explain another time." His voice was quiet, his breath fanning her face.

His hair was also damp, the brown still strange to see. "You washed."

"I did. So did you." His gaze dropped to her body, which was covered in just the towel. Heat settled low in her belly in response. Gods, how she still wanted him.

Did that mean she was fundamentally broken? She wondered. She had a mate, and here she was, lusting over the oversized fae who'd been nothing more than an annoying ass since the moment she'd met him. But she didn't care; she didn't want Aodhán.

She wanted Oberon.

"Sin, you shouldn't look at me like that." But he reached out, touching the bruise he'd left on her neck. He ran a gentle thumb over the mark, and she shivered in response, her skin craving more of his touch.

"Like what?"

His voice was low, rough. "Like you're picturing me naked."

"What's wrong with that?" she asked.

"Sin—"

"Why do you always say my name like it's a curse?" She bit her lip as his hand curved around her shoulder. His fingers swept along the edge of her towel, stroking over the swells of her breasts.

"Maybe it's more of a benediction than a curse," he murmured, eyes locked on her lips.

Sin leaned forward, going to her tiptoes. Gods, how she wanted to kiss him. To feel him pressed against her. To know he needed her as much as she needed him. But his hand gently pushed her back, his hands sliding away from her.

Shock and hurt washed through her at the rejection. Did he not want her anymore? Had he gotten her out of his system now that they'd had sex?

I don't think I'll ever stop wanting him.

The realization made her heart stutter.

"Don't look at me like that, Sin." His voice was rough, a growl coating his words.

"I don't know what you mean." She didn't know how she managed to form the words around the sudden lump in her throat.

"Like I don't want you anymore."

"Don't you?" She barely recognized the bitter sound of her voice.

"Are you out of your mind?" He crowded her, until her back was pressed against the wall. But he didn't touch her. "I want to strip you naked and feast on you until you scream my name as you come apart on my tongue. And that's only the beginning." His nostrils flared as he scented her growing need. "I want to bury myself so deep in you that I don't know where I end and you begin. I want you to think of me—and only me—when you come apart in my arms."

Her core grew unbearably damp, her thighs clenching at his words.

"But I can't do that, because you have a mate." The words sounded torn from him, and he stepped away.

She almost wept at the loss of his touch, of his warmth.

Of him.

"I don't—" He covered her mouth with his hand.

"My panther wants nothing more than to pin you to the wall and take you here and now. But discovering you have a mate has made it territorial. Do you understand?"

She shook her head, her mouth moving against his hand. Unable to stop herself, she swept out her tongue, tasting him. He hissed in response, his eyes flickering orange, then returning to their black hue.

"He will claim you."

Her eyes widened, shock sizzling through her. To be claimed by an alpha shifter would be akin to mating one. She would be Oberon's. And even though she wasn't a shifter herself, if that happened, she would claim him back. Because halfway wouldn't do. Sin wouldn't be able to live with it, if he didn't realize she was as much his, as he was hers. It wouldn't be a mating bond, so she could survive if he died...but it would be a tie stronger than marriage.

She'd never wanted that before.

"You said it would be my choice." Her voice was quiet, muffled by his palm.

His fingers tightened on her mouth. "I did."

She pushed his hand away. "Then why can't we—"

"Because I won't stop it! Do you understand me? I won't fucking stop it." The words sounded torn from the depths of his soul. "I want you, Sin. I'm not going to pretend I don't. I'm not that good of a man, to go pushing you into your fated mate's arms. Not if I get to taste you again." He was utterly focused on her. "So, this is your last warning. Because my panther and I *will* claim you, and then the asshole boy king will want both our heads on a platter."

Her mouth flattened. "I already told you what I want when it comes to a mate."

"Then do what needs to be done. Because there is no 'us' while he's still in the picture." His body radiated tension.

"That's where you're wrong," Sin said, voice low. "There already is an 'us,' even if we didn't want it. At least, not originally."

His jaw clenched. "You have a mate, Sin. Don't fuck it up like I did."

She met his stare, feeling more certain than ever in her choice.

"I won't."

CHAPTER 30
OBERON

The next morning saw Oberon and Sin in the dining hall early. Clearly the High King hadn't wanted Sin out of his sight for any length of time, considering he'd given them a bare five hours of sleep.

Oberon hadn't wanted to leave her the night before, but he wasn't able to stay. Because if he had, he would have given in to the rich, heady scent of her, and claimed her in every way a shifter could.

And she would hate him for it.

He didn't know what choice Sin was going to make now that she was faced with reality. Whether she would accept the pompous ass or reject him. But Oberon had told her where he stood. What he wanted.

If someone had suggested to him even a week ago that he'd be desperate to claim Sin Santiago—of all the people available on Tartarus or Earth—he'd have questioned their grip on sanity. Funny how things can change so quickly.

"I would kill for some huevos rancheros," Sin said as she stared down at the plate of food in front of her.

The dining hall was as opulent as the rest of the palace—with a table large enough to seat thirty people comfortably. This was the "informal dining room," they'd been told by the guards. He could only imagine what the formal room would look like. The table was bedecked with a silk tablecloth, and golden cutlery that had been laid next to their plates, which were made from rare pink porcelain clays that came from the southern continent on Avalon.

A buffet had been spread across one third of the table—large enough to feed a dozen people, rather than just the three of them. Oberon looked at the selection of fruits and the Avalon equivalent of yoghurt Sin had placed on her plate. She had ignored the intricate swirls of pastry, cakes, and other treats that had been positioned in front of her.

It seemed that the fae enjoyed a sweet breakfast. He couldn't even remember what he'd eaten before he'd been exiled. Funny how memory worked—some things were clear as day, while others were lost to the mists of time.

The poverty they'd witnessed yesterday sat hollowly in his chest. He might've been a self-centered asshole when he'd lived on Avalon before, but he couldn't remember ever seeing places like that. Surely, he would've known if conditions were that bad. But it made him realize that this new High King was no better than Titian: living here, in this kind of opulence, while people literally starved on the street. It showed what the High King and the Courts thought of the people.

It didn't sit well with him.

Caius would have never allowed it to happen. Not on Tartarus.

And Oberon wouldn't have allowed it, either.

But here the High King was, enjoying a breakfast fit for a dozen people, and where no doubt the leftovers would be thrown away as scraps.

"No sweet tooth?" Oberon asked Sin.

They were seated near each other, but with at least three feet separating their chairs. He had the feeling that Aodhán would've preferred him to be far, far away, but Sin had chosen where to sit this morning. The High King sat at the head of the table, delicately nibbling on a flaky pastry that somehow didn't crumble all over him.

Aodhán was wearing what Oberon interpreted to be casual clothes; however, they were still ridiculously ornate for a simple breakfast. A silver tunic embroidered with white thread, white dress pants, and a white shirt underneath.

"I'm more of a savory person. I love spice. Food needs flavor." But she dug into her fruit, which looked to be perfectly ripe.

"I've had your sister's tamales. They were delicious."

Sin put her fork down slowly. "You had her tamales? Reagan made tamales, and I didn't get an invite?"

"Reagan and Clara made them. I just had leftovers." Oberon quickly took a mouthful of coffee—the human beverage had apparently made its way to Avalon.

Sin narrowed her eyes but ate another mouthful of food.

"What are these tamales?" Aodhán asked, voice smoothly interjecting. "I can have my chef make it for you."

"It's a traditional dish where I'm from. I doubt that the ingredients for it are here. But I appreciate the offer."

"You could teach us." The High King's smile was charm personified.

Sin scrunched her nose. "I have been banned from the kitchen at home. I'm afraid I'd be of no use."

"Banned? Someone dared ban my mate from anywhere?" Aodhán's expression morphed into outrage.

Oberon absorbed the interaction, noting Sin's body language, her disinterest in the other fae's offer.

Sin shook her head. "I can't cook at all. And my sister is an excellent cook. So, I don't get in her way."

"You have a sister?" Oberon could see the wheels turning in the High King's mind. If there was one Ó hUainín on Earth, could there be more...

Sin shoved the pink fruit around in her bowl, coating it in yoghurt. "Yes."

"Is she a Celestial, too?"

Her hand paused its movement. "I didn't tell you I was one."

The blond king tilted his head in acknowledgement. "I think the aurorae gave that away."

She accepted that, even though Oberon wondered how much more information the king knew about them. "I see. And no, she's not. She's not fae."

No doubt Aodhán's spies on Earth were trying to dig up any and all of her family's secrets. He wondered how they'd react when they learned the sister she spoke of was the new Queen of Tartarus.

The king blinked, then tilted his head to the side. "I don't understand."

"I was adopted as an infant." Her words were clipped.

"Then she is not really your sister. Are you not full-blooded?"

"What?" Sin lowered her cutlery to the sides of her plate, her movements clipped. A hissed intake of breath from the servers alerted them to the faux pas she had just committed, but she ignored them.

"Full-blooded fae cannot lie, so how did you—"

"I am not lying." The air grew distinctly chilly, but no frost formed. She was pissed, but not enraged. "I don't need to share a blood tie to someone to know they're family."

Her opinion of those who only viewed a biological family as family was clear.

Aodhán waved a hand dismissively through the air. "Bloodlines are vital to the survival of our species. It seems the Earthen fae have lost their way. But it does explain why a Celestial has emerged in a death fae line."

"Why are death fae unofficially banned from returning to Avalon?" Sin asked, ignoring his thinly veiled insults.

The king's eyes flashed, and Oberon had the distinct feeling the other male had not appreciated Sin's directness. "There are death dealers still on Avalon, but they are strictly in service to the High King's Court."

That did not answer Sin's question.

Aodhán dabbed the corners of his mouth with a napkin and stood. "I thought we could take a tour of the palace today."

Sin glanced at Oberon. "We have to remain within twenty feet of each other."

"Have you tested it? This binding spell?" Aodhán straightened his sleeves, pretending the question was only of mild interest. But his eyes were intense as they locked on Sin.

"Yes. The worst headache of my life. I thought I was going to die from the pain." Sin's body language was less than welcoming. It soothed the raw edges within Oberon, and made the panther sit up and pay attention to the exchange.

"A tour it is, then. I can probably show Beron how my family has improved the palace since the time his grandsire was here." Mocking green eyes met Oberon's.

"It's been over a thousand years," Oberon replied mildly. "I'm sure there has been quite a bit of change. Whether or not it's for the better remains to be seen."

Aodhán ignored him.

Which was probably for the best.

The High King offered Sin the crook of his elbow when she stood. She paused, and he could almost see the internal war raging within. But eventually, she relented and slid her arm through his. They looked comical—the High King in his finery, and Sin, who was dressed in a pair of jeans and a shirt, with well-worn boots. Oberon had overheard her arguing with the maid that had been sent to her this morning, who'd tried insisting that she dress in something more appropriate.

Aodhán finally seemed to notice the death fae's attire. "Were the clothes not to your liking?"

"No, I prefer to wear my own clothes, but thank you." Sin's voice was polite, but dangerously neutral.

"You are the High King's mate. Your clothing is important."

"I haven't agreed to the mating bond."

The fae's shoulders tensed, but his stride remained unhurried as he began walking. "We must get to know each other first, that is natural."

They walked out of the dining area and into a long hallway. Glancing behind her, Sin watched as the servants cleared the table and took the food away. Oberon followed at a distance, guards falling into step on either side of him and behind.

They were armed to the teeth, and he suspected most of them were fire fae—one of the more offensive fae races. Not that it would matter. If Oberon really wanted to murder the High King, he wouldn't even have to lift a finger.

He was still the High King, even if the fool monarch in front of him didn't realize it. The power of Avalon and its suns and moons sang in his blood, their magic waiting, ready to be used. He was more powerful than he'd ever been, even back when he'd been crowned. He just hadn't had a chance to test his strength yet. But if it came to a showdown between him and Aodhán, he knew he would win.

Oberon walked behind Sin and the king, fingers itching to rip Sin away from the other male. But he restrained himself—barely. He had to give Sin the chance to make a choice, before he gave up waiting and made it for them both.

So instead, he became an inconvenient shadow. The palace had changed in the time that he had been gone. Wings had been added, and rooms had been moved around. Walls were knocked down. He would have trouble navigating it again; he could easily get lost in the altered labyrinth.

It had been a wise decision to keep the binding spell in place, even if it meant keeping Sin on a magical leash.

The biggest change to the palace, as far as he was concerned, was not the structure or the architectural renovations. No, it was the sheer blandness of the palace. Where there had once been a riotous décor of green and black and white, now there was only white.

And not only that, but the people seemed...bland, as well. Ghosts of themselves, uncomfortable with life in a place of power and wealth. The servants and soldiers they passed—even the courtiers—would not look them in in the eye. Hell, they wouldn't even risk glancing at Sin on the arm of their monarch.

They came to a stop in the middle of the great hall where he had once been crowned. This place hadn't changed much; the tall columns still soared to a high ceiling, and the dais that had once been made of the rare multicolored marble remained, although it had been painted.

"This is where all the High Kings and Queens are crowned."

"And is it true that only Celestials can become a High King or Queen?" Sin asked.

"Yes. You would of course be my consort."

Sin stilled. "But I am a Celestial."

The fae male gave her a pitying smile. "There is only one crown. And I already wear it." He patted her arm as it rested in his. "You are part-death fae. You would likely fail the test, anyway."

What. An. Ass.

"I see." Her voice was cool as she took in the hall. "It is rather fortunate for you I won't have an opportunity to try, then, isn't it?"

The High King chuckled, like she'd told a witty joke.

Sin probably had more power than Aodhán in her little finger. Yet the conceited bastard thought she was weak.

"I was always told there were two crowns," Oberon murmured, coming to stand next to them.

Aodhán flicked him a glance. "There is only one High Crown, and I'm wearing it."

"Interesting. So was Helios just a consort, then, to Titian?" Oberon shoved his hands in his pockets.

The fae male stared at him. "He is a god. He was never just a consort."

Is.

Aodhán said that Titian's former lover *is* a god.

So, he was still alive.

Was this High King nothing more than a puppet, then?

CHAPTER 31
OBERON

They had spent the entire day wandering through the palace. Oberon kept expecting nostalgia to hit, but instead, he was left with a sense of purpose. The city was considered the crown jewel of the fae world, but in reality, it was nothing more than a tawdry façade. The beauty, the art—they were watered-down versions of what the fae had once been.

Aodhán had taken Sin to an audience session, where she and Oberon watched as the High King arbitrated petty disputes between Courts, and where he listened to the few subjects who'd been approved to seek his guidance.

It had been...pathetic.

And clearly all for show.

Not one of the cases had mentioned the poverty they'd seen, or the ruined farms and estates. No, it had been wealthy merchants asking for permission to enter new markets, or courtiers wanting to purchase additional lands for their estates.

Then they'd been dragged to a formal dinner, before which the High King had generously allowed them to freshen up. Sin had been sent another dress, but she had also refused it.

"Why don't we visit the lookout? The view there is stunning. Especially at night." Aodhán headed for another hallway that branched off the dining space.

"The lookout?" Sin asked.

Another considering glance. "Yes, it offers a fantastic view of Annwn and the surrounding area. It will help you familiarize yourself with your future territory."

The young idiot was convinced Sin would accept the bond. That she'd be a fool not to. And in most instances, he'd be correct. Mating the ruler of an entire planet? That would be a dream come true for many people.

But Sin wasn't most people.

She cared about her family, her home, and her friends. She helped those who needed it; she'd saved countless children's lives, according to Clara and Reagan. Being a ruler would be a job for Sin, an arduous one with little thanks.

One that she'd also be stuck with if she accepted his claim.

He frowned, the thought striking home, its barbs painful.

By the time they made it to the lookout, Grian had set, leaving Suil low in the darkening sky. They emerged onto the top of a spire on the western wing of the palace. The white marble glowed in the dim light, illuminating the space and the guards around them in a warm, silvery glow. There was still enough brightness from Suil to see the sprawl of Annwn and the surrounding fields that spread to the horizon. Street and house lights glowed golden, creating an interesting pattern on the landscape below.

You would never know poverty lay just beyond the edge of sight.

"It is lovely," Sin said, her voice low. But it wasn't Aodhán she turned to as she spoke, it was Oberon.

The High King shot Oberon a glare that burned, but he ignored it. Sin stepped away from the other fae male, taking a step closer to Oberon, and to the balcony railing that lined the edge of the platform.

The feeling of being watched had Oberon turning to face the spire.

Shock locked him in place.

A man emerged from the shadowed doorway onto the platform, his warm brown hair complimenting his bronze skin. Close to seven feet tall, he looked the same as he had in Oberon's memories. Except this time, rather than leather clothing, he wore traditional Avalon garb, but all in white. Next to him, a woman stood, her proud shoulders slightly hunched, and her once-glossy golden hair lacking the luster and health of youth. She was still beautiful, with sea-green eyes the same as the current High King's, but her beauty was tainted, as if the rotten core within had begun to contaminate her exterior.

How had Titian lived all these years?

Oberon's survival had been a mixture of shadow shifter magic and proximity to a former primordial god. At least, that's what Caius and he could determine. But Titian?

Helios was no primordial deity, not even close. And fae did not live over two thousand years.

Especially if they'd been murdered previously.

"I didn't believe the rumors," Titian sneered, stepping into the light.

Sin hissed a breath at the sight of the former High Queen. "You're a walking corpse."

Between one breath and the next, the guards lining the platform burst into flames, their screams clawing at Oberon's mind as they died. It happened so fast, he barely had time to react. He extinguished the flames, but Helios—or Aodhán—had incinerated them. Bodies dropped to the platform around them; smoking, charred remnants of the people they once were. The stench was...unpleasant.

Sin's gaze met his, and he saw the pain in her eyes, the sense of loss. But when she turned to face Aodhán and Oberon's enemies, she was nothing but pure meteoric steel.

Titian's voice was low and cruel. "You talk of treason, death dealer."

"It's treason to speak the truth?" Sin asked, shoulders back, chin up. She challenged Oberon's former mate with no hesitation.

"You don't know of what you speak." Helios's voice boomed over the platform.

"No? You think I can't recognize when a soul has been tied to a dead husk?" Sin's voice was resolute.

"Sinéad, please." Aodhán stepped between them. "This is the former High Queen, Titian, and the God-King, Helios. They were great rulers, and Titian is my great-aunt."

God-King? So, that's how they got around the loophole of not having the second crown. And then lied, telling everyone there'd only ever been one.

How much of Avalon's history had the two rewritten?

No wonder there were so many fae on Earth. They'd been fleeing tyrants.

Sin's mouth flattened. "I can now see why death fae are banished or bound to your service. You don't want the truth getting out."

Titian turned to Sin. "There was no other Celestial who could rule when I died, killed by my traitorous mate. So, my love, Helios, had me restored to life. But for over fifteen hundred years, no Geal was born who would be strong enough to take the throne. Then, when Aodhán came of age, the crown finally left my head, and I could pass the mantle on to someone else."

So that was the story she spun.

Funny, how the crown hadn't stayed fused to her skull like it had his while he'd been on Avalon. Now, he couldn't get it off his damned finger. Remembering back to the night he'd been exiled, she hadn't worn it then, either. It was like the crown had known she was weak, barely worthy of it. The crown had likely refused to be worn again when another candidate had been born. He wondered how many Ó Duibh and Ó hUainín had died while she waited for the right Geal.

He'd known he would be portrayed as a traitor, of course, but it was different to hear it. He waited for the hurt, the rage, to arrive. But it didn't. He felt...nothing. The betrayal meant little to him, aside from the opportunity to right a wrong from the past.

Titian stepped closer, her gaze glued to Oberon. "It is uncanny. How much you look like him. But it is clear you are not him. Oberon at least had...class. You are just brawn."

Oberon gave a mocking bow, and something almost like recognition, followed by regret, flickered over her features.

Strange, how you could be bonded to someone and they never truly knew who you were. Not that Oberon was the same man as he'd been when he'd arrived in Tartarus. Time changes all people.

"But now we have the opportunity to merge two bloodlines—the Ó hUainín, which we thought lost long ago—and the Geal. Your children will be powerful. Although we have to hope your death dealer power does not taint the children." Titian smiled, magnanimous.

Sin stared.

Then she turned to Aodhán. "Being a death fae is not a taint."

"Of course, you believe that," Aodhán said, his voice meant to be soothing, but it instead came across as condescending.

"Tell me," Sin looked at Titian, "are the death fae in your service the only things keeping your body from rotting away? The only people tying your soul to flesh that should have been destroyed millennia ago?"

Titian's hand shot out. She went to slap Sin across the cheek, but the death fae raised her arm, blocking the strike. "Your insubordination will not be tolerated."

Wrath made his vision haze red, and Oberon began drawing power. It filled him, faster than he could blink.

Sin merely shook her head, lowering her arm, her lip curled in revulsion at Titian's touch. She then met the current High King's eyes. Her mate had stood by and watched his aunt attack her. He had *allowed* his family to do it. It showed her that even though she might be his mate, he did not place her above all others.

Oberon would raze the world before he let someone harm his love. As it was, he wanted to destroy Titian anew—not for her misdeeds against him, but for daring to raise a hand to Sin. And he would.

Soon.

Her voice strong, Sin spoke, "Aodhán Titus Helion Geal, I reject you."

The blond monarch reeled, clutching his chest as if wounded to his core. Titian's gaze locked on her nephew, something almost like concern welling there.

Helios laughed. "Petty, spiteful woman. You will learn your place."

Then the god moved his hands in a circular pattern and hurled the power of the sun at her and Oberon, heat blasting toward them with the strength of a dying star.

"No!" Sin screamed, throwing herself toward Oberon, her hands outstretched, as if she could reach him, protect him.

Oberon's heart stuttered to a stop.

No!

He threw his iron dagger at the god with a flick of the wrist, while he shoved his other hand out, desperate to save Sin, but surprise made him falter. For a moment, the form of a woman in a stained hospital gown flickered into existence, her silvery hair blowing in an unknown breeze, her features reminiscent of Sin. She grew solid as she stood between her daughter and the god, then with a panicked expression, she shoved Sin away, throwing her to the ground and standing in the path of the blaze of pure power.

Love for her daughter was etched into her face as her form vanished in the surge of magic, with Oberon taking the brunt of the explosion. For a brief moment, he met Sin's gaze as he flew back over the railing, the force of the power propelling him into the sky.

Forgive me, he mouthed to her.

Then there was nothing but endless heat and the darkness of night.

CHAPTER 32
SIN

"Oberon!" Sin's scream tore from her throat as he flew backward over the balcony, surrounded by flames. She reached out a clawed hand, trying to throw magic at him, calling on the deep cold of space, but she was shoved back to the ground and pinned down.

Helios.

He was using his magic to hold her in place. Desperately, she tried to look around for her mother, for Oberon, but they were gone.

Mamá!

Oberon!

Pain racked her mind, her entire body, as the binding spell kicked in. Every fiber of her being screamed in protest, attempting to rebel, to fight, but her efforts were futile—her world became a narrow tunnel of relentless torment, where she couldn't think, she could only feel.

And then, as quickly as it started, it stopped.

Sin lay panting on the cold stone floor of the lookout, her face blazing hot, her body screaming with phantom agony. But her heart, her heart ached like she was bleeding to death from a wound that wouldn't heal. Couldn't heal.

Her mind replayed the last few moments; where her mother had become corporeal for a heartbeat of time; where Sin had felt Dianthe's hands on her skin for the first time in memory. Love, a mother's pure love, had kissed Sin as her mamá had shoved her away from Helios's magic, taking the brunt of a god's power.

And then Oberon had been hit with the leftover force of a dying sun.

He'd mouthed something before he'd gone over the edge of the balcony. She thought it might have been "forgive me," but that made no sense.

And no, she wouldn't be able to forgive him.

He was gone.

The binding spell had broken, ending the torture caused by the magic, but not her newly opened heart wound. He'd been engulfed by flames he hadn't extinguished; that he presumably *couldn't* extinguish. Which meant he'd died.

He'd left her.

A broken sob caught in her throat. She'd lost them both. Her mother and her lover. The damned asshole had dragged her here to win his throne back, and he'd left her here with a mate she didn't want and two psychopaths who thought that murdering innocent bystanders was an acceptable pastime. She'd only come to this godsforsaken world to help him.

Because she'd wanted more time with him.

You're a fool.

She'd never told him how she really felt. What she really wanted. And now, he was gone. And she would never get the chance again. He wouldn't claim her, because he couldn't.

A new kind of agony clawed at her, but this pain, she could endure. At least, for a little longer.

No more mistakes.

Oberon couldn't right the wrongs of his past, but Sin could.

She shoved herself to her feet, her hair unbound and hanging over her face as she looked up.

Aodhán still stared at her, shock plain on his handsome features. He still clutched at his heart, like he was unable to believe she'd rejected him. The fool.

She'd do it again.

She'd do it a thousand times over.

Dismissing him, she turned to Helios. To Titian.

Helios plucked Oberon's dagger from his eye. The blade was covered in gore, his damaged socket weeping a trail of blood and clear fluid down his cheek. "You dare not disobey us again, girl—"

Sin flicked her hand, and an orb of pure, crystalline death shot toward the god. He waved it away with a sneer, then locked her in place with his power again. She didn't bother to fight it, or struggle. She'd learned her lesson the hard way when it came to gods and their magic. He could immobilize her limbs, but he wasn't strong enough to bind her power, which was fueled by Avalon itself.

"Did you think that tiny spell would harm me?" Helios laughed, the sound booming. He closed the distance between them, coming to a stop a mere three feet in front of her. The god pointed Oberon's dagger at her. "You can't even move, girl."

"I don't need to move to kill you." She smiled, showing her teeth.

"Sinéad!" Aodhán shouted.

The god frowned, as if seeing Sin—truly seeing her. Sin wasn't just some *girl.* She was a Celestial *and* a death fae who was powered by pure, unadulterated rage. The rage of a woman who'd lost the man she wanted above all others. The rage of a woman who'd had her future stolen from her. The rage of a woman who'd had her mother taken from her not once, but twice.

It felt like the world trembled as her fury washed over her, through her.

She formed a death orb right next to his face, its pale silvery light flickering against his skin. Using just her mind, she flung the sphere of pure death at him.

Helios flinched when it kissed his cheek next to his destroyed eye, before burning it away with his power—but it was too late. She'd formed another three while his attention was distracted, and they burrowed into his body—his legs, his torso, and his back. Their glows flickered out as their magic leeched into him, seeping into his very being.

"That wasn't a tiny spell," Sin whispered. "That was the essence of death."

Helios's good eye bulged as her magic took hold.

"I am a god!" he screamed, tendons standing out on his neck as he tried to fight her. The dagger clattered to the stone floor as his muscles cramped, the tissue dying.

"True." The magic holding her immobile vanished.

She stumbled, and then righted herself. She forced herself to watch as his bronze skin disintegrated, exposing muscle that tried to heal even as the molecular structure binding it together was destroyed. His flesh became tainted with a sickly green hue, while tendrils of silvery-blue magic pulsated beneath the surface of his decaying body. The stench of rotting flesh grew, accenting the putrid odor of the charred guards. Helios's limbs contorted as his corrupted tissue sloughed away, her magic eating him from the inside out. His cries were a symphony of deserved pain.

He screamed until his vocal cords eroded.

All the while, his remaining eye threatened death and chaos until it, too, withered and vanished, eaten by her magic.

Eventually, there was nothing left but bones, which turned to a slimy ash at her feet.

She bent down and picked up Oberon's dagger—the one he'd played with in her house. Sin kicked the pile of greasy powder. "But even gods can die."

When she looked up, Aodhán stared at her, horror bleaching his skin. Titian stood at his side, and Sin threw a wave of power at Oberon's former mate. She pinned the animated corpse to a nearby wall and approached, her mind emptying of all thoughts but one: revenge.

"You are an abomination," Sin said, her voice and steps measured. "That ends today."

"Sinéad!" Aodhán rushed her, and she flung out a hand, her magic slamming into him, and knocking him off his feet. He hit the ground hard, his skull cracking sharply against the stone floor. The crown tumbled to the ground next to him, then rolled over the floor, the metallic sound loud in the silence.

"Me? You are nothing but a whore." Titian spat as her covetous gaze locked on the crown that had once been hers.

"Really? So, you didn't betray Oberon with Helios before you exiled him to Tartarus?" Sin picked up the crown, holding it with one hand as she closed the distance to the former High Queen of Avalon.

The crown was beautiful—the metalwork intricate and mesmerizing in its detail and skillful construction. Stones were encased in delicate grips, and she swore that the ornate headdress beckoned to her.

Titian fought against Sin's magic, but her power was no match for Sin's. He'd been right. She was weak. "Oberon was a fool. He thought that love would fix centuries of war."

She came to a stop in front of Titian, while Aodhán groaned on the ground a dozen feet away. Sin lifted the crown, unable to stop herself. "He wasn't wrong. You'd be amazed at how motivating love can be."

She placed the crown on her head.

Her skull ached as a dozen previously hidden spikes burst forth to bore into her scalp, triggering some sort of spell. Pain soon rose like a cresting wave within her, but it was nothing compared to the heart wound she carried, or the binding spell's induced agony.

Her world narrowed to a dark void, which she dismissed with an avalanche of power. She had little time for this test, or whatever it was. The crown's magic fought her, but she sent another swell of power toward it, and her surroundings returned in a blink.

Titian's face was pallid as she met Sin's cold, cold gaze. The former High Queen was still pinned to the wall, and she reminded Sin of a dead butterfly grasping its beauty, even in death. "You just—that was—"

"The crown accepted *me*." Sin smiled, but the expression lacked any hint of warmth. "And I don't accept *you*."

She met Titian's green gaze and saw the desperation there. "Please—I will do anything—"

"The man Helios just killed? That was Oberon. Your ex-mate." Something dark and avaricious flickered in the other woman's gaze at Oberon's name. Sin held up the dagger, and Titian's eyes grew panicked, like she recognized the weapon, the impending death. "I cannot make you pay for the crimes you committed against him. Not fully. But I can make sure that the death he once wished on you is final."

Sin ran the blade down the dead woman's cheek, slicing the flesh open. Blood refused to well from the lifeless flesh, the wound seeping a clear liquid.

"Please—" Titian's voice broke on the word.

Sin shoved the knife deep into the former High Queen's chest, the bone shattering as the blade found the woman's traitorous heart. "He deserved better than you. So much better."

Sin twisted the blade.

Titian screamed.

Sin turned away from the woman who had betrayed Oberon, who had destroyed a thriving civilization, and who had driven a race of fae to find refuge in another world. All because she hungered for power.

With the barest hint of magic from the twin suns that orbited Avalon, Sin incinerated Titian Geal, destroying the husk that had housed a soul tainted by greed and malice.

Destroying the dynasty she had created.

Oberon's knife fell to the ground, surrounded by ashes, the harsh sound signaling the birth of a new world.

And a new legacy.

CHAPTER 33
SIN

AVALON, TWO WEEKS LATER

Sin stared hollowly at Aodhán.

At the mate she didn't want, and who she still hadn't accepted.

She couldn't stand the idea of him touching her, let alone allowing him into her body. After her rejection, it was the only way to finalize the mate bond.

Over the past week, he'd been nothing but respectful, attentive, and considerate. On the surface, he appeared to be a changed man. One who had seen the error of his great-aunt's ways, and who wanted to do better. He'd stood by her side as she had announced she was now the High Queen of Avalon to the palace staff and the guards.

He had offered her unwavering support when she'd stood before the Lower Courts and the Wild Fae in the great hall when she had proven she was a Celestial and the rightful ruler of their world.

But she just...didn't believe him.

Because when he'd finally staggered to his feet on the lookout, after she'd ended Titian, he'd stumbled over to Sin and tried to rip the crown off her head.

It hadn't budged.

He'd cursed at her, ragefully spewing forth slurs she hadn't even known existed. It was only when the crown had sliced his hands to ribbons that he'd let go.

He later claimed he'd been delirious from the head injury and that he didn't remember much of what had happened on the lookout. He may not be able to lie directly to her face, but she still doubted him and his word. He'd let Helios throw a ball of fire at her and Oberon. He'd been willing to let her burn to death to save his throne.

Those were not the actions of a true mate, mate bond or not.

Titian's and Helios's remains had washed away in the rain that had soon followed, and Aodhán claimed he was now free of their poison.

"Are you sure you want to go on a tour of the continent?" Aodhán asked, grounding Sin back in the present.

They were seated in what was once Aodhán's office, and which was now Sin's. She hadn't redecorated it yet, and she knew it made him uncomfortable to be on the other side of the desk. But he made a valiant attempt at hiding it.

Her guards, Oisín and Cathal, stood just inside the door, their faces impassive as they pretended not to eavesdrop on Sin and Aodhán's conversation. She'd quickly discovered that nothing was private here. No wonder Oberon had learned that sound-dampening spell.

She rubbed her chest, his absence an ever-present and gnawing ache. "Yes. I need to understand how this world works, talk to its people. I can't do that hiding in the palace."

"Your advisors can inform you of this. *I* can inform you of this." He leaned forward, his green eyes earnest.

"I will be listening to all sources of information," Sin replied blandly. Aodhán had denied the poverty she'd seen when she raised it with him a week ago; he'd even excused it with several superficial reasons. But it didn't take a genius to see the truth: the farms were barren, the people were starving, and he'd lived a life of ludicrous luxury.

His mouth tightened, but his voice was friendly. "Of course." He paused. "I heard that you have sent messages to Olympus and Earth that the Ó Duibh and Ó hUainín were welcome back on Avalon."

"I have, but so far, we've had no response." She wasn't sure there were any left. "I can understand if they don't think it's safe."

"Helios said that Oberon had killed all the Ó hUainín. Titian wiped out the Ó Duibh."

"Clearly that is not true, or I would not exist. And...Beron wouldn't have either." While she'd known that Ó Duibh meant black, she'd since learned that the other surnames also represented the families' colors: white for Geal and green for Ó hUainín. It explained the overabundance of white in the palace. Although, she'd noticed that the guards who had begun working with her over the past two weeks had started wearing green on their uniforms; she hadn't asked them to.

"True."

Sin stood. "I have a virtual meeting with Captain Sorrel. Apparently, there's been some unrest near the portal, as of late." Who knew the fae had the equivalent of magical video calls? She hadn't.

Aodhán rose to his feet, graceful and refined. "I'd be curious to hear what the Wild Fae thinks is happening."

She knew he was fishing for an invitation to her meeting.

"I will be sure to let you know." Then she walked out the door, Oisín and Cathal falling in line on either side of her. They'd added a green patch over the center of the breastplate, covering the Geal coat of arms.

She didn't turn back to confirm, but she felt Aodhán's determined stare as she walked down the hall and away from him. He still hadn't rejected her as a mate, even though she had rejected him.

She was willing to give him time, to let him see how incompatible they were.

But she wasn't willing to change her mind. She'd never accept him.

Not when her heart belonged to someone else.

Later that night, Sin swore she could still feel Oberon's soul, still smell his amazing cedarwood and citrus aroma. But it was just her imagination playing tricks on her.

Because he was gone.

And she was alone.

Her mother had never reformed, and Sin had used Clara's spell more than once, trying to call her back. Oberon's body had not been found; the theory was he'd burned until there was nothing left.

Sin lay on her bed, in the former High King's—now High Queen's—chamber. She moved her head, trying to find a comfortable position, despite the ever-present crown. It refused to come off and it made washing her hair a nightmare. Her comfort wasn't helped by Oberon's dagger, which she'd shoved under her pillow.

Rolling onto her side, Sin tucked her legs up to her chest, and grabbed a fistful of the shirt she wore. It was Oberon's, and it still carried his scent. Then, she reached out and picked up the sparkly rock from the nightstand.

The gift from Ayla.

She wasn't sure how to use it, and her fingers played with the stone. The sparkles of light reflecting off the rock made her eyes droop, her mind calm. It was almost hypnotic. Closing her eyes, she drifted to sleep.

"I wondered when you'd come."

Sin opened her eyes and jolted. Ayla stood at the edge of a cemetery, while Sin was in a clearing, surrounded by a forest. "What the—?"

"We're on the edges of the death plane."

"Right." Sin wasn't really sure she understood what was happening, but she accepted it.

"So, uh, what's with the crown?" Ayla pointed at Sin's head.

Raising her hand, she felt the cool metal. Great. It came with her even in death. "I got angry."

The witch snorted. "That doesn't explain anything."

Sin changed the topic. "Did you find out who was hunting Oberon?"

Ayla's dark eyes grew solemn. "It looks like the hit was ordered by a faction of fae on Earth. But we suspect they have ties to Avalon."

"Suspect?" One of Sin's eyebrows rose.

"We're still digging."

"Thanks."

"Are you okay? Is Oberon okay?"

Sin's form began to flicker. "I think I need to go."

An insistent tug in the back of her mind told her something was wrong.

"Sorry, Ayla. I have to go—"

CHAPTER 34
SIN

"Wake up, bitch!"

Sin opened her eyes, groggy. "What—?"

Her brain caught up in the time it took Aodhán to pin her down on the bed. He straddled her hips. "What are you—?"

How did he even get in here?

His expression was cruel as he took in the crown on her head and Oberon's shirt on her body. "You took *everything* from me."

"You stood by and let them murder—" She shoved at him, but he didn't move.

"He deserved to die!" Aodhán yelled. "You think I don't know who he really was? 'Beron Black.' Please!"

Sin blinked at him, stunned. "Then you knew he was the rightful High King!" She shoved him again, and he fell off the bed.

Aodhán stood. "He was a murdering bastard. As soon as we heard Tartarus had opened, I waited for news of him. If anything Helios said was true, he'd be coming back for the throne, provided he'd survived." He leaned down, pressing a hand against her throat, touching the faded bruise on her neck. "You think we didn't know that people prayed to that asshole, thinking that he'd come back and save them? Like he was some hero?"

Sin's breath caught in her throat. The fae had wanted Oberon back?

"Titian knew he was alive?" Sin asked.

Aodhán rolled his eyes. "My great-aunt was weak. But Helios loved her, and he got me the throne. We weren't about to tell her that her mate might return. She lived in fear of Oberon, of what he might do to her. And she was reckless when she was afraid. We didn't want her to expose what she really was. Then we'd have a revolt on our hands."

"Oh no. How my heart bleeds for you." Sin drew magic from the planet, just enough to hurt, but not kill.

"And not only did he come back, despite my sending assassins after him, but he brings *my* mate with him. And you stank of him." Aodhán's lip curled. "He'd fucked you before I ever got a taste."

She threw a bolt of magic at him. He countered it, which told her he was stronger than she'd thought.

"Even now, he stands between us!" He lunged at her, knocking them both over on the bed. The fae male's hands clawed at the black shirt, tearing it from her.

"I rejected you!" Sin yelled, grabbing at the tatters of her shirt and drawing more power.

Crazed sea-green eyes met hers. "Rejection doesn't count if we have sex. If we mate, then I'll still be king. Then it won't matter if you leave."

No.

A million times no.

"Stop!" Sin struggled anew, trying to shove him off her, but he was strong. She blasted him with her magic, but he diffused most of it with a grunt. She was going to have to absorb enough to kill. Or use her death magic.

The scent of cedarwood and citrus flooded Sin's senses, and it was like Oberon's soul was here, trying to protect her. He cared for her, even in death.

She scrabbled back and reached for Oberon's dagger under her pillow. Her hand closed over the hilt as she drew more and more magic, about to blast Aodhán to hell and back when the former king's hand gripped her thigh with bruising force.

She watched, shocked, as two hands grabbed his golden head from behind and then brutally twisted, snapping the fae's neck.

Aodhán collapsed to the bed, his lifeless eyes wide with surprise.

Sin stared at the dead king.

Then she looked up.

Oberon stood at the foot of the bed, dressed in his leather jacket, black shirt, and jeans. His eyes glowed orange and his expression was feral. His hair was its natural color and she ached to run her fingers through it.

She was hallucinating. She had to be. "You killed him."

His voice was a rough growl. "I'd tear apart the world for you. One snapped neck is nothing."

She rubbed her eyes with one hand. That was the most romantic thing anyone had ever said to her. She had a fucked-up life. "You're dead."

"No." He stayed where he was, his body taut, like a wire about to snap.

"I saw you die."

The orange melted into inky blackness. "Did you?"

She thought back, to the flames, to the fall—

"You asshole!" Sin leaped at him, kicking Aodhán out of her way, his body thumping to the floor.

"Whoa! Careful with that." Oberon took the dagger from her hands. He sheathed it, then crushed her to him. She jumped slightly and wrapped her legs around Oberon's waist and gripped his shoulders. He staggered back, then held her to him, his arms a tight band around her back and thighs.

Sin buried her face in his neck, inhaling against his skin, convincing herself that this was real, that he wasn't just a figment of her imagination. When she leaned back, he was staring at her, his expression tender. "I'm sorry."

"Why did you let me think you'd died?"

"I wanted to trick Helios, to have him believe I died, so I could come back and end it. But by the time I returned..." His voice trailed away, as he touched the crown on her head. "You'd already done that."

"Then why let me continue to think you'd died?"

He frowned. "I needed to give you time, to see if you truly didn't want the fool fae. And I wanted to learn more about Avalon. I've been teleporting around the continent, trying to gauge how bad it really is."

To say she was furious would be an understatement. At his idiocy for thinking she'd want Aodhán, to his gallivanting over the countryside...to not telling her he could teleport.

But the pragmatic part of her blurted, "How bad is it?"

"Bad." He ran a gentle hand over her cheek. "But you can fix it."

She narrowed her eyes. "What do you mean by that?"

Tenderness filled his touch as he caressed her. "You'll be an excellent High Queen, Sin. Nobody better."

"I don't want it."

He drew back, frowning. "What?"

"I don't want the damn crown! I just took it because I thought you were dead. And I didn't want them to have it." She thrust a hand back at Aodhán's body.

"I see."

"How did you survive?"

"Helios was a sun god. And it made me realize, his power comes from the sun. But I am a Celestial. I can control that." Aodhán's corpse disappeared.

Sin frowned. "Where did he go?"

"I dumped him in a volcano." He raised his dark brows, then touched her cheek. "Did you know that around the time I 'died,' a series of volcanoes erupted on the edge of the continent?"

"They did?" Surprise had her blinking. So, the world really *had* trembled with her fury.

"Did you know those volcanoes had been dormant for over a million years, according to the scientists I spoke to?"

"No, I didn't even know Avalon had them."

"I suspected as much." Then he smiled, and it was a wicked expression, making her core grow instantly damp at the promise and desire reflected there. "At least I know how you feel, even if you didn't tell me."

"What?"

"Those volcanoes were *you*. Your rage. Your power. Your grief." He gripped her under her ass, hoisting her up, pressing her against the hard length of his erection. "And it's fucking hot."

Surprise had her speechless. Then his mouth crashed against hers, his tongue pressing against the seam of her lips. She pulled away. "I'm not sure we should do this when he just died—"

"You're right."

A second later, they were in a different room. It was decorated in heavy black furnishings and had an enormous bed in the center of the room, carved from some kind of ebony wood. There wasn't a speck of dust to be seen.

"Where are we?"

"This used to be my chamber. I found it walled up in the palace. It seems like they never got rid of it. Just moved the High King's rooms to another part of the building and placed a preserving spell on it." His mouth dipped to her neck.

"It's very...black."

"They took the bloodline thing way too seriously," he murmured, his breath hot against her throat. Then he looked down at her tattered shirt. "You wore my clothes." His grin was smug. "You kept my dagger."

She shoved at his shoulders. "So?"

He let her slide down his body, and she groaned as her core skimmed over the hard length of him. Her feet touched the floor. "I like it. But you know what I like even more?" A brush of power had the T-shirt disintegrating, but her skin remained unharmed.

"Let me guess? No clothes?" She rolled her eyes.

"What was it?" He tapped his chin, then shucked off his jacket and grabbed his shirt, pulling it over his head before throwing it carelessly on the floor. "Tit for tat?"

Sin's gaze roved over his body, unable to fathom that he was here, alive. "I'm only wearing panties."

"True." Oberon kicked off his boots, then shoved his jeans to the floor. He'd been commando. Again.

Sin bit her lip at the sight of all his sleek muscle, at the hard length that she wanted to suck, to kiss, to *feel*.

His gaze was ravenous as he said, "Your turn."

"Mmm, I don't think so." She stepped away, as if to run, but found herself up and in the air. Next thing she knew, she was surrounded by soft linen. He'd tossed her on the bed. She lay on her back, propped on her elbows, her legs spread, knees up.

"Take off your panties," he ordered, eyes locked on the damp fabric at the apex of her thighs.

Her gaze grew taunting. "Make me."

He growled low in his throat and pounced, her underwear falling away from her, as if sliced at the seams. "Fuck, you smell delicious." He laved her with a single stroke of his tongue and groaned.

Sin grabbed his shoulders and tugged at him, pulling him up her body.

He glared at her. "I wasn't done."

"I don't care. I want you. In me."

"I told you what will happen—"

"I want it," Sin said, looking at him, meeting his dark stare, showing him how much she needed him. She grabbed a fistful of his hair. "I want you. Claim me."

His head rolled back. "Fuck."

Sin twined her arms around his neck, then pulled his face down to hers. Their mouths met, hungry and insistent. She inhaled sharply as he pressed his lower body against hers, his cock touching her in just the right place. A deep rumble escaped Oberon's throat, the possessiveness of it turning her on impossibly more.

"I want to taste every inch of you." His words were low and threaded with the panther that lived within. "I don't want this to be a quick fuck."

Sin blew out a breath of air. "We can take our time later. I need you. *Please*." Her voice broke on the last word. She wrapped her ankles around his waist and rolled her hips, moaning at the slide of his cock against her clit.

Oberon's gaze gleamed with feral possessiveness. Her body grew excruciatingly wetter as his need made hers skyrocket. He was hers. She wasn't going to let him leave again. She didn't care that there was no mating bond—hell, she was kind of glad it wasn't there—because she wanted him.

Just him.

She angled her hips as he slid through her slickness to tease her once more, and in the next breath, he filled her completely in one long, slow, torturous move. Sin's mouth parted in a gasp at the sudden feeling of being whole, complete—as if her world rocked on its axis and found a new center of gravity. "*Yes*."

Her nails scraped across his shoulders, grazing his skin, and he pulled back slowly, ever so slowly, to then glide back into her. Rocking her hips to meet his thrusts, she moaned, throwing her head back against the bed, clinging to him, her legs locked around him as Oberon gave her exactly what she needed. Pleasure roared through her with every stroke.

Then he stopped.

"What—?"

The world tilted so fast she couldn't keep track. The next thing she knew, she was on her hands and knees, and Oberon was a wall of heat behind her. "Are you ready?" His voice was a low growl as he guided the head of his cock into her throbbing entrance.

She brushed her hair to one side, exposing where her neck met her shoulder. He growled low in his throat, his hips thrusting more forcefully with each stroke. "*Fuck*." His voice was a strangled groan. "Are you sure?"

She looked over her shoulder, incredulous. "Do it already."

He growled, tugging her torso up, so that her back pressed to his chest. "You're so fucking bossy."

She twisted to face him. "Claim me, Oberon. Now."

His teeth changed, fangs forming as his eyes went nightglow orange. "I love you." Then he bit down on the tender part of her neck.

Sin gasped as pain mixed with pleasure, until the feeling of him inside her consumed her and she didn't know where she ended and he began. She swore she could feel him deep within her soul, tied there. With each wild rock of his hips, her body grew closer and closer to the peak. One of his hands slid down her torso to her clit, circling it over and over again. Tingling spread through her legs, her body trembling as release neared. She shoved her hand over his, pressing his fingers hard against her, and her orgasm raced to the surface. "Oberon!"

Ecstasy poured through her as her inner walls clamped down on his cock, and his thrusts grew feral, until all she could do was ride out a pleasure so intense she thought she might die from it.

"Sin!" His voice was a strangled cry as his cock jerked, exploding deep inside her. She clung to his arms, the only thing holding her upright as he shuddered.

After what felt like lifetime later, Sin collapsed face down on the mattress, limp. She felt...different. Rubbing a hand over her heart, she rolled over to face Oberon, who was on his knees, staring at her in awe.

She chuckled, awkward. "What is as good for you as it was for me?"

Shocked eyes met her teasing stare. "We're—we're mates."

"I feel you in here, but..." Her voice trailed off as realization struck. "We're mates." Sin marveled at the sensation, at knowing he was truly hers. And she was his.

Oberon leaned down and cupped her cheeks, pressing his forehead to hers. His expression was serious, weary. "Fuck. I'm sorry, Sin. I didn't know."

"Wait, what?" She pulled back.

"I know you didn't want a mate, and I claimed you, and you didn't get a chance to reject—"

She shoved a hand over his lips. "Now it's your turn to shut up. I was willing to let an alpha shifter claim me. Do you think that meant I was in this for the short-term?" She studied his face. "I killed a *god* because I thought you'd been murdered. You think I'm going to regret a mating bond after all that?" She tilted her head, a wicked smile blooming on her face. "No, this means you're mine. Forever."

Oberon leaned back, satisfaction clear in his expression. "Good."

Sin's brow furrowed. "Good?"

"Because I'm going to need a High Queen who is scary as fuck. And I don't think anyone fits the bill better than you do."

"Oh, so that's why you claimed me." She kept her voice deadpan.

"No, I claimed you because I wanted you. My panther—the sneaky bastard—must have sensed you were his fated mate long ago. He's wanted to claim you since Giant's Causeway."

"But I had a mate, so how—"

"Second-chance mates. I didn't think I'd get one, because of what I did..." His voice trailed off. "I used that dagger to kill her. The one you kept."

"Huh. I shoved that same blade into Titian's rotten heart." She reached out a hand, running it over the side of his face. "You were a different man then. And you didn't have your panther."

"No. Good thing I killed Aodhán, then. You needed him to die for our bond to kick in, since the ass was never going to reject you." He leaned down, rubbing the side of his face against hers in a very catlike movement.

Sin's eyes widened, and she shoved at his chest. "Oberon!"

"What?"

"You shouldn't say shit like that!"

"I said what I said."

"You can't joke about killing people!"

He gave her a smug smile. "I can. I just did."

She huffed. "Well, you shouldn't."

"Even if I dropped his body in a volcano you made?"

"Even then," she grumbled.

"I wonder what you did this time..." he mused.

Sin sat up, shoving him over. He landed on the bed with a chuckle. "What do you mean?"

"You've got the crown on now, and I rocked your world. I wonder if Avalon is going to have a new continent now." He grinned, then laughed at her outraged expression.

She pounced, pinning him down. Then she bit down on his neck, where shoulder met tendon, until the rich metallic taste of his blood filled her mouth. Only then did she let go, smiling at the sight of the wound, at what it meant.

"Hey! What was that for?" He looked at her like a disgruntled cat, but he lay still underneath her, trusting her.

She ran her finger over the already healing wound. "Tit for tat. You claim me, I claim you."

He quickly rolled and scooped her into his arms. "You're devious. I love it."

She clung to him, feeling remade, fulfilled.

Whole.

"And I love you."

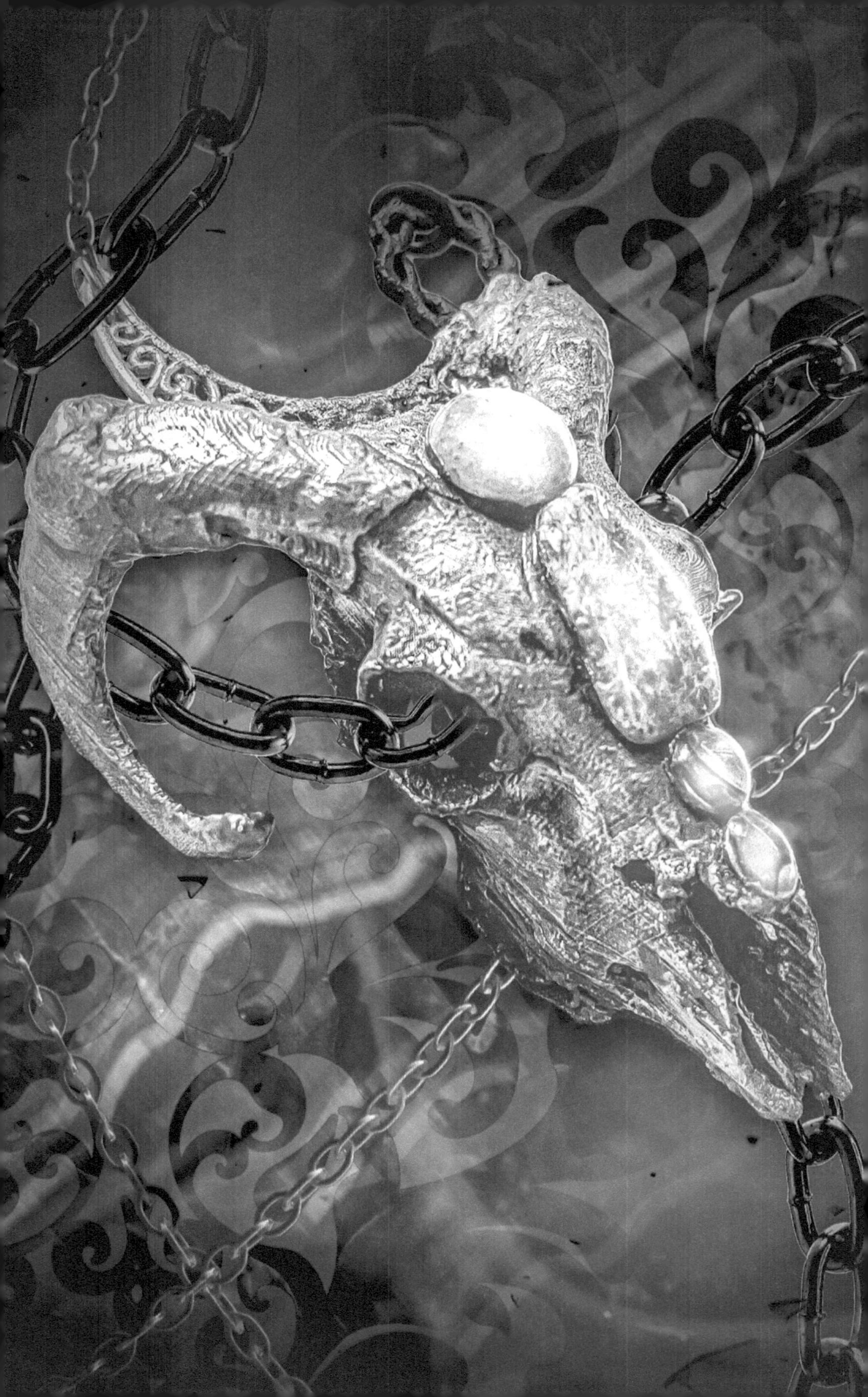

CHAPTER 35
SIN

Oberon teleported Sin to the Earth portal in response to an urgent message that had been relayed from the guardhouse. Apparently, a small army had come to invade Avalon.

Sin walked through the tree line and came to a sudden stop, staring at the large grassy expanse before her and the massive temple that housed the portal.

Madness reigned.

Guards were running left and right as a small black blur chased anyone close enough to bite. Ysabeau St. Claire stood on the steps of the portal temple, sunglasses on and a red leash in one hand. She looked bored out of her mind.

Clara was shooting magic at a bunch of guards that had gotten too close, while Pollux tried to step between her and any enemy foolish enough to approach within striking range. Even Styx was there, guarding Pol's and Clara's backs.

Tía Celeste waved a—was it a wooden spoon?—in the air and swatted at anyone within arm's reach, while Ayla and Aks dodged blows from Captain Sorrel, who strangely seemed to be enjoying herself. Even

Kieran was there, striding through the field in a beeline toward her with a huge broadsword and a look that spelled death for anyone in his way.

Sin's eyes burned and a lump formed in the back of her throat.

Then her dad was in front of her, Alvaro's huge form engulfing her in a hug that spoke of home, of family, of life. A strangled sob escaped her and she clutched at him. "Papá."

He pulled away, his hands on her shoulders, as he looked at her. "*Mija, te quiero mucho.*"

"*Yo también te amo, Papá.*" Gods, how she loved him. He'd given her a life, a home. And he'd shared her with a half-crazed ghost who hadn't been able to let go, not until Sin's life was in jeopardy.

"Mamá is gone," Sin whispered, her throat tight.

Alvaro's dark eyes studied her. "*Oh, hija, lo siento mucho.*"

"She sacrificed herself to save me."

He ran a thumb over her cheek, wiping away a tear. "Your mother only ever wanted what was best for you."

"Sin!" Clara slammed into Sin's side, nearly knocking her and Alvaro off their feet. Sin laughed, hugging her cousin back.

"You're alive!" Pol shouted, slapping Oberon on the back.

Her mate gave the other shifter a droll look. "You expected otherwise?"

"Nog was convinced you were both dead. His handler spent so much time keeping him away from the portal that she decided enough was enough, and that she was going through with or without help. So, the cavalry was called, and here we are." The handsome male turned to Sin. "Sinner, you're alive." He sniffed the air. "And...mated?"

"Pollo, are you dating my cousin yet?" Sin narrowed her eyes.

"What is with your family and that blasted nickname!" He threw his hands in the air.

"So, you aren't dead, chained in a basement, or missing a limb. I see the cavalry was not needed," Kieran's dark voice interjected.

Sin looked at him, surprised he was here. "You here to finish the job you started with our father?"

To her surprise, he snorted. "Hardly. I don't believe in the whole 'sins of the father' crap. Get it? You're Sin and sins of the father? No. Well, I find out I have a half-sister, who then ran off after some fae prick.

I just came to ensure you were okay, and that Jerkface over there didn't need killing."

"Jerkface?" Oberon echoed.

"To be fair, I called you that a few times myself," Sin admitted.

"I remember." His voice was a low growl and she laughed, delighted.

"We're okay. We're okay." She held up her hands, her heart full at the sight of the people who cared about her and Oberon. Who came for them.

"Kasha couldn't come—something about a protection duty—but she told me to tell you she misses you. Reagan and Caius said to give you this." Clara handed Oberon a piece of metal. He frowned, turning it over in his hands. "Caius thinks he'll be able to open a portal to it. He couldn't come because he didn't want the death magic to rip through Earth in his wake. But he said to use the damned thing, because Reagan was driving him insane asking him to set the portal up so she could come see Sin."

"That's not exactly what he said," Pol murmured.

Clara snorted. "Close enough."

"It's from the heart of Tartarus, which Caius created. So, he thinks it will work like an anchor," Styx explained.

"Then we'll have to try it," Oberon said.

"So, uh, what's with the crown?" Kieran interrupted.

Sin raised a hand to her forehead. It had morphed into a circlet, while Oberon's had stayed a ring. When he needed it though, like at his re-coronation, it turned back into a crown. It was like the damned things were sentient. Hers liked being on her head, and his seemed to enjoy being a ring, and hiding in plain sight.

Sin bit her lip, then blurted, "I, uh, possibly killed a god, and a two-thousand-year-old walking corpse, stole the former High King's crown and put it on, and then it accepted me as the new High Queen of Avalon." She may have finished with jazz hands.

"And I faked my own death, and then murdered her fated mate," Oberon added.

"*What*?!" Clara's screech almost deafened Sin.

"Maybe he's not so much of a Jerkface, after all," Kieran muttered, tone approving.

Gods.

He was going to be a pain in the ass, she just knew it.

Nog sat on Oberon's foot.

Oberon sighed. "What did we say about boundaries?"

Nog spat out what looked to be part of a soldier's pants, then woofed a question.

"I became her fated mate because we were second-chance mates," he said to the corgi shifter.

"Wait, did you understand Nog?" Sin asked.

Oberon blinked. "I guess I did. Huh."

A few nights later, Oberon and Sin stood on the lookout where they'd changed the fate of the world.

"Here?" Oberon asked.

"Here," Sin nodded.

It was just the two of them, the air eerily quiet. They'd sent everyone back through the portal, with the promise that they'd visit. Avalon wasn't ready for the chaos that was Sin and Oberon's friends and family.

At least, not yet.

Oberon spoke over the enchanted piece of metal, then he dropped it on the ground near the edge of the lookout. That way people wouldn't be able to sneak into the portal from behind—not unless they had wings, anyway.

Five minutes passed before a small vortex grew in the air above the metal. It expanded rapidly, until a portal big enough for two people formed, nothing but smooth darkness visible from this side.

Tartarus.

Sin stood on her tiptoes, trying to see better.

"They're coming." Oberon put his arm around her shoulder and kissed her hair.

He'd barely finished speaking before Reagan charged through the portal, Caius close on her heels. She skidded to stop in front of them, blinking in surprise. "Clara told me, but I didn't believe her."

"About what?" Sin asked, stepping forward.

"That you and Oberon actually mated. My sister, who was as anti-mate as me." Then Reagan threw herself at Sin, hugging her close.

Something inside Sin calmed at the contact and the familiar scent. It soothed the sharp edges that still hurt after their fight, even though they'd made up. "I love you, Reagan."

Reagan leaned back, giving Sin a watery smile. "I love you, too, sis."

"I guess this officially makes us brothers-in-law," Caius said to Oberon, giving the other male a slap on the back.

"We haven't married yet."

The god chuckled. "No, just formed a bond no law can break." Then he frowned, looking at the spot Sin had killed Helios. "A god died here."

Oberon shrugged and tucked his hands into his pockets. "Sin got angry."

Shocked stares latched on to Sin. She scuffed her foot on the stone floor. "He wasn't that powerful a god."

"Holy shit, Sin! What the hell?" Reagan's mouth hung open.

Sin rolled her eyes. "He was just a sun god. A minor deity. It's not like I trapped the soul of a fae god in a crocheted doll and then let my cousin hump it for the next few months..."

"Hey!" Clara's shout echoed through the portal.

They laughed.

Pol strode through the portal then, ducking as a purple crocheted dog sailed over his head. Clara followed, Nog hot on her heels after the stuffy. Sin winced.

Oberon pulled Sin close to him, putting his chin on the top of her head, tucking her against him. "I love you. Thank you for giving me you."

She turned in his hold, looping her arms around his waist. "I love you, too. Even if it means I'm stuck being High Queen."

He poked her back. "What a declaration."

She laughed. "You're in my heart and my soul, Oberon. Forever."

He leaned down, pressing a gentle kiss to her lips.

"Forever."

The End

Thank you for reading SPURN ME! We hope you enjoyed Sin and Oberon's love story.

The following is a list of character's we saw in SPURN ME and their books:

Sabrina and Kieran is HAUNT ME
Reagan and Caius is MATE ME
Styx is SHADOW ME
Legion is HUNT ME
Kasha is in CAGE ME
Ayla is CHASE ME

MORE BY AMANDA PILLAR

Immortal Vices and Virtues
Haunt Me

The Tangled Threads Series
A Court of Tangled Threads
A Crown of Tangled Thorns (coming December 2024)

The Heaven's Heart Series
Deadly Passion
Benevolent Passion
Winged Passion
Ascending Passion
Secret Passion (coming soon)

The Graced Series
Graced
Captive
Survivor
Bitten

MORE BY AMANDA PILLAR

Ashes
Freedom

The Moonlit Hills Series
Winter's Curse

ACKNOWLEDGMENTS

Unlike the last time when Kel Carpenter asked me to participate in the Immortal Vices and Virtues world, I did not let my enthusiasm get the best of me. At least, I didn't think I did. Turns out I was wrong.

Ghost romances, like Haunt Me, are hard to write.

But having to write the story of a fae king from legend?

Yeah, it was no small task.

Look, I know I'm no Shakespeare, so this fae king may not be anything like Oberon from A Midsummer Night's Dream. But parts of his backstory find echoes in the sixteenth century play, and I wanted to make him slightly evil, dangerous, and sexy. But he needed a heroine could match him step for step—and who better than Sin?

Thank you to everyone who supported me through this book. First and foremost, thank you Kel. Thank you for asking me to participate in this universe, for listening to my crap, and reading the first draft. Thank you, Theresa, for your amazing edits and to Rachel Theus Cass, my wonderful proofreader. A special thank you to Sara and Francis Henriquez, who helped me with the Spanish elements of the book. Any and all mistakes are my own (I studied Spanish several years ago, and now only use it to talk to my beautiful niece, who is one—she doesn't care when I make mistakes, lol). I also want to thank Heather Renee, Annie Anderson, Mila Young, Lexi C. Foss, and Heather Hildenbrand for all those plotting chats.

And last, but certainly not least, my husband and family. May our children never read this book.

About the Author

Amanda Pillar is a *USA Today* Bestselling author and award-winning editor, who lives in Australia with her husband and two kids. She's the author of the unique Graced series and the paranormal romance adventure series, Heaven's Heart. She is busy working on her next book and has plans for many more to come, all with lots of snark. Because snark.

She has had over a dozen short stories published and has edited nine anthologies over the years. People say it's because she's an 'overachiever' but in reality, Amanda doesn't understand the concept of 'relaxation'. (Please feel free to explain it to her. Use small words.) Compounding this issue, Amanda also designs book covers and has commenced work on a PhD. Because she's crazy.

Oh, and in her day job, she's an archaeologist.

For more information and to join her mailing list, please visit http://www.amandapillar.com

www.ingramcontent.com/pod-product-compliance
Lightning Source LLC
Chambersburg PA
CBHW020249030826
48979CB00030B/2669/J
9780648793540